A Soldier's Wind

A Soldier's Wind

A novel by

Stuart Riddell

ISBN: 978-1-941066-09-6

Wordrunner Press

Cover and author photo by
Emily Riddell Photography
www.emilyriddell.com

Book design by Jo-Anne Rosen
www.wordrunner.com/publish

Acknowledgments

I owe a huge debt of gratitude to the following: Guy Biederman, editor, guru and teacher, who made the manuscript lose weight and feel much better; Dr. Carol Kreuger, orthopedic surgeon (Ret), who knows a lot about many things; Robert Van Blaricom, world sailor, for his helpful nautical experience; Taylor Teagarden, for her expert editing; and most especially to my wife, Emily, of fifty-five wonderful years (ten years at sea), for solving the mysteries of computers and her ability to put up with me. Thank you, one and all.

A Soldier's Wind

A name given to the wind when it blows on the beam of a vessel under sail, and, therefore, calls for no tacking or trimming of the sails. It is a wind which will take a sailing vessel there and back again without much nautical ability. [*Oxford Companion To The Ships And The Sea*]

Therefore, it is said that even a soldier could sail the vessel.

1

A small flock of seagulls flew over the water, singing their early morning symphony to the residents in the marina. From the open window of one funky old floating home came a sweet female voice singing. "I knew a man Bojangles and he'd danced for you in worn out shoes." Then all was quiet, save for the squawking gulls continuing their endless search for anything edible.

Trish threw off the duvet and looked at the reflection of her body in the mirror that was housed in the canopy of her four-poster bed. She smiled, rolled over slowly and headed for the bathroom.

It was 6 a.m. when she sat down at her desk, as a gray smear of daylight appeared over the Tiburon hills. "Good morning, planet. It's the fifteenth of April, two thousand and twelve. So, many happy returns of the day on your forty-fifth birthday, Mary Patricia Cameron."

Trish was looking at the screen-saver on her laptop, featuring a photograph of *Bojangles;* the old family schooner. She finally decided this was the day to follow the advice of her best friend and mentor, Dr. Helen Boyle, who had suggested she should write her memoir.

"Helen." Trish had objected. "People don't write their memoirs until they're in their dotage; I haven't been out of diapers that long, for God's sake."

Helen was wise. She'd said that Trish needed a catharsis, to be set free from the pain that had dwelt for so long in the hairline cracks of her psyche. A top-of-the-line shrink, Helen, a renowned therapist and author, had suspected that Trish was hiding from a deep melancholy, but successfully playing the role of an outgoing professional. "It's like a dormant cancer cell in your body. Let's flush the bugger out, my dear, I've seen it in your eyes."

"Oh, I don't know, Helen." Trish had replied. "Aren't we all a little sad occasionally? I think about Mom and Daddy. Really, dear, it's no big deal."

"And that is why you should write about it, purge it from your mind. Put it where it belongs. I want to pass on to you my favorite mantra, and if you like it, I'll sell it to you for a nickel. It's by Johann Wolfgang von Goethe. 'Whatever you can do, or dream you can, begin it. Boldness has a genius, power and magic in it'. Begin it by writing a letter to your mom and dad, telling them how much you love and miss them. Start your memoir on your birthday. A year from now it'll be complete, and you'll be reborn."

That conversation had been replaying in her mind. "I'll be reborn. Begin it. Begin it Trish. Power, genius and magic."

"Alright Helen, here goes."

Dear Mom and Daddy:

How strange, this will be the first letter that I have ever written to you because I was never away from you. Daddy, the first thing that comes to mind is the constant sadness I feel for your tragic and untimely death. The last time I looked at you, you were rounding the windward mark at Crissy buoy. You gave me your last smile. I remember that the guys on the main sheet lost control when you jibed onto port tack. The booms swung over and hit the shrouds so hard it shook the whole rig. I just lost my grip on the shrouds and ended up in the drink. The next thing I saw was a life ring thrown to me, and then, you diving in to save me. You were so brave; I couldn't imagine that you weren't going to be in my life any more. Part of me died with you that day, Daddy, and I'll miss you and love you for the rest of my life.

I can understand why you didn't tell me that you had a dicey ticker. Of course you didn't want to worry me. Mom told me after the memorial service that your doctor was sure the cold water stopped your big heart. He said he'd advised you about the serious nature of angina and not to do anything strenuous, including sailing. But that's like telling a bird not to fly, or fish not to swim. Sailing was in your blood, and I remember you saying that you were going to win the Master Mariners race if it killed you.

Tears rolled down her cheeks and onto the keyboard.

Mom, when the Coast Guard couldn't find him after a day of searching, it was like someone had thrown a hand grenade into our lives. Our bodies lived, but our hearts were shattered. I understand why you drank; it was all too much for you. We just had each other. Then, as time went by we put on stiff upper lips, and somehow carried on. Daddy would have expected us to be brave. I tried to comfort you, Mom, but sherry was your only comfort. Sally and weed were mine. I don't remember too much of that year. I would never have made it without Sally, because she was my rock and my lifeline. She helped me through my grief and always loved me like a sister. I don't know if you knew that we sort of fell in love; but that's for another day. I know you're with Daddy, and I expect you're sailing in the trades on a broad reach in Bojangles, roaring down following seas heading for Tahiti and Moorea. Someday, I hope I'll be at anchor in Cook's Bay and we'll have a great get-together. So until the next time, I send you enormous love.

Your loving Trish.

P.S. Mom, I hope you've forgiven me for breaking your pelvis when you delivered me. I guess a ten and-a-half-pound baby was just a little too much.

She smiled as she looked at the screen. "Well, Helen, it's a beginning."

Trish slipped into her jogging suit and sneakers and walked out to the dock. Fog was pouring out of Tennessee Valley. The sun peeked through cumulous clouds, which hovered over the Tiburon hills. A few early commuters were power-walking along the dock, intent on catching the ferry to San Francisco. Briefly greeting her friends and neighbors, she continued on her own power walk. Her daily outings were not only pleasant, but also necessary. She would often see a large blue heron, a few pelicans or some egrets picking in the mud for some morsel. She was grateful for the foresight some locals had given to preserving these wetlands so that the birds could survive and the walkers and joggers could enjoy them forever.

Returning home, she opened her front door to hear the phone ringing. Gasping, she hit the speaker button.

"Hello."

"Trish, dear, did I get you at a busy time?"

"Oh, Helen, no, I just got in from my walk. What's up?"

"If you have a few minutes, I wanted to give you a heads-up on David Avent? The fellow I referred to you the other day."

Trish put the kettle on, poured some muesli into a bowl, and covered it with blueberry yogurt. "Oh, yeah, thanks for that. I'm seeing him tomorrow."

"Anyway, Avent is a recent widower; he lost his wife to ovarian cancer about a year ago. I gather it was very bad and shook him up a lot, poor chap. Anyhoo, he says he's impotent. He had a romp with a woman long after his wife's death, but failed. Typical case of erectile dysfunction, I guess; and maybe he's afraid to get out there and get involved with another lady. They were married for twenty years or so. He really needs a sex therapist to get him on track again, and he's adamantly opposed to trying a working girl; can't say I blame him. And, as you don't do surrogate anymore, I thought you might work with him and refer him to one of your surrogate pals. I only talked to him on the phone and that's all I know, except he's fifty and I gather he does some plucky work with the elbow, which could account for some of his E.D."

"Yeah, I talked with him a little, mainly to make the appointment. He's obviously depressed. So, I'll check him out and let you know if I can put him on the road again. What's plucky work with the elbow?"

"Oh, it's an old British expression that an actor said in a movie; it means he likes the bottle, hence moving the elbow to pour."

"Cute, I love it. You know, Helen, it seems I haven't seen you for ages; could you come here for lunch today? I'll have some of that scrumptious Thai chicken salad delivered, and we could do some plucky work with our elbows, but with iced tea."

"That's a wonderful plan, what time?"

"Oh, noonish, suit yourself."

Trish smiled. She'd known Helen for twenty years. She thought about her own graduation from the Institute for Advanced Study of Human Sexuality with a well-earned Master's degree. After graduation she couldn't wait to see Florida in the rear view mirrors when she headed west to the San Francisco Bay Area in her dad's classic Mercury convertible.

She would never forget the day she met Helen in Sausalito, armed with a solid referral from her professor. They became friends immediately and had remained close ever since.

She called the Thai restaurant and placed the order for the salads, then prepared the iced tea.

Trish finished her report on one of her patients as she glanced at her watch. The ship's bell rang at the front door. She smiled as she looked through the glass. Helen was smiling at her through the door window.

"There you are, dear soul, give me a big hug. I need a Trish fix right now." They embraced in the doorway and kissed. "I've missed you so much," Helen said in her broad Australian accent. "How are you?"

"Never better." Trish led her upstairs and into the spacious living room with its breathtaking view to the upper reaches of Richardson's Bay, and Mt. Tamalpais to the north.

"God, how lucky you are to live in this heaven on water. You must be in rapture every time you look at Mt. Tam."

They went out onto the redwood deck and sat in the lounge chairs under the awning. "Well, dear, if someone has to do it, it might as well be me, but I'll share it with you any time. I feel so guilty that I haven't called you, but my cup runeth over with so much stuff going on. It's been wild and I can't even remember the last time I got laid. Well, I do, but that's best forgotten."

"I thought you were seeing some guy with a strange name. Bim, Zim or Zam, what about him?"

"Oh yeah, Bim Walters, he was too weird for me. He had a taste for bondage; I being the one he insisted on binding. No thank you. I'm just not meeting any men that I really want to spend the rest of my life with. They either have enormous egos or they're off-the-wall nuts, or divorced four times or still badly married. Maybe I'll try on line or put another ad in the Coastal Sun? And maybe not, we'll see."

The doorbell rang. "Oh, that'll be the salad, I'll be right back."

Helen walked over to the deck railing. Multi-million-dollar mansions hugged Strawberry Point across the channel. She saluted the sleeping maiden atop the summit of Mt. Tamalpais.

Trish returned and placed the tray with salads and iced tea on the table.

"My, there's a lot of sailboat action out there today. How lovely. Oh, Trish, before I forget, I have a little love gift from Eros, the great-spirit above, especially for you, dear." Helen removed a baggie from her purse that contained several small bags of dark powder, and handed it to her. "This is Magic Medicine Two or MM Two. I've tweaked the recipe a bit and added more of another classified ingredient. Let me know how it works for you. Same dose, take the first one and about two hours later boost with half a dose and then if you are still with it, one more boost two hours after that. It's right out there."

"You absolute sweetheart, thank you, it couldn't have arrived at a better time; I'm so ready for a vision quest. I love you for this and everything else about you."

Trish recalled when Helen told her how she decided to find the ultimate aphrodisiac. She had a Ph.D. in Pharmacology, and over the years she had combined this profession with her psychiatric practice. When she first started her practice many years ago, she learned about the incredible properties of MDMA and its therapeutic potential. After researching that psychotropic compound, she'd decided to create her special recipe and using only herbs, roots and bark, to create the ideal love potion that did not contain outlawed drugs. She started mixing her own witches' brew, as she liked to call it, just after the Drug Enforcement Agency put MDMA on schedule 1, and in the same category as heroin, cocaine, meth, crack and marijuana. She was constantly reminded about the government's failure during the prohibition years when hundreds of thousands of people made their own home brew, bathtub gin and moonshine. Obviously prohibition only made people want booze all the more. The Feds chose to ignore the axiomatic law of nature. "That which is forbidden makes it all the more desirable." Finally, after a period of trial and error, Helen made a breakthrough and mixed an amazing herbal aphrodisiac that she called Magic Medicine. She only gave it to her close friends, and had an ironclad rule that she would never sell it nor divulge the formula. It was a gift of love to those who would benefit from its therapeutic qualities.

Helen grinned. "Let me know what you think of this batch, still no side effects. I'm positive I've made it this time, so put a notch on the bedpost every time you pop. I'll be very interested to know from a clinical point of view if it's as good as I think it is."

Trish laughed. "Sure will, and I'll take notes and maybe do a video."

"Good for you. Then, when I'm sure it's perfect, I might anonymously slip the recipe to the website High Up There. And then maybe I'll turn the whole bloody country on to it. Perhaps I'll recruit a volunteer-army of do-gooders to spike every reservoir in the republic. Or patent the formula and send it to the DEA. How's that for a plan?"

"Sounds like a plan, and I promise I'll visit you every week in the crow bar hotel, that is, if you're locked up in the Bay Area. I don't commute to distant correctional facilities."

Helen sipped her tea "Thank you. Oh, I almost forgot, happy birthday. Have you started your memoir and do you have anything for me to read?"

"I started it today and it's the most difficult thing I've ever attempted, especially, Daddy's death. I've always felt it was my fault that he drowned. As you know I went into a meltdown depression. So I wrote them a letter as you suggested, and that felt very good. I pictured them reading it. But, Helen, the worst part will be spilling my blood and guts onto the page, and confessing my addiction to cocaine, booze, pot and sex. I was appalled at my debauchery, and if it hadn't been for your good friend, Phoebe Nell, God knows where in hell I'd have ended up. I told you she got me on MDMA and helped me kick the coke and booze? I'm sure she saved my life with that incredible stuff."

"And of course, I'm eternally grateful she saved your life."

"So am I, but even though I was loaded most of the time she persevered."

"Now look at you. You have a thriving healing business; you're living in a heavenly place. Can it get any better than that?"

"I guess not. I have a lot to be thankful for, especially to you."

"It was my pleasure, and with that I'll take a big hug and get out of here. I have a two o'clock with a gal who needs Prozac or a stick of ginger up her butt to get her going. Thanks for the scrumptious lunch. It's been so much fun to catch up with you, and I'm delighted that it's all working out."

Trish took Helen's hand and walked her to the door.

"By the way, were you ever able to track down your old friend Sally?"

Trish shook her head. "Afraid not. I tried everywhere, zero, nada. For all I know, she could have married some goat farmer and moved to Plentywood, Montana, and had six kids, human kids. It's so sad, because she was so much a part of my life from three to eighteen. It's a big blank in my life. I've got to talk to a missing person's service and see if they can find her. I keep putting it off because—Well, I'm afraid that she's—"

"I think you should do that, because she's either alive or dead. You need closure, love."

They hugged again. "You're right, as usual. Thanks for coming over, and especially for the Magic Medicine. I love you." Trish smiled and waved as she watched her friend walk away along the dock.

2

It was a clear, windless day, perfect for the mile walk into town to her Tai Chi class. Trish grabbed a bottle of water and headed out at a fast walk over to the waterfront. The boat yards were full of power and sailing yachts preparing for their summer cruises and the racing season.

She walked to the bottom of the street and hesitated for a moment, trying to decide whether to go up to look at the old family home. She glanced at her watch, then quickly turned and went up the hill and stopped in front of the house. It was the only home that she had ever lived in until she was eighteen. She looked up at the dormer window to her bedroom, and then down to the second floor and the large bay window that was her parents' bedroom. Her eyes moved slowly as she scanned the front wrap-around veranda on the first floor. She remembered the happiness that filled their home and the fun times they had together; Mom and Daddy, their friends and Sally Brown who had lived four doors away when they were three years old. Again she stared at her bedroom window where the rape had taken place, then quickly looked away.

Trish turned to leave, then quickly stopped in her tracks. She gasped when she saw a large schooner lying at anchor in the roadstead off the Sausalito foreshore. It was the anchorage where her dad had often anchored their schooner. She walked as fast as she could down the steep winding street and headed south on Bridgeway, arriving at the small grassy park next to the Yacht Club. She greeted a few of the early members of her Tai Chi class. She kept looking at the schooner that was flying a large Canadian ensign from the flagstaff on the stern rail. It looked like a larger model of her dad's old schooner.

The last stragglers joined the group. "Do you know who owns the fancy yacht?" One man asked her.

"I have no idea, but I'd say a very wealthy Canadian. Alright, guys, shall we get started?"

They formed into three rows; Trish took her place facing the class. They all put their hands together and bowed as a sign of respect to each other. "Start with *Part the Wild Horse's Mane* followed by *Crane Cools its Wings*." Trish started in a slow, carefully choreographed series of moves. Most of the class followed her moves precisely. A few made mistakes but gradually caught up with the others.

Fifteen minutes into the exercises, Trish noticed a very tall bearded man watching the class from the pathway. He was wearing what appeared to be a buckskin vest, tan canvas pants, and sandals. His long hair was drawn back into a ponytail. He sported a beaded headband with two feathers hanging from it. His leather shoulder bag revealed vegetables inside.

She decided he must be one of the local characters from town. She had seen many of them over the years. Sausalito had been the Mecca for beatniks and hippies in the fifties and sixties. Now, some of them hung out on patched-up old boats anchored on either side of the main navigation channel that led into the upper reaches of Richardson's Bay. Drugs were being used and sold by some of the resident mariners; an occasional murder had occurred, and some deaths from drug overdoses. Most of them were a pretty docile bunch, and the police left them alone unless they got out of hand. This big guy with the feathers was different from the run-of-the-mill locals. He appeared to be neatly dressed and good-looking. He was watching her as she went through the intricate moves of her Tai Chi routine. The class was used to having many spectators observe their Friday classes.

"*Brush Knee; Play the Fiddle.*" Trish called out the routines and the class followed her graceful moves. She glanced over her shoulder, but the man had gone. A short time later she saw him sculling a Whitehall pulling boat in the direction of the schooner.

Trish turned to watch the feather man as he stood ramrod straight in the stern of the boat, sweeping the oar back and forth. He brought the boat alongside and he stepped onto the platform where he secured his boat.

"That must be one hell of a rich Canadian anchor-out; man, that's a big yacht." One of her class said. "Maybe he's one of those retired Canadian casino Indians."

Trish looked at the yacht. "What makes you think he's an Indian?"

"The feathers and buckskin; the only thing missing was the tomahawk."

"Could be. Well, that's it, enjoy the day. See you all next week, guys."

She looked at the beautiful gaff schooner for a long time, and heard the faint sound of a big band playing Glenn Miller's In the Mood floating the classic song over the water. She smiled, turned and headed for home.

3

At seven the next morning Trish started typing. "Okay Helen, this is for you."

THE MEMOIR OF MARY PATRICIA CAMERON
CHAPTER 1

The first time I was born, I broke my mom's (Janet's) pelvic bone because I was 10 pounds 8 ounces. It really wasn't my fault, because I just wanted out. The OBGYN and all the nurses bet that I was going to be a boy because Mom's belly was slung so low.

Daddy (Alan) wanted a boy so much he'd convinced everyone that I'd be one; but then I came into this world as a girl, Mom was wrecked and Daddy was dazed. When he first held me, he said to Mom, "Say hello to our new best friend."

The second time I was born at the age of fifteen, I was a tall, beautiful lesbian. At least that's what I thought I was. I had no idea that there was such a thing as bisexual; more about that later.

I first met Sally when we were three years old. Her family moved into the house a few doors away. Mom thought she was so cute when she said, 'My name is Thally, whath's yourths?' From that moment on, we became sisters. We played together, ate together, bathed together, slept together, attended pre-school and kindergarten, and we cried together when one or both of us were scolded for something we did wrong, or when we skinned our knees. We were inseparable. And Sally called me Trishy.

When we were six, Sally's parents decided to enroll her in a convent up county. It was a boarding school, so we only saw each other on weekends. I remember we were both in tears over that terrible separation. Sally became unmanageable in her prison, so her parents decided to pull her out and we became classmates again. Sally told me the nuns were very strict and some were mean. She became an instant atheist because, as she explained to me, "If there was a God, he would never put nuns on this planet." I became an atheist in sympathy and have been one to this day. Well, maybe I was an agnostic. I couldn't really prove there was no God. Just not for me.

We decided that we didn't like Sally's mother, so she spent most of her time at our house.

My mom and dad drank scotch mostly, but sometimes they drank rum, bourbon, gin, vodka, aquavit, rye whisky, red wine, white wine, pink wine, champagne, brandy, Cointreau, crème de menthe, crème de cacao, beer and a lot of other stuff. My mom and dad and their friends became very silly when they drank this stuff at parties. Sally's Mom and Dad only drank wine and they were never silly, so we didn't like them much because they never made us laugh.

Daddy always owned wooden sailboats. He liked the feel and smell of wood. He sailed in lots of races and won a lot because he was such a good sailor. He even taught Sally and me to sail, and that was lots of fun, except when Sally got seasick over the side. Mom never sailed when Daddy raced because he always shouted at her to pull this or push that. But she would always come along when he took Sally and me cruising for two weeks up the Sacramento Delta. We would anchor there, swim, barbecue and have lots of fun, especially skinny-dipping. Daddy was a partner in a boat yard in town, he knew most of the yacht owners, and he was very popular so they gave him their business.

I think Daddy treated me like a boy because I sort of became a tomboy, which I guess was the next best thing to having a son. I know he really loved me because he used to wink and smile at me a lot and give me hugs and kisses that I liked best of all. I used to help him on the boat, like sanding the bright work, and I even learned to varnish, not as good as Daddy, but he used to say, "Good enough for gumint work." He even taught us what to do if someone fell overboard by falling overboard himself, so we'd have to rescue him under sail. Of course he'd always wear a life jacket when he did this, just in case we couldn't rescue him.

Then, when I was fifteen, Daddy bought a big classic gaff-rigged schooner named Lilly that was in bad shape, and needed a major refit. This gorgeous yacht was built in Scotland by the famous yard Fife of Fairlie in 1935. Daddy didn't believe it was bad luck to rename a yacht just because everyone else said it was. He said he'd be goddamned if he was going to own a schooner named Lilly, so he broke a cheap bottle of beer over her stern and declared, "I un-name thee Lilly, because I don't even know anyone by that name." Then he asked me to re-christen her. We went up to the bow, where he handed me a bottle of good champagne. He told me exactly what to say for the ceremony. Mom and Daddy and about fifty or so sailors and local wharf rats were standing by. I remember I was really nervous because I was afraid the bottle wouldn't break, which would really be bad luck.

I really wound up like I was going to hit the ball out of the park and took a mighty swing. "I re-name thee Bojangles; bless you and all those who sail in you." The netted bottle hit the bow and exploded and sprayed champagne all over the place. Wow! I did it, and everyone cheered and they let the newly painted schooner slide down the ways into the bay.

Mom and Daddy had an outrageous party on board, which went on all afternoon. There wasn't a sober sailor on board, including me. Daddy said it was okay for me to celebrate on this special day. Sally and I got a little drunk on champagne for the first time. It was one the best days of my life, because Daddy was determined to win the Master Mariners race and I was going to be his wind spotter and first mate. What an honor. I was in seventh heaven. Daddy named her Bojangles because he liked Sammy Davis Jr. and he loved how he sang the song. So did I.

Trish signed off on her memoir when the nautical clock chimed eight bells. Her phone rang as she was pouring a smoothie into a bowl of Muesli. "Hi Helen, how are you?"

"Just fine, dear. I called to ask you for dinner next Friday; we had such a short visit the other day."

"My calendar's clear. I'll bring a bottle of Kangaroo Red. Oh, by the way, I'm coming along pretty well with my memoir, ten pages. It really is a relief to get it all out. I'm actually enjoying it."

"Wonderful, I look forward to reading it when it's ready. How about six thirty?"

"Perfect."

4

The week had evaporated when Trish realized Friday was upon her. She was running late with one of her patients, so she rode her dad's Indian motorcycle to her Tai Chi class and met with the group in the park. The big schooner was still anchored there. She assumed that it was a cruising yacht that had put in to re-provision on a voyage to southern oceans. The Canadian ensign still flew from the staff and the small American courtesy flag flew from the starboard cross tree halyard. She noticed that the pulling boat was not tied to the stern, but a small dinghy was, and there was no evidence of any crew or passengers on board.

She greeted the class with the respectful bow and started the exercises. With a smile, she took them through the moves when she noticed the big man she had seen the previous week. He was walking along the path beside the park when he stopped and put his leather bag beside the path to watch the class. He was not wearing the beaded headband with the feathers hanging from it.

Trish glanced at him from time to time and noticed that he was staring directly at her. It was during one of these brief glances that she was surprised to see he was doing the exercises in complete unison with her. She asked one of her class to take over and walked over to him. She put her hands together and bowed. "Good afternoon, friend, you're welcome to join my class if you like." She was surprised that he was much taller than he had appeared.

He smiled and returned the bow. Trish looked over at the vessel. "Is that your schooner?"

"It is."

"She's beautiful." Trish looked around at the class. "Would you excuse me? I have to finish with the class, and if you have time, I'd like to talk to you some more."

"Sure, I have all day."

"I'll be about ten minutes. Come on, join us, why don't you?" Trish took her position before the class. The big man took a place at the end of the front row. Trish called out *"Part the Wild Horse's Mane."*

The class and the stranger went through the exercise and several more until the end of the session. Trish announced, "Guys, if it's raining next Friday, come to my place." They all bowed to each other. Trish waved to her class and walked over to the stranger.

She looked at the yacht. "She's beautiful and has the lines of a Fife or a Milne. That looks like a dragon's head on the forward cove stripe."

"How do you know about Fifes?"

"My dad had an eighty-four-foot Fife gaff schooner."

"Really, what was her name?"

"Bojangles"

"Jesus!" He exclaimed. "That would be Alan Cameron, right? So you must be—Trish; I'm Gilley Cornwall."

Trish's face lit up at the sound of his name. She held out her hand. His big hand swallowed hers. "The Tahiti race seventy-three. Of course I remember you. You came on board our boat after the race to congratulate Daddy and the crew."

He smiled. "Well, I'll be damned, that was about twenty-eight years ago, how about that?"

She returned the smile. "You had a crew cut and no beard. This absolutely blows me away. Wow!" She studied his weathered face and bright blue eyes, noticing some scaring on his right cheek.

His short beard melded with his long gray hair with touches of white at the temples. "Gilley, this calls for a big hug."

They hugged quickly, with a few back pats. "You know, when I first saw you with your class last week, I wondered if we'd met in another life. I couldn't help staring at you, and you're very easy to stare at. But I couldn't put it together and I've been wondering all week. You grew up, Trish. It's really good to meet you again. This calls for a celebration! Would you like to come aboard for a cuppa and a look see?"

"I'd love to. What's her name?"

Gilley picked up his bag and started walking toward the small boat-wharf in the marina. "*Romayne*. She was designed and built by the 'William Fife yard in Scotland, away back in nineteen thirty one. I've just completed a three year stem-to-gudgeon refit in Costa Rica."

Gilley stowed the bag in the bow of the Whitehall. He cast off the painter and inserted the oar into the transom notch and sculled out of the harbor with a rhythmical sweep of the oar from side to side, propelling the boat toward the schooner.

"What a lovely name. Where did it come from?"

"It was her original name, named after the owner's mother. I was told it's a Romany gypsy name meaning romance. But I'm not sure. I loved the sound of the name when I found her. She's the first yacht I've ever owned, and damn well time; I'm lucky to have her."

Trish glanced up at him. "You sure are. She's big."

"She's one-hundred-and-eight feet on deck, twenty-foot beam, and draws fourteen. Your dad's Fife was the first one I'd seen. At that time I decided if I was ever going to own a schooner, it would be a Fife, and that's why I had to buy her, so we can sail off into the wide blue yonder together." He laughed. "Yeah."

Gilley approached the schooner, landing alongside the companion ladder. He held onto it as Trish stepped out and up to the deck. He followed her with the bag and made the painter fast.

Trish was in complete awe as she slowly surveyed the deck, varnished masts, doghouse and polished bronze fittings. She turned around to him. "Wow, she's really squared away, I can't believe what I'm seeing. She's absolutely magnificent, like new. Did you replace the deck?"

He stowed the bag in the doghouse and joined her at the helm, where she stood holding onto the big wheel. "We removed every deck plank and some beams; we found that all but a few were sound. So we refastened, caulked, filled the seams with Thiokol and sanded about a sixteenth of an inch off. We also took off every hull plank, replaced some cracked frames, refastened her with copper rivets, put her all back together and Bob's your uncle."

As they slowly walked around the deck, Trish examined and touched everything as if it were gold or fine jewelry. "Gilley, I don't know if you knew about my father's death. Had you heard?"

They stopped at the foremast. Trish looked toward the city, a sparkling tapestry of buildings. Gilley stood beside her. "Yes, I'm sorry to say I did hear. I was very fond of Alan. He was a prince of a man. I really didn't think he was the dying kind."

She turned to him with teary eyes. "I remember he was very fond of you, Gilley, and the fun parties you all had during the Bastille celebration. What a crazy two weeks, and both of you joined the Tahitians in their pirogue races and the spear-throwing competitions. I remember him saying about you that he'd found a fine new friend." Trish wiped her tears with her hand. "Then Daddy got you into an arm-wrestling match on the quarter deck, and surprisingly, he beat you. I found it difficult to believe that you didn't let him win."

"Trish, he had a strong arm and was very determined in everything he did. He beat me two out of three. It was fair and square."

They continued the slow walk around the deck as Gilley described some of the improvements he and his shipwrights had carried out. He pulled a Meerschaum pipe out of his coat pocket. "You're not in law enforcement, are you?"

"God, no, far from it." He paused and lit the pipe, and some of the aromatic smoke from the hashish wafted over to her. He passed the pipe to her.

"Not right now, thanks, I'm riding home on Daddy's old classic Indian bike."

Trish was standing beside the forward hatch and was surprised to see a young woman emerge with a cup of tea in her hand. She nodded to Trish and Gilley.

She spoke to Gilley in a manner that indicated she was deaf. Trish noticed a nasal quality in her tone. "Got teapot on, skipper, and I put new tea cozy on like you told me."

"Thanks, Fern. Shake hands with an old friend, Trish Cameron, she's a blue-water sailor; I met her in seventy-three when her dad won the Tahiti race." Gilley spoke very slowly and moved his lips so that she could read them. "Fern did a lot of work on the schooner when we refitted her, and now she's the schooner's bright-work superintendent." He winked at her. Trish shook Fern's hand, which was rough as sandpaper.

"It's nice to meet you, Fern. I've been admiring your beautiful varnishing." Trish caressed the varnish on the hatch coaming. Fern's smile showed crooked teeth. Her face had a masculine appearance, with a few chin hairs showing. She wore her long brown hair in a ponytail.

"I glad you like my work. I use special camel hairbrush from China. You have schooner?"

Trish noticed Fern's clipped and missing words and shook her head. "No, but I have a Whitehall like Gilley's. Maybe you'd like to varnish the seats and cap rails for me?"

Fern looked at Gilley with a mock frown. "I guess I never finish on this goddamn schooner. Gilley want five coats, this number four, right Gilley?" She laughed and took a sip of tea.

Gilley pulled hard on his pipe as if he wanted to send the smoke down into his toes. "Yup, one more coat, Fern, and I'll cut ya loose." He took his wallet from his pocket and pulled out some twenties and handed them to her. "So, Fern, don't go and spend it all on beer in the bar. I'll see you Monday and you can give her a last coat. Have a good weekend, aye?"

"Thanks skipper. It nice to meet you, Trish."

"You too, Fern." They continued aft, where Gilley stopped beside a mechanism mounted on the deck aft of the helm. It had a varnished plywood paddle attached vertically. "This is Arthur, my secret weapon, commonly known as a wind vane. We didn't have these in the good old days. It replaces six crew and steers a way better than any helmsman, it doesn't talk back, doesn't get drunk, eats no food, doesn't use electricity and, best of all, it won't steal your girlfriend in port."

Trish laughed. "I love it, won't steal your girlfriend in port."

"This particular incredible contraption was invented by an old friend, the late Arthur Whitfield from Australia. He singlehanded his ninety-eight-foot gaff schooner from Sydney via Cape Horn to the Caribbean."

Trish studied it. "It looks complicated; how does it work?"

Gilley lifted a small latch and rotated the bronze mechanism in a full circle, then locked the latch. "It's really simple. Once the sails are trimmed to the course you're steering, you rotate this gear until the wind vane is directly in line with the wind, then lock it in, let go of the wheel and Arthur does the rest. Arthur steered most of the way from Costa Rica to here."

Trish liked his smile, which radiated confidence. He looked at the vane and disconnected it. "So what are you going to do with *Romayne* now that you've restored her?"

"First thing on Memorial Day, I'm going to enter her in the Master Mariners regatta, which I'm sure you're familiar with. That's four weeks from Sunday. We've got some serious competition with the hundred-and-sixteen-foot gaff schooner *Maverick*. But we'll give it a shot and see how she goes. So, Trish, let's go below."

He led the way to the doghouse, ducking his head to clear the hatch. Trish heard the ship's clock strike seven bells. "Your clock is right on three-thirty." Gilley tapped the matching barometer, watching the needle move slightly to a higher pressure.

"It loses about a minute a week." He preceded her down the steps into the commodious salon.

"Oh my God, look at this!" She examined the darkly polished wood paneling. "It's huge, and absolutely beautiful."

He grinned. "The salon is paneled with French-polished African mahogany by William Fifes' master shipwrights. It was still in usable condition when I found her. It just needed cleaning up, rubbed and polished. The leaded-glass panes in the cabinet doors, the countertops are Italian marble and the paneling behind the fireplace is mosaic tile, real leather settees. Would you believe the previous owner used this schooner as a storage hold for all the crap they didn't want in the farmhouse? The piano is also original, but needs tuning, salt air is tough on pianos." He played a quick scale and closed the lid.

Trish stroked the polished wood as she looked toward the oil painting of old schooners on the forward bulkhead. "Looks like a serious painting." She examined it closely, looking for the artists' signature. "I can't read it, but it's beautiful. It reminds me of Monet. Do you know if this is an original?"

Gilley glanced at it. "Damned if I know, I just love the look of it."

"I'll get the tea and some cookies." She followed him into the galley.

He took two Pyrex measuring cups from the overhead hooks and filled them.

Trish laughed when she saw the cups. "Very original, Gilley." They settled into easy chairs.

"So where did you find this incredible schooner?"

"Well, an old friend of mine and crew were delivering a ketch from Panama to San Diego. We were beating our stupid brains out. So we said screw it and pulled into Golfito Bay in Costa Rica, and there was *Romayne* tied up to a wharf of a big date plantation. We were waiting for the norther to turn fair, so we went ashore and met the elderly British lady who owned the plantation and the schooner. She and her husband had bought the Fife for a world cruise. On their way north to British Colombia and Alaska, they stopped in Golfito for weather and found this plantation for sale. I guess they had a piss-pot full of money and were looking for an investment in the tropics. They bought the plantation, hired a manager and farm workers and had just got the operation going when her husband had a massive stroke. He died a year later. Apparently she didn't like England and decided to stay and run the farm." He refilled their cups. "She and her three kids lived there for about twenty years. I asked if the Fife was for sale. None of her kids wanted it. She was asking a hundred grand. The schooner had been left alone for too long; she was numb and dying. I was very interested; but she needed a lot of work because she'd been in the tropics for twenty years. You just can't do that to a ship. Finally, my friend said to me, 'Gilley, if you have the ability to buy and restore a classic Fife and you don't, you're a goddamn fool'. So that did it, he made me do it. I bought her then and there for seventy-five grand including the painting of the schooners."

Trish had been admiring the salon during Gilley's account of his acquisition. She noticed a shelf around the upper section of the paneling with twenty or so full bottles of liquor securely mounted on it. "That's an interesting way to set up your bar."

"It's not really a bar, Trish, but old friends the bastards, they're there to tempt me."

They both laughed. "So you know about temptation, do you?"

"Unfortunately, I've had too much experience with it. What about you?"

She gave him a smile. "Well, according to Oscar Wilde 'The best way to get rid of temptation is to yield to it.'"

He laughed. "That's great; to get rid of temptation, yield to it. Ya hear that, ya bastards?"

Trish laughed. "Yeah, I've had a lot of temptations, and a lot of fun and trouble yielding to them. I agree with good old Oscar; he was really out there. So what are you going to do with this beauty after the race?"

"So, what am I going to do with her? Maybe we're going to chase sunsets in the northeast trades down to Tahiti; I haven't been there for a while. Then, over to Cook's Bay in Moorea, which, in my opinion, is the most beautiful bay on the planet. Of course you remember, we were all there together. Maybe we'll run down some more westing to Auckland, meet up with some old pals. Come on, I'll show you the rest of her. Bring your tea."

They walked forward into the full-width galley. "This is the original cast-iron Aga stove, which used to burn coal. I converted it to diesel because I don't want to store coal."

She could feel the heat radiating from the cast-iron top.

He led her forward to a cabin with separate head and shower. "Originally this was meant for a paid captain and his wife. Across on the port side was the mate's cabin. Forward was the four-berth crew quarters with a head and shower. "I installed four water-tight bulkheads with locking doors, just in case we hit a whale, or a log. The previous owners had a paid crew, maybe three or four."

"Let's see, where were we? Oh yeah, then after New Zealand, I'm going down to the roaring forties and around the Horn. I've never been in those waters." They walked aft. "Actually, we're going to double the Horn."

"That sounds ambitious. How many crew?"

Gilley continued walking aft to the owner's and guest cabins. "No crew, just Arthur McWindvane and me. Remember, Arthur is the same as a crew of six."

"You're kidding. You're really going to single-hand a hundred-and-eight-foot schooner?"

"Well, I'm thinking about it. We'll see."

"But God, the gear and sails are all so big. What if you get hurt or—?"

"Arthur single-handed his schooner, as I told you, around the Horn. Trish, don't you think we all have to take risks in this life? I'm sure you've taken some, like when you sailed with your dad in the Tahiti race. I remember he told me that he wanted to transit the horn someday. You knew that, right?"

He showed her the four double aft cabins with heads and shower.

"Yeah, I knew he wanted to do the Horn. I would have gone on that cruise, too—but it wasn't meant to be." Trish paused for a long moment. Did you ever hear how it happened? I mean, how he died?"

They were standing inside his cabin. She looked at it without really seeing it, except for the beaded headband with the eagle's feathers hanging on a hook. Beside it was an old, grainy framed photograph of a tall man wearing a cowboy hat and chaps and a short woman with Indian features, holding the hands of a small boy who appeared to be about four years old. She reached up and felt the feathers.

"I heard there was an accident on *Bojangles* and he drowned. I'm so very sorry, Trish, I know how you worshipped him. We all did."

They walked forward to the salon and sat down. He filled their cups.

"It was the year after the Tahiti race and the second time we'd entered the Master Mariners race in *Bojangles*. Daddy had Alfi Fowler as first mate and a big crew, and my friend Sally and I were on board. Anyway, I became pretty good at spotting the wind lifts and headers. He used to call me his secret spotter. So, he had me up on the mainmast crosstrees where I could really see the lifts. I'd call the information to him and he'd either come up into the wind or fall off. He was so gung-ho to make that windward mark on one tack. We had the topsails set and the schooner was going like a train. We'd passed all the other boats in our class and were coming up on the mark at Crissy buoy for the jibe. The mainsail crew lost control of the sheet; when Daddy jibed, I was just climbing down to the deck when the main and gaff booms jibed over and hit the shroud that I was holding onto with a hell of a whack. I lost my grip and went into the drink. When I came up, I saw someone throw me a life ring and then Daddy dove in."

Trish hesitated and looked at the carpet and back to Gilley. "He never came up, Gilley. The next thing I remember, I was being pulled onboard, hysterical that they couldn't find him. We searched. The Coast Guard searched. They were sure that he'd had a heart attack and drowned. His body must have been taken out the Gate with the ebb tide."

"God, Trish, I had no idea, how terrible for you."

"The worst part of it was he had angina, a heart condition that I never knew about. Mom said he didn't want me to know. He was always thinking of me, my brave hero. His doctor told him that he shouldn't sail. Of course, sailing was in his blood, and I remember him saying that he was going to win that bloody race if it killed him." Trish wiped her eyes with her hand.

Gilley shook his head in disbelief. "I can't imagine anything worse for you and your mother. You must have gone through hell."

"We did, but we finally got our lives back together after a year or so. My good friend Sally helped me a lot." She paused and appeared to be deep in thought. "Dear Sally, I've lost track of her for too many years. Oh well."

She glanced at her watch. "Well, Gilley, it's been great to meet up with you again after all this time. A lot of water has passed under our keels. Thanks for the tea and the tour of your amazing schooner. Maybe next week I'll launch my Whitehall and row down for a visit. I'd like to hear more about what you've been doing for the last twenty-eight years. God almighty, that's over a quarter of a century."

"It's been a real treat to see you again, Trish. Sure, row down for a visit. The teapot is always on. I'd like to find out about what you've been up to."

Gilley pulled the Whitehall to the companion ladder. He offered Trish the stern seat and took the middle thwart, to be in the rowing position; the wind had freshened a bit from the north, kicking up slight chop.

He rounded the corner into the marina and landed the boat at the wharf.

She gave him a hug. "I look forward to seeing you again." He released her from the embrace and held her hands momentarily. "Trish, I don't know if you'd be up for it, but I'd be honored to have you aboard for the Master Mariners race, and I could sure use you to call the lifts and headers; I'll even provide a safety harness."

She gave him a smile as she turned to walk away, and then looked back. "Thanks, Gilley, I'll think about that. I haven't been sailing for quite a while." She mounted the Indian, kicked it into life, waved and roared away.

5

Gilley went into the heart of Sausalito and walked past the small-treed park on the main street. He crossed over and started up the easement steps two at a time. He needed the exercise and felt his leg muscles tighten. By the time he hit the top step, his muscles were in knots. He sat down on the top step and massaged them for a long time before he felt like walking again. Finally recovered, he walked along the street and stopped in front of a small cottage.

He wondered how many sheets to the wind Julie would be this day. He shrugged and knocked on the door. Carol, Julie's friend and caregiver, a short middle-aged woman, held the door. "Oh, hi Gilley, come in. I'm just finishing up here. So long, Julie, I'm off. See you tomorrow. Maybe we'll go shopping if you like?"

He walked into the small living room where his wife sat in a wing chair facing a panoramic view of the yacht harbor and the anchorage. Her wheelchair was parked in the corner; two crutches were leaning against the wall.

She glanced at him quickly and asked sarcastically, "Well, who is she?" She took a deep drag from her unfiltered cigarette, and blew a smoke ring at the window.

Gilley pulled up a chair across from her and sat down. "What are you talking about?"

"The tall, good-looking redhead with the big tits."

Gilley glanced at the binoculars on the table that would give a commanding view of the schooner and any activity that took place on deck.

"Oh, that was Trish Cameron. You remember me telling you about her dad, Alan, who was drowned in the Master Mariners race." He detected booze on her breath. Her eyes were lazy. He decided she was three sheets to the wind this day.

"Did you put the blocks to her?" She grinned, still looking out at the Bay.

"For Crissake Julie, why do you have to be so goddamn crude?"

"Because that's what you sailors do when a sexy woman comes aboard. I should know, after being married to you for eight years." They had only lived together for three of those years. The remainder of that period he was overseas driving millionaires' yachts. Annoyed, Gilley went into the kitchen for a glass of water.

"You want water or whiskey?" He delivered the question with as much sarcasm as he could. He drained the glass, and stood watching two sloops beating up the channel.

"Go to hell, Gilley, my drinking is my business, so knock it off."

At one time he had enormous sympathy for her, especially after the fall and broken hip. He felt guilty about how badly he had conducted his relationship with her. They had argued endlessly about her drinking and her firm refusal to take lithium. He finally realized there was nothing he could do to help her. The doctor had told him that her deep depression was partly a result of her inability to deal with life. He'd also diagnosed Julie to be bipolar. This dual combination had ended the remote possibility of bringing any joy into her life or their marriage. The doctor had prescribed lithium for the manic depression and a barbiturate for the insomnia. Julie told him she wouldn't accept the diagnosis or take drugs. The sleeping pills were the only drug she would take. He had also told Gilley privately that if his wife continued to drink and smoke, her future was very dim indeed. And that's where they left it.

"Listen, Julie, I've got to apologize for my—insensitivity; if I'd just tried to walk a mile in your moccasins. You're only fifty and I know you've been dealt a lousy hand."

She had told him all the horror stories that went down with her father. A drunk and an abuser, he had stuck the business end of a shotgun in his mouth and blew out his alcohol-soaked brains. Julie, awakened by the blast, found him. She was orphaned at fifteen when her mother had died of an overdose. She ended up with an unloving aunt, became pregnant and had an abortion at sixteen.

"I'm not interested in a pity party, Gilley. Get to the point or get out."

"Okay, my point is that there are some very kind friends who want you to get better. Try to listen to what they're saying. Dr. Benson told me you have nothing to lose by trying lithium. I beg you to give it a try, Julie. What do you say?"

"He's a quack and I don't trust him or any of those goddamn idiots. They can't even fix my constant pain when I'm on crutches. At least I'm not in any pain sitting here."

Gilley looked at her. "Well, sleep on it, will you? All I want to do is help."

He thought back to the day he'd had a call from Carol that a drunken Julie had tripped in the bank, falling hard on the marble floor, and broken her hip. All the time she was in recovery, she continued to drink. Later, X-rays revealed that her hip joint was not healing.

Gilley had been working in the Mediterranean as skipper on a yacht during his wife's recovery. The orthopedic surgeon insisted that she stop drinking because bone will not heal with alcohol in the system. When Gilley returned on leave a few months later, he was shocked to see how her condition had deteriorated. The surgeon told him that her hip joint had failed to heal due to osteomyelitis and inflammation of the bone marrow.

"Gilley, I appreciate your support and renting this pad for me, I really do, but just let me be. I'm really at peace here."

He leaned over and kissed the top of her head. She took his big hand and gave it a feeble squeeze. "Take care, Julie."

"Yeah, you too."

He walked along the tree-lined street to the top of the steps and stood there looking down at his other lady, lying peacefully at anchor.

6

Trish finished an hour of therapy with a middle-aged client and walked with her to the door. After this last appointment of the day, she wrote up her notes on the session, then changed into shorts and a T-shirt. She glanced at herself in the mirror. "Trish, it's time for a row."

She lowered her Whitehall in the davits onto the rollers on the float and eased the boat into the water. She tossed a bailing scoop, water bottle and life jacket into the bottom of the pulling boat and shoved off. The oars felt good in her hands again. She pulled hard. The boat glided easily through the calm water along the Sausalito waterfront. Looking over her shoulder to avoid any boats, she saw Gilley's schooner lying at anchor.

She slowed the boat as she approached. "Gilley, are you aboard?"

From the companion ladder she heard his deep voice. "Yeah. Oh, it's you, Trish. Throw me your painter." He held it until she stepped on deck, and secured it.

"Hi there, Gilley, I'm out for some much-needed exercise, but I developed a mighty thirst. So, I'll take your offer for a cup of tea and a hug."

"Great, I'm calling it a day. Welcome, you're just in time." He took the Meerschaum pipe from his pocket, lit it and passed it to Trish.

"Why not?" After pulling on it, she held her breath for a few moments, and then blew smoke into the breeze. "Um, nice."

"B.C. Bud, dynamite stuff. Come below, I'll have a pot of tea ready in no time or, coffee if you like?"

"Tea's fine. Say, Gilley, if the wind spotter-job is still open, I accept, but I'll definitely need a safety belt."

"Terrific. Alan Cameron's daughter will be sailing on my schooner. We'll dedicate this race to him and have a perpetual cup in his name. What do ya say?"

"I'd be over the moon with joy. Did you hear that, Daddy?" She looked up at the sky and gave Gilley a high five.

"Great, we're going to do a trial run on the Saturday before the race, mainly to get familiar with the tides and the course, so put that on your calendar. So far I've got a damn good crew of about twelve local sailors, but I need ten more heavies strictly for rail meat, about two thousand pounds of movable ballast. Oh, and Alfi Fowler is back from his brother's funeral, and he'll be onboard. That should do the trick."

Trish faked a frown. "Captain Cornwall, sir! I'm really disappointed, I thought it would be just you and me and old Arthur over there. What's all this about a crew of twenty-five?"

Gilley laughed. "I'll tell you what, after the race we'll dump the crew ashore, because for sure they'll want to get loaded and party all night. Then you and I can take off and sail down to Tahiti and Moorea. I'd say for about six months. Can you block that out on your calendar?"

Trish laughed. "I'll check and get back to you right away. Give me your cell number; you do have a phone?"

"I do, and I'll give you my card when I get the tea underway."

Gilley set the teapot on the table and covered it with a tea cozy. Two measuring cups and a plate of cookies completed the presentation. He picked up the teapot and cups, then took a card from the chart table and gave it to her. "Let's go on deck. It's nice this time of day when the wind's down. Would you bring the cookies?"

They sat opposite one another at the big horseshoe-shaped cockpit table as he poured the tea.

"Gilley, I have to ask you about the headband and feathers you were wearing the other day, and your gold earring. What's that all about?"

He smiled. "Well, my mother was a full-blooded Canadian Chilcotin Indian, or First Nation as they call them now. My father was British, so I'm half Canadian, half Brit. That head-dress I wear from time to time was given to me by the chief of our tribe when I became a young man, traditional tribal stuff. The earring can be worn by sailors who have sailed the South China Sea and not gotten their asses hijacked by pirates."

She studied his face. "Really? I had no idea. Wow, so you're, ah—?"

"Half-breed. I look like my father, who was six-foot-four, blond and didn't look like a British remittance man. My mother was five-foot-five, had black hair, and was very loving. They were great parents. The headdress feathers came from a live bald eagle that I captured on my rite of passage, and I have the scars to prove it." He rolled up his sleeve and touched his cheek.

"Incredible; you did have a battle." She touched the scars on his arm.

"I was sixteen when I was instructed by the tribal elders to go out into the bush alone without food for as long as it took for me to complete my vision quest. I went up to a mountain lake about five miles east of our place. I built a small shelter under a big fir tree that had an eagle's nest in it. I'd seen the eagles flying to it, so I snared a chipmunk and tied the little bugger on the top of the shelter, and left an opening in the roof where I could see an eagle coming for the bait. The little chippy was making a hell of a noise and jumping around. When an eagle finally landed to take the chipmunk, I reached up and grabbed one leg. He worked me over with his beak and claws on his other foot, blood all over the place. I managed to pull a feather out of each wing so he could still fly, and let him go. I'll tell ya, I was one hell of a mess when the battle ended."

"What happened to the poor chipmunk?"

"He was a lot luckier than I; he never got a scratch. I thanked him for his good work and cut him loose. But I got the feathers and I didn't have to kill the great bird. My mum had told me how her dad had done that very same thing many years before."

"Amazing. What about your wounds?"

He laughed. "Oh, I got some moss, soaked it in the lake and made a bandage. That stopped the bleeding fast. I think about that time in my life often. I stayed another two days and the hunger kinda went away. I had some incredible visions about my life, and everyone I knew. Finally, I dragged myself back home wearing a birch-bark headband with the two feathers. Mom and Dad were very happy to see me. The tribe had a little pow wow to welcome me into manhood with the new name, 'Rainbow Lightning Eagle.' So that's how I got the headdress. My mother made the beaded headband. It keeps me grounded, so I wear it once in a while just to keep on my life's course, if you know what I mean?"

"Yes, I do. I love your story. What an amazing experience for a young man."

"I decided on my vision quest that I'd try to be the best person that I could, just like Mom and Dad. You know, honest and helpful to others. It's sort of my mantra. So, Trish, tell me about you?"

"I'm really a healer, and I decided a long time ago that I wanted to help people professionally. After Daddy died and a year later, Mom died of a heart attack, I was an orphan at nineteen. I chose psychology after I met a very good woman psychologist who sort of lured me into it. I got into the University of Miami and came out with a degree in psychology. Now I have a private practice, which I run out of my floating home at the north end of town. Fortunately, I have a full stable of patients and I thrive on healing them."

He topped up their cups. "So, your medicine wheel is in sync with your life, and all is in order. Did you ever marry?"

"I was married for seven months, and sadly, he was killed in a car crash. We never even had a honeymoon."

"Oh, I'm sorry."

"He was in a head-on with a driver who was so loaded that the police figured he must've passed out. The son-of-a-bitch lived and Dan died; go figure. After all the dust settled, I headed back to Sausalito, which had always been my home. I set up shop here, and you know, I can't believe how fast the years just slipped by. The last two decades have simply vanished, but here I am, forty-five, unmarried and happy. So, enough about me. I'm very interested in your mom and dad; how and where did they meet?"

Trish glanced briefly at the small town over Gilley's shoulder and then back at him. She remembered the old picture of his father holding his small son's hand and his pretty mother holding his other hand.

"Well, it's an interesting story how they met. My father, George, had graduated from the Royal Military College at Sandhurst in England. He joined a regiment in the British cavalry. Then, as he told me many years later, he was caught putting the blocks to the adjutant's wife when the adjutant was away on military maneuvers, while father was on non-military maneuvers with his wife."

Trish laughed. "Putting the blocks to the guy's wife; what a great way to put it. I'm sorry I interrupted you."

"Yeah, it's a good one. It was Dad's expression. I guess his hormones were raging at that age and the wife was ready and willing while her hubby was doing his thing. Anyway, he was damn lucky he wasn't shot on the spot. Apparently, the wife was a little loose and had an eye for younger officers. So Sub-Lieutenant George Cornwall was cashiered and drummed out of the army for that and his hard drinking. He told me the whole saga when I was old enough to understand how serious this was for a young career officer. He had disgraced the regiment and his parents. His father was a retired Colonel in the cavalry and was so ashamed of him that he sent him off to Canada, supposedly never to return. That's what they did to loose cannons in those days. He was paid a small stipend every year not to come back. He became what was known as a remittance man. So, he shipped out to Canada as a deckhand on a tramp steamer. He found work on farms as a laborer picking fruit, stooking grain on the prairies, and finally ended up in British Columbia, where he found work on a big cattle ranch. He became a range rider. He and an Indian were issued horses and hired to keep an eye on a large herd of cattle on the summer range.

"Anyway he and this Indian, Seymour Pettell, shared a tent on the range. The rancher gave them a grubstake, a carbine and a few extra dollars, and they lived on deer meat and beans and bannock, which is sort of a bread pancake. Then one day they were rounding up strays when they got between a grizzly sow and her cubs. Seymour's horse spooked and bucked him off; the bear went after him and mauled him a bit. Dad, who had learned to use a rope, got a loop around the bear's neck and dragged him off Seymour with his horse. Then the bear went after Dad, and he got bucked off and the bear went to work on him. He was badly mauled on his arms and shoulder and neck. Then Seymour, who had the rifle, shot the bear. The next thing Dad remembered was waking up in bed in a log cabin on the Indian reserve, and being cared for by Seymour's sister, Tatla. She nursed him back to health. Dad said she saved his life."

"God, what an amazing story. How did Seymour get him back to the reserve?"

"He made a travois with two poles lashed to the saddle, which was dragged behind the horse. It's an old Indian way to bring their wounded warriors home. He was almost dead. It was months before he was back to normal. He was a hero to the tribe because he saved Seymour's life, and yet, Seymour saved his life.

"They became tribal brothers, and he was made an honorary member of the tribe. Not long after that, Father and Tatla were married in a tribal wedding ceremony. In those days, a white man who marries an Indian was called a cloochman. So he was a remittance man, cloochman and a mountain man. He considered all the titles to be badges of honor, and I agree. I was born on the reservation to two of the best parents a kid could ask for, and there you have it. Someday I'll tell you the rest of the story if you like."

"What fascinating history." She reached over and took Gilley's hand. "Your dad was quite a man."

"He was, for sure."

Trish heard the ship's clock ring three bells and looked at it in the doghouse. "God, it's five-thirty already. I've got to be at a friend's for dinner, I'm sorry to say, but I'll see you Saturday for the practice run. What time?"

"I'll have the schooner alongside at the visitors' berth at Toadfish Marina. We'll cast off about ten. I'll have sandwiches and sodas aboard for lunch, so dress warm. You remember it gets cold out there."

Trish stepped into her Whitehall, set the oars. Gilley waved as she rowed north up the bay.

She shouted. "Thanks for the tea and good company."

7

Trish walked in through Helen's open door. "Sorry I'm late, love, but I met an old friend I knew from the Tahiti race." They embraced. Helen led Trish by the hand into the living room.

"Don't give it a thought, I had a late patient, and the lamb's in the oven. Bruce is out with his writing class tonight, so we have the place to ourselves. Let's start with something special in a glass."

Glasses clinked and they sipped their Scotch. "So who did you meet from Tahiti, pray tell?"

"I'm not sure if I ever mentioned Gilley Cornwall. Anyway, we met in seventy-three, when he came aboard our boat in Pape'ete to praise Daddy for winning the race. He's a big, extremely charming Canadian, and owns an enormous schooner. He's sixty-five, but looks a lot younger. And get this; he has a museum of full bottles of booze around the salon panels, which he calls 'old friends the bastards; they're there to tempt me.' I'm still reeling from the experience. It's not often you meet someone after twenty-eight years. I had the feeling that my Dad was on board. I guess it's because the last time I saw Gilley was with Daddy on *Bojangles*. It's kind of spooky." She drained her glass. "And I just learned he's half Canadian Indian, but you'd never know it to look at him."

"It's wonderful to meet an old friend like that. Let me top that up for you. My, aren't you thirsty tonight?"

"Thanks. I hardly ever drink hard stuff, but tonight this Red Label goes down nicely. I'm just so thrilled about meeting him aboard his beautiful Fife. By the way, Daddy's schooner was a Fife. And would you believe, Gilley asked me to sail in the Master Mariners regatta as wind spotter aloft?"

"Really, I assume he knows about the situation with your Dad?"

"Oh yeah, I told him the whole sad story. I think he's just being kind, and of course, he knows a good wind spotter can make a hell of a difference to windward in a race."

Helen winked at her. "Especially, a gorgeous one like you."

"Go on with you. But you know, I remember an old saying. 'When you get bucked off a horse, you damn well better climb right back on again.' And I think it's about time I got back aboard a sailboat again. I told him today that I'll do it, and yippee, I get a safety belt."

Helen went to the kitchen to take the lamb out of the oven. "It'll do you the world of good to get your feet on a deck after all those years on the beach. Now, would you pour the wine and let it breathe while I carve? There's the decanter."

"You know, I'm actually excited about sailing again. "I've been in denial about it all those years. I guess I'm doing it in tribute to Daddy, and I want to throw a rose to him when we round the windward mark at Crissy buoy."

Helen held up her glass "Oh, that's the best thing in the world for you right now, especially as Gilley was a friend of your father. Here's to them."

"God, that got to me. Oh well, it's good to keep the tear ducts open. What's new and exciting with you?"

Helen filled their glasses. "Same old, same old. Have you tried the new Magic Medicine yet?"

"Not yet, but it's on the top of my list. I want to take it when I do sweat lodge and vision quest; you know, the full deal, all day. I want to reel back my life script and review a lot of old stuff, and then put it to rest in my memoir. I also want to take a good look at the present, my practice. I'm ready to pick the ideal time to hang up the gone fishing sign, lock the door, turn off the phone, and let it all happen."

They finished their dinners and Trish poured the last of the wine. "That was absolutely delicious; you are a chef extraordinaire. Is that another of your secret recipes, too?"

"Thank you, it was good, and it's in Julia Child's cookbook." She reached for Trish's hand. "Now back to your vision quest. You certainly have a very good grasp of your life force and what you're all about."

"Anybody home?" A soft shout announced Helen's husband, Bruce, had arrived. "Good evening, you sweet ladies, I'm sorry I couldn't be with you. Did I miss any juicy gossip?" He leaned over to kiss Helen and then Trish.

"No, dear, just girl talk." Helen's face was flushed. "Why don't you pour us some of that delicious port? I'll get the dark chocolate."

Bruce held up his glass. "All for one and one for all."

After slowly sipping two glasses of port, Trish stood up unsteadily behind her chair. "Helen and Bruce, dear friends, I don't know when I have been so royally wined and dined by such charming hosts. Helen, thank you for your excellent dinner. I love you. But alas, now I must away on my flying machine to be with you yet another day. God, that was very good port; I must buy a case on the morrow. Sweet dreams darlings."

Helen looked into her eyes "Are you sure you're okay to ride the Beast? The spare room has your name on the door if you—"

"I'm fine really, lots of wind in my face and it's all downhill. Thanks for dinner, next time at my place."

They watched her start the Indian. Then, in a cloud of smoke, she roared off into the night.

"Bruce, I think our friend Trish is in love."

8

Trish's phone rang. She checked the I.D. number but didn't recognize it.

"Hello."

"Trish, it's Gilley, good morning. How are you?"

"Oh hi, Gilley, I'm fine, thanks. What's up?"

"I forgot to ask you the other day if you liked jazz, boogie, rag time and the Music Box?"

"I love all of them. And I haven't been there for ages. Are they still playing that good stuff there?"

"They sure are. Would you like to check it out with me Friday night?"

"I'd love to, how sweet of you to ask. Let me check my calendar here." She knew her calendar was blank as it had been for months. "Terrific, my dance card's empty."

"Great, so let's meet out front, say, six thirty. They start playing at seven."

"Terrific, I'll be there."

"Right on. I'll see you then; look forward to it."

"Me too. Thanks for calling."

"Well, Trish, a date with an old friend and why the hell not? You're going out with a fine schoonerman. God, what'll I wear?" She laughed. Over the years she had accepted dates that seemed interesting at first, but usually ended in disappointment. Helen once joked about her being a guy magnet, but after dating so many letches and losers, she'd elected to go into seclusion, keeping one eye open for the suitable mate, male or female. So far none of either sex had made the cut.

Trish firmly decided that it was now the time to contact her old childhood friend, Sally Brown. She also wanted to reassemble the story of her life and discover what mattered, or didn't. Sally definitely did matter.

After phone interviews with three private investigators, Trish settled on Betty Lindley. It wasn't cheap, but if $500.00 up front and $125.00 an hour would locate Sally, the price was worth every nickel.

Lindley was a retired F.B.I. Agent who seemed highly motivated. She had a great track record locating missing persons, living or dead, and verified by the closed-case files she had shown her. She wanted Betty Lindley to start immediately, but the former agent was committed to helping her 86-year-old mother to get situated in a retirement home in Camden, Maine. They agreed to proceed in two weeks. Trish smiled as she thought about Sally. "My love, you are about to be found."

Trish decided designer jeans, sweater, black leather coat and cowboy boots would be cool for the Music Box and practical for the bike. She roared along Bridgeway and pulled up in front of the famous bar, parked the Indian and chained it to a tree.

Gilley walked toward the bar with two other men and one woman. He was easy to spot in a crowd, as he was so much taller than the others. Trish recognized Alfi Fowler, who had just returned from his brother's funeral in Washington. An old friend, Alfi had been first mate on her dad's schooner. She had looked after the old guy for years, often bringing him several plastic containers of Irish stew to tide him over for a while. Every now and then, Trish would also slip him a hundred dollars for rum, fun and incidentals. He was always extremely grateful to her, and she, in turn, was delighted to be in the company of this dear old friend of her family.

Trish greeted Alfi first with a hug. "Welcome home, dear. I'm so sorry about your brother; I hope he was comfortable."

"Yes, he went nice and easy, just like the rest of his life. He was a great guy. Thanks for your card."

Then, she gave Gilley a hug. "It's great to see you, Gilley. Thanks for getting me out off the boat. I was going into terminal cabin fever."

Fern was standing beside Gilley; Trish offered her hand to her, but was quickly enveloped in a bear hug. "I like hug too, you know."

Gilley introduced Ishmael, a tall, blocky Jamaican with dreadlocks "He's the best goddamn shipwright on the planet, and was the main man on our refit. Bloody good sailor, too. I suspect he may be related to William Fife. So, Ish, shake hands with Trish, who navigated her dad's Fife schooner in the Tahiti race when she was seventeen."

"It's nice to meet you, Ishmael." She shook his large, strong hand, and like Fern's, it was rough as sandpaper.

Gilley held the door open for his crew and found a table for them close to the stage. He ordered a round of drinks and looked over at the musicians, who had just arrived. They touched glasses.

The bandleader blew his trumpet and held his hand up for quiet. "Welcome, ladies and gentlemen, it's great to see you all again. Unfortunately, our piano player had a death in his family and won't be with us tonight. I know this is very unusual, but it's worth a shot. I want to ask if there is anyone in the audience who can really tickle the ivories, mainly to play the background melody, and if not, I'm pretty sure we can still make music."

He scanned the faces for a few moments, and his face lit up when Gilley shot his arm up. "If the piano's in tune, I'll give it a shot."

"Terrific, come on up here, friend. What's your name?"

"Gilley Cornwall."

Gilley leaned over Trish's shoulder. "Did I mention that occasionally in emergencies like this, I fill in if the regular piano player can't make it? Sometimes I forget those little details."

"I'm sure I'd remember a little detail like that." With a pat on her shoulder, he mounted the stage to join the six other musicians. He shook hands with them and took his place at the piano.

"Welcome, friends of the Music Box. We are the Rag Timers, and it's our pleasure to rock this old place off of the foundations for a while. Please welcome our new member to the band; Gilley Cornwall at the piano, Jim Dignall on soprano sax, Bill Samson on trombone, Don Henderson on clarinet, Hall Donavan on drums, Sammy Riley on the banjo and guitar, and I'm David Whitfield on this brass thing, whatever it is. So, Gilley, how about warming up that old thing and we'll play along with whatever you've got."

Gilley glanced at the bandleader, and then winked at Trish. "Folks this is Dizzy Fingers; it's the best ragtime piece ever written by Zez Confrey about 1923. Gilley hit the keys at full-syncopated speed. It was Gilley's signature piece, which he had learned from his piano teacher at the age of nine. He'd been practicing scales that day in one of the music rooms at school when he heard the fast ragtime piece being played in the next room. He'd rushed in to see his piano teacher, playing the most exciting music he had ever heard. He remembered standing in awe as he watched Mr. Batt's fingers fly over the keys. From then on, Gilley was hooked and determined to learn to play Dizzy Fingers. His teacher had suggested that maybe he could try to play it in a few years. Mr. Batt soon learned that Gilley had an ear, and was astonished when his student learned to play it well in three months. It was then that Mr. Batt realized he had a very gifted lad in his music class.

Trish and the others watched in fascination as Gilley and the band ignited the audience. She was the first to stand up and clap frantically when they finished the piece. The bandleader joined in the applause and shouted. "Ladies and gentlemen, tonight we have a piano player, and that's for damn sure. Thank you, Gilley; you're the first person that I've heard play that piece in years. Like wow!"

For the next hour, the audience was treated to the best ragtime, boogie and jazz that anyone in the Music Box could remember hearing. Trish and her companions were enthralled, and roared their appreciation for the amazing talent on the stage. Gilley joined the table at the end of the first set. Trish took one of Gilley's big hands in hers and patted it.

"God almighty, Gilley, you never said anything about what these big hands can do to a piano. Incredible."

He laughed. "I had a really good teacher. Glad you liked it. Are you guys getting enough to drink here?"

Alfi put his empty glass on his head, which was his personal signal to the waitress for a refill. "Here's to ya, captain, you're in fine form tonight. And, here's to the ships and the women of our land, may the first be square rigged and the second well manned." They all touched glasses and shouted their approval to Alfi.

Fern looked puzzled and leaned over to Trish. "What Alfi say that so funny? I don't get it."

Trish looked straight at her face and spoke slowly as Fern watched her lips. Her eyes smiled when she understood. She laughed at Trish. "That funny, I think Alfi a little drunk." She leaned close to Trish. "You very beautiful, Trish, I really like you; yeah. I think skipper like you too."

Trish took Fern's hand and squeezed it. "I like you too, Fern, you're very sweet."

They smiled at each other. "Gilley tell me you sail on *Romayne* with us in Master Mariners race?"

"Yup, I'll be onboard; I'm going to be wind-spotter up the main mast."

Gilley pulled up a chair beside Trish. "So who and where was this amazing piano teacher?"

"Well, that was a few years ago at school. Sammy Batt was a classical musician, but he loved ragtime and jazz. It turned out I did, too, so we worked together for a few years. I didn't dig classical, so he cut me loose on the good stuff and the rest is history."

The bandleader came by their table. "So are you guys having a good time?"

Trish spoke for the group. "We're having the best time. The music is unbelievable. Thank you, David."

"You're welcome. We sure landed a live one here with Gilley; we gotta sign him up. So, we'll rock the joint again in about ten."

Gilley grinned at the bandleader as he moved on. "He's got one hell of a band."

Alfi sipped his drink and laughed, "Looks like you've got yourself a job, captain."

"I might play the odd gig once in a while; we'll see."

Several people in the audience came by their table to thank and congratulate Gilley. He thanked them and shook their offered hands.

Finally the musicians mounted the stage when David Whitfield made the last announcement. "We'll be happy to play some of your requests." He held up a few pieces of paper that had been given to him. "Here's an old one called Honky Tonk Train. Gilley, I'll bet you know it."

The band members nodded to each that they all knew the piece. Gilley started off and the others joined in. When the piece ended, he leaned toward his mike. "I want to dedicate this next piece to a dear old friend who is no longer with us. Alan Cameron was one of the best schoonermen who ever sailed the ocean, and his daughter is with us tonight. Trish Cameron. They sailed and won the Tahiti race in his schooner, *Bojangles*. This is for Alan's memory and Trish's presence."

Gilley started Bojangles solo for the first few bars and sang the lyrics in his deep voice. The band picked it up and played softly in the background.

He looked down at Trish and winked. She let the tears flow down her cheeks then reached over to Alfi and put her hand on his and held it.

Alfi leaned over to speak into her ear in his squeaky voice. "Alan was a prince, he was loved by everyone, and you're a princess, Trish."

She smiled at Alfi and looked up at Gilley as he finished the piece. The audience cheered, and many of them stood up and clapped, as did Trish, Alfi, Fern and Ishmael.

One inebriated young woman in the audience called out. "Will ya play anything by Jerry Diner, puh-leeze?"

Gilley looked around at her. "Right on! The late Jerry Diner wasn't just a one-night stand, baby, he's forever." He started playing and singing one of the great love ballads. Gilley's voice was almost the same as the late Jerry's raspy baritone. The young woman was obviously overwhelmed, swaying with her own private passion for the music. She screamed with delight when it ended.

The band played nonstop for the remainder of the set. David Whitfield thanked the audience. He held up the Rag Timers C.D. to remind them it was for sale. He signed off and waved to the crowd. "We'll cut another with Gilley on it, for sure. Good night, all."

Gilley joined his group and sat down. Trish leaned over and kissed his cheek. "That was so sweet of you to honor Daddy and me like that. It was just beautiful, Gilley, I'll never forget it."

"Well, Alan would have been right at home here tonight.

I've been wanting to do that for some time, so it seemed the right time and place."

The waitress brought another round of drinks. "Gilley, I really dig it." He smiled at her as he stuffed a tip into her hand. "Our pleasure, we'll be back next month, and thanks."

Alfi leaned over Trish and grabbed Gilley's arm. He'd been drinking Mount Gay on the rocks continuously since they arrived, and was well on his way. "Ya done good, captain, you really got my old feet a stompin' tonight."

Trish took Gilley's arm. "You should go on the road with that band, you're right for them. God, that's the best I've ever heard anywhere. Did you ever think of that?"

"Yeah, I gave up sailing and went on the road for a short spell. It was a good band and we did pretty well, but there was way too much boozin', carousin' and temptation. I was blown out in three months, and I had to go back to sea to sober up. So I play for pleasure for my friends and folks like these. About ten years ago I played a gig with old retired farts, and any cash that got in the jar went to cancer research."

"That's wonderful. I love that kind of philanthropy."

Trish looked over at Alfi, who was barely able to sit straight. "Oh man, it looks like the President of the Pacific Ocean should be in his bunk. I better take him home."

Gilley loaded Alfi on the buddy seat behind Trish. She wrapped his arms around her waist and kicked the Beast to life.

She took Gilley's hand and pulled him to her face and gave him a decent kiss. "You're a dear man, Gilley, and thanks for the best time I've had in years. So I'll see you tomorrow alongside the guest berth. Can't wait."

Fern approached the bike and hugged Trish. "You my new friend, Trish. Goodnight."

Trish threw one arm over Fern's shoulder. "And you're my new friend. Good night, Fern, and Ish, it was great to meet you. Hang on, Alfi, we're heading for the barn."

She pulled away from the curb slowly, made a graceful U-turn and headed for Alfi's ark.

9

Trish was awakened by the same horrifying nightmare when her father drowned, after she fell overboard and he dove in to save her. Then blank, nothing. She tried to shake it off. When she was unable to drop off to sleep, she would turn on the radio, hoping the steady drone of National Public Radio would lull her to sleep.

The alarm went off at 7 A.M. She got up slowly and turned the shower on full blast. "Come on Trish, get a grip for God's sake. Remember the saying, 'You worry most about the things that never happen.'" The sports page in the *Chronicle* gave the lineup of yachts that would be sailing in the Master Mariners regatta. There it was: *Romayne,* Canadian schooner, Owner Capt. Gilley Cornwall. She didn't recognize any of the others in the lineup, but she was sure she'd get to know some of them before the day ended.

Trish parked the Indian in front of Alfi's waterfront ark and chained it to a fence post just as Alfi stepped out of his front door. "Morning, Trish. So are you ready for the big day?"

They headed toward the yacht harbor, walking slowly side by side. Trish stood a head and shoulders taller than her 84-year-old shipmate "Yeah, I'm a little nervous and I'm sure you know why."

"You'll do just fine, honey, just like you did yesterday; the windward leg to Crissy should be pretty smooth today. The forecast is northwest, fifteen to eighteen knots. She's really a close-winded old girl, especially with the topsails up. That was a damn good sea trial yesterday, but we didn't have all the rail meat on board like we will today. Gilley's rounded up about ten more big guys, so that'll make her stiffer than a wedding prick; excuse my French, it was one of Alan's expressions."

Romayne was moored alongside at the guest berth. They approached the schooner and saw ten or so sailors on deck and several more approaching along the dock. Trish watched Gilley directing his crew to their positions. He looked up as they stepped aboard.

"Now, we're getting some talent here. Mornin', Alfi, and welcome aboard, Trish. I'll be with you in a few minutes, I want to get these new guys organized. Tea and coffee, pastries on the cockpit table." Gilley went forward to instruct his expanding crew.

Trish saw Fern approach. They hugged. "Hi Trish, so you wind lady up mast. You hold on tight, okay?"

Trish smiled at her. "I sure will."

Gilley came aft and touched Fern on her shoulder. "Good job on the anchor lashings."

Gilley turned to face forward and shouted to his crew. "All right, lads, it looks like we're squared away now. I want to introduce those who weren't aboard yesterday to two good friends of mine. Trish Cameron will be our wind-spotter aloft; she's a blue-water sailor."

They all clapped, some whistled.

"I also want to introduce another guest: Jon Ewer, chief of Sausalito's finest. So, you better be on your best behavior. Some of you may not know it, but today *Romayne's* a pure sailing schooner. There are no race rules about having a crew of twenty-five to give us about two thousand pounds of moveable ballast. When we come about I want you ballast guys to get onto the weather rail right away. The main sailing crew will take care of the sheets and running backs. It looks like we have just enough wind to sail her off the dock. So, Ish and your boys, give her the main, the foresail and the staysail." When the sails were all hoisted, Gilley called forward. "Ish, stand by on the bow line." Gilley looked directly at Fern and mouthed. "Stand by on the stern line." She nodded.

The sails and sheets hung slack as they sweated up the gaff throats and peaks. Gilley stood behind the wheel and watched the sails take shape and fill as the gaff boom jaws settled on the copper mast bands. "Let go forward." He watched the bow slowly fall away from the dock as the staysail filled. "Let go aft." Fern pulled the stern line aboard and coiled it neatly in the scupper.

"Sheet the main and fore and stand by to give her the inner jib first, then the jib topsail." Trish and Alfi watched the crew harden up the main and foresail sheets. The schooner gradually picked up speed and heeled over to port as the jibs were hoisted and filled. Gilley checked the set of the sails as he laid the course to San Francisco. He shouted to the mid-deck crew. "Harden up the main backstay, then give her the topsails, sweat down the main and foresail jigs, and ease the lee topping lifts." Trish grabbed Alfi's arm as the schooner accelerated noticeably when the topsails filled. "Wow, she's really going." Alfi nodded. "Remember, she was doing twelve yesterday by GPS." Alfi pulled a small hand-held Garmin from his pocket, and passed it to Trish. It read ten knots. "Wait till we get some wind through the Gate. She'll go like a scalded cat." Gilley looked over at Alfi.

"She's all yours, Alfi, take her over to the City, then head her up to the bridge, I want to do a couple of practice jibes up there. We've got an hour till the start. Let's go forward, Trish." Alfi moved over to the big wheel as the relief helmsman. Gilley and Trish went forward, he to check all the lines for fouled sheets or halyards, and she to watch him and see how he became an integral part of his vessel.

The ballast crew was sprawled along the weather-side deck. "Good job, you guys. We'll be coming about in front of the yacht club, so stand by the jib sheets and be quick on the back-stays; you know the drill."

Gilley and Trish leaned over the bow to watch it cut the waves like a sharp rigging knife. "This old girl's in her element, this is her day. Yeah."

Trish looked over at him. "And this schoonerman is in his element. This is your day, Gilley."

She pulled a red rose out of her jacket and handed it to him. "This is for Daddy when we round the mark at Crissy."

He nodded, stuffed the rose in his pocket and looked toward the bridge. "We'll sail this one for Alan."

10

The 42-foot Grand Banks Europa *Bacchanal* pulled out of the Sausalito Marina, turned to starboard and set a course to the city front. Aboard were the owners, Jotty and Mary Linden; Sterling Sanderson, the sports broadcaster for the KABR radio station; Harry and Jan Schofield, the owners of KABR; and several guests. The owners of the station were going to cover the Master Mariners Regatta as they had for the last decade.

Jotty pushed the throttles into the corner and the handsome trawler surged ahead at 10 knots. He knew that two of the big schooners in the race could sail faster than his top speed, so he would pilot his vessel inside the course so that the announcer's boat could intercept the racers at the turning buoys. He would stay well out of their way to avoid any chance of interfering with the race.

Sterling came on live ten minutes before the starting gun. He followed some of the classic yachts with his binoculars. "Good morning to our nautical audience that is waiting for news on the classic yacht race; the Master Mariners Regatta. This is Sterling Sanderson with KABR. There are sixty sailing vessels racing today. Most of these classic yachts were built before World War Two; most of them are built of wood, and two, I am told, are steel. All of the yachts are sailing back and forth in the area of the starting line, jockeying for the best position to sail across the line just after the starting gun has fired. If they cross the line before the gun, they have to make a full circle turn and start again, losing valuable time. It will be a staggered start, which means the smaller, slower boats start first; the next class will start five minutes later, and so on until all classes have crossed the line. The two larger schooners, which are over one hundred feet, will start fifteen minutes later to give the smaller ones time to be well on their way, and they'll be sailing a different course, which is the race that I will be announcing today."

Sterling focused on the small sloops as they rallied behind the starting line. "There goes the gun for the nine smaller Bear boats to cross the line. The wind is blowing seventeen knots from the northwest, and there is a slight chop, so it should be a very lively race today. The two big schooners have just sailed by us, heading west for the Golden Gate Bridge." He focused his binoculars on them as they tacked to starboard.

"The first is *Maverick,* the one-hundred-sixteen-foot gaff schooner owned by Richard and Muriel Jensen from L.A. She's a steel hull built by Camper and Nicholson in 1938. The next is the Canadian flagged 108-foot gaff schooner, *Romayne,* owned by Gilley Cornwall. This classic yacht was built by the Fife yard, in Fairlie, Scotland, in 1931. So we're going to hold here around the inside of the starting line to watch the two big schooners cross the line. The handicap is given to *Romayne,* which is eight feet shorter than *Maverick.* She has to give *Romayne* five minutes. However, they will both start at the same time, making it a match race. All the smaller boats have started and are off on their own course."

Five minutes later, Gilley was standing behind the wheel. He was in position to start running for the starting line just two hundred yards offshore from the St. Francis Yacht Club. He looked to starboard to see *Maverick* getting into position for her run to the line. He had never met the owners, as they had just sailed up from southern California a week ago on their way for an Alaskan cruise. One of the two vessels would have a trophy cup at the end of the day. Gilley wanted to be closest vessel to the windward mark to round it, and then set a course to the first mark at Harding buoy.

"There goes the five minute gun. Haul everything in a skosh and we'll be on our way. Ish, let me know how she's lined up for the mark, I can barely make it out."

"Come a little to port, hold her there, you're right on, Gilley." Trish put her safety belt and life jacket on and was ready to go aloft to the main crosstrees when Gilley gave her the word. She gave a red rose to Alfi. "This is for Daddy at Crissy." He squeezed her hand.

Alfi looked at his GPS and showed it to Trish. They both glanced at *Maverick*, which was sailing about a hundred feet behind on their starboard quarter. Gilley checked his stopwatch. "One minute to the gun." He shouted to his crew. "Harden up the sheets for a close reach." He watched the booms and sails come in. "That's good." Ishmael called aft. "One hundred yards to the line." Gilley aimed the bow just to the right of the committee boat, and then slowly turned the wheel to port. The starter's gun fired with a puff of white smoke. *Romayne* crossed the line seven seconds later, and *Maverick*, five seconds later. "Here we go, lads, be ready to come about at Harding in about ten minutes. We'll be hard on the wind, so strap her in tighter than an Arab wrestler's jock strap." He looked over at Trish. "Okay, Trish, shout real loud when you see a lift or a header. Good luck." He held up his thumb. Alfi patted her back.

Trish climbed up onto the port cap rail and up to the ratlines; she held the shrouds tightly as she climbed ninety feet up onto the crosstrees, where she slipped under the round steel safety rail and clipped on her safety harness. She looked down at Gilley and raised her thumb.

She had a full view of Harding buoy ahead and *Maverick*, which had closed on them and was sailing abeam and slightly faster. Gilley held his course, trying to keep *Maverick* from crossing his bow and getting to the mark first.

Romayne was sailing at ten knots, but was slipping behind *Maverick* as she pulled ahead and took the lead to the buoy, which she rounded thirty seconds before *Romayne*. "Ready about!"

Gilley spun the wheel. The schooner sailed through the wind; as the booms came over, the heavy sheet blocks hit the ends of the traveler stops with a loud bang. The schooner quickly settled on to her new course directly behind *Maverick's* stern. Gilley looked over at Alfi. "Goddamn it, we're getting her dirty air. Trish better give us a lift soon."

"Sterling Sanderson back again. The big schooners are sailing hard on the wind, heading for Crissy buoy about two miles to the south."

He paused. "*Maverick* rounded Harding less than a minute ahead of *Romayne*. She's obviously a bit faster due to her longer water line. We are following directly behind *Romayne*, although slower, but sailing closer to the wind. We have learned over the years that races are often won to windward. We'll know in two hours. And that could be an advantage on this leg to the next mark. Both schooners are being affected by the last of the flood tide, which is setting them to the east. They won't feel the effects of slack water for a half hour. So I expect both boats will have to tack over to starboard and back to port to lay the windward mark."

Gilley couldn't quite lay the course to Crissy buoy as the flood was setting them to the east. Trish was surprised to see a lift so soon, but there it was, moving toward them. She shouted to the helm. "Gilley! We've got a lift at two o'clock; it's a big one." He looked over his starboard bow and waited for Trish to give him an update. She shouted. "Here it comes, go for it!"

He turned the wheel to starboard and came up about ten degrees, then eased the wheel back to center. The lift was a very strong wind shift from the beam, which heeled the schooner over until the lee rail was momentarily awash. "Hang over the rail, lads." The ballast crew kicked their legs over while holding tightly to the lifeline. Gilley looked over his port rail to see *Maverick* falling further down-wind and well below the mark. They didn't get the benefit of the lift.

Trish shouted to the deck. "There's about a hundred yards more of it, Gilley. You can come up a bit more." *Romayne* had gained from the lift and was sailing above the windward mark.

He looked over at *Maverick* and smiled as he saw her come about on a course toward the Marin headlands and the north tower of the bridge.

Ishmael shouted from the bow. "You're above the mark, but hold that course, Gilley. We've still got some flood."

"Thanks, Ish, we needed that." He could see Crissy buoy to port; the sea was pouring around the buoy and leaning it over from the force of the wind and the flood tide.

"That's the end of the lift, Gilley." Trish shouted. "You can make the mark like gangbusters now."

Romayne was half a mile from the mark and Gilley held his course. "Get ready to give her the ballooner and the fisherman as soon as we round. Stand-by on the main and foresail ready for the jibe."

When Gilley shouted, "Stand by—jibing!" he spun the wheel hard to port and the schooner cleared the buoy by twenty feet. The gaff booms jibed over to starboard and the main and foresail sheet blocks hit the traveler stops. Trish took a red rose from her pocket and threw it over the side to leeward and into the water where she had fallen overboard so many years ago. She put both hands up to her lips and blew a kiss to the memory of her beloved father. She watched Alfi throw a rose to the water, and then he took the wheel as Gilley went to the side and threw his rose to his good friend. He looked up at Trish and shot his clenched fist into the air.

Alfi saluted and went to work steering the downwind leg as he had in so many Master Mariners races over the years.

Trish unhooked her safety belt, grabbed the main throat halyard and slowly lowered herself to the deck hand over hand with her legs wrapped around the halyard. She walked aft to the helm to join Gilley and Alfi and wiped the tears on her hand. Gilley put an arm over her shoulder. "Alan would have liked the way we did that." Then he walked forward to check the set of the big nylon ballooner jib and then looked up at the fisherman, which was drawing well between to the mastheads.

Fern and Ishmael opened up two coolers that were lashed to the cockpit table. Fern signaled to her captain that lunch was ready.

Gilley shouted to his crew. "Alright lads, we've got about fifteen minutes till we round Blossom. So dig in to beef or turkey sandwiches and sodas. Save room for beer when we cross the finish line."

"Well, race fans out there in radio-land, that was the best sailing maneuver I have seen in many years. *Romayne* made a tactical coup and took a wild ride with an enormous lift, which allowed her to claw up to windward and make the first mark without having to tack. Unlike *Maverick,* which, for some reason didn't see the lift. So they had to tack and go over to Marin, losing about eight minutes. They are now well on their way on the downwind leg to Blossom buoy. *Maverick* is just now rounding the buoy, exactly ten minutes later. She will really have to put her skates on to catch up. She has just set a spinnaker and a fisherman. So stay tuned, we will break for the commercials and the news."

During the next leg, *Romayne* sailed flawlessly, partly due to having sailed the course the day before and also due to the excellent sail handling by the strong young crew. They were having the time of their lives. Some had cameras and camcorders to preserve the images of the day and to talk about for years. The schooner had rounded Blossom buoy and reached up the west shore of Angel Island and into Raccoon Strait. *Maverick* was slowly catching up, was now five boat lengths astern and had just set her genoa. Alfi had the helm and was steering a course to catch the last of the flood tide off-shore of Angel Island.

He knew that he would get a four-knot assist from the current. He was concentrating on keeping the schooner dead downwind. Gilley looked aft. "She's gaining on us slowly. Alfi, does this current curl around the east of Angel?"

Alfi looked aft quickly. "Not much, but I hope we get a kick as the westerly blows over the top of Angel. He looked back at *Maverick*. We want to hug the shore in flat water so when we get clear of the point Blunt, we'll be in position for the beat to the finish line."

"We're back live on KABR. Here comes *Romayne* around the south shore. She's just got a blast of wind over the top of the island, and she's going to clear point Blunt momentarily as she heads over to the city front for the final leg of this very close match race. *Maverick* appears to be closing the distance, and is about three boat lengths behind *Romayne*. The schooners will have to tack to windward passing Alcatraz, then along the city front. We can see hundreds of spectators and boats over there with their binoculars and cameras."

"Close haul this old girl as tight as you can. Get on the rail, boys, we've got more wind now." Gilley looked aft. *Maverick* was now about two boat lengths behind and was catching turbulent air from *Romayne's* sails. Suddenly *Maverick* tacked over to port to get out of the dirty air. "Ready about! Be fast now, here we go." Gilley made two turns of the wheel and the sails came over quickly as his schooner covered *Maverick* so that she would again be taking turbulent air, keeping her a boat length behind *Romayne's* transom. "We've got a tacking duel here, lads, so stay lively. Alfi, tell me when they tack, I want to show him nothing but our transom. Trish, take the helm, I want you to sail her over the line."

Surprised, Trish took the wheel in her hands and focused on the committee boat, which was anchored to the right of the finish line. "You bet."

"She's tacking right now." Alfi shouted in his squeaky voice.

Gilley glanced over his shoulder quickly. "Alright, Trish, give her about two turns to starboard, then head for the finish line."

"Ready about!" She shouted to the crew as the schooner came onto port tack. *Romayne* gradually accelerated. Gilley looked back at *Maverick*, directly astern. It looked as though *Maverick* was aiming to drive her bowsprit into *Romayne's* transom.

"Here she goes again, Gilley." *Maverick* started to tack and was half way through, when she altered quickly back to starboard. "Hold it, it's a bluff! Don't tack, Trish." She was just starting to turn the wheel.

"Sneaky bastards, they're trying every trick in the book." Gilley could see that they couldn't lay the finish line on this tack and they were about five boat lengths from it. He looked back at

Maverick, focused on the helmsman and saw him turn the wheel hard over. "They're tacking. Okay, Trish, let's do it."

"Ready about!"

The wind speed had increased. Water washed down lee scuppers. "Gilley, I can lay the mark now."

He looked over at her and smiled. "Go for it, Trish. They won't tack again." She altered a little to port and held that course.

She kept her eyes riveted to the mark and steered slightly to the left of it. The air horn on the committee boat went off with a high-pitched screech. The race was over. *Romayne* and her excited crew had won by two boat lengths. They all shouted at once. Alfi danced a little jig on the aft deck.

Trish hugged Gilley and kissed him. "Oh God, what a race, what a schooner, what a crew. Gilley held onto her and buried his face into her hair.

"That was for Alan, we won it for him." Gilley put his arm around Alfi's thin shoulders and hugged his old friend. "Ya done good, Alfi, that's one for the history book."

Alfi nodded and smiled. "Good job, Gilley and Trish. This is one hell of a schooner; fine crew too."

They all watched *Maverick* cross the line thirty seconds later as the horn sounded for her finish. Gilley led Trish and Alfi to the rail and started clapping. "Let's give 'em a hand, lads." The crew shouted and clapped, then shook hands with one other. Gilley took the wheel and turned hard a-starboard. "Ease all sheets, get the topsails off her. We're headed for the barn."

"Well, folks, that was the closest and most exciting finish I've ever seen. They beat the scratch boat fair and square. On the first windward leg they rode a big wind shift and made that leg in one tack. *Maverick* lost that leg by having to tack and lost about ten minutes. But due to her greater speed, she caught up and became a real threat to *Romayne,* which immediately started a tight tacking duel and covered *Maverick* on every tack. *Romayne* won on elapsed time by thirty seconds, and *Maverick* has to give her five minutes. Now they are all sailing over to Sausalito for the trophy presentation dinner and party at the yacht club. That's it from KABR for this year's Master Mariners race."

It was midnight after the close of the presentation dinner when Trish rolled into her bed, physically exhausted and happier than she had been for many years. Of all the events of the day, the best was that Gilley gave her the ultimate honor of sailing his schooner over the line. "We won it for you, Daddy. It was like you were there, and it was so wonderful to throw our roses to you. I love you."

She thought about Gilley. What an amazing man. He's in the twilight of his life and really enjoying it. He and his dream schooner won the race today, and he told me he's going to chase sunsets in the trade winds down to Tahiti, and then, the Horn. "It doesn't make sense for a gregarious guy like him to sail single-handed. Why?"

11

Gilley was looking at the clock as it chimed six bells. Then he heard the tune of Oh Canada playing from his cell phone. "Cornwall." He sat up and swung his feet to the sole.

"Gilley, it's Carol. Oh, God, there's no easy way to say it— Julie's dead."

He stood up and walked into the salon. "Jesus Carol. What—how?"

"I don't know. Can you come up to the house right away?"

Twenty minutes later he arrived at the small cottage, out of breath, leg muscles burning. Carol greeted him and held his arm as they entered the living room. Julie was sitting in the winged chair, her head tilted to the side on the wing. They looked down at her lifeless body. Carol handed him a piece of paper with the single word in sloppy cursive, Good-bye.

"Good-bye?" He shook his head slowly as he looked at an empty bottle of Scotch lying on the floor beside the chair. He nudged it with the toe of his shoe. "Jesus; what do you think killed her; surely not one bottle?"

"Well, if she drank the whole bottle, I suppose that could do it. I really don't know, they'll have to do an autopsy. This is so sad—but you know Gilley, she was terribly depressed, what with all the pain, and freaked out about another major operation. I couldn't stop the booze coming in. She had a cab driver buddy who'd take her shopping. She was doing a lot more drinking lately, and God knows I tried to talk her out of it, but she wouldn't listen. She just wanted to stop the pain of living. When

I said good night to her last evening, she gave me a hug and just said 'good-by, Carol.' I thought that was kind of odd. That's why I came to see her early this morning. But you know, Gilley, after all is said and done, it's kind of a merciful release in a way, don't you think?"

"Yeah, I guess it was for her, poor soul. Look at the scars on her wrists. She told me she fell on the rocks when she was a kid, but those are razor cuts. She tried to kill herself long before I met her. So what do we do now, call the police or what?"

"I think you should, just to find out what the procedure is. They'll tell us what to do."

"Carol, were you still giving her one sleeping pill a night, and did she have access to the pill bottle?"

"Absolutely, one pill a night and I had the pill bottle with me all the time. But I guess she could have faked taking it and saved them. She could have had twenty or thirty pills and then taken them all at once with the whiskey. Lights out; it's just a possibility."

"Well, I guess I better call Jon Ewer and find out where we go from here."

They looked down at his deceased wife as he pulled out his cell phone.

Chief Jon Ewer and detective Lynn Duke arrived at the cottage thirty minutes after Gilley's call. They examined Julie's lifeless body and took a careful look around the interior of the cottage.

"Well, Gilley, from our examination there doesn't seem to be any sign of a crime here. If she drank the whole bottle of Scotch, she may have had a cardiac arrest. We've seen cases like that, no glass around, I assume she just drank from the bottle. We'll have to get the coroner's report after the autopsy is complete. I'm really sorry about this, Gilley."

Lynn took several digital photos of the deceased and the bottle of whiskey. "That's all I need, Chief, nothing else seems necessary." She slipped a pen into the bottle's neck, flipping it into a plastic bag. "I'll get prints from this."

"Here's the coroner's number, Gilley. They'll arrange for the autopsy and help you get a funeral home in the loop."

"Thanks, Jon, I appreciate your help."

Two days later, the autopsy report revealed that Julie Birkett Cornwall had died of a massive overdose of sleeping pills and a bottle of Scotch whiskey. It was estimated that her final cocktail was enough to kill six people. The coroner's report stated unequivocally that Julie's death was suicide. There was no evidence of foul play.

Gilley sat in *Romayne's* salon looking at the box that contained Julie's ashes. Then he shifted his gaze to the bottles on the shelf encircling the salon and removed a bottle of Bell's scotch, just to feel the texture of the glass and study the label of the whiskey. How many of these had he consumed in his life? A hundred, two hundred? He returned the bottle to the shelf.

His alcoholism had probably been as destructive to his brain cells as it had been to his late wife's; except that he was very lucky and alive. And she, the poor sad soul, was terribly unlucky and dead, her ashes residing in a synthetic box, which was the only time she had been aboard his schooner. Now, thanks to a very astute investment banker and good friend living on the Isle of Man, his estate had grown in fifteen years to two-and-a-half-million dollars, making him a rich man with a fancy yacht worth another million or so. He wondered how and when to sail away, but most important of all, could he single-hand a one-hundred-eight-foot schooner, or did he really want to at this time of his life?

12

"Trishy, call me as soon as you get this message. A patient of yours, Agnes Rogers, who's a friend of mine, just by chance mentioned your name. Call me right now!" Trish's mouth opened.

"My God! I can't believe it." Trish replayed the message for the third time. Her hands shook as she wrote the phone number.

"Sally! It's Trishy. You just about gave me a heart attack." She started to cry. "Where are you?"

"Greenbrae. Oh, Trishy, it's so wonderful to hear your voice. I'd really given you up for—if I sound crazy, it's because I'm in serious shock. We've got to meet tonight. Where do you live?"

"Oh, Sally, I'm blown away happy. Yes, yes, let's meet tonight. I live in Sausalito, on a houseboat in Richardson's Bay Floating Homes Marina. Would you like to come down here, you tell me?"

"I know where that is; tell me which dock?"

She gave her directions to Skookum Chuck dock. "I'll be waiting for you there."

"Trishy, I'll be there as fast as I can."

She walked quickly to the entrance of the dock. A few minutes later a small European van crept up to the dock portal. It slowed and stopped with a squeal of brakes. When the driver saw Trish, she opened the door and yelled, leaving the door open.

"Trishy!" They ran into each other's arms, yelling and crying. They hugged, swayed and kissed as if they were in a new dance for the first time. Finally they separated, staring at one another partly in disbelief, but mostly with unrestrained joy. Tears poured down their cheeks. They rubbed their soaked faces together, melding their tears. They had difficulty forming cohesive words.

"Oh, my darling Sally, I never thought this day would come. I really gave you up for lost. Where have you been?"

Sally muffled her sobs until she could answer coherently. "I've been living in Napa, but I've been working at County General forever. Oh, and I was married, so you couldn't have known my married name, Sally Brown Poser."

Trish gasped. "You married John?"

Sally wiped her eyes with the back of her hand. "Yup, I did, big mistake. Anyway, let's not talk about that now. My divorce'll be final next week. Let's celebrate; I'm the happiest person in the world right now. Hold me and squeeze hard. I just gotta make sure I'm not dreaming."

"You're not dreaming. I'm here and I'm never going to lose you again. Come on, let's park your car, there's a space right over there."

They walked to the end of the long dock with their arms around each other. "Here we are, this is my floating home. I call it poor-man's waterfront. It's kinda funky, but I love it, and it's all mine."

Trish took Sally's hand and gave her a quick walk through her large, three-story home. Sally's eyes glanced at the home, but she only saw her old friend.

"You're still so beautiful, Trishy, and your lovely red hair shines like gold. And you're taller." She leaned over and buried her face in Trish's hair and inhaled the fragrance.

Trish turned and faced her. "You're the beautiful one, I always thought you'd go to Hollywood and be a sexy movie star."

She studied Sally's tear-stained face and reached up to caress it lightly with her fingertips. She examined her short gray hair, the chipped front tooth and the scar over the eyebrow. Her nose was a little crooked. She touched it tenderly and wondered how these wounds had been inflicted. "You said that you were at County General: are you a doctor?"

"I'm a surgical nurse. You might remember Dad always wanted me to be a surgeon. He kept telling me I had the hands. I was in premed at UC when Mom and Dad were—" She paused for several moments. "They died over Lockerbie, Scotland. Maybe you remember, Pan Am One Zero Three, in eighty eight. Everyone died. One day I was in med school learning to be a doctor, the next day I was an orphan and I dropped out of school. The scary part of it was, I was meant to go to Africa with them. Dad was doing a month or so of volunteer cosmetic surgery on kids. He used to go to some Third-world country every year. I just didn't want to go to Africa, so I stayed here. I don't know—if I had gone with them. I felt a lot of guilt and grief, still do."

"Oh, honey, I'm so sorry, I didn't know. I tried to reach you so many times by phone. Your number had been changed, and I wrote you so many letters but never heard a peep. Your mom really didn't want me in your life. The few times I actually talked with her on the phone, she made it very clear that I was not to call anymore. I remember her telling me that I was evil for what I had done to you. Why did she hate me so?"

"Oh, you know how Mom was, she flipped out over everything."

Trish held her and remembered that she had always been the stronger of the two. When Sally fell and skinned her knee or broke her wrist, it was Trish who always kissed her better and carried her to safety. They were the same age, and Trish was like the big sister, always the healer. She led Sally up to her bedroom suite, where they sat on the loveseat. Trish opened her dresser drawer to remove an ornate porcelain box and took out a joint.

"Let's celebrate and get elevated, or would you rather have a glass of wine?"

"No wine. I'd fall flat on my face. And I haven't smoked pot for years."

Trish lit it, took a drag and passed it to Sally.

"Oh God, Trishy, the last time we smoked this stuff our lives went upside-down." She looked at the cigarette for a moment. "Why the hell not." She took a deep drag, inhaled, held it for a second and coughed it all out. They passed it back and forth until finally Sally could hold the pungent smoke without coughing. "Damn, I'm so yesterday, I forgot how to smoke."

She took another drag and held it without coughing. "Fine, I needed that." A happy smile lit up Sally's face as the drug embraced her.

Trish went out onto the deck to remove the cover from the redwood hot tub.

"Want to take to the waters? It'd do us good." She returned to the bedroom and handed Sally a kimono. Trish peeled off her clothes, and stood naked before Sally. "Last one in is a ninny poo. Remember that?"

Sally giggled. "Sure do, and you're a ninny poo too."

"Wow, you look absolutely mawvlus." Sally stared at her breasts; the nipples were pierced with gold rings. "So you had a boob job, Trishy? They're absolutely beautiful."

Trish glanced down at her breasts and cupped the undersides lifting them slightly. "Actually I had a breast reduction. They were too big and heavy. My main squeeze for a while was a plastic surgeon. She took out some excess fat and inserted small saline bags underneath to shape them. You can just barely see the scars." Sally looked at the scars. "Can I touch them?"

She took Sally's hands and brought them to her chest. "Of course you can, you were never shy before."

Sally touched the breasts tenderly and lifted them up to inspect the hairline scars. "Did she put in the rings as well?" She touched the rings.

"Yeah." Trish paused. "Tragically, I lost her a few years ago. She of all people had breast cancer. It wasn't discovered until it reached stage three. By then it had metastasized to her lungs. I actually found the lump on her breast. She was only thirty-eight. That's when I was absolutely positive there was no intelligent design and no God."

"That's so sad."

"Yup, it was. I just couldn't believe it when the doctor told her." Trish faked a smile. "Now, are you going to get naked or do I have to rip your clothes off?" Trish approached Sally with a wicked grin.

Sally struck a sexy pose. Her bra and panties were the last items to drop on the love seat. Trish examined Sally's lithe body and smiled. She wondered about the bruises.

They lowered themselves into the steaming water. "My boobs never got any bigger. Mom's were small, too. And I came that far from having a boob job, but I got cold feet because of the cancer flap. Apparently they've proved that it was all bullshit, now it's too late, and who the hell needs it anyway? Any more than a mouthful is a waste. Well, maybe someday, I don't know."

Trish laughed. "They're lovely."

Their eyes locked and smiled happily. Sally put her arms around Trish's neck.

"Oh, God, it seems that everything I get involved with goes haywire. I really shouldn't have married John, even though he was fine at first. You know—he drank a little — well, maybe more than a little, and didn't take drugs except pot, we both did. His mom was sweet and his dad was an egomaniac asshole who apparently beat him when he was a kid. I didn't find out about that until much later when we went into counseling. And I had no clue he could go right off the deep end. He did my front tooth; eyebrow, these bruises, the broken nose. I couldn't take it anymore and moved out about six months ago. I got a court injunction against him."

Trish shook her head as she listened to Sally's sad story. "Do you remember he got smashed at our grad prom and gave me a bad time in the front seat of his mom's car?"

"Yeah, I do. He really went after you, and you walloped him. That should have been a warning for me. I was really stupid, you know. I thought I loved him. Oh, hell, it's all water over the dam now; you don't need to hear about all that." Sally looked at her for a moment as she tenderly stroked Trish's face. "Oh, one more thing about that God-awful day; I've got a confession to make. You just asked why my Mom was so horrible to you. Well, remember when your mom's boyfriend, what's his name—Taylor? Tyler, walked in on us?"

Trish nodded. "Damn right I do, I'll never forget it, we were terrified."

"And he beat the hell out of us with his belt and kicked me out of your room. I got dressed and ran home hysterical. Mom found me in my room crying, she asked what had happened. I told her some stupid lie, which she knew immediately and insisted I tell the truth. You remember her, she was such a forceful woman and I was always a little afraid of her. I just broke down and told her what happened, the joint we smoked and Tyler finding us naked and making out, and then him whipping the be-Jesus out of us. Trishy, I was such a coward. I just caved in. I was always programmed to tell the truth, and Mom went absolutely bonkers. She was furious and especially with you, when I had to tell her it was your joint. She said that you were evil, and had made me evil too. I couldn't stop her. She grounded me for a month, damn near bread and water. Dad was mad as hell and said that Tyler did the right thing. Finally Mom dragged me to church and made me go to confession. I was devastated that I betrayed you."

"Sweetheart, don't beat yourself up, I sure as hell would've blabbed if your mom had me by the ear. I was scared of her, too. So what did the priest say about it?"

"He said that I had sinned, you know, do a half a million Hail Marys and made me take a complete indoctrination. For a long time I really thought that I had sinned, and finally I repented and was forgiven by my parents. But Mom never forgave you. But the best part of it was, we lost our virginity together and I loved every minute of it. I still think about it. We were the only two people in the world until that drunken bastard arrived."

They climbed out of the hot tub and put their robes on. Trish passed Sally a bottle of water. "I guess you didn't get any of my letters?"

"Nothing. Mom must have intercepted them, and of course, she never said anything about them." They climbed onto the bed and lay down, using the pillows for back rests.

"Well, here's what happened to me. After Tyler kicked you out, I tried to put my jeans on, but he knocked me on the floor, pulled them off. I broke away, but he caught me by my hair and forced me down. He was in a rage. He tied my wrists with his belt and the son-of-a-bitch raped me."

Sally sat up and stared in disbelief. "Oh, no!"

"Yup, and while he was doing me he said, 'It's about time you learned that women don't lie with women, they lie with men, and this is what men do with women'. I was still stoned and he kept at me for a long time until he splashed. I looked over at my dresser and saw my softball bat. He finally pulled out and stood holding his dick, covered with my blood. I'd just got my period. So I jumped off the bed, grabbed the bat and had batting practice on his crotch. By then I was in a total rage. He was screaming his head off and puking. Then he just moaned and cried, and I shouted at him: 'This is what women do to men who rape them'. I really got off on that."

Trish relit the joint, took a hit and passed it to Sally. "I can remember it as clearly it as if it was yesterday, and I don't think I was his first rape. I always thought the only reason he dated Mom was to get at me. He was such a devious prick. Always saying stuff like, 'How's it going, beautiful', he always called me beautiful instead of my name."

"So then what?"

"I took a shower, packed a couple of bags. All I could think of was to get the hell out of there, fast. He was doubled up in agony. I told him to get dressed and get out.

" Then after he'd left, I saw his wallet on the floor. I took all the cash, about two hundred bucks."

"Jesus. I guess that's why he was limping and stooped over when I saw him going to his car. So I assume you didn't know he jumped off the bridge a few weeks later?"

"Well, good riddance, a fitting end for a very evil man. I've never hated anyone in my life, but I hated him from the get-go when he dated Mom. You remember she went back to Florida to look after her sister and she asked him of all people to keep an eye on the house and me. I called Mom and told her what had happened, and that I was driving to Florida. I also called you, but your mom answered, that's when she told me I wasn't welcome in her home again and hung up."

The ship's clock on the wall chimed two bells. They both looked at it. "Two bells, one o'clock, and all's well. I hope you don't mind sleeping on the port side, sweetie." Trish threw her robe onto the foot of the bed and climbed under the duvet.

Sally did the same. "Port side's fine. It's so great to be with you again. I can't believe how it happened."

"And I'm so happy you found me and we're together again." She took her hand. "So tomorrow, sleep in because I've got a client at nine for an hour, so help yourself to anything in the kitchen. Sleep well, my sweet Sally. I love you." She leaned over and kissed her friend tenderly.

"Client?"

"I'll fill you in tomorrow. That last toke really zonked me. Good night, sweetie."

"Good night Trishy, I love you too. God, just think, I found you through my friend."

Sally lay on her side facing Trish. The moonlight shone through the skylight directly on Trish's face. She reached over and touched her cheek gently. "Trishy, are you gay?"

13

The seagull symphony was in full chorus as they flew over the floating home community. Some were swooping in circles in their search for breakfast. One large white gull perched on the railing outside of the sliding glass door to the bedroom deck. It was obviously annoyed about some avian injustice. The decibel level coming from it was extremely loud. Sally rubbed her eyes and watched the bird for a while, then looked up at the mirror on the canopy and smiled. She chuckled as she sat up on the bed and reached for her kimono.

The note stuck on the mirror read, Good morning, sweetie. Towel and toothbrush are on the counter. I should be through about ten. Can't wait to visit and catch up. She had drawn a heart with an arrow through it.

Sally smiled and leaned over close to the magnifying mirror to inspect the scar on her eyebrow. She looked at the chipped front tooth, and remembered that she would have her new cap installed on Tuesday. She let her kimono fall to the floor, and looked at her bruised body. Each orange or purple mark was the result of a solid punch or kick inflicted by a drunk and violent husband. She turned around to look at the bruises on her back, then turned to face the mirror and cupped her breasts and felt for any sign of unwelcomed lumps.

She pulled on the kimono and sprinkled water on her face, then made the bed and went down to the spacious living room. She stroked the Steinway baby grand piano and touched the violin in its case. Outside on the wide deck, she observed the round teak table and four lounge chairs, then returned to the kitchen and sat down at the kitchen counter and picked up the *Chronicle*. She flipped through it and found the funnies. Doonesbury was up to its usual bizarre satire attacking the president.

She was sipping tea when she heard Trish's voice downstairs.

"Well David, you're well on your way. I think it's time to try it out there. Call me and let me know how it goes. Good luck, I'm very proud of you."

"Thanks, Trish, I really appreciate your help, especially with the grief counseling. I feel like a new man."

Trish walked into the kitchen. "Good morning, love. I'm sorry, the session ran longer than I expected." She put her arms around Sally. Now we have the whole weekend to catch up, where to start? I'm so goddamned stoked I can't believe it."

"Me too. I guess I should be calling you Trish, now that we're grown up?"

Trish poured a cup of tea. "Sally, you can call me whatever you want, it's the name you gave me a hundred years ago. And when I hear it, I'll always know we're back together. Let's go out on the deck, it's so nice out there."

"Good idea. So how did your meeting go?"

"Very well. The poor guy lost his wife of twenty years to ovarian cancer, and he was almost going down for the third time. I managed to get him off the booze, which wasn't easy. Then I had him in treatment for serious booze-related erectile dysfunction. So I sent him to a urologist for evaluation. He was tested and given a prescription for penile injections and shown how to inject himself. Complete success. And, as he wasn't in a sexual relationship, I referred him to a professional sex surrogate, to make sure he could go all the way. He's been with her several times, and now he's able to perform very well. He's on the wagon and his depression's gone, and finally he's raring to go. Look out, ladies, he's back and on the hunt for you know what."

"Wow, so that's what you do, amazing."

"Absolutely, and after a few treatments, the surrogate taught him a lot about his and a lover's body and how to really please a woman. Our team effort made all that possible for him, and I happily cut him loose. Yes, that's what I do, I bring sexually dysfunctional men and women back to good sexual heath. Strange, eh?"

Trish reached over and stroked Sally's hand.

"I've never heard of a sex surrogate before, is she a hooker?"

"No, these ladies and gentlemen belong to a professional surrogate association, which is all perfectly legal. I was a surrogate for a year until I got my degree in advanced human sexuality."

"Amazing, you've been involved in every part of sex. Obviously you like it?"

"I love the healing. So I've done everything from making love with you as my first lover. Then for my further sex education after our beautiful session, I was raped, which I didn't need. And now, here we are together again; stay tuned folks."

"Yes, stay tuned. So Trishy, last night after you turned the lights off, I asked if you were gay but you'd fallen asleep. Are you?"

Trish laughed. "Funny you should ask. You know, I wondered for a while if I was, especially after you and I became lovers. But after I'd been around the block a few times in Florida, I discovered that I was happily bisexual. I love being well fucked by a passionate, considerate man. But a soft, sexy woman is something else. So I enjoy the best of both worlds, but making love with you has always been my favorite fantasy. I want to relive that with you today. How about you?"

"Absolutely."

"Okay, now we're going to walk fast for half an hour to get our juices flowing, and when we get back, we're going to medicate with a special erotic brew, which is made by a dear friend, Doctor Helen Boyle. She's a fair dinkum Australian psychiatrist with a degree in pharmacology. So Helen has synthesized her amazing witch's brew, with no side effects. It's also a powerful aphrodisiac, which she calls Magic Medicine, and we take it on an empty stomach, so no breakfast. Orgasms are beyond belief and the psychedelic effects bring out amazing emotional feelings. She won't tell me how it's made except that it's all natural herbs, roots, no illegal substances, and it's safe. We'll do it when we get back, if you like."

Sally gave her a big grin, "I like, I like. I better get dressed."

They power-walked on the bike path along Richardson's Bay, past the seaplane base where they stopped to watch a Beaver float plane winding up to full revs and taking off to the south.

There were several egrets and blue herons wading slowly through the wetland marsh grass, making lightning-fast strikes to pick up some small morsel, and then they'd repeat the process. Two pelicans peeled off from aloft, dove into the water with quiet splashes to quickly devour a wiggling fish. Several mallards paddled along in a loose formation, occasionally plunging their heads under water with their tails and yellow feet in the air. A large flock of coots darted in and out of the marsh grass for their share of the menu.

"Trishy, I forgot to ask you last night. Did you ever marry?"

"Yes, when I was in Florida, to a terrific guy who I really loved. Tragically, he was killed in a head-on with a drunk driver. So I've been on my own ever since, except for a few guys and some gals, but none of them blew my socks off. Then, sometime later, stupid me, I got knocked up and had a badly botched abortion, so bad that I ended up in the E. R. to have a hysterectomy. So, no kids for me, and actually, with all said and done, I definitely didn't want children. I've been single-handing ever since, so to speak. Until, a month ago, I re-met a very interesting guy, Gilley Cornwall, who we'd met in Tahiti when we did the Tahiti race on *Bojangles*. You remember all that. Anyhoo, I'm just getting to know him again." She grinned. "We'll see."

They stopped at a bridge spanning a narrow creek that drained the wetlands. They leaned their elbows on the railing as speeding bikers whizzed past them. "I never wanted kids either. It was all I could do to manage my own life. And I haven't done a good job of that; neither has John for that matter. He started to run with whores, and snort coke, meth, boozing, and gambling, all the bad addictions. Anyway, he began to knock me around; slaps at first, then body punches. He's hung up on anal, but he was just too rough. I'd slept with his cruelty too long, and I had to find a way to escape his madness and his disrespect for me. So I finally refused to do it anymore. That's when he got nasty and violent."

"How do you know he was running with whores?"

Sally watched the duck family. "We have separate checking accounts, thank God, so I got snoopy and went into his banking file. And lo and behold, I discovered regular five hundred buck cash withdrawals, and as he wasn't bringing any five hundred dollar suits, food, or other expensive goodies into the house. It didn't take a genius to figure out what the money was used for."

Trish nodded. "That's the going rate for a call girl, according to my sources."

"That's exactly what I found out from one of my pals who used to be a working girl and now is a nurse's aide. So, long story short, one night John was in one of his bad drug moods and we got into one hell of an argument, he went nuts and knocked me around again. I moved out that day and shared a studio with one of my nurse pals. John's still living in our house in Napa. He's one very sick puppy."

"Oh, sweetie, that's terrible. You were smart to get out, and I sure hope he can't find you." Trish looked at her watch. "Let's start back." Trish reached for Sally's hand.

"No, he doesn't know where I live and he isn't interested. He's agreed to the divorce. Now all we have to do is settle the financial part next week with our lawyers. He's almost broke because he pissed everything away. He has a family trust fund, which pays him about thirty grand a year, his whoring and dope slush fund. We're closing escrow on the house on Monday, and we split the proceeds. Fortunately, I've been saving my earnings separately in my IRAs, and I'll be so relieved to get this over with, so I can get on with the rest of my life."

"Sally, you're my first love, and this is the first day of the rest of your life and we're sharing it. I'm so excited." Trish let out a wild shouting chant and Sally joined in as they hugged and twirled around several times as a few amused walkers watched them.

At the houseboat, Trish hung the 'Gone Fishin' sign on the front door, locked it and switched off the doorbell and phone ringer. She turned on the stereo for her favorite country music.

Trish's black cat, Robin, stretched from her rest and walked beside Sally's legs. She leaned over to stroke her. "Meet my old kitty, Robin. Now, my sweet, we have complete privacy. So after I make the magic tea, we'll go upstairs, for our date with destiny. Just us."

Trish poured the boiling water into the cups with the dark tea bags. "I'll let it steep for a few and then add this unknown white powder. Then, about twenty minutes after we drink this, gangbusters, up, up and away. You'll love it."

Sally sniffed the steam from the tea "You really are too much."

They blew on the tea and took small sips. "Okay, let's go up to Le Boudoir." Trish threw her clothes onto the love seat. "Now, my darling, are you ready?"

Sally threw her clothes on top of the pile. "Bring it on."

Trish stood beside Sally. "Soon we'll be entering Nirvana, the most wonderful place in this world. So, what I have planned is we do sweat lodge in that little hut I built."

"It's Indian?"

"Yup, so we'll sweat out all our toxins and feel—well, you'll see."

On the other side of the hot tub was a low, round, domed structure framed with bent willow boughs tied together with raw-hide lashings. It was neatly covered with a rawhide fitted cover with a flap opening for entry. Outside the opening to the hut was a steel crucible like a wok that contained several smooth granite rocks. Trish ignited the gas burner under the crucible, then put the cover over the rocks. "They're a cookin' now, honey."

Sally held her hand over the rocks. "Another first with you, a sweat lodge."

"In a real Indian sweat lodge, they'd heat the rocks over a wood fire. Now, we shower and by that time the rocks should be ready." They stepped into the large double-headed shower and soaped each other's bodies, then sprayed the suds off with squeals of delight. "Oh, this is fun, I love the feel of your beauti-ful bod. Sooo—soft."

Sally watched Trish pick up the rocks from the crucible with padded mitts and put them into another crucible in the center of the lodge.

"Crawl in and don't touch the rocks." Trish followed her in and sat cross-legged opposite Sally. She sprinkled water on the rocks. They watched the steam fill the interior of the lodge. She handed the water ladle to Sally. "You do it now, and try to imagine this as a sacred place where all good things begin in the world. Close your eyes and take deep breaths and slowly let it out through all the pleasure zones of your body."

They inhaled the scented steam, their bodies dripping with perspiration. "You're about to be re-hatched, my love."

They were deep in their own private meditations. Trish gave a slow, soft chant that filled the lodge and mixed with the steam. Finally, wilting from the intense heat, she reached for Sally's arm. "Now open your eyes, we're done in here. We finish with a cold shower to close the pores. The natives would jump in the lake or roll in the snow." They shouted when the cold water blasted their skin and rejoiced as they dried off.

"Oh ho, ho! I've just arrived."

"What?"

"The Magic Medicine just kicked in, you should be there soon. I forgot to mention you might feel a little unsteady on your legs at first, like when you do mushrooms, but not to worry, it'll pass soon. Come on up on the bed, and say hello to us in the mirror."

"Oh, yeah, I see what you mean. I think I'm there too."

Sally looked into Trish's eyes. "Your pupils are enormous." Trish looked into Sally's blue eyes. "Yours too. In a few minutes we'll be all the way up in euphoria land and your inhibitions will eee-vaporate, and it'll make us horny as stoats, so my sweet, you better watch out."

Trish leaned over Sally and looked into her eyes and kissed her, first tenderly, then passionately. They stayed locked together then gradually exchanged little pecks on eyes, ears and noses. "How do you like it so far?"

"Unbelievable. Where'd you learn to kiss like that?" Trish smiled and ran her fingers over Sally's scar and kissed it.

"How could you forget, we were about fifteen and you French kissed me in my bedroom. That was our first real kiss. I've thought a lot about that one."

"Yeah, I remember that day. It was raining and we had just

| 86 |

started our homework, and of course, never finished it. Your mom and dad were away for the weekend, and we had a sleep over. Trishy, let's put the clock back to when we got stoned for the first time and when you pulled that joint out of a ballpoint pen; I'll never forget that. Oh man! This is amazing stuff. I've never felt like this, I feel like running naked down the dock. Kiss me again."

Robin jumped onto the bed and started to rub herself on Trish's leg. "Robin, would you please vamoose? All right, you can stay, but settle down. We're going to be busy here. And now, my love, it's time to get intimate, and as you're the honored guest in my home for the first time, I am going to seduce you on my love bed, so just relax."

"Oh goodie, but please be gentle, I'm quite sensitive in some areas. Oh, Trishy, your tongue is absolutely magical. Oh, that's perfect; I so desperately need this. Yo, Saint Peter, look at us; two ladies in love really getting it on. I hope you don't mind us doing this up here, and even if you do, nobody can stop us now. More, more, hold on, here comes the big one. We're flying, and I'm looking down on us, we're making love away up in space. Oh here comes another one, keep going, darling, it's getting better, oh Jesus. Yes, yes, yes. Yeeees."

Trish grinned as she came up for air "Wow, you really are sensitive."

"Oh yeah, that was just a-amazing, I've never exploded like that."

"As they say, it's all the way you hold your tongue. So let's have a time out, we need some liquid before we go for round two."

Trish opened the mini-fridge and returned with the juice. "Guava okay?"

"My favorite."

The love-filled hours slowly seeped away. They were deliriously happy together and completely unaware of time passing. First, Trish the lover, showing her beloved every nuance and method in the Tantric philosophy. Then the student charming the teacher and re-learning the lessons of love. They slowly forged ahead on their voyage with no destination in sight or required.

Occasionally a soft hand and delicate fingers would soothe a cheek, caress a back, pinch a buttock, tongue a breast, a run through flowing hair, then be brought to a nose to savor the beautiful scent. All was done that two lovers could learn and enjoy.

They slipped their kimonos on, and Sally followed Trish downstairs "Let's see, where did I leave off before we started to love ourselves silly?"

"Ah, I think you were a cocktail waitress in a strip joint."

"Right, I'll give you some details about that. So I did that for a while, then I got promoted to full-time stripper and I just loved it; of course, we were ripped all the time. The guys and some gals stuffed five and ten-dollar bills in our G-strings, all of them trying for the big score. Some nights I'd make a hundred bucks. Some of the gals were doing some extracurricular hooking after the show, which was absolutely crazy because some got the clap, and one got badly roughed up."

"You were smart to stay away from that. So did you have a boyfriend then?"

Trish laughed. "Hell, no, I'd never even been with a guy, except for Tyler raping me. But I had a little thing going with one of the strippers who was bi. We shared a dinky studio for a while."

They climbed the stairs, carrying a large bowl of popcorn and juice. Trish sat up on the bed to face Sally.

"After Aunt Mini died, Mom was living in her rental in Lauderdale. Then, a few months later I got a call from one of her neighbors to tell me that my wonderful, darling Mom had passed away in her sleep. Heart failure. Bang, I became an orphan as you did."

"Sally hugged her. "Oh, Trishy, first your dad's heart and then your mom's."

"Yeah, I couldn't believe it. Mom's autopsy showed she had arteriosclerosis and obviously didn't know it. Her heart just shut down. It was terribly sad. I just had to get that off my chest and finish my tribute to her. Anyway she's with Daddy now."

Robin woke suddenly, as if her feline dream had ended; she stood up slowly, stretched one back leg at a time and promptly lay down again. Sally petted her and giggled. "She's quite a cat, sleep and eat. What a life."

Trish sat on the edge of the bed. "You know, I'm still a little high after that boost and I'm starting to come down to a soft landing. I really don't want to boost again; are you okay if we just ride it out?"

"Sure, that's fine. God, we've been up what, five hours? It was a wonderful ride. Right now I feel like I'm hovering slowly and I keep wondering if we're really here together. I know we are, but I feel like we're in a dream together. Kiss me again so I know it's really real." Their bodies folded together like two pages in their favorite book.

Sally reached for her hand. "So what about this schooner guy, what's his name?"

"Gilley Cornwall. A little over a month ago, he dropped anchor here in his big schooner. And right now I'm at the stage where I'm a lot more than just fascinated with him, in more ways than one."

"I hope it works out. Have you—?"

"Not yet; we'll see. He's about as perfect a man I could ever hope to meet. He's absolutely authentic. Twenty years older, but looks a lot younger. And I think he's firing on all eight cylinders. Lots of raw horsepower. He's handsome, and get this, he's an incredible pianist and played a gig at the Music Box and blew the roof off. I don't know where this will go, but I wanted you to know that he's in my sights and the path is open."

"Yeah, let whatever happens, happen."

"You're so cute to say that. Maybe we'll row down to his schooner tomorrow; I'd like you to meet him if you like?"

"Sure, he sounds interesting, and I also look forward to meeting Helen; anyone who womps up medicine like that is a genius."

"Terrific, and we have the rest of the day and tomorrow to ourselves. We can do whatever you want." Trish led her out to the deck and squinted at the overcast sky. "Looks like we've got some weather coming in. When it comes from the south, it often blows for a couple of days. We might have to scrub our visit with Gilley tomorrow. Anyway, we still have a lot to catch up on. I want to find out all about you. Everything!"

They went back to the bed and pulled the duvet over them as a sudden chill had settled in.

"Well, it took me awhile to get over that horrible Tyler situation, then Mom's rage and you leaving. I was devastated without you. But at least Mom did tell me that you said you were driving to Florida to be with your mother. So after Mom and Dad cooled off, I got a job as a nurse's aide in Dad's hospital, planning on going to medical school in the fall. I became very proficient at emptying bedpans, giving bed baths, soothing butt sores and moving very heavy fat patients in and out of wheelchairs. It was backbreaking work. I'd crash into bed every night after my shift. Anyway, the big day arrived. Med school was more than I bargained for, but I was determined to stick it out. A few in the class bailed or failed before the end of the first year."

"Yeah, I've heard that a lot of students can't stand the pressure. Not enough sleep."

"It was very hard, two or more hours of homework every night. Then, when Mom and Dad were murdered over Lockerbie, I literally came apart, physically and mentally. I was totally depressed, medicated up the ying yang. I actually had to go to the hospital for a few days, where I met a senior nurse. She was so compassionate, spent time with me after her shift ended. She gave me soothing massages, and what came through most was real love. Agnes had eyes that immediately inspired trust. She's the angel who influenced me to go into nursing."

"How great for you. I've been lucky enough to meet a few neat women like her. Totally giving people who just serve others. And look at you now, serving people. Do you visit your patients after surgery?"

"Yeah, some of the time, it's not really part of the post op, but because of Agnes, I like to do it on the human level. Patients are so drugged, confused and sad. I just like to hold their hands, let them know that I'm there for them."

"If I ever get sick, I'll insist that you be my personal nurse."

Sally shot her a happy smile. "So anyway, I entered the General Hospital School of Nursing, and four years later I was a registered nurse. I did post-grad training in surgery, and I've been in operating rooms for twenty years. I'm at the point where I want to do something else, but I haven't a clue what."

"You'll do just fine. I was actually going to hire a private detective to find you; I even interviewed one. Now here we are, best friends and lovers again. Maybe there is a God after all."

"So, do you believe in God, Trishy?"

"No, I don't. I think the God theory is totally illogical. But if there is or was one, I think she laid down some good rules, then split town. Man has been plagiarizing them ever since. Voltaire wrote, 'God is a comedian who is playing to an audience that is afraid to laugh.' And what kind of a God would allow so many religions to go to war and kill people who believe in their own God? I just don't buy it. But I certainly understand why so many people do and are comforted with their God. Good for them."

"I couldn't agree more. I left the church years ago and haven't looked back since. The only thing I still believe is, we all go to heaven and we get our hell right here on earth. But you know, Trishy, I still pray, not to a deity, but I just pray, it helps me. And of course I always prayed that we'd find each other. And here we are. Wow."

"You pray real good, honey; I know you always prayed for me, and that's another one of the many reasons I love you so much."

They chatted for a while between yawns when Trish heard little gasps from Sally and glanced over at her. She was fast asleep.

She leaned over to look at her, first, the scar above her eyebrow, which she kissed tenderly, then her broken nose, and she kissed that. Sally's mouth was open as she snored. She put the tip of her tongue on the chipped tooth. "How could anyone hurt you, my love?" She whispered. "You'll be safe with me. This will never happen to you again."

After a leisurely breakfast, Trish led Sally down to the front door and held her tightly, then looked into her eyes and stroked her hair. "Can you believe we found each other after all of those years, and now there's nothing to stop us from being together. I mean really together, so how would you like to move in here with me?"

"Oh, Trishy, that would be absolutely wonderful. My mind is getting blown just thinking about living with you. But, what was I going to tell you? Oh yeah, one more thing before I leave.

I think I mentioned that we're closing escrow on our Napa house tomorrow. And the divorce on Friday and then I'm free as a bird. If it's okay, I'll finish off the week at Greenbrae because it's a stone's throw to the hospital, and then can I move in with you, say, Sunday? Saturday I've got to clear all my stuff out of the Napa house. And I pray that John won't be there, but it'll be a good time to get rid of a lot of my crap to Goodwill. Yippee! My dream is coming true, thank you, thank you."

"Sunday will be perfect." She held Sally's face and kissed her.

"Well, Trishy, I better scoot, places to go, things to do. I love you with all of my newly repaired heart."

"I'll see you Sunday, and I'll have the chili and a bottle of red open. I love you more than words can say."

14

Trish rowed through the southerly chop along the Sausalito waterfront. She maneuvered the Whitehall alongside *Romayne's* companion ladder, and was surprised to see that Gilley's Whitehall was rigged for sailing with a short mast and a furled mainsail.

There was no jazz coming from the deck speakers.

"Gilley, are you aboard? There was no response; she called again loudly. She heard a throaty, garbled reply.

"Yeah, who goes?"

Trish started down the stairs, then poked her head into the salon. She gasped when she saw Gilley sitting in the captain's chair half-naked with a Tahitian pareu wrapped around his waist. There were liquor and wine bottles scattered on the rosewood table along with paper plates, leftover cold cuts, raw vegetables, and potato chips. It looked like the aftermath of a long, hard drinking binge.

Gilley looked up with unfocused, bloodshot eyes. Trish couldn't find the words to greet him, she was so shocked by his drunken state. "Gilley, are you alright?" He tried to get up but failed and fell back into the chair.

"Welcome, Trish, it's good to see you. Have a drink with an old drunken sailor." She sat on the settee facing him.

"Gilley, what's going on, I thought you were on the wagon?"

"Well, Trish, I think something you said, or was it that Wild Oscar guy? I don't remember. Now let's see if I can get it right. 'In order to overcome temptation, one should yield to it'. So I yielded. Have a wee draught of Mount Gay, the best sippin' rum in the world." He reached for the bottle. "Did you know they've been making this great stuff since seventeen fifty three? Let's see, that's over three hundred years, right?"

"Right, three hundred years. But, no thanks, Gilley, not right now."

He started to get up again when his pareu slipped to the floor. He reached over to pick it up and pitched forward onto the carpet, flat on his face. "Whoops, I'm not too steady on my pins today. 'Scuse me, Trish, this is no way to greet a pretty lady."

He attempted to get up on his knees and balanced precariously when Trish got up to help him back into the chair. He sat there and looked around for the pareu. She retrieved it and draped it over his lap. "Oh, yeah, maybe you'd like a cup of tea. I don't think I can make it to the galley right now, so Trish, just help yourself, the kettle's always hot."

Trish gave him a look of exasperation. She didn't expect or need to be with a drunken sailor today. Then it gradually occurred to her that this very kind, decent man appeared to be in trouble. She could see that several bottles had been consumed.

"So, what's the celebration for Gilley?"

He looked at his glass, then at her. "It's not really a celebration, Trish; it's more like a wake." He paused. "My wife died by her own hand last week."

She gasped, "Oh, I'm sorry to—"

"She was a very, very sick woman, poor soul."

She looked into his sad eyes.

"Our marriage was over a long time ago. She wouldn't give me a divorce. She was a full-up Catholic, end of ball game. Yesterday, I sailed out to the Gate in the Whitehall and spread her ashes into the southerly." He took another sip. "Alfi was here with a few of her friends. They had all pretty much given up on her. I just paid the goddamn bills."

Trish focused on his face, now much changed from hard drinking and grief. She understood why he had slipped off the wagon — the sudden termination of a sad and bankrupt marriage.

He looked up, toasted the sky and drank. "She's in her Catholic heaven now." She saw tears on his cheek. He leaned his arm on the table and rested his forehead on it. His big shoulders heaved as he sobbed. She wanted to reach out to comfort him in his grief, but knew it was better to leave him alone and let him get it all out. Finally he raised his head and wiped his eyes with a napkin. "I'm so sorry, Gilley, death is hard to take." She stroked his hand. "It sounds like she'd programmed herself to end her pain."

"It wasn't Julie I grieved for, it was for others. I still grieve for my father. He was such a fine man and he died such a terrible, unnecessary death. I think I told you a little about him. When I was home from school at Christmas, I used to go out with him on the trap line. It was a big production, you know, snowshoes; we carried heavy grub backpacks. He'd built two small log cabins on the trap line to camp in because we'd be out five days at a time, in all kinds of weather, sometimes below zero. We'd clear and reset the traps, skin the animals and take the pelts back to one of the cabins and put them on stretching boards. Then we'd move on until we had all the furs that we could pull behind us on sleighs and head for home. I'd finished school for good, so that summer I'd been working underground at Vidette gold mine. Dad wanted me to help him on the trap line, but the money was so good at the mine that I kinda begged off."

He poured himself a drink. "Dad said he'd hire an Indian from the reserve to help him. So it worked out for both of us. I'd work at the mine and bring money home. I worked like a dog six days a week; hard rock mining wasn't for sissies. Drill a dozen holes, load 'em and blast out the face. I became a man that year.

He squinted into his glass and swirled it. "Just to tell you how great my folks were, they put my wages in the bank and made me use it to buy my first car, a '29 model A Ford. They wouldn't take no for an answer. I'll never forget that, never."

He sat there gazing at the painting of the schooners, then back at her. "I didn't know that he hadn't hired an Indian. So he went out on the line by himself. After about eight days, Mum got worried and had her brother Seymour go to the mine to bring me home. We found him in the last cabin, dead and frozen. He'd written a farewell note on a chunk of cardboard with the lead point of his last cartridge. It said, 'Hip broke, can't move. I love you Tatla and Gilley. Not where I want to die.' He didn't use the last bullet for himself. He froze to death; there was no fire wood left for the heater. He'd fired off all of his cartridges to alert anyone that he was in trouble. That's the hunter's distress signal, three quick shots. Mom heard them and knew it was Dad. That's the grief that always lives in my heart. I felt responsible because I didn't go with him."

"That's the saddest story I've ever heard." She laid her hand on top of his. "God, Gilley, we both lost our fathers in tragic accidents."

"Yeah we sure did, and I have vision quests about my Mum and Dad; it helps to smooth out the rough times."

"Yeah, I do too." She paused as she held his big hand. "Gilley, do you know about sweat lodges?"

"I do."

"Well I've made a real one on my upper deck. I wondered if you'd like to row up to my place, say Saturday morning. We could do a sweat lodge, and have a vision quest—You know, solve some of the problems of the poor old world, and— maybe ours too?"

"You bet, sweat lodge, and a vision quest would be perfect right now. I haven't done one for a very long time. How do I find your place?"

"Up the bay about a mile, it's the big old three-story float-ing home. I'll have a small maple leaf flag hoisted on the mast. I think a vision quest would be good for both of us, show us the path wherever in hell that is." She took both of his hands in hers and kissed him tenderly. "It's my turn Saturday, how about eight in the morning, and don't have breakfast. I have something to make the vision quest special."

He gave her a genuine smile. "Eight bells it is, see ya Saturday. Can I bring anything?"

"Just your pareu."

15

Trish hung the 'Gone Fishin' sign on the front door, turned off the doorbell, removed the clinger from the ship's bell. She went out to the main deck and looked south. She could see a sailing dinghy reaching up Richardson's Bay. She had hoisted the small Canadian flag to the yardarm of her flagstaff. Then she remembered when she was last aboard *Romayne,* Gilley's Whitehall was rigged for sail. Of course he would sail; only a fool would row a mile when he had a fair wind.

Finally she could see him — he was wearing his feathered headband and sitting in the stern. She went down the ramp and onto her float to watch him approach for the landing.

Gilley threw the coiled line, which she made fast. He lowered the sail and removed the rudder from the transom.

"Top of the morning to you, Trish."

"The same to you, Gilley." They pulled the Whitehall onto the float. Trish kissed him on both cheeks and took his hand. "Welcome, come aboard and take a look at my funky old home."

They went up the ramp to the lower floor. "This is my office, which was a living-room, and two bedrooms on the left with bathroom, laundry and storage room, small kitchen. Before I bought the boat, I rented this unit for a couple of years."

He followed her upstairs to the living room and surveyed the expanse of the large octagonal space with windows giving a water view. His eyes took it all in; the panoramic view of the bay, Mt. Tamalpais and the mansions on the Strawberry peninsula.

"What a terrific location, a beautiful paradise on the water."

They walked out to the spacious deck with the teak table and lounge chairs. "I could see your Whitehall all the way down the bay from here; looks like you made it in one tack."

"Yeah, fair wind all the way." They returned to the living room. "This is truly amazing."

He ran his fingers lightly across the top of the baby grand piano. "I didn't know you played."

She chuckled. "Chopsticks. I took lessons for a couple of years; I just got bored doing scales and trying to read music." She stroked the fiddle case. "So I took up the fiddle. You remember Daddy played and taught me. I love the fiddle and bluegrass, they fit together."

He lifted the cover over the piano keys. "Is it in tune in this salty environment?"

He played middle C and a quick scale. "Now, do you think that I'm the kind of person who would invite a musical gentleman on board to play a piano that was not in tune?"

He smiled. "No, definitely not." Next, he inspected the cleverly crafted erotic bronze lamps. He reached over and touched the rough finish. "You sure as hell don't find these in your average lamp store."

"No, I sculpted them in clay and had a friend who had a foundry on his boat make the molds and pour the bronze. I may take this up for my next hobby."

They moved into the dining room, where Gilley stood looking at the antique table and chairs. "What a beautiful table. The rosewood inlay is incredible. Where did you find it?"

"Believe it or not, at a garage sale, of all places." They moved into the kitchen. "Gilley, the other day I forgot to ask if you've ever taken MDMA? It's known as ecstasy on the street?"

"Yeah, I had some sessions with a healer for my drinking problem. She called it the 'Lion's Path.' By the way, I apologize for the other day; I really slipped off the wagon. I thought I'd put the goddamn lion back in the cage. I guess Wild Oscar sort of gave me the go-ahead to yield to my temptation, but I'm back on track and the lion's back in his cage. Yeah."

"Good for you. I know how it goes with booze, one drink leads to another and another and then we lose control, and yielding to temptation is easier than getting rid of it. The reason I asked about ecstasy is because my dear friend, Helen Boyle, synthesizes an amazing brew with herbs and whatever. Actually it's a powerful tea, better than E with no side effects like jaw clenching and no impotence. She calls it Magic Medicine, with a capital M, and, it's not on the DEA list of controlled substances. It's a wonderful way to do our sweat lodge and vision quest. Would you like to try it?"

"You bet; anything you say is fine with me."

"Did you have breakfast?"

"No, I never eat on a vision quest."

"Good, it's best to do this on an empty stomach." She reached into a kitchen cupboard and took out a small box that contained some bags of dark tea. She filled the kettle and plugged it in. "So after the tea is brewed, and cool enough, down the hatch. It takes about twenty minutes, then up, up and away."

"Sounds good to me; it's fun up there gliding around in space."

She unplugged the whistling kettle, filled the cups, and dropped the tea bags in. "We'll give it about ten minutes and then add a few tea spoons of this white powder. Helen won't tell me, or anyone else, what's in the tea or the powder; she only gives it to good friends and, she won't sell it. She's left the formula to me in her will." She passed a mug to him. "Let's go upstairs and I'll get the sweat lodge stones heated up."

He followed her up to the bedroom suite with the canopy bed and a beautiful sign hanging from it, which read: *THIS IS A HIGH CLASS PLACE. ACT RESPECTABLE.* He grinned. "I love the sign." He slowly took in the beauty of the room, the full picture window with the mountain well framed in the center. They went out onto the deck with the covered hot tub and the domed sweat lodge. He examined the hand-stitched rawhide cover and the bent willow boughs inside. "This is a perfect lodge; you made this yourself?"

"After I did my first sweat lodge at a pow wow and vision quest, I just had to have one. So one of the elders of the tribe cut the green willows and showed me how to use the rawhide strips to tie it together. Like it?"

Gilley smiled as he ran his fingers over the rawhide. "It's beautiful; you've got another hobby, making these."

"I'll think about that." Trish lit the propane burner under the iron crucible that contained the smooth stones, and covered them with the metal top.

Gilley looked around the deck and shook his head. "Incredible. You really did it right. So how did you find this amazing place?"

"When I moved back here from Florida about twenty years ago, the old gent who owned it had the small unit for rent on the lower floor. The price was right and the location with this view was absolutely magical. Also, this floating home community was so friendly. I fell in love with all of them. Sadly, about two years later, Jimmy, the owner, was diagnosed with pancreatic cancer and he passed away six months later. I was able to buy it from his estate because his daughter didn't want it. I finally burnt the mortgage in the fire place last year."

Trish went over to the deck railing and placed two deck chairs to face the mountain. "Let's relax and let the Indian maiden on the mountain take us while the stones heat. I often meditate up here and do Tai Chi. Now the tea is steeped, so here's to you, my friend, fair winds." They clicked mugs and sipped. "Gilley, I have two questions that have been gnawing at me. First, was the reason you came to the Bay Area to visit your wife? Finally how did you meet Chief Jon Ewer?"

"Yeah, for the most part, I just had to get the divorce finalized once and for all. Our marriage had been over for a long time. She told me she was thinking it over when she decided to end her life."

"Well, that was a strange but definite way to divorce. I'm sorry, it was a sad way to end it."

"Yeah it was, but now it's over, so as they say: 'Onward and upward.' The other reason I came here was to see San Francisco, because strangely, I'd never been here on my travels. Also I had Alfi's and your Dad's address in my book, so I wanted to meet up with everyone. I thought I could find Alfi and maybe you. And as luck would have it, I found you, or you found me. And, Chief Jon was the first person to welcome us to Sausalito. He has a small gaff schooner having a refit, which he couldn't sail in the Master Mariners. We hit off right away, so I invited him to sail on *Romayne*. He's really a terrific guy." He touched his tea mug to hers again. "Here's to you, Trish."

"And to you, Gilley; it's wonderful the way it happened. So can you tell me what you want to cover on your vision quest, just the general idea of where you want to go with it?"

He studied the mountain for several moments before he spoke. "It's strange that you ask, because today is the eighteenth year since I was shipwrecked on a voyage to transit Cape Horn. It's a long, tragic story. Do you want to hear it?"

"Of course, I want to hear everything about you."

She watched him as he started his story. "Well, at the time I just got the job as skipper of a one-hundred-thirty-foot iron gaff schooner that was laid up in Pape'ete for a major refit. I had about four months to waste while the yard went to work re-plating her. Then one day I was in the Vaheria with some friends. I'm sure you remember that great watering hole on the waterfront. Anyway, I met a Brit and his pretty wife, Reggie and Daphnia Whitfield. They owned a small Milne schooner and they'd just moored her beautiful stern to the seawall in front of the bar. They were on the last part of their circumnavigation. The rumor was they were looking for a strong, personable, able-bodied schoonerman to give them a hand. They had a ten-year-old daughter, Claire, and her black cat, Bear."

He glanced over at her. She studied his face as she sipped her tea and smiled..

"Well, after too many Hinanos and wondering if I could ever sail with a black cat called Bear on board, I finally signed articles on the schooner *Maruffa*. They only needed me for the Horn transit. I would sail with them to the Falkland Islands. They were a nice, together family and I developed a fairly serious crush on Daphnia. She was quite beautiful, and sweet as honey. Reggie seemed pleasant, but a tad moody, and occasionally put his wife down, which I didn't like. According to waterfront scuttlebutt, which travels like lightning, he was wealthy and was having a great time spending it."

"Don't stop, Gilley." Trish got up to check the temperature of the stones and returned to her chair. "Not long now, but we should finish our tea. Go on with your story, it's fascinating."

"Well, the Whitfield family stayed in Tahiti for a few weeks. They were very popular on the quay, partly because Reggie often shouted the drinks for the local cruising sailors who were mostly on tight budgets. Even the daughter, Claire, found some playmates on cruisers who were either going to New Zealand or continuing with their voyages. Finally, on departure day we topped up with water, diesel and provisions and cleared customs. And, with fond farewells to the cruisers, the bar girls, and wearing Tiare leis up to our chins, we split for Cook's Bay for some R and R. We spent another week making baggy wrinkle and leather chafe gear everywhere. I've always been paranoid about chafe. I also rigged a series nylon storm drogue with cones to hang off the stern in case we got a bad blow. We did a final stowing and set a course for the roaring forties and latitude fifty six south."

Trish got up to check the stones. "How do you feel? Are you getting a message yet?"

He stood up slowly. "Better by the second, whoa, I'm getting airborne here."

"Same here, the stones are hot for us, shall we?"

He grinned. "Absolutely."

"Okay." Slowly they stripped off their clothes and viewed each other with happy smiles and stood next to the lodge opening. Trish picked up the scented water bowl and climbed inside. Gilley crawled in and sat cross-legged opposite. She took his hands in hers, then leaned over and kissed him.

"Welcome to my lodge, Gilley, and may you realize your vision quest here." She handed him the water bowl. "Would you do the honors?"

He took the bowl from her and splashed water onto the hot rocks. The steam immediately filled the space in the lodge. The rawhide cover was translucent enough to allow muted light in so they could see each other.

He started a very low Aboriginal chant, first in a whisper then louder. "Chant with me, Trish."

She picked it up right away and stayed in tune with his deep gravelly voice. Their glances melded as they chanted the melodious tones. He continued sprinkling the stones with the ceremonial water. They never spoke, but went on with the chant. Small streams of sweat poured from their bodies. They ended their chant as the steam stopped rising from the cooling stones. "That was beautiful, Gilley, I loved it."

She crawled out and waited for him, then led him into the double-headed shower.

"Whoa, you've got cold water here! Feels good, though." After a short time of the slow torture, Trish turned off the water, handed him a bath towel, and together they dried their invigorated bodies.

She took his hand and walked slowly to the bed, where they lay on their backs, looking up at their reflections in the overhead mirror. "This is the first time I've ever looked up at myself in a mirror, and I sure like what I see." They laughed and waved at their images.

"Me, too. So how do you feel?"

He looked at her in the mirror for several moments. "I'm in a dream, right?"

She rolled over on her elbow and looked into his eyes. She caressed his face. "Let's find out." She leaned over and gently touched her lips to his, then put her arm around his neck and kissed him passionately.

His arm encircled her shoulders. She teased his lips with her tongue as a parting gesture and rubbed her nose on his like Eskimo lovers do.

"Some dream. I'm in yours and you're in mine." She fell back on the bed. "Tell me about that chant you sang."

"Oh, it was just me asking the Great Spirit to tell me this wasn't a dream. Actually, it's one my mother taught me when I was a youngster. The chant is like a prayer asking the Great Spirit to guide us and give us the wisdom of how to behave with all people and animals on the earth. To help others and to take only what we need from the earth. It was my mother and father's mantra, and they passed it on to me."

"I loved it, and it was wonderful to hear it in my sweat lodge. Now it's a sacred place for us, and for all the others who enter that space. You've made it complete. Thank you, Gilley, from my heart. So now, my dear, what do you say we let our libidos out for a little trot?"

"What a wonderful thing to do."

Trish slowly threw a leg over his body and straddled him. "Now, this is how I want to behave with one special person on this earth. I don't know if you were aware that when I first met you on *Bojangles*, when I was seventeen, I had a bit of a crush on you. Did you by any chance pick up on that?"

"Well, now that you mention it, I sort of wondered why every time I looked at you, you were looking at me. Is that what it was all about?"

She smiled down at him. "Yup, that's what it was about then, and that's what it's about now." She leaned over and kissed him, then slowly sat up and placed his hands on her breasts. "Don't be shy."

He caressed them tenderly as he watched her head rhythmically go from side to side. "If these were mine, I'd play with them all day. They're truly beautiful, especially the gold rings."

"They're yours now, Gilley, and you can do what you like with them."

Trish moved her hips slowly, waiting for nature to take its course. She was becoming aroused from his delicate caresses. She put her hands over his and started a slow gyration.

"Oh yes indeed, our dream is improving by the second, and his majesty has entered a warm, friendly place to explore."

He grinned. "Let the dream play on; I'm captive to it."

Their smiling eyes fused like invisible lasers. The cadence of her slow movements increased as her passion rose steadily to a quick, explosive orgasm. They were on the starting line of their new love dance as her first gun went off, followed by another, and finally, a continuous orgasm took complete control of her body. Her face and chest glowed with a pink hue. She gasped and wailed loudly, then leaned over his face and devoured his mouth just as he exploded into her.

"Oh Jesus—some dream!"

She lay on top of him, panting. "That—my dear Gilley—has been on my to-do list for twenty-eight years."

He pulled her face to his. "That was the best loving I've ever had in this life, and probably the next one."

They lay on their backs looking at themselves in the mirror. "I can't wait for round two and three and so on, until we dissolve into mere shadows of our former selves."

Gilley laughed. "Let the loving continue."

"So in about an hour or so, as we start to glide down, we'll boost with a half dose of tea to keep us up here. That should just about take care of the day. I'm delighted that you're here to share it with me. It's a very special day." She made a slow move to the side of the bed. "We better get some juice into us or we'll dry up and disappear. I'll be back in a flash, don't go away."

"Ha, not much chance of that. I'll just be floating around here someplace."

Trish set the glasses of juice on their bedside tables. "So, before we flew up here to the troposphere, you were telling me about *Maruffa* and the interesting family."

"Oh, right. Well, we left Moorea and set course for the Horn. Everything was going great in the southeast trades. *Maruffa* was fast and a dream to sail with the gollywobbler up. As we sailed further south, the trades were taken over by the variables and the gale force westerlies. We were shortened down to staysail, and ran before fifty-foot seas. We got into the roaring forties and battened down for a blow. Reggie, Daphnia and I were doing three on and six off, by now we're under bare poles, surfing, and doing about ten knots. We finally set the drogue to slow her down. We kept on through the night, with the wind and seas really building. By daybreak we figured it was honking seventy and enormous seas breaking. The sea was like white smoke as the tops were blowing off. We couldn't breathe facing the wind. We had to scoot on our butts to get to the helm and lock our safety harnesses to the deck cleats. What a ride; the biggest seas I'd ever seen. Scary."

Trish sat cross-legged while Gilley related his story. She watched his face intently, occasionally leaning over to kiss him. "I hope I'm not distracting you, Gilley. If I am, don't pay any attention, I'm still just a wee bit horny and I find you sooo easy to love."

He laughed. "So am I, and I can't believe that I'm with you after all this time, and if I heard your invitation correctly, we're going to be together tonight?"

She leaned over and whispered in his ear. "Yes, and all day tomorrow when my best friend, Sally, arrives."

He grinned and kissed her on the nose. "Anyway, Reggie agreed with me that we would make the drogue fast to the stern mooring cleats and then a few wraps around the anchor windlass as a backup, just to make sure."

He gently stroked her face. "God, you're so beautiful, and we're in heaven together. So where was I?"

"Ah, something about a drogue and winches, I think."

"Right, so it was the nine-to-twelve morning watch. Daphnia relieved me at the helm, so I crawled into my bunk, which was a small cave-like pilot berth aft of the salon. I was in a sort of half sleep."

He kissed her eyes. "You are so beautiful; I think I told you that; you still are. I digress. Oh, yeah, I'm sure you remember what it's like when the schooner's doing her thing well. She'd rise up on a big wave that passed under her, then slowly slide down the trough, hardly any roll. It was just a nice, controlled ride. I must have really zonked out, because in my dream, I felt her sliding sideways off a wave like she was going over the edge of the horizon and I couldn't wake up. I heard the sound of wood ripping. The next thing, I was rolled onto the deck head and slammed back onto the bunk. I crawled out backward and stepped into water up to my knees. I knew she'd rolled. I found Reggie slumped on the salon settee with a bleeding gash on his forehead."

"How terrifying."

"It was. His nose was bent onto his cheek. I could see his upper arm was broken and lying at a weird angle. He was groaning and coughing blood. The hull was half full of water. I went forward. The foc's'le hatch had carried away, the cat was howling under the bunk. On deck, the doghouse where Claire slept was also wiped clean off. The masts were hanging off the port side and the sharp stump of the main mast had pierced the hull into the head. The wheel, compass binnacle and the helmsman's seat all carried away. Daphnia and Claire had been washed overboard. I was sure we were done for. Waves were breaking on deck. I knew she'd fill soon and go down."

Trish watched him intently as he relived his horrible nightmare. "I just happened to glance at the anchor winch, and the drogue wasn't on it. I couldn't believe that Reggie would have taken the drogue off the windlass. The stern mooring cleat had just ripped out of the deck, which let the drogue hang from the starboard cleat, causing enormous drag. Obviously Daph lost control and couldn't steer her straight down-wind, so the bow must have rounded up, then slid down the face of the wave and buried her bow into the trough. She just pitch-poled, then rolled. When she came upright she was headed into the wind. The dismasted foremast had become a sea anchor."

She saw tears on his cheek.

"Poor Daph, she never had a chance. I couldn't see more than a boat length. There was no way that she and Claire could have survived. I went to the forward cabin, grabbed the cat, then went to carry Reggie on deck. He was unconscious. Somehow I got the life raft inflated, then put him and the cat in. I found the yacht's log book, emergency raft bag with spare hardtack and water and chucked it in, then cast off. *Maruffa* went down very soon after we got in the raft. It was a non-ballasted life raft, so the goddamn thing got picked up on waves and was blown ass over tea kettle, several times."

"God, Gilley, I can't imagine how that would be. What about Reggie—was he still out cold?"

"He'd been coughing bubbles of blood. I'm sure he had broken ribs, probably punctured his lungs. He didn't suffer long. He was dead soon after I cast off. I buried him at sea. I cried and chanted for a long, long time. They were a nice family, and they were wiped out, and their dreams and their schooner went with them. Bear Cat and I became raft mates." Trish watched the tears roll down his scared cheeks, then leaned over and kissed them away. They lay together silently for a long time.

"I'll never know why I was spared. Bear and I spent thirty-eight days in that raft. I had plenty of time to think about that and many other things in my life. But what came from it was I had a very long vision quest as the raft was taken north, well off shore by the Chilean current. I made a solemn vow that someday I would go back to that place where they all died and give them a proper memorial. And now I have the schooner to do just that. But I'm haunted by the ferocity of wind and seas in the southern ocean and Horn—I haven't figured out if I can finish the voyage for that family."

Trish's looked into his sad eyes. "What a horrible tragedy." She nestled with him.

Stroking her hair gently, he kissed it. "During those thirty-eight days, I fired off flares at three freighters; none of them saw the flares. Obviously they were on autopilot and maybe watching movies. I'd read about that sort of thing with other shipwrecked sailors in life rafts whose flares weren't seen either. Finally, a Norwegian freighter saw my last two flares and rescued Bear and me. As luck would have it, they were out bound from Santiago for Tahiti. Trish, I feel like I'm flying up there and watching us a way down here; it's weird, and very beautiful. Anyway, I was able to spear and catch mahi-mahi, tuna, and flying fish. It was a sushi diet without the rice and sake, so I got some protein and some moisture from the fish, but I lost about forty pounds. Bear was in seventh heaven, and gained weight on all that fish. I rationed what little water I had, but it finally ran out. I collected some rainwater, but I was very dehydrated and hallucinating when those guys rescued us. The Norwegians sure looked after my sorry and blistered ass—herbal baths. They shaved me and fed me the best food I've ever eaten. They treated me like a long-lost son from the sea. They even had to teach me to walk again because I'd been on my backside all that time and my legs and hips were atrophied and almost seized."

"Did you ever think you weren't going to make it, after those three ships went adios over the horizon?"

"No, no, I figured I was going to make it as long as I could still catch fish."

Trish refilled their glasses. "What about the Whitfield's parents, they must have been frantic when they went missing all that time? How did that all play out?"

"I was able to call Lloyds of London from the ship on their single-side band to report the sinking of *Maruffa* and the deaths of the family. Lloyds then made contact with the relatives and put me in touch with Reggie and Daphnia's parents. Those were the most difficult conversations, and we all shared our mutual grief. About two months after I was able to function again in Tahiti, Lord and Lady Whitfield, Reggie's parents, invited me to join them in England for their Memorial service. They were very gracious and more than generous. They not only paid my plane fare, but also insisted that I accept five thousand pounds for my so-called tragic ordeal, as they called it. I had a true bond with all of them."

"So in spite of the tragedy, it sort of had a closure for you and the family. Thanks for sharing your story. I know it was hard to relive it again."

Gilley smiled as he took her hand and kissed it. "You're an amazing woman, Trish; I've never met anyone like you. I want to know everything about you—when you were a kid growing up, your father, who taught you to sail and navigate. I want to know what your vision is."

"Well, I've l got my therapy business and Tai Chi, which keeps me busy. Now, my dear, I'm starting to lose altitude slowly and I really don't want to do another boost. How about you?"

"Sure, I'm fine with this, floating back to earth in a gentle glide."

16

They went down to the kitchen, where Trish made green tea. He touched her mug with his. "Here's a toast for you. A cheerful glass with a cheerful lass is a mighty fine thing together. But a cheerful lass with a cheerful ass, to my mind is a damn sight better. So, here's to the lass, the glass and the ass, may all three come together. Drinking the glass, feeling the ass and making the lass feel better."

She roared. "I'll drink to that."

"It's the sailors' toast."

"I've gotta learn that one, Sally'll love it."

"She's your old friend you grew up with?"

"Yup, we finally got together, after having lost touch with each other for too many years. Anyway, hard to believe, but then out of the blue last week, I got a call from her on my message center. It turned out that she'd been living in Napa, just thirty miles from here. And what a meeting we had, catching up on those lost years. Now she's divorcing a very nasty good-for-nothing wife-beater, and thank God, she's moving in here with me tomorrow. The creep really knocked her around, broke her nose and front tooth, bruises all over her body, just terrible."

"What is it with these guys beating up on women? I don't get it."

"They're badly screwed up, and in his case, Sally told me, he was beaten constantly by his old man. It passes from one generation to the next; very sick. He's also an alcoholic and into drugs. She's a surgical nurse, and shares an apartment with a nurse pal, where she's out of hitting range."

She leaned over to face him. "Gilley, there's something I have to tell you."

"Okay."

She paused for a few moments. "Well—I'm bisexual. I hope that isn't a problem for you." She searched his face and found a smile.

"No, problem here, I'm happy for you. You have the best of both worlds. So you and Sally?"

"Yup, we're lovers. I'm so relieved you feel that way. I don't want any secrets between us. Sally and I became lovers back then. We thought we were lesbians. Boy, was I wrong about me. And now, she's sure she's gay. She's my oldest and dearest friend; we were three when we met."

She leaned over and kissed him. "And now, dear Gilley, you and I are lovers at last. How about that?"

He smiled and took her hand. "What a great day this has turned out to be."

"Wonderful. Now, my dear, would you like to play the baby grand?"

"I'd love to."

"I'll get my fiddle going and we'll have a concert. I'm still high, and this'll be a first; I've never played high before. Here's to first times."

Trish brought their pareus, which she wore on her hips and topless; Gilley wore his on his hips. They moved to the living room. He sat at the piano and started with Happy Birthday.

He sang the words while Trish picked up her fiddle played the melody.

"How about that, I still can play. Does it sound alright to you?"

Gilley finished the song. "Great, how about Bojangles?"

Trish nodded. "Daddy, are you listening?"

They played and sang the song in harmony. "Hey! That sounded terrific! Maybe I could play with the Rag Timers at the Music Box?"

"Why not? A fiddle would sound great."

During a pause in their jamming, Trish held up her hand. She turned and walked through the dining room into the kitchen. She heard pounding on the front door. "There it is again. Not today, whoever you are."

Trish was reluctant to call out the kitchen window to ask who it was, because the last thing they wanted today was to be disturbed. "Maybe they'll buzz off; let's just wait a bit."

A few minutes later the pounding started again. Trish whispered, "I'm damn well not going to answer it." She tiptoed over to the window. "I can't see anyone."

"Trishy, I know you're in there. Sweetie, please let me in."

Trish opened the window more and shouted, "Sally, I'll be right down."

She turned around slowly, walked to the head of the stairs and re-wrapped the pareu to cover her breasts. "Goddamn it, I told her you'd be here today. Oh well, she probably forgot; she's got a lot on her plate."

Trish opened the door and was shocked to see Sally with a bandage on her head, a neck brace and a cast on her wrist. Her left eye and cheek were badly bruised. "Oh, Trishy, thank God you're here."

"Sweetheart, what's happened to you?" Sally fell into Trish's arms. She could smell the disinfectant from the bandage as she cradled Sally's head, then slowly pulled back to look at her face.

"Poser—the bastard, he went right off the tracks this time." She put her arm around Sally's waist and struggled to help her up the stairs.

Trish glanced at Sally's small overnight bag. "I'll get your bag later. I've got you now, just give me your arm." They slowly made it to the top step and into the kitchen.

"Sally, this is my old friend, Gilley Cornwall." Sally gave him a cursory smile.

"Hello, Gilley, it's nice to meet you at last."

"Same to you, Sally; do you need some help Trish?"

"We're okay, thanks." Trish led her into the living room and sat beside her on the couch. "Now tell me, what happened?"

"Trishy, do you have a joint, I really need to—you know, before I get started here."

Sally nervously rubbed her hands together and looked forlornly at her friend.

"Gilley, would you look in the top drawer to the left of the fridge? There's a baggie with some joints in it. I think it's under the dish towels, some matches, too."

He returned with a joint from the bag. She lit it, took a couple of puffs and passed it to Sally, who took a drag, inhaled it and coughed. "Goddamn it, I can't even smoke without coughing. I'm so out of it."

"Just take little bites, sweetie. It's really strong weed." Sally tried again and held it in, then exhaled. "Have a couple more, that should settle you down. Okay, from the beginning; tell me what happened."

"Let's see, the day before yesterday, we settled the divorce, all signed and closed. So, John went back to the house. He'd rented it back from the new owners for a month. I certainly wasn't going to spend the night in that house with him, so I went to a hotel in Napa."

Sally started to look more relaxed. "So the day before yesterday, I bought some moving boxes and went back to the house to pack up my stuff. He was there and obviously drunk or stoned.

Finally I ran out of boxes, so I went back to town to get more and have lunch. When I got back about two hours later, all of my boxes were dumped out on the floor. Trishy, he'd gone through all my things. So I hit the roof; I was furious. Then he came after me. Held me by my neck and slapped my face hard several times."

Trish gasped. "Oh, Sally, no."

"So he goes into a bloody rage and accused me of taking his meth and starts to beat the crap out of me. I can't believe how he just exploded. I started to run out of the house, but he caught me and dragged me back; Trishy, I really thought he was going to kill me. The last thing I remember he picked me up and threw me head-first at the fireplace. That's where I woke up, my head and shoulders were in the goddamn fireplace."

She reached up to touch her bandage. "Lots of stitches, mild concussion, cracked wrist, buggered up neck. I don't know how long I was out, maybe an hour. Blood all over my face. I crawled out of the fireplace, I couldn't stand up, and he was gone. I was so out of it, my head was splitting. I was able to crawl to the phone and called nine-one-one." She paused for a long time, looking first at Trish, then Gilley.

Trish and Gilley sat speechless, open-mouthed, and then looked at each other.

"Unbelievable." Trish held Sally's hand in hers and stroked it.

"They got me to the E.R. right away and put me back together, such as I am. The best part of this is OxyContin, no pain, great high. Anyway I got a cab and here I am, damn lucky to be alive, and please forgive me for crashing your vision quest, but I really didn't have anywhere to go. My roommate rented my room."

"Oh, honey, no problem. I'm so relieved we're here for you. Would you like anything, tea, juice, whatever?"

"Tea's fine, and another toke, actually several, that's great weed."

Shortly after Sally had finished her tea and took a few hits, she put her mug on the coffee table, yawned and happily fell asleep on Trish's shoulder. "Gilley, our guest has had a very bad day. I'll let her sleep right here." Trish removed Sally's shoes, lifted her legs on the couch and covered her with a blanket. She kissed her friend's bruised cheek and closed the drapes. She joined Gilley in the kitchen.

"She's completely exhausted. My God, can you believe what she's been through?"

"No, I can't, and she is damn lucky to be alive."

"It's going to take her a while to get over this."

Trish went down to the front door, picked up Sally's bag and a folded flyer sticking under the door and returned to the kitchen. "Well, love, I guess we'll have to put our concert and vision quest on hold for a while, but it was wonderful what we had. And I really look forward to the replay." She casually opened the flyer, read it and gasped. "Jesus, Gilley, look at this."

She watched his face; he frowned as he read it aloud. "Roses are red, violets are blue. I've killed before and I'll kill you too. Soon BITCH."

Trish stared at him with a blank look and slumped down on a counter stool. She reached for the paper. "It's a prank. Has to be some crackpot, why would anyone do this?"

"Trish, I don't think this a prank; I think it's the real thing. This is serious; we better call Chief Jon Ewer."

She started to shake. Her lower jaw chattered as she tried to enunciate the words. "Gilley, this—can't be happening, are we on a bad trip or what? I'm starting to crash here."

Gilley put his arm around her. "Take deep breaths. Relax, okay? Let's get dressed."

She looked up at his face with tear-filled eyes.

17

Gilley opened the door for Jon Ewer and Lynn Duke. "It's good to see you, Jon and Lynn."

"You too, Gilley."

They followed him up to the kitchen.

"Jon, you remember Trish Cameron, our wind spotter on *Romayne*. And Trish, this is Lynn Duke." They all shook hands.

"Thanks for coming by Chief and Lynn. This is it."

Trish handed the death threat to the chief, who, before taking it snapped on a pair of rubber gloves, as did Lynn. "Humph, short and to the point." He handed it to Lynn, who read it and placed it in a plastic bag, then into her briefcase.

"So Trish, Gilley said this was slipped under your door. Do you have any idea when it might have been delivered?"

"I don't, I haven't been out all day. The first time I went to the front door was to let a friend in about an hour ago. I noticed it when I went down to get her bag. So I guess it could have been delivered today or even last night, I really don't know."

"All right Trish, can you think of anyone who you would consider an enemy? Or have you had a serious altercation with anyone lately?"

"Well, let's see. No enemies." She ran her fingers through her hair.

"I'm concerned about your safety here Trish. You're extremely vulnerable on the dock, also from the water side. My first concern is the easy entrance into your place through the Dutch door window. Unfortunately, we just don't have the resources to provide you with a security guard. You would have to take care of that yourself." He looked at her, then Gilley. "The safest solution of course, is to relocate to a safe place away from the marina, a friend's home or whatever."

"Oh yeah, the Dutch door." Trish sat down at the counter. "An altercation, yes about two weeks ago this creepy hair storm of a guy was ringing my ship's bell, and kept at it till I opened the door. He asked if I was the sex therapist Trish Cameron. Now I don't take patients unless they have a referral from therapists I know. Then I would call them and interview them by phone. So right away a red light goes on and I asked him how he got my address. He mumbled the VA, and he's a 'Nam vet, had a leg and a nut blown off with a land mine. All this is rapid-fire talk. I could hardly understand what he was saying. He was really speeding, and obviously high on something. He said he needed help, can't get a good hard-on. He said the VA told him maybe I could fix him up."

She rested her head on her hands for several moments. "So then, let's see—"

"Take your time, Trish."

"Oh yeah, he said he wanted to get treated. I told him no and that I was with a patient. I just wanted to get rid of him. He kept looking inside behind me, and I'm getting nervous. Anyway, I told him that he'd have to get a referral from a doctor or psychologist. Then he said he'd wait till I'm finished with my patient and he makes a move to come in. I held his shoulders to stop him and he tries to grab me, I got one of his arms, turned him around to put a half-nelson on him and shoved him out the door onto the dock. Now he's in a rage, shouting every name in the book at me. I told him to leave the dock or I'd call the cops. Then he picks up a flowerpot and chucks it at me. I ducked as it smashed against the wall and just missed the door. Then he limped away on a peg-leg."

Jon glanced at Lynn. "Sound familiar to you, Lynn, lots of hair, prosthesis, stoned?"

She thought for a few seconds and looked at Trish. "No, there are usually a few guys around town with lots of hair, but no whacked-out stoners that I can recall. This guy may be a drifter. I'll ask the crew at the station. Anything else, like scars?"

Trish looked at her. "He had very bad teeth, upper front teeth missing and he had a droopy left eyelid. He didn't give a name."

Jon nodded and made a note in his small book. "Well, Trish, I suppose this guy could be a suspect. I say that because if he's a 'Nam vet, there's a good chance he killed over there. He should be registered with the VA. And it's a possibility that he might have it in for you giving him a half nelson. Lynn, would you get on to the VA and see if they can come up with anything on this so-called hairy poet. 'Roses are red violets are blue.' Well, it's a start."

Trish reached for Gilley's hand. "Oh, God, this is unreal; I've lived in this community for twenty years, and now someone's pulling the rug out."

"This is a tough situation, Trish, but in the meantime, I recommend you move off the houseboat now. Stay with someone you know, and buy a canister of pepper spray and keep it in your purse."

Trish buried her face in her hands. Gilley embraced her. He whispered in her ear, "You'll be safe on the schooner; no one'll know you're there."

She nodded and wiped her eyes. "Sally too?"

"Of course, and your cat."

Gilley turned to face the chief. "Jon, Trish and Sally can stay aboard the schooner. We'll head there just as soon as possible."

"Good plan, Gilley, that's a safe place. And Trish, I advise you to keep a very low profile, hide for a while until we can get the investigation going. Leave as soon as possible after dark. Lock the windows, doors and leave some lights on and maybe a radio or TV. Lynn, would you get Trish and Gilley's fingerprints? We need to see if there are any other prints on that note beside theirs."

Jon and Lynn were satisfied that Gilley's exit plan was a good one. They exchanged forced smiles and handshakes.

"So, Trish, if you really have to go ashore, take the big guy and the pepper spray with you and wear sunglasses, hat or whatever you can to disguise yourself. Okay? We'll be in touch. Take care, you two."

"Thank you, Jon and Lynn, I really appreciate this."

Trish found it difficult to comprehend the gravity of her new predicament. She ordered her drugged brain to take charge, to get her moving. She kept peeking behind the blinds in the kitchen. "'Roses are red violets are blue. I've killed before and I'll kill you too. Soon BITCH."

18

Trish left the radio tuned to National Public Radio and turned on several lights.

As soon as it was dark, Gilley guided Sally down the ramp onto the float and helped her into the transom seat in Trish's boat. He decided to sail his boat and tow Trish's.

"Fresh beam wind, we'll be alongside the schooner in no time. You all set, Trish?"

"Yeah, let's cast off." There was just enough light to see the small Canadian flag flying from the yardarm and the large American flag flying from the masthead.

Trish and Gilley methodically unloaded the boats and stowed the provisions in the galley. Unable to help, Sally sat at the cockpit table with Robin in her lap, trying to calm her down from the bouncy voyage. Bear jumped onto the table and cautiously approached Robin; he sniffed the new arrival and hissed.

Finally Trish came back on deck and slowly walked past Sally up to the bow. She sat on the bulwark rail, staring at the lights of the City across the bay.

Gilley sat beside Sally, picked up Bear and rubbed behind his ears. "Where's Trish?"

Sally pointed toward the bow. "She's in shock." Gilley stood up to leave the cockpit. "Gilley, wait here please, I'll go to her." She walked to the bow and put Robin in Trish's lap, then put an arm around her shoulder. "You alright, sweetheart?"

Trish kissed her cat. "No, of course I'm not alright. How

could I be? Some bastard wants to kill me, Sally. You should know. Poser tried to kill you, for God's sake. And I've been forced out of my home. "Why do people hate? Who is this idiot who hates me?"

Sally gently massaged her friend's neck and back and whispered in her ear. "Trishy, we're safe out here with Gilley. That's all that matters now."

Trish turned to put her arm around Sally, holding Robin with the other. "I'm sorry sweetie, I didn't mean to be short with you."

They held on to each other for a long time. Sally sniffed the air. "Do you smell what I smell?"

Gilley's deep voice called up through the galley hatch. "Soup's on, ladies, come and get it."

They all sat around the dimly lit cockpit table and inhaled their first meal of the day. Sally smiled at him. "Thanks Gilley, I was about to die of starvation."

"Sally, I've learned over the years that an unfed crew usually leads to mutiny. And after today's terrible events, I'm not about to let that happen."

After dinner, Gilley reached into the table drawer for his pipe and filled it with hashish. He looked at Trish and winked.

"Oh yeah, I might as well get good and ripped." Gilley lit the pipe and passed it to Trish, who took a hit and handed it to Sally, who examined the intricate carving on the bowel of the Meerschaum pipe for a moment, then took a small hit. Again she coughed the smoke out. "Damn, I've got to learn how to do this." She tried again and held it, then blew the smoke out as she spoke. "Ah, yeah, that's better, just little bites."

Gilley took the pipe from Sally for his turn. "Oh, before I forget, there are three double cabins so you can take your pick or bunk together, whatever you like. Two cabins have heads and showers. I'll show you how to work them when you're ready."

Trish stood up and put her hand on Sally's shoulder. "Come on, let's go below and check it out." She led the way and looked into the port cabin that had a double lower berth and a single upper. Sally looked into the starboard cabin, which had the same configuration.

"Oh, Trishy, he's just amazing, and I understand why you want to be with him."

"He really is." She studied Sally's bruised cheek and black eye and kissed her cheek.

"So where do you want to sleep?"

"Well, sweetie, I don't think I'd be very good company tonight."

"Of course, I know you're freaked about this. I sure hope the cops can do something about it soon."

"Me. too. I've got to call a few patients tomorrow about the next two weeks. I'll just have to postpone their appointments, and I have no idea what to tell them. Obviously I can't tell them what's going on. I suppose I could tell them I have to look after a sick relative, who's terminal. What do you think?"

"Sure, you could get away with that."

They watched Gilley carry the dishes into the galley, then he returned. "Did you get it all sorted out?"

"Yeah, Robin and I are taking port and Sally starboard." She whispered in his ear. "Thank you for being here for me. I worship our sweat lodge and our unfinished vision quest, it was wonderful. We'll do it again for sure."

He grinned. "It was wonderful and I treasure it too. I'll be here for you all the way. Sleep well."

Sally embraced her and whispered in her ear. "Same to you sweetheart. I love you."

19

Within a few minutes Trish started to fall asleep. Sally covered her and closed the door, and joined Gilley in the saloon.

"She's absolutely exhausted. What a hell of a thing to go through."

"Terrifying. I just hope the Chief and his gang nab the son-of-a-bitch. The scary thing is that he was right there at her door to deliver the death threat. He must have been there at night, because he sure as hell wouldn't want to be seen around there during the day. Scary dude."

"Yeah I agree. So, Gilley, are you sure it's alright for me to hang out here with you?"

"Of course Sally; Trish needs you as much as you need her. She told me all about you two growing up together and then losing each other for all those years."

"Thank you, I appreciate your hospitality. And now, I just can't believe we're together again. It's like it was meant to be. And she told me all about you Gilley, how you met in Tahiti when her dad won the Tahiti race. It's strange how things have turned out for you and me? It's so unreal." Slowly she got up from her chair to look at the painting of the schooners. "Gilley, I have to ask you. Are you in love with her?"

He looked directly at her as she turned around to face him. "You don't beat around the bush, do you?"

"I like to have things out in the open, especially now. Just so we all know where we stand."

"Well, Sally, this is a place I've never really been before; she's just beyond belief, the most amazing woman I've ever known. Yes—I am."

"Did you know that I'm in love with her too, and have been all of my life?"

"Yes, she told me that you grew up together since you were little kids, and you're lovers. It's not difficult to fall in love with Trish Cameron." He paused momentarily, deep in thought. "But beyond that, Sally, I think we need to give this some time and see how it goes. I'll stand by her in any situation. I'm glad that she was there to take you in and help you, and I'm happy that we finally met."

"Yes, I'm happy that we met with Trish to—you know."

"Anyway, during the short time we were together, we became soul mates. I'm fully committed to her, and she is to me. And more than anything, Sally, I would like to have your blessing as Trish's best friend."

She stood calmly for what seemed like an eternity, and then nodded her head. "Yes, you have my blessing, Gilley, because—she loves you."

"Friends, is that a deal?"

She returned to her chair. "Yes, yes, I like that. It's a deal, a good deal; of course I want you for my friend." She held out her right hand with the cast, then withdrew it and offered her left hand. He smiled as he took her small hand and kissed it. "I'm happy about this Sally, and Trish will be too."

"Yes, she will."

20

Sally was sitting on the anchor windlass cover watching clouds drift slowly over the bay. A light breeze from the south made a slight chop on Richardson's Bay. Flocks of ravenous gulls, pelicans and sea lions were gorging themselves on a school of herring. She was fascinated by the incredible activity that was taking place directly around the schooner's bows. First, one sea lion would break the surface to fill its lungs with air, then disappear below the surface to take in another mouthful of herring. Then another sea lion would repeat the process. A flight of brown pelicans observing the feast below folded their wings and dive-bombed into the water for their share of the bounty. The surface was alive with seagulls squawking and fighting for the leftovers.

Sally removed the neck collar and slowly tilted her head from side to side. She reached her hands up to massage her neck and was startled to feel soft hands on hers. "Looks like they're having a herring feast." Sally turned her body around as Trish kissed her cheek.

"Good morning, sleepyhead, how do you feel?"

"Shitty. Awful dreams. I'm a fucking wreck, and my cell phone battery is dead. It's not the way I want to start my day. Where's the captain?"

"He said he was going to work on the gardener, whatever that means. Trishy, Gilley and I had a long talk last night, and I've got tell you: he's—well, just wonderful. I can understand why you're soul mates. I gave him my blessings, and that goes for you, too. That's all I need to say about that. I'm happy for you.

Apparently you told him about us. Are we going to—you know, still have our special time together?"

"Oh of course, I'd tell you if he wasn't, I really couldn't be with him if he didn't accept you and me together. And I think it's simply wonderful how this all happened so quickly, without any fuss."

"Oh that's great, I never thought we'd be in a love triangle, if that's what we're in. Tell me, how old is he?"

"Sixty-five, the same age as Daddy would be."

"Amazing. I'm so happy for you; he's very sweet and damn handsome."

"Thanks. I'm still in a bit of a daze about it, and here's the kicker—I had fantasies about him when we first met in Tahiti. God, if I knew then what I know now. So, enough about me. Tell me about your long talk."

"Well, he told me a little bit about your vision quest, and I asked him if he's in love with you. He said yes, that he's committed to you all the way. So I approve, he's a keeper."

"I think so, too, and it was beautiful. We were just coming down from our Magic Medicine and having a musical duet and there was this pounding on my door, and the rest is, well here we are." She looked directly into Sally's eyes and put her hands on her shoulders. They silently studied each other.

"But now sweetie, I think we're in real trouble, both of us. I'm terrified of this death threat, and I want to get as far away from here as possible until this blows over. I have to talk to Helen right away. Did you get a new phone yet?"

"No I didn't. Gilley's got one."

Trish looked over Sally's shoulder and caught sight of a man with binoculars looking at them. She quickly ducked down out of sight behind the bulwark "Oh shit! Some guy's looking at us with binoculars, get down, let's go below."

They ducked down onto their knees and crawled to the forward hatch and down the ladder. "This is scary. I don't want to be seen onboard. I'm gonna find Gilley."

Trish rushed aft and up to the deck, where she crawled out of sight and slipped down the engine room hatch. Gilley was leaning over the Gardener engine, polishing the copper pipes. Before he had time to greet her, she blurted out. "Gilley, some guy's spying on me with binoculars. He's freaking me out."

He mopped his forehead with his sleeve and chuckled. "Don't worry about it, sweetheart. If I charged a dime for every tourist that looked at *Romayne* with binoculars and took pictures of her, I'd be a rich man. But it's a good idea for you to stay below during the day, or in the doghouse where they can't see in. Remember, Jon said stay outta sight. So, how'd you sleep?"

"Awful nightmares, one after the other. I've never been so scared. I've got to talk to Helen about this. Can I borrow your phone? My battery's dead." He passed his Nokia to her. She punched three wrong numbers before she reached Helen. She gave Helen all the details of her death threat and Sally's horrible situation. "I'd give a lot to see you right now, dear. Gilley could meet you at the Jib Topsail restaurant and bring you aboard." She nodded and glanced at him. "He'll be there at the dinghy dock; he's tall, with a beard and ponytail; oh, yeah, and he's handsome. You can't miss him."

Half an hour later, Trish spotted Helen waving her arms from under the ponderosa pine tree. A few minutes later, she was hugging her friend under the blue awning.

She introduced Helen to Sally. "It's wonderful to meet you Sally. I'm delighted that you and Trish reconnected after so many years. Now I know that dreams do come true."

"Yes, it's hard to believe that we only lived thirty miles away from each other."

"What a wonderful day for both of you, absolute magic. Now, Trish, tell me about this death threat. I don't like the sounds of this one bit."

Trish told her the details, including the visit from the police and the chief's advice to move away and onboard the schooner.

"Can you believe some idiot wants to kill me? This situation is a lot worse than any nightmare, at least a nightmare ends." Trish and Helen sat at the cockpit table, Trish with her back to the shore. Gilley sat opposite them with Sally.

"Stone the crows, darling, this is bloody serious. So, Gilley, what's to stop some deranged dingo from climbing aboard in the middle of the night and doing the nasty?"

"Well, Helen, I pull up the companion ladder at night. So if he made it to the deck, he'd have to break these two-inch teak doors down to get below, and if he was stupid enough to try that, he'd walk into the business end of a twelve-gauge shotgun blast. We'd be scraping his filthy guts off the deck for a month."

Helen laughed at the description of the carnage that Gilley would render. "Well, that would certainly solve the problem. So the chief of police thinks this is the safest place? The reason I ask is because Trish could stay at our place up in the quiet hills of Mill Valley. She'd be safe up there, no one would know she's there, and we have two golden retrievers that would shred the bastard to bits faster than you could say 'good on ya, mate.' Well, at least they'd bark and show their fangs."

Trish took Helen's hand. "Well, I don't see why not, I could certainly hang with you. You know, Helen, I feel like I'm in a continuous roundabout of terror, and I don't know how to exit the bloody thing."

Tears formed in Trish's sad eyes. Helen put her arm around her and pulled her head to hers. "I know this is going to be very difficult love, you've been through more than any normal person could handle." She paused and looked ashore. "But all these years I've known you, you've proved yourself a tough Sheila. Now you find yourself in a situation that you can't fight, because you can't see your enemy face to face. So you'll have to trust the police to do their job. The worst part is the waiting, not knowing if the threat's real, or if this is just a nasty prank to unravel you."

Trish wiped her eyes. "You're right, I have no choice but to hide and wait, but I'm so jittery. I can't sleep because of the God-awful nightmares. I wake up exhausted in a cold sweat."

Helen studied Trish's tired eyes. "I can give you something for that later. Now, can you think of anyone on the verge of going over edge? You know—spooky wild eyes, strange sudden movements, very different."

She told Helen about her encounter with the hairy poet. "They're going to talk with the VA and see if they can identify him."

Helen glanced past Gilley to see a Whaler approaching the schooner. A man in uniform was at the controls, with a uniformed woman beside him. "Looks like you have visitors Gilley."

They all looked aft and saw the small vessel approach. Gilley stood up and went to the companion ladder. "It's Chief Jon and Lynn." The chief eased the boat to the companion ladder and Lynn threw Gilley the painter. "Hello, Jon and Lynn, welcome aboard."

"Chief Jon Ewer and Detective Lynn Duke, this is Doctor Helen Boyle and Sally, Trish's friend."

They all shook hands and sat at the cockpit table. "So Trish, there were no fingerprints on the note except yours and Gilley's. Absolutely clean, he must have had gloves on. Also, the Sheriff's Department has been patrolling the dock and your place. The VA is still trying to get the lowdown on this character, so they'll get back to us."

"That's a relief, Jon. Thanks for making that happen."

"So how are you doing, Trish? Is your support team looking after you?"

"Just fine, thanks. Good food, good company. But I've decided to stay with Helen for a while, just to get out of town."

"Good plan, so just keep out of sight. I've got your number, so we can keep you up to date on the investigation. Well, folks, that's it from us for now. It's been great meeting you Doctor Boyle and Sally. Take care Trish. It's always a pleasure, Gilley."

Gilley cast off the painter and waved as Jon and Lynn headed back to their station.

The ship's clock in the doghouse struck four bells. Helen glanced at her watch. "Well, dear, I've got a three o'clock. So we must be away." She leaned over and hugged Sally. "I'm delighted to meet Trish's long-lost friend." Helen reached for Gilley's hand. "Gilley, I'm so happy to finally meet you. Next time I'd love to inspect your beautiful yacht if I may. I have a special thing about schooners, especially gaff schooners with a Canadian flag."

He smiled. "Of course Helen and I look forward to seeing you again."

Trish kissed Sally. "I'll call you every day." She picked up her cat. "Robin, you be a good girl now, Sally'll look after you." She picked up her overnight bag and stepped into the Whitehall with Gilley and Helen. Sally waved and watched until they were out of sight behind the point.

Gilley helped Helen ashore, then held Trish, nestling his nose in her hair and whispering in her ear, "I love you, Trish." Helen looked on and smiled.

Trish grinned through her tears. "I love you, too, Gilley." She slowly released from him and glanced at Helen. "I better go, Helen has an appointment."

21

They sipped iced tea in Helen's living room, enjoying a full view of the sleeping Indian maiden reclining on the skyline of Mt. Tamalpais.

"Bruce and I often sit here and watch her up there. She seems to be saying, 'You will be well, and safe from fear and evil. Love is the path that leads to good health and happiness.'"

Trish looked out at the long-haired legend for a long time. Helen watched her nodding imperceptibly when she saw her tears.

"That's right, dear, let the tears flow; you've been on that rocky road alone, but now you have support from a lot of people. We'll climb up Mt. Tam tomorrow. It won't take long, and every step will be a new feeling of confidence until you reach the summit. Drink the tea mixed with your tears. It'll invigorate you. Now dear, how would you like to slip into a bath? Let the Jacuzzi jets soothe you, I'm sure you'll want to wash your hair."

Trish took a final sip of her tea and stood up slowly. "Okay doctor, lead the way."

"First, I want you to take a happy pill. It'll relax you as you soak in the tub. And then we'll start to work on you, get your head and your life straightened out."

Trish soaked in the big tub; the jets massaged and relaxed her exhausted body. Helen brought her a white capsule with a glass of fruit juice. "Take this. I call it HOPE. It's similar to MDMA, but it's my own brew with a few extra molecules. It's much better; you'll feel it in about fifteen minutes. Enjoy; I'll be out on the deck."

"Helen, I really appreciate this. I'm at the stage where I can't think straight, I just want to dig a hole and hide in it."

"I know this is all so traumatic. Just close your eyes and relax, take deep breaths and let the energy circulate through your body. There's a kimono on the back of the door. Shout if you need anything."

It was at the start of her hair-drying session when she felt the drug coming on. She looked at her dilated pupils in the mirror and smiled. She pulled her hair into a neat ponytail and went out to the deck. "It just kicked in; what a smooth entry. Helen you really have a talent for making the most amazing drugs."

Helen smiled. "Thanks. I try to make them work for people who need help. Now, lie down on the chaise, I'm going to start to put Humpty Dumpty back together again. Close your eyes and relax."

Trish felt secure with Helen sitting beside her as she lay under the awning. Another look at the sleeping Indian Maiden and she closed her eyes. "Whoa, this stuff just ramped me up a notch. I'm flying here."

"I'm right here, just go with it, let it all out."

Two hours later the drug was losing its effect. Trish opened her eyes to glance at Helen, who smiled and took her hand.

"Well, I must say you have summed up your whole life history in great detail. You verbalized your memoir perfectly. I learned some wonderful things about you that I didn't know. Especially that part about you diving off the pier in Sausalito to save the little girl and her dog that fell in. You certainly have been through a lot; and, of course, the tragic drowning of your father, who dove in to save you. What a hero he was; and then, the untimely passing of your mother, all within two years. My God, then you discovered cocaine and promiscuous sex. That was your escape from the torment and pain of losing your parents.

But here you are, very much alive and on the path to being the wiser for it. "

Trish nodded.

They were startled to hear Helen's cell phone playing Waltzing Matilda. She glanced at the message window. "It's Chief Ewer, dear. You should answer it."

"Yeah, it could be important. Hi Jon, what's up?"

"Trish, we've got some very interesting information from the VA about the hairy poet. He's a Viet Nam vet, his name is Pinky Urqhart, he's an anchor out and lives in a converted WWII landing barge out on the bay not far from your place. The harbormaster here told us he's a real loner, seldom talks to anyone; he just nods and grunts at people when he walks past them. He gets his mail at the Toadfish marina office; apparently he doesn't have a bank account; always pays cash. Now, we just talked to one of the marina crew, who told us that he's positive he's dealing drugs because there is a lot of small boat traffic making short visits back and forth from his boat. Now, that changes the whole dynamics around this guy, which means were going to consider our law enforcement options here. Anyway Trish, I just wanted to keep you in the loop, and Lynn or I will give you updates. So how is it going with Doctor Helen?"

"That's very interesting information Jon. And yes, Helen is really looking after me. I really appreciate what you're doing for me on this case."

"That's what we're here for, Trish. You take care, and give our best wishes to the good doctor."

"Will do Jon, and my best to Lynn."

Trish turned to look at Helen. "Well, apparently I have a nasty, anchor-out, drug-dealing neighbor close by my boat who doesn't like me, and scared the bejesus out of me. And I certainly don't like him."

"I'm sure our finest will take care of this nasty dingo so that you can get on with your life again. I have another mantra from Alexander Graham Bell. This one's free. 'Sometimes we stare so long at a door that is closing that we see too late the one that is open.' It's human nature, but it's time for you to walk through that open door. Try to visualize doing that. I assure that it will set you free of the nasty past, and you won't look back again."

"I like that, now I just have to find that open door."

"I assure you it will appear." Helen helped Trish's to her feet, then walked her over to the veranda railing. "Look up at the Sleeping Maiden; tomorrow morning, we're going to pack a lunch and visit with her to sit where her heart is and have a chat."

Trish squinted at the bright sky. "What a great idea. All the years I've lived here, I've never climbed Mt. Tam. And I didn't know you could actually be with her, like that."

"Bruce and I climb up for a visit once or twice a year. It's a vigorous two-hour hike, and worth every minute. Now I want you to have a rest."

22

The next morning Trish and Helen left the house as the sun rose above the Tiburon peninsula. The summit of Mt. Tamalpais was shrouded with a thick veil of fog clinging to the trees and jagged rocks. They both carried daypacks containing sandwiches, fruit and several bottles of water. Helen had added a small emergency first-aid kit, her cell phone and a pair of binoculars. She had given Trish Bruce's hiking poles to help steady her on the steep trail up the mountain.

"Bruce and I usually make up it to the Maiden with one pit stop. Are you ready, dear?"

"You bet." Trish followed her at a steady pace, planting one pole after the other on the rocky soil. "Do you think that fog'll burn off?"

"Too right it will. By the time we get half way, it should be gone."

"Helen, I like your suggestion about the door closing behind with all the bad stuff locked away forever. I'm still thinking about that. I'll keep working on it, because I'm ready for the next door."

"You're in for an enlightening experience."

As Helen had predicted, the fog had lifted when they rested at the halfway point. "Another hour and we'll be on top of the world. It's the highest point of land in Marin County. Some days you can see a hundred miles in all directions. Are you ready for the last stretch?"

"Let's do it." Trish looked ahead and wiped the sweat from her brow.

They were gasping for breath when they reached the summit, where they sat and massaged their tortured leg muscles.

"Just over here is where Bruce and I sit. That's where we think her heart is." Helen walked to the spot, with Trish beside her. They sat on the soft grass and drained their water bottles. She took her binoculars from her pack. "You can see our house right where those tall redwoods are; have a look."

Trish swept the area and finally found the Boyle's house between the redwood trees. "I see it. Your dogs are lying on the veranda." She moved her line of vision to the floating home marina. "There's my boat, I can just make it out."

She scanned further south to the schooner. "There's *Romayne*. I can see Gilley's Whitehall tied astern. These glasses are great, oh, no wonder they zoom a way up."

"Would you like to call Gilley and Sally to tell them that you're looking at them from the mountain?"

"Not right now. Maybe a little later. I just want to lay up here and think a bit."

She lay back on her pack and quietly dosed off.

Suddenly, muffled sobs from Helen awoke her. Shocked, she turned to her friend.

"Helen, what is it, dear?"

"Not to worry, I just get a little sad up on the mountain. Bruce and I often shed a few tears and then feel better for it. There's a little sadness in everyone's life, don't you think?"

"I've never known you to be sad."

Helen looked down at the grass. "There's something I've never told you, Trish. Maybe I'm in denial. Even shrinks are permitted to experience it."

She looked over at Trish with reddened eyes. "We lost our five-year-old daughter to leukemia many years ago. Today they would have been able to save her. In those days, they didn't have the drugs. So Bruce and I come up here to grieve for our sweet little girl, and the Maiden gives us strength to go on. I have a photo of her in my locket here."

"Oh Helen." Trish crawled over to kneel in front of her. "I had no idea, there was no mention of it in your memoir."

"That's one chapter that I couldn't write. It's behind the door that I can't close. I keep looking back at our little girl."

Helen handed the gold locket to Trish. "Oh, she's adorable." She studied the sweet face for a long time, then returned the locket and embraced her.

It's strange, Trish, but she would have been the same age as you are now."

Trish gasped quietly. "Oh, Helen, it's terrible losing a loved one. I'm sure that thinking about her is what helps you and Bruce over the years."

"Yes, it's why we come up here." She wiped her eyes. "Now, why don't you just lie back on the soft grass, close your eyes and breathe deeply. I always visualize the Maiden up here, and I talk to her."

Trish placed her backpack under her head, shielded her face from the hot sun with her hat, then laid back and closed her eyes. "All right, I like that."

Sometime later Helen woke and glanced over at Trish, who was fast asleep. She looked at her watch. "Stone the crows, we've been out for an hour! Trish, wakie-wakie, it's time for some nosh."

Trish turned her head and yawned. Helen passed her a sandwich and a bottle of cold tea. "I had the most bizarre dream. I was standing on this mountain looking at an enormous billboard with a photograph of Gilley's mother and dad. They were holding his hands between them. Gilley has this photograph in his cabin. In my dream, they just stepped out of the photo and stood right in front of me and pointed to the Bay. Then his mother and father said, 'Help our son on his long journey. You are young and strong and he needs you.' Then they stepped back into the photo, chanted and faded away into a cloudy background. Do you suppose—?"

Helen nodded. "Yes, I'm sure you had a vision from your subconscious. You must have been thinking about Gilley, had you?"

Trish took a bite of her sandwich. "Yes I was. I think about him a lot, so how can I help him on his journey? He hasn't said anything about it since I first met him, and I have no idea if he's still planning to chase sunsets to Tahiti and do the Horn. We haven't talked about it at all."

"Well, I think you two have some serious talking to do, and the sooner, the better."

Trish stood up and stretched her arms. "I guess you're right; maybe that's what's behind the open door."

Helen stood beside her and put her arm around her shoulders. "Just take it one day at a time. I'm only a phone call away and a twenty-minute drive. Now let's get our stiff butts down off this amazing mountain."

"Thanks for bringing me up here to meet the Maiden. I am on top of the world and I'm ready to get busy."

They made much better time descending the mountain, as their stressed muscles complained all the way down.

"Trish, I've been thinking about Sally. I'd like to offer her some stress counseling. Like you, she's had a bloody terrible shock. I thought she could come up here for a few days after you go back to the schooner. Also, you need some personal time with the good captain. What do you think?"

"Sure, I'll ask her. I know she needs all the help she can get. You know, I think we're making a pretty good team here, what with a high voltage schooner captain, a top-of-the-line shrink, a terrific chief of police, a banged-up surgery nurse, and me, such as I am. Look out world, don't fuck with us."

They laughed. "That's a good way to put it. Come on you silly girl, we only a have short sprint to the hot tub and a bottle of red."

As soon as they entered her kitchen, Helen turned the oven on. Then, after inserting a few garlic cloves into the roast, she slid it into the oven.

Trish came into the kitchen wrapped in a bath towel. "Can I help?"

Helen took a bottle from the wine rack and handed it to her. "You can pull cork on this, and you'll find big glasses in the cupboard above the dishwasher. Pour some of that most exquisite Malbec into said glasses and come up with a suitable toast."

Trish handed her a glass and touched it with hers.

"I have one of Daddy's. 'Here's to the ships and the women of our land. May the first be square-rigged and the second well-manned.'"

Helen laughed as they eased their tired bodies into the hot tub. "What a fitting toast. You must write it down for me. Well-manned indeed." They smiled at one another and sipped their wine.

"This Malbec is like sipping satin."

23

Gilley was exchanging waterfront scuttlebutt with one of the yacht captains when Helen parked her car close-by and waved.

He shook hands with the young man in parting, and was immediately embraced by Trish. "I've really missed you, love, and it's only been three days."

He put his arm over her shoulder and gave Helen a hug with the other arm. "It's good to have you back and thanks Helen, for looking after her. Sally and Robin are waiting for you."

Sally took the painter and passed it to Gilley as he came on deck. Trish helped Helen onto the companion ladder and followed her to the deck.

Sally embraced her. "Trishy, it seems like you've been away for a week, you look like your old self. Doesn't she Gilley?"

"She does. So Helen, would you like a look-see below?"

"I'd love to."

Trish took Sally's hand and led her to the forward hatch, where they sat under the awning. "The reason I look better sweetie is because Helen, bless her heart got my head straightened out. And she's offered to take you up to her place and help you with your situation; she knows you're stressed. You have no idea how steady she is in guiding people through major life changes, and I've known her for twenty years. I never thought I'd be on her couch."

Sally looked over at the City for a few moments. "Of course I'll go with her, she's terrific."

Helen quietly approached them from behind. "I didn't mean to eavesdrop on you two, but I couldn't help hearing you Sally.

I'm delighted that you'll visit with me. The truth is, I really just want company while Bruce is away." She winked at Trish, "Now, let's join the captain for tea and scones."

"Gilley, I forgot to mention, I'd like to abduct Sally for a few days; just a little tune-up for her psyche. I trust you'll grant her shore leave?"

Trish sat happily listening to the joyful banter passing over the table. "Arr. Captain, methinks she should do double duty when she returns. The lass has been slacking her work on the schooner. She's not even swabbed the decks or polished the brass. She'll give the ship a bad name, I declare, sir."

"Aye, you're right on the mark. So, Miss Sally, you'll sure be doin' double duty when you return. I've decided to grant you medical leave, and you're to bring back a goodly supply of scones and croissants to this neglected ship. So there!"

"Of course captain, but where is the bakery?"

"It's right across the street from the big restaurant yonder, ya can't miss it."

"My, you do run a tight ship Captain." Helen added, "I'll have her back on board, ready to do her duty, in two days. And now, may I request a shore boat sir?"

"Right away." He disappeared below, and Sally excused herself to pack an overnight bag.

"He is a darling, adorable man, and I'm so happy for you, Trish. You're both so well suited together at this time in your lives, and remember what the lady in your vision said to you."

Trish nodded. "Yeah, these few days together will help."

Sally arrived on deck carrying a small backpack. She stood on her toes and gave Gilley a hug. "I promise I'll try to do better when I return Captain, I really will. Thanks for everything."

Helen took Gilley by his arm. "Gilley, please make sure Trish eats her spinach. it always helped Popeye. Bye bye."

24

Trish sat in the cockpit holding her cat on her lap and looked at her little town, which resembled a small seaside village on the Cote d'Azur. Her dad used to call it a five-minute town when her parents first moved there several years before she was born. He said it took about five minutes to drive from one end of town to the other. Now, Trish called it a twenty-minute town, particularly if one hit all nine red traffic lights.

She walked around the deck slowly, admiring the excellent craftsmanship of the old-school shipwrights. They had followed the naval architect's plans to the letter, but their callused hands had transformed the raw teak into an object of beauty. She put her arms around the base of the main mast and lightly kissed the varnished spruce. Looking up, she noted that the spar was straight and true, and the leather-covered oak mainsail hoops were sitting neatly at rest atop one another. She wondered when the mainsail and the jibs would next be hoisted to drive this incredible schooner to some far-away shore. Would it chase sunsets, as Gilley had imagined when he was showing her around the vessel that unforgettable day three months ago?

She was startled when she heard Gilley's footsteps behind her. "Is the mast straight, or do I need to tune the bow out of it again?"

"Looks straight as an arrow, but the topmast has a slight bow forward, see?"

Gilley looked aloft and smiled as he put his hand on her shoulder. "Ah, the running-back stays are a little slack when she lies at anchor. Soon as we bend sail on her, we'll harden up on the back-stays and it'll be right on."

Trish patted his hand and held it. She gave him a happy smile and led him aft to the cockpit were they sat side by side.

"Helen's an amazing woman. She seems to look right into you, and knows what makes you tick. What did she do to make you like your old self again?"

Trish looked at Mount Tamalpais and the sleeping maiden lying in repose at the summit. "She's a shaman, firewoman. She spent a few months with aborigines down under and Native Americans here. She studied their cultures and learned all about their spirituality and sexuality. A lot it of rubbed off on her, and some of it onto me. That's how I discovered sweat lodge and vision quests; Helen and I were together with the tribe, and among many things, we learned that we're all brothers and sisters on the earth."

"I remember you said at our sweat lodge that you've been involved with Native American culture with its amazing spirituality."

"Yeah, I try to play the part that I believe in so strongly. Helen also took me to an event sponsored by the Ojai Foundation council. It was fascinating, and we learned about the natural sacred laws of Cherokee Nation. Also about the medicine wheel, and that sexuality was right in the center of it. It was the hub. I began the journey of the Sweet Medicine Sundance path. You may be familiar with some of these teachings, such as everything is born of woman and nothing can be done to harm the children. Native Americans and Canadians lived this way for thousands of years."

"Yes they have. My mother and the elders taught me about the way of the Great Spirit. I've also tried to play the part that I believe in, so we're kinda kindred spirits."

He leaned over to kiss her and she lightly touched his scarred cheek. "Soul mates?"

"Definitely."

Gilley reached in the drawer under the table and brought out his Meerschaum pipe. "Speaking of spiritual, I think it's time for us to get spiritual and elevated." He passed the pipe to her. She examined it for a few moments, then looked ashore. "I guess we're far enough out here, aren't we?"

"Haven't been busted yet, and besides, we know the chief of police, right?"

"Right." Trish drew on the pipe and handed it back. They exchanged it again, then Gilley snuffed it out and returned it to the drawer.

"When I called you yesterday from the mountain, remember I told you I'd fallen asleep lying on the maiden's heart, and I had an incredible vision?"

He nodded. "What was it?"

"It was bizarre. That photo in your cabin with you and your parents when you were a toddler. In my dream, you all appeared on a big billboard and walked out of the photograph and stood right in front of me. Then your mother and father turned and pointed at the Bay and said together, 'Help our son on his long journey. You are young and strong, he needs you Trish.' Then they raised their hands, chanted for a while and faded away."

He grinned. "That's one for the dream catcher, a keeper for sure."

"It really is, and it's something to think about."

"Yeah, I've had dreams about that picture too, but without any words being spoken."

"Well, maybe some night we might end up in the same dream." Trish took his hand and stroked it. "Well, now that we're elevated, let's go aloft to look at my beautiful town from up there and watch the sunset; what do you say?"

He grinned. "Well, if the lady wants to go aloft and inspect her town, why not?"

They secured their safety belts. He followed her up the rat-lines to the main-mast crosstrees, where they clipped themselves in the safety hoops. "Gilley, look where I'm pointing, up there on the hill. See that three-story brown house with the dormer windows and the white flagpole? That's our old family home, we lived there for twenty years or so."

Gilley looked where she was pointing. "So that's where you were raised? You've always been a water person like me."

"Yup, I must live not more than a city block away from salt water or I can't function. We had some very happy years in that house. Sally and I were together most of the time."

She looked back to the mountain again. "Then there was that terrible year when Daddy died, and some other bad stuff. That's all gone now, locked away forever."

Trish turned around slowly to face him and put her nose up to his. "I've been up a few masts in my time, but there's one thing that I've never done aloft." She had an impish grin on her face.

"You don't mean—?"

"No, no, I mean I've never been kissed aloft." She put her arm around his waist. They kissed for a long time, then slowly separated. "Yes, I like it up here and not just for wind spotting." Trish laughed. "I suppose it's possible to get it on up here, but with safety belts on, I think they'd get in the way, don't you?"

He giggled with her; they were behaving like childish teenagers on their first date.

"Yeah, and what about all the tourists ashore, watching us with binoculars. I don't think so. But, just maybe in a secluded anchorage somewhere. It's food for thought."

He wrapped his arms around her and the mast. They watched the sun slowly sink below the Tennessee Valley hills. High wispy mare's tails appeared to burst into flame and ignite the whole sky above the ridges.

"Red sky at night, sailors delight." He kissed the top of her head.

"None better."

"We can't chase that one, but what about all the others you want to chase on your way to Tahiti? I think you're going to need a backup navigator on that run down the trades."

He was momentarily silent as he considered the meaning of her statement.

"Well, I've kinda put that on the back burner for a while, Trish. You know there's a hell of a lot going on here, with your dicey situation, and of course Sally's too."

She turned around to look at him. "I know all that. We'll help Sally with her situation and mine. God knows how, but, oh well—"

"We need to get a plan going. Let's think about it when things clear up a bit."

"Okay, but when that's all cleaned up, I'm free, Gilley. I've had a real vision that tells me to go to sea with you. I miss it all, the trade winds with the porpoise diving under the bow, the speed of a big schooner on a broad reach with a bone in her teeth. I miss the waterfront in Pape'ete, the beauty of Tahiti, also to be anchored in Cook's Bay with the aroma of the tiare flower, the colorful pareus, and the beautiful Tahitian vahines with their flowing black hair as they sit side-saddle on screaming Vespas. I want to do it all again, but with you this time. And then the Horn; remember I told you Daddy was going to do the Horn? Now I want to do it for him, with you. Besides, your mom and dad asked me to help you on your journey. So there."

They watched the fading sunset together, then his gaze slowly moved to her. "You're serious?"

"Yes, absolutely. Chasing sunsets, I love that expression, and I mentioned it to Alfi a few days later. He didn't think it was a good idea, single-handing a big schooner. In fact, he—"

"Yeah, he rowed out and told me I'd been smoking too much hash. He said, 'Never heard such a goddamn cockamamie idea in my eighty-four years.' So that did it; I gave up the idea right there. We had a drink on it and haven't talked about it since."

"I'm sorry. I shouldn't have mentioned your idea to Alfi, but I sorta wondered what he thought about it."

He nodded "That's alright, you did the right thing. I was little stoned when I told you about single-handing the old girl. It was a stupid fantasy, you know; Gilley gets his name into the Guinness book of World Records: The first Canadian Indian to single-hand a one-hundred-eight-foot gaff schooner around Cape Horn both ways. Three cheers for Canada and Sir Gilley Cornwall. Knighted by the Queen in Buckingham Palace. Alfi just knocked some sense into me. Bad plan, back to square one."

"Yeah, single-handing this old girl was a fun fantasy for a while. So how about sailing with a small crew and Arthur McWindvane, who you said wouldn't steal your girlfriend in port. Wouldn't that be a start? I hope you haven't given up on having that very important memorial for your shipmates."

Gilley shrugged his shoulders and reached for her hand. "I've been mulling this whole thing over and over ever since the shipwreck. But it's the damn nightmares of the crash. I wake up in a sweaty panic, get up and take a few turns around the deck, have a couple of tokes, then I go back to bed, but I don't sleep. I just lie there looking at the deck-head, and I don't know what to do about it. I can't explain why I lived and they all died. It's like post-traumatic crash stress. I keep seeing their faces, and I cry and cry some more, it won't go away."

"I'm not surprised that you're still having nightmares after all these years. I'm sure Helen could help you out with your nightmares."

"I was thinking about asking her if she has a magic pill in her bag of tricks for rogue nightmares."

"Darling, she has pills for everything. Of course you should tell her. She'll certainly find a way to help you. Then, maybe she'll march you up the mountain to meet the Maiden who can really help you with her magic."

"Yeah, maybe I'll ask her when she brings Sally back."

Two mornings later Trish had a call from Sally. Helen told her that the healing had gone well, and wanted to meet at the pine tree by the restaurant around noon.

Their wonderful morning love-making exercise was followed by some preventative maintenance exercise. Gilley and Trish hauled many buckets of salt water over the bulwarks and sloshed it onto the teak deck. This regular procedure kept the deck planks swelled to prevent any seams from opening under the hot sun. Finally, they wiped down all of the varnished teak with chamois skins soaked with fresh water and vinegar until it shone like a piano.

Gilley washed the hatches and doghouse windows, and Trish polished the schooner's brass bell and compass hood. She stood back to admire the bright shine with her distorted reflection and suddenly burst into song. "She polished up the brass so carefully that now she's the ruler of the Queens' navy. Well sir, she's ready for inspection, unless there are other duties to perform?"

"No, my pretty maid, she's well squared away; we can stand down. Oh, before I forget, I wondered if Helen might be having lunch with us."

She bent down to look at the ship's clock on the doghouse bulkhead. "They'll be here pretty soon, so let's plan on it. I'll go down and rustle up a tuna salad."

"Terrific. I've gotta finish up here, I'll keep an eye out for them."

She dressed and tossed the salad and put it in the fridge, then loaded a tray with plates, cutlery and condiments and took it up to the cockpit table.

Gilley was securing a detached awning lanyard to the back-stay. He glanced ashore, raised his arm and waved. "They're here. I'll go pick them up."

Shortly after Helen and Sally came aboard, they all sat at the cockpit table enjoying Trish's salad. "Gilley, I must say, the nosh onboard this vessel is delicious, and you've certainly trained your crew very well."

"It's not easy to find good help these days Helen." He faked a frown. "And thanks for the scones and croissants; we just ran out."

"So, Sally, how did it go with our favorite guru?"

"Well, as Trish said, she's an amazing healer. My stress simply dissolved, it was magical." She leaned over and hugged her new friend.

"I loved having you at my home, dear, and I'm so excited to see you moving on in your life's journey."

Trish passed the salad to Helen, who patted her tummy and passed it to Gilley. "So Gilley, how is your voyage plan shaping up?"

"Oh, it's on the back burner for a while, Helen. We've got a few things to take care of now."

Trish interrupted. "Excuse us, Helen, we're going below to clean up. The lass has been shirking her duties on the schooner the last few days, so you and Gilley have a nice visit."

Gilley filled their water glasses. "I know Trish told you about the crash and sinking of the schooner I was on. The owners and their daughter were killed. I wake up shaking; but I don't sleep, I just lie there. But when Trish and I are together, no nightmares. Maybe she's my cure."

"Well, it could be just that simple. She's a loving person, and very much in your life right now. I'm just thinking out loud, but I wondered if you and Trish could make that trip around the Horn, or would you need more crew? Just a thought, Gilley."

He shot her a grin. "Funny you should ask, because she told me the other night that she wants to sign on as backup navigator. I have to admit that I've lost my nerve to do that Horn passage. Maybe we should just book passage on a cruise ship and see the Horn from a deck chair while we drink Margaritas and snack on caviar."

"Have you really lost your nerve, Gilley? I'm surprised to hear that after all those years you've spent at sea."

"I have a real horror of Cape Horn and hundred-knot winds. It's like a friend of mine who was bitten by a rattlesnake and damn-near died; he wouldn't go outside for months."

"Phobias are very strange, and some people have them all their lives. Gilley, I think you and Trish should have a good down-to-earth talk about all this. You simply have to face your phobia. I've suggested this to her as well."

He nodded. "Yeah, I guess we should."

"But to put your mind at rest, Bruce and I took a cruise ship around South America a few years ago. The dreaded Cape Horn was as calm as a mill pond."

"You're right, we'll work it out. I appreciate your good advice, and maybe you can recommend a magic pill for nightmares? Hash doesn't work."

She patted his hand and held it. "No it doesn't, just cut it out, and make love often, Gilley." They both laughed as Trish and Sally joined them.

"What's funny, you two?" Trish looked at Helen, but sidled over to sit on Gilley's lap.

He smiled. "Oh, I was just telling Helen your dad's great joke about the dying Scotsman and his helpful friend."

Sally looked surprised. "I haven't heard that one. How does it go?

"I'll tell you later, sweetie. Now, Captain, the lass did good cleanup work in the galley, and I think she's ready to be trained in the art of cooking, but only with your approval, sir."

Sally played along with Trish's little theater, then blurted out, "Hey, Trishy! I told you I'm a Cordon Bleu graduate; I'm fully qualified in the culinary arts. Give me a break here."

"That's good to hear, Sally. Now, I suggest you prepare the evening meal as a trial run. And I'll decide if you're qualified for full employment. That will be all."

"Thank you, Captain, I hope my work pleases you. I also know a little first aid, sir."

"I can certainly verify her talents in the kitchen." Helen laughed. "I'm sure she'll do very well in your galley. And with that, dear people, I must be away to pick up my beloved Bruce at the Airporter; he's returning from down under. Thank God."

Trish offered to ferry Helen ashore. She put on her Tilley hat and sun glasses.

She rowed slowly. They hadn't spoken one-on-one for some time. Helen's serious expression puzzled her.

"What is it?"

"I'm concerned about Gilley. He told me he's scrubbed his voyage plan because of his fear of Cape Horn, which is understandable. He's reliving that horrible shipwreck. And he's trying to cope with the nightmares by smoking hash. He said he told you about this. Does he smoke a lot?"

"I'm concerned, too. I'm not sure how much he smokes, maybe two or three times a day. I can't really say. He could be a little high all the time."

Trish docked the Whitehall at the wharf. "I see, he could be depressed about that. But steady use of cannabis always exacerbates the problem. It's the same as chronic alcoholism. I must say, it is a little troubling, dear. Your quitting will not necessarily stop him, but he wouldn't have a buddy to smoke with. So you might help him by your example."

"I'll give it a try."

"Yes, just have a nice, loving talk with him, and make love often; I suggested that to him as well."

Trish helped her onto the dock and embraced her. "We do, and we will for sure. Thanks so much for helping Sally and me over the rough patches. My love to Bruce."

"I'll look forward to hearing how it goes. Remember, no hash. Ta ta, dear."

Later that afternoon, Trish took her Whitehall out for a fast row over to Angel Island to get some exercise. As she returned to the schooner, she veered off course to get a better broadside view of the vessel. The generator exhaust was spitting out a stream of water and gray exhaust. She remembered how she and her dad had often admired *Bojangles* at anchor the same way. He used to say, "Just look at the fine entry of her bow and how it gently curves up to the cap rail and gracefully aft along the sheer without any fuss until it joins with the incredible sexy stern." *Romayne* had the same beautiful Fife lines. Now the masts are sitting straight and tall, but idle. The sails asleep and neatly furled on the booms, waiting for crew to hoist them and get this old schooner under way in search of a fair wind and a destination.

She watched Gilley fussing with something on the foredeck. He looked over at her and waved. "What are you doing out there, lost?"

"Just enjoying her incredible lines; she's so beautiful." She joined him on the foredeck.

"Where's Sally?"

"Galley duty, rustlin' up some killer chili for dinner."

"Cool, I'll give her a hand." She secured the Whitehall and went below.

"Hey there, sweetie, need any help?"

"Sure." She slowly stirred the pot. "Would you get the plates and stuff together? I'll get a salad going and some bread. I brought a bottle of red to go with the chili."

Trish watched her old friend, happy that she was fitting in as a functioning member of this unusual trio. After they devoured the delicious chili dinner, they watched the sun setting; igniting wispy mare's tails into a dark red glow as it slipped below the hills.

Gilley reached into the table drawer for the Meerschaum, lit it and passed it to Trish, who shook her head.

He offered the pipe to Sally, who looked at Gilley, then at Trish, who moved her head side to side so subtly that Gilley didn't see it.

"No thanks, the wine's fine."

They sat in silence with their private thoughts, gazing at the red sky as it faded to gunmetal blue. Trish reached under the table to find Sally's hand and squeezed it.

"So it's time the serving maids went back to work here." Sally piled the plates and glasses onto the tray.

Gilley patted his stomach. "Thanks for the great dinner and wine Sally, the best chili I've ever had."

"Thanks. I'm glad you enjoyed it."

Trish picked up the bottle and her glass. "I'll give the serving maid a hand or God knows what she'll do."

They entered the galley; Trish poured a glass of wine and handed it to Sally. "For you, sweetie."

Surprised, she smiled and took a mouthful, and with it still in her mouth, put her arms around Trish's neck and kissed her, transferring the wine into her mouth.

Then Trish, with the bottle in her hand, wrapped her arms around her friend and passionately returned the kiss.

"Oh, Trishy, I've missed you so much. Can we—?"

25

Sally covered her mouth with her hands to muffle her cry. Then, between gasps of ecstasy, she shouted, "Oh God, oh yes, yes."

Trish whispered in her ear. "Another one?"

Sally rolled over on her side and grinned. "Oh no, that was beautiful; God, I hope Gilley didn't hear me. Was I loud?"

"Who cares?"

Trish watched Sally's eyelids close. "Not me. Wow, I'm ready for some shut-eye; must have been the wine."

Within minutes Sally was sound asleep. Trish covered her bruised body and kissed the scar over her eye. "Sweet dreams."

Trish dressed and joined Gilley at the cockpit table. "She's still a bit brittle, but she fell asleep happy, and that's all that matters for now."

"I'm glad she's on the mend. She's terrific; I like her a lot."

"Trish snuggled under his arm and rested her head on his chest. "Thanks for being so cool with Sally and me. She just needed some loving. I'll always be there for her when she needs me."

"I'm happy for you both, just keep lovin'."

"Yeah, I guess so, but this is the first time I've had two lovers back-to-back of both sexes at the same time, so if you can handle it, then so can I. Now that she's out of the closet, I hope she'll find a main squeeze one of these days."

"Absolutely. Keep her happy, she needs it. When did you find out she was gay?"

"She was never really interested in boys at school. I guess we were seventeen when we had our first real love affair. We both kinda thought we were gay, and then several years later after we lost each other, she married, because it was the thing to do in those days. She always had strong leanings to girls, and later she kept befriending women, but stayed in the closet. Who knows, maybe I started her on her way. She doesn't like sex with men, particularly her ex, who was very rough and literally an ass man."

He reached for his pipe on the table and ran his fingers over the face and beard of the carved sculpture on the pipe bowl. "This was my dad's old pipe, which I gave to him many moons ago."

She watched him light it. She decided that this was not the time to encourage him to quit. He passed it to her; she held up a hand and shook her head.

"You're really quitting?"

"Sweetheart, I've been smoking weed since I was seventeen, it's time to move on. Helen told me in very definite terms that it's time to quit. You know I have the highest respect for her opinion; she's my mentor."

She caressed his big hand, then kissed it. "So that's my new resolve. It'd be too easy for me to smoke with you now. But I'm not going to do it anymore. I have a new path and I'm happy with that."

He took a drag, snuffed it out, and put the pipe on the table. "Trish, the reason I started smoking this stuff was to wean me off the goddamn booze, which was taking me down to the depths of hell, fast. I'm sure I told you a good friend got me in some lifesaving sessions with a very smart shrink. She was giving treatment sessions she called the Lion's Path."

"Yeah, and I did the path in Florida just before I hit rock bottom with coke and booze. My therapist was also a very savvy lady. And after about five sessions she had my head straightened out. I was able to identify and acknowledge most of my worst personal flaws. By then, when I was well on the road to recovery, she referred me to her old friend Helen, when I graduated and moved back here. Meeting Helen was the most significant transformation in my life. She sort of put the finishing touches on my wobbly character and helped me to get established in my therapy business. She kind of adopted me, and you know the rest. I'm sorry; I interrupted you about your healing. Would you like Helen's number?"

"She's already suggested that I quit smoking and substitute you, lots of you. Who ever heard of a shrink telling a guy to screw his brains out? Is that far-out or what?"

Trish carefully unwound herself from his arm and whispered in his ear, "Is it, Gilley? Is it really far-out?"

26

Trish got up slowly, dressed and went into the salon. Sally was eating a scone and looked up at her. "Good morning, sleepyhead. Croissants and scones are in the oven; join me."

"Morning, love, I will. Where's Gilley?"

"He went ashore to get something for Mr. Gardener, which I just found out is the diesel engine. Now I understand what he meant when he said he was going to make love to his Gardener; funny man."

Trish filled her breakfast plate and poured a cup of tea. "Yeah, he is, and he loves that engine. He showed me how to start it with a hand crank if the battery dies; it's amazing. Now, what are your plans for the day?"

"Well, as I'm still on medical leave, I'm trying to figure out how I can get my stuff out of the Napa house, and my van. But I can't go alone, because if Poser is there—I can't take the chance, it's too damn scary. I'm really stumped, and I think I told you the bastard always carries a loaded pistol in his pouch."

"Well, in that case, you definitely need several armed cops with you. I think you should tell the police that Poser damn nearly killed you, and you should have charged him with assault, for God's sake. Why didn't you?"

"I didn't simply because I never wanted to see him again or have anything to do with him, period. Also, I was in no shape to be involved in a bloody assault case against a drugged wife beater. And as you well know, I was in a lot of pain and really out of it. That's why, and I still dread being anywhere near him again, even with cops there. It's just too fucking dangerous. So that's what I'm not going to do today. Any ideas?"

Trish refilled their cups and took another croissant. "Well, when you put it that way, no I don't. You could ask Chief Jon what he'd recommend, he'd certainly advise you. Think it over."

Sally looked up as they heard footsteps on deck. "It sounds like the captain's back."

Several minutes went by and Gilley entered the salon. "Good morning, ladies." He leaned over to kiss Trish and held Sally's shoulders. "Fortunately they had the fuel filters for the genie. How are you two doing?"

Trish told him about Sally's perplexing dilemma, which he pondered as he stroked his beard.

"Well sure, Jon would tell you the best thing to do, and he'd probably know who to talk to at that station." He put his phone on the table. "Give him a call."

"Maybe later. I want to mull it over a bit; besides, he's a very busy man, and anyway, there's no hurry. Trishy, what are you going to do today?"

"Not sure, I've polished all the brass on board, we've watered the deck, and I've made the bed. Is there anything that needs to be done, Gilley?"

"No. I think we're squared away. I'm going to change filters and run the genie. So take it easy, read a book or, write a book. So, I'm off to the ER. Sally, that's engine room, not emergency room."

"Great idea, I'll work on my memoir for Helen."

"Well, my next project is to change my name back to Sally Brown, and I'll burn the name Poser; I never liked it. That'll boost my morale a lot. So Trishy, do I start with my driver's license?"

"That's wonderful, I never did like the man and name either. Now, I know one thing you'll have to do. I think you have to get a court order to change your name. Then, you have to legally inform your credit card companies, your bank, the DMV for your driver's license, your HMO, your passport and God knows how many other documents you'll have to change. Just don't ask me to help you, Ms. Sally Brown. Oh, one more thing: if you ever get married again, don't change your name."

"Okay, I'll hire someone to do the paperwork. Yes, Sally Brown, you're about to become a new woman. What about your plans?"

"Oh hell, I'm not sure, except that I'm so in love with him, which keeps me busy, it's just perfect. So I'll just let it ride for a while and see what happens with the crazy Pinky dude. It's so weird we both have crazy men who want to kill us. But what the hell, we're together again, and that means a lot to me right now."

Sally smiled. "Me too, I feel the same way, and Trishy, I'm almost free. Yippee! So, if you'll excuse me, I'm going to retire to our cabin and read my book. See you later."

27

Trish got up slowly, stretched, picked up her laptop and went up to the doghouse. She opened her memoir and reviewed the last few paragraphs. She made a few corrections, added a few lines and saved it.

MEMOIR CHAPTER 9

I couldn't believe the bizarre dream vision I had on the mountain with Helen. Gilley's mom and dad were beckoning me to help their son on his journey. Where did that come from? Sure I saw the family photo of the three of them. They were holding Gilley by his hands, aged 3 or 4. It obviously made an impression on me. Now, he's 65 and there's no one to hold his hands, except me. Is it up to me now? And then, Helen sitting beside me on the Sleeping Maiden was crying. That really upset me. She's not the crying type. She told me that they had lost their 5-year-old-daughter to leukemia. Then, a big shock, her daughter would be my age today. Her birthday was the same day as mine. This has blown me away. Is it possible that Helen secretly adopted me? Maybe so, it's definitely should be up to her to tell me. I'll just have to wait and see. So, there are some strange things going on in my life, and then there's Sally. My plate's overflowing. I'm in love with a wonderful man. I'm very, very happy.
"I won't give this chapter to Helen."

Trish picked up her fruit juice and went out to the cockpit, where it was cool under the awning.

Gilley climbed out of the engine room and joined her at the table. "Well, it's a good thing I got the filters changed just in time. The old ones were really loaded. I must have taken on some dirty diesel along the way."

He took her hand. "Anyway, Trish—I've been thinking about us and what you said about chasing sunsets and Cape Horn."

"Great!"

"Well, it's time I leveled with you." He stroked her hand as he looked into her eyes. "I love you, Trish. God, who would ever think thirty years ago we'd be sitting here, in love on my schooner? It's one for the book."

"It sure is, and whoever is writing our script so far is doing one hell of a good job."

"They really are, but there's more, Trish. It's time I told you some things about—well, this may take some time."

"For you, I have as long as it takes."

"How about a few turns around the deck? These old legs need some exercise."

They walked, arm in arm, toward the bow.

"Well, you remember about my vision in the life raft; that if I ever had a boat and the opportunity to go down to the crash site, I'd give the family a memorial ceremony?"

"Yes I do, to lay three wreaths in their memory."

"Yeah, but it'd be four wreaths."

She nodded. "Right, one for the schooner."

"No." He paused for a long moment and looked toward the city. He appeared to be struggling; then slowly turned to face her.

"Daphnia was pregnant."

She gasped and put her hands up to her face. "Oh my God, Gilley."

"Yup, that's what happened."

Tears welled up in his eyes. She wrapped her arms around him and held him as he sobbed and let his grief drain onto her. They stood together under the awning for a long time. Silent.

Gradually, they found their footing again and returned to the cockpit. She reached up to wipe the tears from his cheeks.

"You've been living with this horror all these years. Oh my darling."

He turned to look at her. "I really need you to help me through it. I just couldn't find a way to tell you before. Now, maybe I can move on with you."

"Of course you can."

"Yeah, I better pour it all out."

They sat side by side, looking at the little waterfront town.

"Well, when I signed onboard the *Maruffa* with the British family in Tahiti, I didn't tell you that Daph's husband got a telegram that his father in England had had a stroke, so he flew back to England to be with the family. When he left, he indicated that he'd stay as long as necessary. He told me to take the schooner to Cook's Bay in Moorea. Apparently they'd befriended a nice Kiwi family with a daughter the same age as Claire. They'd rented a summer house in Cook's Bay. Reggie wanted his family to be with them. And he wanted me to get the schooner ready for the Horn passage. Daph didn't like Pape'ete—too much boozin' and cavortin'. Well, we anchored in that great bay and tied our stern to a couple of palm trees. I got into a lot of deferred maintenance that he didn't want to tackle. One evening Daph's Kiwi pals invited us to join them for dinner at the upper boozer at the head of the bay. The joint was full of yacht cruisers and a bang-up party was roarin', everyone doing the tamure with the vahines. We closed the place when the Hinano beer ran out and we staggered back."

"Brings back memories."

"Yeah, we were all plastered. Daph's daughter stayed with the Kiwis for the night, and when Daph and I got back to the dinghy, she whips off her T-shirt and shorts, throws them in the dinghy and says, 'Gilley, I'll race you back.' She dove in and made it back before I could even get the goddamn oar-locks in. I'll tell you Trish, it was the last thing this drunken sailor expected. She met me on deck with open arms."

She shot him a grin. "What do we do with a drunken sailor, eh?"

"Yup, run or get busy. It turns out that Reggie hadn't been the jolly faithful husband he appeared to be, and she was up for a good old romp. I just happened to be on deck at the right time."

"She seduced you. I'll bet she wasn't the first lady who took you to her bed."

"I was her first since they'd married."

"Oh God. So when did Reggie come back from being with his family?"

"Well, his father died, so Daph and Claire flew home for the funeral, and a few weeks later, returned to Moorea. As the eldest heir, Reg had to stay to manage the estate's vast holdings. They had thousands of acres, two huge farms. So while Reggie was away managing the estate, and no doubt sowing his wild oats, Gilley and Daph did their thing, and damned if we didn't fall in love. Couldn't help it, she was so sweet, kind, gorgeous, and she told me she didn't love him. Oldest story, they'd married because she was pregnant. And, with two old-line British families love wasn't as important as duty, keeping the old bloodlines together. Anyway, Reggie inherited the title of Thirteenth Baronet of some damn thing or other. And he stayed with the family for about four months to run the show. And I was running my own show, dividing my time between the refit on *Te Vahine* in Pape'ete and working on *Maruffa* in Moorea. And you can guess where I spent most of my time."

"Well, you were sort of between a whatever and a loving soft place. While the Baronet was away, the mate did play. I can't imagine what that poor lady was going through, being pregnant and estranged from Reggie, who would eventually return to his family and—how sad for her. Did you ever see any signs of unpleasantness when they were together?"

"Oh, yeah, they had a few nasty spats, usually when he'd had ten too many, when I first got to know them. He was the big party man who shouted drinks for the yacht cruisers. I mean, they were cordial, but not lovey-dovey. He used to grab her by the butt when he was loaded; she'd scold him and slap his hand away. He'd do this in the bar to show off for the yachties who got a kick out of it. They slept in separate bunks even though they had a double and a single in the aft cabin. I doubt if there was much marital activity going on."

"So the owner's wife moves to the first mate's bunk for a roll in the hay. Did the daughter have any idea what mummy was up to?"

"She stayed with the other family ashore most nights, but sometimes she and her friend would sleep aboard. We had a real close call one morning. Claire and her friend surprised the hell out us when they swam out to the schooner about an hour after we'd done our happy deed for the day. She wanted to ask mummy if she could go on the ferry with the family to shop in Pape'ete. Luckily, I was in the galley at the time and Daph was in my bunk. She asked where mummy was. Then Daph quickly called to her and said. 'I'm in here darling, come and give mummy a kiss.' So she went in to see mummy and asked. 'Isn't this Gilley's cabin'?"

"Oh man."

"You wouldn't believe what mummy answered. 'Good gracious, no darling he sleeps in the dog-house. I'm sleeping here until he's fixed the leak in my cabin.'" He gave a hint of a chuckle for the first time.

"I was crazy in love with her, but of course we didn't want to think what would happen when his nibs returned. I knew she was unhappy in their marriage. She said that she'd definitely divorce him when they returned home. We never talked about it again and just let it happen. Maybe Claire suspected something was going on. Anyway, she asked me privately one day. 'Gilley, do you love mummy?' God, aren't kids intuitive about adults?"

"They really are. So what did you say?"

"After I picked myself up off the deck, I think I said. 'Your mother is a very special lady and I like her very much,' something like that. So, we played it very cool when she was aboard."

"Yeah, she was pretty sure that Gilley liked mummy a lot more than very much. Kids can read expressions on adults' faces. You must have shown something the way you looked at each other."

"Yeah, I suppose we did. But we sure cooled it when Reggie returned."

"What happened when he came back, did he have any idea what was going on?"

"No, he was anxious to get underway. But she put on a great act, showed no interest in me. Even got a little rude and bossy, but she'd wink at me when she was sure he wasn't looking. Anyway, I had the vessel ready for sea, so we went back to Pape'ete to top up and re-provision. We headed south for the Horn a week later. I'd made up a heavy-duty storm drogue with canvas cones. He thought it was ridiculous. All he would do in a big blow was drag tires."

"So you sailed away, and when did she tell you she was pregnant?"

"About a month before Reggie came back. After missing two periods she went to the doctor to make sure. She told me right away."

"Oh no, I can't believe how you both dealt with that time bomb. Was abortion an option?"

"I asked her if she wanted to have one. She was absolutely against it, and told me she wanted to have our child. That was it."

"Jesus."

"Also, she said she'd understand if I didn't want to sail with them. I told her I'd stay with her come hell or high water." He put his face in his hands and sobbed. "And—that's exactly what we got."

"God almighty."

Trish held onto his arm. "Darling, now I understand why you don't want to sail down there."

Gilley was still choked up and had to clear his throat several times before he could even whisper. "So my fear is not really the Horn, but how could I handle going back to where they all died, and I lived? I've gone over a return voyage in my mind many times, awake and in my dreams, sober and stoned. The dream always cuts to the crash. Crazy, eh?"

"Not at all, it's a natural reaction. It stayed with me for years. I kept dreaming about Daddy's death and then, when I was awake, I tried to visualize what I could have done to prevent it. I know now I should have stayed aloft until we were on the next tack. But no, I came down just as they were jibing her. I know what I did killed him, and I have to live with that."

He draped his arm over her shoulder. "That's very hard to live with, Trish. You told me about the jibe, but it wouldn't have happened if the guys on the main sheet hadn't lost control."

"True, but I have to take the responsibility for what did happen. I was in the wrong place at the wrong time."

"I hope you can put that to rest now."

"I have finally, thanks to Helen."

"Yeah, and like you, I keep thinking what I could have done to prevent the crash. I couldn't believe the cleat pulled out of the deck. All I can figure is the through bolts might have been corroded and failed. Then I think I should have taken the watch instead of Daph, and I would have made damn sure the end of the drogue was secured to the winch. I remember asking her if she felt up to it. She insisted that she loved steering down the big waves, so I sat with her for a long time to make sure that she was okay. She was steering perfectly straight downwind. She was a better on the helm than Reggie or me."

He looked at Trish and took her hand.

"I gave her a final kiss and went below to my bunk. An hour later, it was all over. I didn't really sleep; you know how it is when you get into your bunk. Most times the rhythm is so constant that you fall asleep. But even when asleep, you're aware of the motion. Before I dozed off, I remember hearing Reggie letting out more of the drogue, which really wasn't necessary. I had no way of knowing if he'd secured the bitter end. It turned out he hadn't."

Trish shuddered and whispered, "I can't bear it."

They sat holding each other silently for a long time.

Finally, she said, "I don't remember if I mentioned to you when I told you about Daddy's accident, I was so paralyzed with grief that Mom took me to a shrink. The woman told me more or less what I just told you that the grief and guilt will always be there, but will fade with time. She suggested that I should do what I feared the most, sail in another Master Mariners regatta. I told her that I wouldn't get on board another boat at gunpoint. And I didn't, until you asked me to crew that day. Thank you for that."

"Oh, I had a feeling that you wanted to sail again, and it was obvious to me you had a big thing with this schooner. You're a born sailor."

"The schooner and, her captain. It's true, and it only took thirty years to get over my fear."

"I really appreciate that you offered go with me on this voyage. I'll just have to give it more thought."

"Well, you won't be going anywhere without me, sweetheart, you can count on that."

"You're a true friend, and I want to be with you." He opened the drawer under the table and reached for the pipe. He fingered the intricate carving and looked over at her, grinned, then focused again on the pipe.

She was surprised when he put it back in the drawer.

"I almost deep-sixed it the other day, but it's the only memento I have of him. I decided to quit when the hash ran out. It really never helped; I still had the nightmares. You were right, so it seems you and I are kinda on the same boat, aye?"

"We really are."

28

Trish opened one eye; the other was buried in the folds of the pillow. She moved so she could focus on his slow, rhythmic breathing. He snorted and slowly opened his eyes, then gave her a grin.

"Good morning, sweetheart. You know, I've been lying here thinking. We're going to have to make about a mile-and-a-half of baggie wrinkle for this old girl. And maybe, just maybe, we could shanghai Sally into helping us. What do ya think?"

Trish rose up on her elbow, her mouth opened as she stared at him. "Gilley."

"Besides that, we'll sure need a Cordon Bleu chef, and a nurse. Won't we?"

She leaned over to him. "You're serious, you amazing man. How did you ever turn yourself around?"

He pointed at the photograph of his parents holding his hands and then looked at her "Well, it's like this: it was what you said last night. 'Do what you fear the most.' And you showed that you had the guts to go aloft again after all those years of fear and grief. That's what turned me around."

"You really are incredible, brave and—I'm plum out of adjectives."

A wide grin lit up his face. "It's about time this old girl stuck her nose outside the Gate so we can mosey on down south and find the trades."

"Yes! Yes! Yes! I can't wait for that. Did you hear that, Daddy? Oh, I'm sooo happy."

Trish could hardly contain her joy. She leaned over and kissed him.

When he finally came up for a breath, he laughed. "So am I. Let's have breakfast."

Gilley leaned back in his creaking Captain's chair and sipped his tea as he glanced at Sally. Trish spread marmalade on her muffin. "Well, are you going to tell her?"

"I think you should, you've known her all your life."

Sally watched them as she munched her muffin. "Well, Sally, ah, how did you sleep?"

"If you really must know Gilley, alone damn it. So what the hell's going on with you two?"

"Well Sally, there's scuttlebutt on the local waterfront that you're a recently semi-retired lady of considerable means who's looking for adventure. So, I decided to ask if you'd consider signing onboard the good schooner *Romayne* for a southern Pacific ocean voyage, you know—around Cape Horn and Tahiti kind of adventure?"

There was a long pause as she surveyed their faces. "Have you been smoking, Gilley?"

"No no. You see Sally, the thing is; Trish has just signed on as first mate and navigator, and there is a position open on board for a Cordon Bleu chef and a ship's nurse. But I have to tell you up front, the work is hard, the hours are long, and the pay is low."

"It sounds exactly like the goddamn position I had for the last twenty years. But the part about Cape Horn sounds fascinating. Would we see any polar bears? I really love polar bears."

Trish broke up. "Polar bears, for chrissake!"

Sally looked at them with a happy smile "Oh, Trishy, I can't lose you out of my life again. Yes, I'll sign up, on two conditions.

One, I'll need help in the galley, two, I want to make sure that the ginger cure works for mal de mer."

"Terrific." Gilley said. "That's wonderful. You'll have all the help you need in the galley, and don't forget, Trish and I can cook, too."

Trish hugged her. "Oh Sally, how great, we'll be shipmates again, a crew of three and two kitties. Fantastic. Oh, yeah, I've heard ginger is very effective for motion sickness, and so is sitting out on deck in the fresh sea air, watching the horizon."

"Welcome aboard, Sally. I figure we'll set out in about six weeks. I have a lot to do on the schooner to get her ready for the southern ocean. And I'm sure you probably have a few loose ends to tie up; I know Trish does."

"Right. Now Captain, as first mate, I have a bit of a concern." She leaned closer to him and took his hand.

"What's your concern?"

"Are you positive three of us can pull this off on this big vessel? The Horn is notorious for hundred-knot gales and ninety-foot seas. That's not exactly schooner-friendly, is it?"

"Good point. Well, it's more than likely we'll find a full gale with our name on it in the southern ocean. But I always reef early, usually two reefs, and if that doesn't settle her down, I'll run downwind under staysail. And if we get some hundred-knot kick-ass stuff, we'll set the storm drogue and put out oil bags and run before it. This old girl can take anything."

She looked at him for a moment. "Sure she can, but can we take it Gilley?"

He nodded. "Yes we can, we're strong and we've got lots of winches to do what our bodies can't. So before we take off, we'll take her out the Gate for a two-day shake-down, find out where we're weak and fix it." He pointed up to the deck. "Remember, we have Arthur McWindvane up there, who adds another six helmsmen to the crew while we rest."

Trish nodded in agreement. "Oh right, and he won't steal the captain's girlfriend in port. I love that part. Gilley's girlfriend. I haven't been anyone's girlfriend for a long time."

"And I haven't had the pleasure of being a boyfriend for longer than I care to remember."

Sally laughed. "Well it's settled, then, and I'll be happy in this semi-retirement type of adventure. I like it."

Trish cleared the breakfast dishes and deposited them into the sink; the sink that had recently received the contents from ten of Gilley's bottles of booze, which together they'd drained into Richardson's Bay. She smiled as she patted the sink and remembered his comment. 'The seals and fish are going to have one hell of a knock-out party today.'

29

They were startled to hear a short blast from an air horn beside the schooner. They hurried up to the deck and were surprised to see Chief Jon at the wheel of the Whaler, and Lynn beside him. "Permission to come aboard sir? I bring glad tidings."

"No permission required sir, get your butts onboard without delay. We can provide tea or coffee for your pleasure."

"Thanks anyway, Gilley, we just finished breakfast." They all sat around the cockpit table. "Now, Trish, I'm very happy to tell you that the hairy poet, Pinky Urqhart, is no longer a threat to you or anyone else, because he's presently rattling bars in the county jail."

She gasped. "Really Jon, how?"

"Remember I mentioned that the VA finally found his file and told us that his mailing address was Toadfish Marina? Well, we followed up on the scuttlebutt and discovered that he was an anchor-out and rumored to be dealing drugs. We set up a video photographer to watch for any traffic to and from his houseboat. There was a total of eleven visitors in four hours, making short visits, which obviously weren't social calls. So we got a court-ordered search warrant. Lynn and I and a few armed officers pulled up beside his houseboat and ordered him to appear on deck unarmed, which he did. Long story short Trish, and I can give you more details later, but he surrendered without so much as a burp. We had him under guard outside while Lynn and I and our search party went to work."

"Oh Jon, I'm so relieved and grateful. I can't thank you enough. So, was he dealing?"

"Big time, we found a large inventory of many drugs. They also found a strongbox with thirty four grand in cash under the floorboards, also a fifty caliber assault rifle, five hand grenades, pistols, ammo and porn."

Lynn handed Trish a file folder. She opened it and removed a carbon copy. "Oh, for God's sake. A copy of the death threat, so it was him. The bastard really had it in for me."

Jon grinned. "It's anyone's guess if he actually planned to carry out the threat, Trish, or to scare the hell out of you."

"Well, it worked. He did scare the hell out of me. Well, it's over. Thank you, Jon and Lynn, from the bottom of my shattered soul, and thank all the other men who assisted you." She leaned over to hug Jon. "Oh, I can do better than that." She got up on her knees and kissed his cheek, then leaned over him to kiss Lynn. "I really love you two."

Lynn smiled at her. "Thanks Trish, we're just happy we got him. So you can go home now and get your life back together."

Gilley clapped as he looked at Jon. "Well done. So Jon and Lynn, this poet will do some time; any idea how long?"

"First of all, he'll lose everything; they'll confiscate his loot, his houseboat and guns. And as to the time he'll serve, it depends on the judge. It was a big bust, and they'll squeeze out of him who supplied him with the drugs, so this could be huge all the way down the chain. He'll do many years, probably making license plates, and we don't know yet if he has any priors. You'll never see him on this Sausalito waterfront again, so now you guys can breathe easy. And with that good news, we must be on our way."

Sally held up her hand. "Before you go, Chief, I have a question for you."

"Sure, Sally, what is it?"

"Well, as you can see, I have a few battle scars, which I got from by ex-husband. I don't need to go into any details except that he was drunk and really lost it, and I took a beating. I didn't report or charge him with assault because I don't want any involvement with him ever again. Now I need to clear out my possessions in our former house where he still lives in Napa. Jon, I'm terrified to go there alone, because he could definitely attack me again. Do you think it's possible to have police protection while I get my things packed up and leave in my van, which is still there? And—he's always armed."

"Absolutely. You definitely need to be protected; the man is obviously dangerous, and he should be charged with assault. Were there any witnesses to the attack?"

"Only the ambulance rescue team that took me to the hospital. My ex had left the house before I came to. But the hospital has the case records. I've had no communication with him since. Do you know any of the officers in Napa?"

"Sure, the chief's an old friend." He took a card out and wrote the man's name, then referred to his notebook for the phone number. "Give him a call and send my best wishes. Now, Sally, I strongly suggest that you file charges against your ex, because he could assault someone else. It sounds like he's a time bomb with a short fuse ready to—well, who knows? They should also find out if he is permitted to carry a concealable weapon."

"Thanks Jon, I really appreciate your help. I'll give him a call."

They watched them leave in the Whaler and waved. Tears formed on Trish's cheeks. "I worship those two, they're so brave." She glanced up at Gilley as he put his arm around her.

30

Trish and Sally packed their bags and put Robin in her carrier, then took them up to the deck where Gilley loaded everything into Trish's Whitehall. She put her arms around his neck. "Well, sweetheart, it' been a very interesting visit and we loved being onboard *Romayne*. Thanks a million for being here for us. It's absolutely amazing how everything got resolved. Oh, before I forget, Sally and I are going to organize a full up celebration dinner party for all the players for whatever night that Jon and Lynn are available, just to announce your voyage. We have a lot of people to thank. Does that sound like a good plan?"

"It's a great plan. How about Ish and Fern, too? They're part of the family."

"Of course, they're on our list. Okay Sally, are you ready?"

"Yup." Sally reached up on her toes to kiss Gilley. "Thank you dear man, you are absolutely wonderful, and I'm honored and delighted to be involved with your voyage."

"Sally, it's my pleasure, I loved having you aboard and so did Bear Cat."

They took their seats in the Whitehall. Trish gripped the oars and pulled her boat away from the schooner as Gilley waved to them. Twenty minutes later, she eased the Whitehall alongside her float. "Well, here we are, sweetie, safe and sound." They pulled the boat onto the float, took their bags, and the meowing cat, into Trish's home. They settled onto the easy chairs on the living room deck. Trish plugged in her phone and handed it to Sally. "Do you have the Napa police number?"

Sally nodded. "Oh, Trishy, I'm so dreading this, I really can't bear to see him, even if I can get an officer to go with us."

"I know, but you have to do it. Maybe you could request the officers to keep him out of the house while we pack your boxes; it shouldn't take us long."

Sally found the Chief's card and punched in the number. "Good morning, may I speak to Chief Lipsett?"

"Your name please?"

"Sally Poser, I was given his name by Chief Jon Ewer of the Sausalito police department."

"Thank you, please hold."

Thirty seconds later she heard a deep voice. "Lipsett here, good day Sally Poser. How is my old pal, Jon?"

"He's fine and sends you his best wishes."

"Terrific, and thank you. Now what can I do for you? Poser— Poser; that name sounds familiar. Can you hold for a minute?"

Sally looked at Trish. "Oh, God, he put me on hold. I wonder why the name's familiar; maybe he was busted?"

"Alright, I'm back. Well, this is not good news, I'm sorry to say. We've just received an accident report; your husband, John Poser, has a red Mustang convertible?"

"Yes."

"Well, Mrs. Poser, here are the findings from the report. Your husband's car was found yesterday by a hiker at the bottom of a deep ravine on the old county road. It was almost hidden in the bushes. His body was discovered about a hundred yards up the hill from the car. Obviously he was ejected when the car rolled. No seat belts. The coroner determined that from the decomposition of the body, the accident would have occurred approximately two weeks ago. The deceased is presently at the city morgue, and the autopsy revealed that he had been under the influence of methamphetamine. I'm sorry to have to break this to you Mrs.

Poser, but it's the only way, and this will no doubt be difficult for you, but—would you be able to identify his body?"

Sally looked at Trish and frowned. "Ah, yes, but I'll have to let you know when. Could it be in a couple of days?"

"Certainly, and please give my best to Jon. No, hold that, I'll call him myself. I offer my condolences to you, Mrs. Poser."

"Thank you Chief."

MEMOIR Chapter 10

I can't believe how things have turned out for Sally and me. Sally's life had been turned inside out and upside down because her late ex-husband had almost beaten her to death. Then she was told by the police that he had driven away from their home and onto an unpaved county road under the influence of meth. He apparently skidded off the road and was thrown out of the car, which must have rolled over him as it went down into a deep ravine. Sally was just able to identify his face and body, although it was terribly mangled by the crash. Her life is almost back to normal, and her injuries are much improved. Both of our lives are getting better by the minute, especially because we have been invited to join Gilley Cornwall aboard his schooner Romayne to sail down to the southern ocean and transit Cape Horn. I can't begin to explain our unbelievable good fortune, except that it's part of our lives and some clever being is writing our life scripts, which we will happily follow.

31

The weeks had flown by when Trish picked up Alfi up at his ark. He always got a great thrill to ride on her classic bike.

Helen and Bruce were the first to arrive. Bruce handed Trish a bottle of Malbec, and was rewarded with a kiss. Finally, coats were hung up, loving embraces were exchanged, glasses of wine were distributed and toasts were given.

"Helen and Bruce, I'm sure you remember Alfi, my Dad's first mate, who holds the prestigious office of President of the Pacific Ocean."

"Of course I do." Helen took his hand. "How good to see you again, Alfi. I trust the Pacific is in good order?"

"Well Helen, it's been a lot better, I'm sorry to say. Ships are losing too damn many containers, some sink, some don't. Pollution is out of control, what with the Pacific gyre out there. Millions of tons of plastic, rope, nets and general garbage the size of Texas circulating in an endless loop."

"Yes, I've been reading about that, I hope they can do something about it."

The last guests to arrive were Ishmael and Fern, with Chief Jon and Lynn, now out of uniform. Trish greeted them happily, issued them with wine and held up her glass. "Here's to all of you, now bring your glasses and let me show you around before Gilley gets here." Trish led them up to her palatial bedroom and out to the deck railing, where they all scanned Richardson's Bay.

"Isn't that the most incredible view you've ever seen, Bruce? And look, there's a little boat sailing up the bay."

"Helen, it's Gilley. Poor man, he doesn't own a car, so he has to sail everywhere. Ahoy there, you're just on time." They watched him land his Whitehall alongside, furl the sail and pull it onto the float.

They returned to the living room just as Gilley walked in. As soon as he saw Helen, a wide smile appeared as he embraced her. "Helen, it's great to see you again."

"And you Gilley; you haven't met my hubby, Bruce. This is the famous and most recent addition to the Sausalito waterfront, Captain extraordinaire Gilley Cornwall, from British Columbia."

"Gilley, it's a pleasure to meet a Canuck from the colonies."

"Bruce, it's always good to meet a lad from down under. It's a wonderful country full of excellent blokes and lovely wild Sheilas."

Gilley reached over to Alfi and gave him a bear hug. "Good to see you, Alfi, how are ya?"

"Never better skipper, this liquid gold is improving my morale by the minute."

They all followed Trish out to the deck. She took Gilley's arm and Sally's on her other side. "Everyone, I can see you're chomping at the bit. Now, about the news I mentioned to you. Gilley has invited Sally and me to join him onboard *Romayne* on a voyage to the southern ocean, where we'll have a special memorial ceremony for his shipmates who lost their lives there many years ago."

Helen raised her glass. "What wonderful news! Bravo! I'm so happy and proud of you, absolutely delighted."

The guests raised their glasses. "Thank you all, now captain, over to you."

He looked at all of them in turn before he spoke. "Well. I've been putting this trip off for one reason or another. Trish got me back on course again, so how could I ignore that kind of help from such a great friend and fine sailor? I have all the confidence that we can pull it off. We had a little difficulty in convincing Sally to join the crew, because she really wanted to see polar bears. Anyway, she finally settled for penguins, whales, albatrosses and porpoises. Thank you, Sally, we really need you. Now, Trish just told you about the ceremony we'll have at the crash site. Then, we'll transit Cape Horn, find the safe anchorage I've been told about and hang out for a while to rest up. Then, we'll sail east to west around the Horn and head for Tahiti and the islands for some R and R. That's basically the voyage. I'm not sure how long we'll be gone it's really open-ended. So, good friends, it'll be over when we drop the hook here in Richardson's Bay."

Chief Jon clapped, and was joined by the others. "Excellent. It sounds like a wonderful cruise, Gilley."

Alfi nodded. "Good for you, Gilley, she's a great schooner and she deserves to do the Horn with you and the ladies. The only suggestion I can give you is, install radar; there's hell of a lot of traffic out there."

"Thanks, Alfi, I'm having one installed next week."

Trish showed them to their seats. Helen took a bite of her dinner. "Sally, this salmon is beyond delicious."

"I'm glad you like it; I'll give you the recipe."

"Arr, arr." Gilley laughed. "After some basic training on yon schooner, the lass made quite an impression on me, what with her amazing expertise in the galley, considerable medical knowledge, and very good looks. Well, I just had to sign her on for the trip. It turns out she also has a wonderful sense of humor, and rumor has it she plays a mean bagpipe."

Sally laughed and held up her hand. "The truth is, he shanghaied me. Somehow he twisted Trishy's arm to sign on, and as I'm absolutely useless without her, what the hell could I do?"

After two hours at the table, Helen had a little trouble getting up from her chair and sat back. "S'truth, darlings, woe is this old lady, now—I regret to say that we must away before the three bears come and eat us up. Bruce, will you help me out of this most comfortable chair?"

With little effort and mock grunting, he helped his inebriated wife to her feet.

Bruce held Gilley by his shoulder. "Gilley, you are a fine gentleman. It's been wonderful to finally meet you on such a great occasion. I'm envious of you being able to sail out the Gate and head for the trades."

Trish and Gilley walked with their guests to their cars.

"Thank you for the loveliest of all evenings," Helen said. "Now, Alfi, would you show us the way to your ark?"

Gilley put his arm around Trish's shoulder as they waved goodbye. "That was a great party you had for them. Your heart's bigger than you are. Come here."

32

Trish slid her legs over the edge of the bed and glanced at Sally, still sleeping soundly. She put on her kimono and picked up her phone and called Gilley. "Hi, sweetheart, how are you?"

"Well, I slept till eight. Must have been the port or the chocolate. That was a great evening."

"Thanks. It was a lot of fun. Now, the reason I called was to ask what Sally and I can do to help you get up and running for the voyage."

"Not much right now, but you might think about making lists of food for us for about four months; we won't be in a port to resupply until Pape'ete. Remember, I've got a big deep freeze and fridge. Sally should make up a list of all the medical supplies she'll need. By the way, I'm funding everything, so spare no expense, we'll go first cabin all the way. I just wanted to get that out of the way. Anyway, I'll be coming up to your place shortly."

"Oh, goodie, two kept women. That's very kind of you." Sally joined her in the kitchen. "How about that? Gilley's funding everything."

"Wow, so he's generous, too. What a guy."

From her float, Trish heard Gilley singing an Indian chant loudly as he pulled his Whitehall up. She grinned. "Oh, hi there, come on up."

They sat side by side on the deck chairs. "So did you get your teak and rope supplies?"

"Yeah, they'll deliver it tomorrow. By the way, a good berth came available that Ish found, so we'll move the schooner to Toadfish Marina. She'll be alongside on their old pier. Then, next Tuesday I'm having her hauled to replace the anodes and installing a new feathering prop to eliminate the prop drag. You might want to come down to see what the old girl looks like with her pants down."

"Sure, we'll be there, and when do we start making baggie wrinkle?"

"Tomorrow. Fern and Ish will be onboard too, so the three of you should knock it off in a couple of days."

"Now, I have good news." Sally said. "My pal, Doctor Dansel called to say he'll have the medical kit ready Friday, with all the meds, instruments and bandages. I'll pick it all up together. And mark your calendars; I've made appointments for physicals and blood tests for all of us on the same day."

MEMOIR Chapter 11

It's hard to remember what we've accomplished these last 6 weeks. First, Fern, Sally and I made up a lot of hemp baggie wrinkle, and Sally volunteered to wrap it around the shrouds and topping lifts. This was her first time in a bosun's chair, and she really enjoyed the experience. Gilley is very pleased with our efforts, he's sure there will be no chafe on the sails and running rigging. Ishmael made two teak deck boxes to store the storm drogue that he and Gilley created; the boxes can also be used for seats. We also took Sally's three doctors, with Helen, Bruce, Chief Jon, Lynn, Ish and Fern, and of course, Alfi, for a lovely sail out the Gate to the Farallon Islands. (Saw two great whites, one really big.) We returned to anchor on the lee side of Angel Island for a scrumptious lunch. Now every locker onboard and the hold under the galley sole are full. We even bought 200 pounds of cat kibble, and sand for kitty litter. We have gone over the lists several times, and believe me; if we don't have something, it hasn't been invented. We had our physicals with Sally's doctor friends. No concerns except that Gilley's LDL is too high. He absolutely refuses to take a statin drug to lower it. He'll have to go on a very strict low fat diet. But good news, Alfi has formally resigned the office of President of the Pacific Ocean and has passed it to Gilley, so now I get to sleep with the President. My next news will be Trish's Journal on Romayne on the Pacific Ocean, Yea!

33

"Well, this is the big day, ladies. The weather report said twenty knots and six-foot seas at the Farallons. Did you both take your ginger?"

Trish nodded. "Don't worry, I took four tablespoons. How about you Sally?"

"Yeah, I'm addicted to it, and I wash it down with ginger ale. This girl will not hurl!"

Gilley took the halyards off the belaying pins. "The tide is ebbing as we speak, so when you're ready, let's give this old girl some sail."

"Okay, Trish, you hoist the peak and I'll take the throat. Just keep the gaff boom parallel to the deck until I two-block the throat, then the peak." He looked aloft.

Together they hoisted the large mainsail, belayed the halyards and coiled them neatly, then looped them onto the belaying pins. Sally took the slack out of the main sheet and looked at Gilley, who gave her a nod.

They repeated the procedure for the foresail. They had just belayed the halyards when they heard a familiar squeaky voice shouting from the dock.

"Avast, heavin' there me hearties, ya can't sail her worth a damn when you're still tied to the dock for Chrissake. I thought you knew that." Alfi was laughing as he stepped aboard.

Gilley grinned at his old friend. "Well damn it, I wondered why we weren't movin'."

Alfi sauntered over. "She's fresh out the nor-west, so you got a fair wind to get you goin'."

"Right Alfi, we'll get the fore lowers up and wait till we get out the Gate and maybe set the topsails."

Helen and Bruce approached the schooner, carrying a packaged box, then behind them, Ishmael and Fern with a small package.

Bruce handed the box to Gilley. Helen took Trish's hand. "Just a little token of our affection for you in your first anchorage. You must not open it till you've rounded the Horn."

Gilley grinned. "Thank you Helen and Bruce, I'm sure it'll be enjoyed."

Ishmael and Fern joined the group. "Now skipper, this is a present for y'all. I found this in a used bookstore on account it's outta print. I hope ya gets some time off to read it."

Gilley took the gift. "Ish thank you, we'll think of you and Fern when we read it. You're great friends, and we'll miss you."

The two big men embraced. "Fair winds to you, Gilley, we'll miss you too. This be the first time you be sailin' without me. I love you, Mon."

Alfi came over to Trish and handed her a small box wrapped in a piece of an old chart. "I know the big guy doesn't use a GPS, but this is just in case both sextants quit on you." He whispered. "And you can also measure wave heights with it. Go safe, my sweet girl, I love you." Trish hugged her old friend for a long time.

"I love you, and I've got Helen and Bruce to keep an eye on you and bring you an Irish stew. Take care."

Helen wrapped her arm around Trish's waist and whispered to her, "A little offering from Eros, just in case you get becalmed in the doldrums and don't know what to do with yourselves." She slipped a small package into her jacket pocket and kissed her cheek. "I'll miss you terribly Trish."

"I'll miss you more than I can say. And thanks for the offering; I'm sure we'll find something to do in the doldrums; who knows, maybe we'll have a vision quest?"

Trish hugged her dear friend. When she finally looked up, she saw the weathered face of Chief Jon and the smiling face of Lynn approaching them.

"Hey, what's all this weeping about on such a great day?"

"Hi Jon and Lynn, you know what it's like when old friends have to say goodbye for a while. Thanks for coming by."

"Wouldn't miss this farewell Trish, and I have something for this great schooner."

They all gathered around with Gilley.

"Captain Cornwall sir, I took the liberty of looking through your flag locker the other day and noticed that you didn't have the Chilean or the French courtesy flags. Now, I'm sure you know that flag etiquette is strictly enforced in those countries. So here's a French flag from my locker, which I probably won't need for a while, if ever. I didn't have a Chilean flag, so I had one made. It's a pleasure to present it to *Romayne* and her fine crew. Broad reaches and safe anchorages, my friend."

He embraced Jon and Lynn. "Boy, you sure know how to get to a guy. I completely forgot the courtesy flags. Thank you Jon, you're a great friend. Hey Trish and Sally, we better go over the damn list again, maybe we forgot something important here."

Gilley put one arm around Trish and the other around Sally. "Well, you wonderful friends, we want to tell you how much we appreciate your coming to see us off. Sorry that it had to be so early, but you know the tide waits for no one. We thank you for your good wishes and gifts. And, as soon as we find a phone along the way, we'll call. So now we gotta catch this ebb and that fair wind out there. We love you all, and stay well."

Helen watched and let their departure scene develop through her tears. In slow motion, Ishmael released the bowline to Sally, then Fern let go the stern line to Trish. Gilley slowly turned the wheel and the schooner quietly came to life as her sails filled with the westerly. A bow wave gradually materialized, and was soon followed by a ripple off her quarter. They all silently watched the jib go up, and then fill as strong hands sheeted the eager sail. The three sailors waved to their friends as the Canadian ensign fluttered its red maple leaf to them.

It was silent on the aft deck of *Romayne*, except for the rush of water on the hull. Trish, now at the helm, moved the wheel a spoke at time, feeling the schooner picking up speed until the needle kissed eight knots. She glanced over at Sally and gave her a smile.

"Happy?"

Trish nodded. "Very, and sad, too; it really isn't fun to say goodbye to such wonderful friends, but you know, sweetie, we're not running away, we're running forward."

Trish picked up the binoculars and held the wheel in place with her knee. A large container ship was dead ahead in the center of the ship channel. "Okay, big guy, might has right." She eased the wheel a couple of spokes to starboard to make her change of course certain and known to the pilot on the bridge. "Red to red, go ahead." She watched Gilley hoist the big working jib and trim it. There was no pressure on the wheel, only a noticeable increase in speed. "Great ten knots, she really wants to go."

Gilley joined them, wiping his forehead and adjusting his cloth cap. "So here we go, how's the helm?"

Trish took her hands off the wheel and waited. "I'd say you trim very well."

"Yeah, she likes this wind." He picked up the binoculars and watched the approaching ship. "We're going to get a wave off that container ship, Trish; we'll take it on the beam."

They waved to the Korean crew just as the schooner felt the ship's bow wave lift the hull up and roll her onto her beam ends, sending a small river of water along the lee deck, which quickly drained through the scupper ports.

Finally, they left the last channel buoy to port. Gilley streamed the taffrail log from the stern, which would record the nautical miles traveled through the water.

"In a little while, we'll alter to one-nine-zero and hopefully we'll be on that course till we find the trades."

Trish took her last look at the Golden Gate Bridge and threw a kiss to it. "How many days do you figure?"

"Oh, she'll probably average ten knots maybe more, depends on the wind. We have El Niño this year, so it's anybody's guess what the hell we'll get. If all goes well, I'd say roughly two to three days."

He looked around for ship traffic. "Trish, you can alter to one-nine-zero now and let Sally drive. Stay with her till she's comfortable with the wheel and compass. Then we'll trim the sails and set Arthur McWindvane. It's about time he started earning his keep."

Trish looked into the compass binnacle and turned the wheel to port until the lubber line found 190 degrees and went past to 200, then brought it back. "Steering one-nine-zero, sir. You take it, Sally, I'll be right beside you."

Sally focused on the compass and watched it move off course to 180. "Now give it a little correction to starboard, which is to the right. Remember, if you want to make the number increase, turn to starboard. And of course, the opposite if you want to decrease the number. That's it when you get it on course, you only need about a quarter turn either way to keep it there. See, the lubber line is right on. Just play with it a bit."

Sally nodded. "Got it."

"Okay, are you happy with it now?" Trish watched her for a few minutes until she was sure Sally had control. "Okay, I'm cool with it."

Gilley eased all the sheets until he was satisfied with the set of the sails with the fresh nor-westerly filling them.

Trish watched him making his rounds, ensuring that everything was in order, no lines or sails were chafing. He came aft and eased the main sheet. "Everything looks good; we've got a nice reach. It's time to put Arthur to work."

Gilley rotated the mechanism until the vane was facing directly into the wind, then engaged the latch to the vane. "Okay, Sally, let go of the wheel; you're relieved, Arthur's on duty now."

She took her hands off the wheel and kept watching the compass. Gilley, she's steering one-eight-zero, how come?"

He made a small adjustment to the vane mechanism. "How's that?"

"It's coming back; there it is, right on course." He leaned over her shoulder and looked into the binnacle.

"That's amazing. It looks like it's averaging one-nine-zero; Arthur is a very clever guy."

They all went up to the bow and leaned on the bulwarks. Sally looked down at the bow wave kicking off the port bow. "I love the way she cuts these waves, very powerful." She looked forward with the glasses again. "So, am I on watch?"

Gilley nodded. "Sure, I figure we'll do four-hour watches, eight off. So every eight bells on the ship's clock will be the change of the watch. Sally, you'll be off at noon, okay?"

"Sure, that's fine. The sandwiches are in the fridge. So I'll serve lunch, and then what do I do?"

Trish laughed. "Well, you could read, you could sleep, write in your journal, cook, take your pick. It's your time."

"Great, I'll stay up here and watch for the enemy. See you later."

Gilley leaned over her shoulder. "Now, Sally, if you see the enemy, that's too close. Get back to Arthur as fast as you can, unlatch him quickly and steer away enough to miss whatever it is. But always call me and let me know if you see something threatening. When it gets dark, we'll have the radar on, for about eight hours. But to make you feel better, I've logged close to four hundred thousand miles and haven't hit anything, and I know a few blue water sailors who haven't either. So, I just want you to sleep well at night."

"Okay, if you're not worried, then I'm not."

"You're doing fine, Sally, and I'm really happy to have you aboard."

Gilley and Trish came on deck with their sextants and faced the rising sun. They held them up to their eyes and adjusted the micrometers to measure the exact angle of the sun to the horizon. He lowered his first and took the time with his wristwatch. Trish lowered hers. "It's ten-twelve and thirty-six seconds." She followed him to the chart table in the salon, where they read the sextant angles and wrote them down. "I have forty-five degrees, thirty-five minutes and forty seconds, what did you get?"

"Forty-five degrees, thirty four minutes, thirty seconds."

"Close enough." Gilley sat at the chart table and flipped through the pages of the nautical almanac, ran his finger down the page, then wrote down a number. He selected a page in the HO 214 volume and wrote more numbers. He passed the books to Trish, who repeated the process. A few minutes later, he drew a ruled pencil line on the plotting chart and looked over at Trish.

"What are you estimating the height of eye above water?"

"Eleven feet's close enough. Here's the plotting sheet, might as well use the same one."

She worked out the problem, took the pencil and ruler, and carefully drew a position line on the chart approximately a quarter of an inch beside Gilley's.

"How about that, we made our first sight and position lines together, and look how close they are! Are we good or what?" She put her arms around his neck. She kissed him. "God I'm so happy we're together like this."

"So am I. It's damn seldom I get a fresh fair wind to start a passage, and the five-day forecast said we'd be in this high for a day or two." They joined Sally at the helm. "Then, there's a tightly wrapped low right behind it. I hope to hell we make enough southing to miss it."

Sally took a couple of gulps of ginger ale and belched. "Scuse me, so what's a tightly wrapped low?"

"It's a low pressure weather system with the isobars close together, which tells us that the wind speed will be higher, maybe twice what it is now, and depending on where the low is situated, we could get that wind right on the nose. I figure we'll be in a tight race to get us into the northeast trades before we get hit with the low. Then, as long as we're in the shipping lanes, as we are now, we need to keep watch for ship traffic. Most of these ships are doing fifteen to twenty knots, and that means we go from seeing nothing on the horizon to being a target of a hundred thousand ton ship twenty minutes later. So it's up to us to see him first. The radar on should give us plenty of time to get out of his way. I'll get you up to speed on that come sunset."

Trish flinched as Robin jumped in her lap. "Jeezs, Robin, don't scare mummy like that." She picked up her cat and kissed her head. "Has anyone seen Bear lately? They're usually together."

"He's flaked out on my bunk, and so was Robin. They seem to hit it off."

Sally grinned at Gilley and collected the plates and glasses. "Well, as I'm officially off watch I think I'll retire to my bed for a nap, I mean my bunk. Then, how about dinner at six, I mean four bells? "

34

Romayne sailed through the star-studded night almost due south at a steady 11 knots with a wind blowing 23 knots out of the west. She was heading for the northeast trade winds. Her master had a serious addiction for trade wind sailing and knew where to find them. He'd had the incredible rush of pleasure that they gave him on numerous ocean passages, long after he'd started sailing as a deckhand on a tuna fishing schooner out of Vancouver many decades ago.

The faint glow from the port and starboard running lights illuminated the frothing waves alongside. They sent out a visual alert to other mariners that this schooner was under sail. *Romayne* was on her way to the great southern ocean and would proceed while her crew performed a real memorial service for sailors long gone. Gilley leaned his elbows on the forward bulwarks and wondered about his rendezvous at 83° 20' west longitude, 54° 32' south latitude. He thought about his other true love, Daphnia, and wondered if he would have full closure from his lingering grief.

He glanced at the compass, satisfied that Arthur was steering on course, then slowly swept the horizon with the glasses. He saw a brightly lit, heavily laden oil tanker heading north. Quietly he entered the doghouse and put his face to the shielded radarscope. The tanker was five miles off their starboard bow, doing 16 knots. There were also five small blips 12 miles ahead to port, probably fishing boats moving at trawl speed, possibly out of San Diego. He smiled when he heard Trish snoring contentedly, then turned and went below to the salon and checked the barograph on the chart table. The inked nib left a distinct line on the recorder paper showing a definite drop in pressure to 29.2 inches in two hours. He noted it in the logbook and returned to the deck.

The eastern sky was awakening with a faint pink glow that appeared on the horizon. It would alert the people who lived on the northern hemisphere that the quiet darkness was in the process of ending. He loved the dawn watch, because he was the only human on the planet at this precise location to witness a new day evolving. And this one developed into a spectacular red sky.

He heard the clock chime six bells. Glancing into the doghouse, he saw Trish leaving her bunk and disappearing below. Shortly after, she appeared beside him, warmly dressed in a hooded parka and gloves. She poured two steaming mugs of cocoa from a thermos.

"Good morning, love. I thought I had the four-to-eight watch, and it's seven o'clock."

"Morning, sweetheart. There was a lot of traffic out there last night, so I decided to slalom through it and let you gals get some shuteye. You were exhausted."

She looked into his tired face. "I guess I was, because I went out like a light, what with the excitement of all the goodbyes and hoisting sails. At least we can enjoy our first sunrise watch together. I really love this watch."

"Yeah, me too. It's been a while since I've had one, so I thought I'd take it to get myself back into sea mode. The traffic will thin out when we get about a hundred miles offshore, and we can relax a bit. Also, the glass is dropping fast and the wind has picked up. We'll have to tuck in a reef or two before too long. We're sailing right into that low."

She sipped her cocoa and looked up at the sails. "Oh, yeah, look at that sky. 'Red sky in the morning, sailors take warning.' I remember that sailor's rhyme from Daddy."

He looked up at the wispy cirrus clouds in the western sky. "Yessiree, those mares' tails up there tell me there's a front coming in and we'll get some rain and wind."

"I'll wake Sally. She's been down for about eight hours."

Two hours after breakfast the wind had picked up to 32 knots, the seas were ten feet with whitecaps rolling, and the sky was partially overcast. Gilley and Trish eased the mainsail halyards until the gaff jaws were resting on the copper mast band at the second reef. They belayed the halyards and secured them. Then, standing on top of the doghouse and table, they tied the reef lines under the boom. Gilley secured the tack and the clew outhaul.

"Not bad, we did that in eight minutes. Now the foresail."

They repeated the procedure on the foresail without any difficulty; then returned to the helm seat where Sally was watching the compass.

"Gilley, she's steering two-four-zero, how come?"

"The wind's veering, Sally, with this low coming at us. We're gonna get slammed right on the snout before too long."

Trish and Gilley sheeted the main and foresail with the winches, then the jibs. A tap on the barometer in the doghouse sent the needle down to 28.2 inches.

Mares' tails in the eastern sky were being chased by the overcast fast approaching from the south. "Mackerel sky and mares' tails make lofty ships carry low sails," he sang. "Trish, let's get our safety harnesses on, we gotta dump the jibs. That front is rolling in way too fast for my liking."

Sally stood to watch the action of the flailing arms on the fore deck and grinned.

With considerable effort, Trish finally captured the flogging staysail, furled it, and tied the canvas gaskets around it and to the lifeline. When she got to her feet, Gilley was wrestling with the big jib as it tried to flip him off his perch. She unclipped, climbed out onto the boom and clipped on again. "Hold on, I'm coming to the rescue."

"This son-of-a bitch is trying to kill me," he shouted to her over the howling wind.

She clawed at the flapping sail, which immediately pulled away from her fingers and took a part of a fingernail with it, then slapped her hard across her arm. Finally, she got her arms around it and lay flat on top of it on the boom, and bumped her head on his. "Shit!" she shouted. "This is gonna kill both of us!"

Gilley started to laugh. "Are ya having any fun yet?" He looked into her face, just inches from his. "Fancy meeting you out here—I did say the work was hard."

"I don't remember that."

A rogue wave with their names on it blasted up through the net and drenched them. Trish shouted, "Okay, that does it. Fuck it, I quit, let's go back home."

Together they furled and lashed the sail into the boom, then unclipped and crawled back to the fore deck. "Thanks, I was in trouble out there."

"Glad to help." She looked at her fingernails. "Damn it, I just lost half a fingernail; I meant to cut 'em and forgot. Gotta put it on the list."

After coiling and securing the halyards, they returned to Sally at the helm.

"Well, we got the buggers down just in time. That wind is sure honking."

Sally needed a full turn of the wheel to hold the course. "Gilley, there's a lot of pressure on the wheel since you dropped the jibs, she wants to come up."

"Weather helm." He eased the mainsheet several feet. "Let go of the wheel, see what it does. Is that any better?"

"Okay." Sally took control and brought it back on course.

He felt the wheel and the pressure. "Yup, she's got too much main up. So have you got enough juice left, Trish?"

She shivered as the wind blasted her. "Maybe, if I don't die from hypothermia first."

Trish's' Log, day 1 & 2.

We certainly got off to a great start, a happy but sad departure. We are happy to finally begin our big adventure in this incredible Fife. Sad to say goodbye to our dearest friends: lots of tears, even Chief Jon, who says cops don't cry.

One is always anxious before heading out onto big blue. I certainly was, because I wasn't absolutely sure that one big strong man and two women could sail this enormous schooner and double the Horn in her. I lost my anxiety when the three of us did our two-day shakedown cruise with very few problems, except Trish (the seasoned sailor) hurled and Sally (the novice) didn't.

So, here we are on day 2, in a 45-knot southerly blow, triple reefed foresail, heading due west. Gilley had been up and busy for 28 hours without sleep. He wisely decided to heave-to under reefed foresail and backed staysail with the helm up. Now his crew and ship can rest until this nasty storm blows out and goes east. Romayne is lying 90 degrees off the wind; we're safe, resting, watching and waiting.

Happily, we all get along and work very well together, and now I have much more confidence that we can pull it off. Reefing is much easier with the help of the great lazy jacks. Sally has really taken over in the galley. She loves the diesel-fired Aga stove, which also gives us heat and hot water. I'm on K.P. duty, which is fine. We've got a rhythm now. Actually, the way Sally cooks (especially her whole-wheat bread,) we will probably put on a few lbs. Only the scales that we don't have won't tell, so we'll never know.

My exhausted darling Captain is fast asleep on the doghouse settee right across from me. When I accepted his invitation to sail in the Master Mariners regatta, my fear vanished. One thing led to another—falling in love, this thrilling voyage, Sally (what a trooper) with me again, after an unbearably long separation. We all have a mutual love affair with this amazing schooner; it simply doesn't get any better than this. I treasure all of it.

I wonder about the memorial service and how Gilley will deal with throwing the wreaths to his beloved Daphnia and their unborn—Sally and I will play "Amazing Grace"; tears will fall.

The generator is running almost silently, charging the large battery bank which gives us power that runs the fridge, deep freeze, and any number of electrical gadgets. Thank goodness for modern technology. Arr! Wouldn't William Fife III be blown away to see the three of us, with all the modern toys, about to double the Horn in the largest yacht his yard ever built?

Robin is trying to climb onto my laptop. She must think a cat atop a laptop is politically correct. Not on my watch. She gives me a hurtful look when I push her down to warm my feet.

Gilley thinks as soon as we're out of this blow, we can stream a line from the starboard main fishing pole. Here, mahi-mahi, try this feather jig. There is nothing as delicious as mahi-mahi in the pan half an hour after it hits the deck and gets walloped on the noggin with a winch handle.

Signing off for now to help Chef Sally with her pre-frozen dinner of Irish stew, avocado, and spinach salad, freshly-baked bread.

Trish clipped her harness onto the jack line, then leaning into strong gusts, she slowly walked to the bow. The sun was making a slow dive for the western horizon on its way to warm other lands, and gave off a pink glow followed by a dark red sky. She shouted down the salon hatch. "Ahoy, you two; red sky at night, sailors delight. Come see."

A minute later they were on deck to hear what Gilley assured them would evolve when the storm moved on through.

Trish swept the horizon slowly with the glasses, then joined them on the aft deck. "How about that, a good omen or what? So, how long before this wind settles down and goes fair?"

Gilley surveyed the clouds. "By the looks of those clouds to the south, I'm sure we'll get some rain before it's over. Remember, 'The wind before the rain, soon make sail again.' These low-pressure areas generally move pretty fast. I figure sometime after midnight or later, and we can get sail on her and head south again."

"That's good to hear. Anyway there's a tanker over there heading north. And a container ship passed before us heading west, that's all I've seen. I'll check the radar for any small stuff. Go finish your dinner before it gets cold."

Shivering, Trish ducked into the doghouse to get out of the cold wind. She looked into the radar. The scanner was rhythmically rotating around the scope, the two ships now well on their way to foreign ports. She was just about to leave the radar when she noticed a blip on the edge of the scope approximately 30 miles east, heading in their direction. She decided to track it, checking the clock on the bulkhead. The oil tanker was no longer on the scope and the container ship was nearing the edge of it. She went down to the salon and sat beside Sally. The gimbaled table swung slowly, assuring the diners a steady meal.

"Um, smells good. So, Gilley, we've got a new target heading our way from the east. It's about thirty miles away."

Gilley finished the last of his dinner and wiped his mouth. "Sally, that Irish stew was delicious. I thank you, and my stomach thanks you. So excuse me, I'll check out the new target."

He looked into the scope. "Yeah, it's definitely heading our way at about fifteen knots. I left some stew for you sweetheart. Go ahead, I'll keep an eye on this vessel. Enjoy."

Sally put her feet up on the settee and leaned against the pillow. "So I gather Gilley got a good six hours of solid sleep. He must have been completely knackered."

"Yeah, he was ready for the bunk, but he usually does fine on six hours. He sure has remarkable vitality for sixty-five. I hope I'm that strong at his age."

Trish cleared the table and washed the dishes. "I've got two more hours on my watch, and then he has it until midnight. Why don't you hit the sack and get a good sleep—Sally?"

She peeked into the salon to see that the super chef was asleep. Trish found a blanket to cover her, then dimmed the lights on her way to the deck.

Gilley was standing braced against side of the doghouse with the binoculars up to his eyes.

"See anything?"

"Not yet, but whatever it is on radar, it's coming right for us. I just wondered if it could be one of your nuclear subs; they really move. Man, it's cold out here, I'm gonna get my windbreaker and gloves. The temperature's dropped a good ten degrees in this cold front."

She chuckled. "I thought Canadians never got cold."

"Huh, only the stupid ones who don't know enough to get inside."

35

Trish's log, Day 3

My noon fix 18°32' north, 126°20' west. Wind SW@ 15 K. Speed 9.5K. Course 180°. Sea, 6-8 Ft. Sky, cirrus, a hint of cumulus. Bar 29"and rising. Same Lat as Guadalajara, Mex. Hooray, we've finally got a decent wind on a close reach. She's flying full main and fore, forestaysail, inner and outer jibs.

Gilley and I got the golly wobbler and ballooner on deck. They're in stops, bagged and ready to hoist. Trade winds, look out, this schooner is ready to give us one hell of a thrill, soon.

We're so ready to find the N.E. trades to give us the ultimate ride. I'm betting Romayne will hit 18k; Gilley thinks 15. He figures at this speed and with luck we'll get the first whiff soon. Arthur is steering like a champ; what an incredible invention. But I still love to drive her myself, just to really get the feel of the schooner and her enormous power. I feel a genuine intimacy with this great vessel. So does Sally, she loves to drive, she's a terrific helmswoman. We aren't getting much exercise except hoisting and sheeting sails. I think I'll do a few spins around the deck, maybe a push-up or 10. We certainly have great teamwork going, and we're getting enough sleep. The first two days were difficult, until we got our sea legs and found the rhythm. I've been getting some very good footage of the action with the video camera, and I hope I'll have enough to make a short documentary at the end of the voyage.

The vessel that was speeding toward us was the enormous ocean-going U. S. Coast Guard cutter. They boarded us last midnight, for a very thorough search and safety inspection. The last thing we ever expected, but we realized that our coasts are so vulnerable to drug smugglers or who knows what. I'm glad to have had the experience of being tossed (inspected). The cute young lieutenant with dreamy eyes was at first quite authoritative, as he should be, but he was very friendly at the end. He is a sailor, and crewed on a gaff schooner to Tahiti and all the islands for a year. He swooned over the beauty of Romayne.

We've had a lot of traffic—oil tankers, container ships, cruise ships, some large tuna trawlers, one ketch about 45', homeward for San Diego from Panama. Gilley talked to them on the VHF, two guys and their ladies. They'd been in the Caribbean for a year of fun and sun.

Gilley always sleeps dressed in the doghouse with weather-cloth up. He wants to be close to the deck in case something goes wrong. I've decided to take the other settee, because I want to be near him. Stay close to the one you love. I've made a date with him for some serious intimacy tonight, on Sally's watch. Should be fun; we've hardly touched each other since we left except a few kisses. I'm sure Sally would enjoy a little romp soon. God, what an enormous responsibility; as the ship's working girl, I have to service the captain and the cook; what the hell, someone has to do it. Well, journal it's 8 bells. I've got to relieve Sally, I have the 4-8 watch.

The wind direction continued to change and finally blew steadily from the northwest quadrant. Trish sat beside Sally on the helm bench and held her mug of tea to warm her hands.

"Hi, sweetie, see much traffic?"

"Oh, about three ships, all heading north, and a few trawlers."

"So it's still pretty busy out here. Gilley says all this traffic is coming from the Panama Canal and heading for the refineries on the west coast. And look at us, using wind power to get to the Horn, just like the old-time mariners did."

"So what do we do for wind in the doldrums?"

"It's mostly flat. Sometimes there's a little wind, but it's all over the place. When we went through the doldrums in *Bojangles*, we carried sail all the way, but they were at a narrow band. We slowed down for a couple of days. Also, there's always some current flowing south, so Gilley says we'll soak the decks, hang out under awnings and rest for a few days until we get wind. Hey, we can skinny-dip, eat, sleep and—whatever. "

"Sounds like fun, especially whatever. Speaking of which, when are we going to get together? I'm a tad horny."

"Well, I have a date with El Capitan tonight, so how about sometime tomorrow, on Gilley's watch? I'll be at your service darling. I'm just the ship's happy hooker."

Sally put her arm around Trish's shoulder. "You are the happy healer, and you love every minute of it. Okay, I'm done, the watch is yours, it's eight bells, and the course is still one-eight-zero."

Trish watched the compass for a while to make sure Arthur was performing properly, then put the binocular strap around her neck and walked to the foredeck. Two albatross glided past, their wingtips barely missing the wave tops, then landed a few hundred feet in front of the schooner. They were just sitting and watching the schooner sailing by and seemed to be inspecting it with real interest.

"So we have Mr. and Mrs. Albert Ross." She felt Gilley's big hand on her shoulder.

"Oh hi; yeah, they're amazing. We saw a lot of albatross on the Tahiti race. They used to do the same weird thing, fly alongside ahead of the boat, land and look us over.

They walked back to the helm, where Trish checked the compass heading and sat beside him. He squinted at the anemometer.

"The wind's picked up to eighteen; it's starting to smell like the trades to me. Those cumulus clouds are the first sign of friendly trade winds." He fussed with the outer jib to get the trim just right, then secured the jibe preventers from the boom ends to the foreword cleats.

"How does that feel, any weather helm?"

"Feels okay, she's doing eleven, so when do we hoist the big guys?"

He studied the sails. "Soon as it blows steadily from the northeast. Tomorrow for sure, we'll hoist 'em all up first thing in the morning. Maybe she'll kick up a rooster tail."

"Well, I think I'll lay me down for a spell. I look forward to our date tonight."

She grinned. "Me too."

36

Trish's Log, Day 4

*My noon fix 23° 38' N- 126° 41' W. Speed 13-K. Sea 8-10'.
Wind N E @ 18-20K. Days run 305 NM. Sky cumulus. We are
at the Lat of the Tropic of Cancer, My fix 6 NM west of Gilley's.*

*I got a noon fix from the GPS that Alfi gave me. It was right
in between our fixes; not bad. Sooo, here we are sailing fast at
13 knots. So far, so good, touch teak.*

*It was not so good for our late-night date. The lighting was
perfect, the mood was soft and mellow, our bodies showered,
Arthur steering perfectly and Sally was on watch. We were just
getting into our lovemaking when, BANG! We heard a sail flapping like crazy and Sally shouting. The outer jib halyard had
parted and the jib came down, making a hell of a racket. Gilley
turned on the spreader lights so we could see what we were doing.
He told Sally to stay on course, then without safety harnesses or
anything else on, we went out on the jib boom. After a lot of mur-
derous flapping, we captured the jib and lashed it down. So much
for the best-laid plans to get laid. It always seems that halyards
part and sails blow out at night. Luckily we had lights, but we
were so reckless, we didn't even think to wear safety belts. If one
of us had gone over the side, that would be one lost, drowned and
very dead sailor. I still shudder when I think about it.*

*After we got our clothes on and warmed up with multiple
cups of cocoa, we had a damn good laugh that helped to relieve
the terror we both felt. Sally started laughing first. She said, 'I*

couldn't believe my eyes when I saw your bare asses climbing out on the boom. So I guess from now on, when you have a romp you should wear your safety harnesses.'

Anyway, that event completely dimmed our libidos, so we both took to our bunks in the doghouse and slept. Gilley was up when the wind shifted into the northeast. He said it was 0500 on his dawn watch when the trade wind kicked in solid. After breakfast, Gilley, who thinks of almost everything, had a spare jib halyard from the double fore stays. We bagged the outer jib, replacing it with the enormous ballooner, and set the whisker pole from the clew to the foremast fitting. Then we hoisted the main topsail in stops, then popped it to its gaff block. It balanced well, we only had to trim the main. Then Gilley noticed a squall on our windward quarter, so he decided to wait until it passed by our lee. (It nailed us for about ten minutes.) I took the helm and steered dead downwind with everything up. That squall packed 40 knots of wind and rain, driving the old girl at 16K. There wasn't time to get the ballooner down. Gilley said, "Hold on, folks, we're in for a wild ride, and if the jib blows, we have a sewing machine." The rain laid the sea down a lot, and man, what a ride. Nothing broke.

37

Three times a day the three sailors were awake and enjoying one another's company. Breakfasts and dinners were social times and their opportunity to make sure they were all physically fit and spirits were high. They were all in their element and had developed a warm and cohesive relationship. They had found their ideal groove with *Romayne,* the sea, and loved all of it. They were getting enough sleep, plenty to eat, and now that they were sailing in the trade winds, they all loved to drive the schooner. Arthur McWindvane was temporarily on vacation for a well-earned rest while Sally steered.

Gilley put a hand on Sally's shoulder. "Sally, I'm going to give Arthur a little lubrication; he's been working pretty hard the last few days. And Trish, as soon as I'm finished with our friend here, let's go aloft, I want to check a few things out. Are you up for it?"

"Sure, I want to get some video from up there."

After Gilley finished the maintenance on Arthur, they went aloft to the main mast crosstrees. Well secured inside the mast hoops, Trish focused on the sails that were pulling like Clydesdales. She zoomed in on Sally, who was happily steering and leaving a very respectable wake astern. Sometime during the day, they would be passing over the Tropic of Cancer, the most northerly latitude and vertical sunrays. Gilley carefully checked blocks, shackles, halyards and sails for signs of wear or damage on both masts and found none.

"Let's go down, it's time to fly Mr. Gollywobbler."

As soon as they reached the deck, they dropped and furled the foresail as the open space would be filled with the gollywobbler. They attached the halyards, sheet and tack onto the gollywobbler. He shouted to Sally, "You might feel some pressure on the wheel, so be ready for it."

They wrapped the halyards around the winches. "Trish, if the sail breaks out of the stops before we get it all the way up, don't worry about it, we'll just winch the monster up. You ready?" She nodded.

They pulled the halyards until the heads of the sail were tight to their blocks and prepared to break out the sail. "Okay, let's pop it."

They cranked their winch handles as fast as they could, and watched the enormous rectangular sail fill with wind and find its proper place between the masts. Gilley trimmed until he was sure the sail wasn't touching any standing rigging that could chafe through it. Out of breath, they went back and sat on either side of Sally. "Well, that's it ladies, this old girl is now under full sail." They all looked at the knot meter and watched the needle settle at 16.2 knots.

Trish shouted. "Wow sixteen, she really loves the golly. She's picked up two knots; fantastic."

Gilley squinted at the compass quickly. "Right on course. Now, Sally, let go of the wheel." He felt the pressure on the wheel and grinned. "Well how about that, she's trimmed. We got lucky."

They watched the frothing water cascading down the lee scupper and spewing out the ports. "She's heeled over quite a bit. No wonder, that's one hell of a big sail. She's really got a bone in her teeth."

Trish stood up, raised her arms and shouted at the top of her voice. "Dad, we've got everything up but the cook's drawers, she's doing sixteen knots on a broad reach in the trade winds, and no one's steering. It's a Soldier's Wind!" They all shouted. "The last time this happened was on *Bojangles*." She looked up at the sky. "Hey Dad, check this out."

They snapped their safety harnesses to the jack line, and wiped the spray from their eyes. They moved forward, grabbing hand-holds as they went to look at the sails, showing off their magic. The energy from the wind-driven sails converted their immense power to the schooner's hull, speeding it through the water. "God almighty!" Trish shouted over the noise of the wind. "This is un-believable; I wonder what William Fife would think about his famous schooner cracking off sixteen knots?"

Gilley looked aloft and grinned. "He'd probably say, 'stop showing off, you bloody idiots, you're driving her too hard, and you better shorten sail at sundown me lad, or else.'" They walked forward to the bow, which was kicking up a large bow wave that immediately belched it to leeward. They leaned over the windward side, when a school of porpoise broke the surface as if they'd been commanded to show them the way. They dove under the bows, crisscrossing back and forth with lightning speed.

Trish went aft to the doghouse to get her video camera and started shooting the aquatic activity.

"That's it; I'm coming back in the next life as a porpoise, for sure."

Gilley glanced abeam and saw hundreds of porpoise jump-ing straight up out of the water. They watched in awe at these amazing mammals pierced through the surface and twirled, some performed full summersaults. It was obviously playtime.

"You know we're doing sixteen, they've got to be doing twen-ty-five. See how they get ahead of us." Some of the large school joined the bow group, perhaps to find out what this enormous white whale was doing out here. It soon became apparent that the reason for the sudden migration heading toward them was flying fish, hundreds of them just ahead of their hungry pursuers. They broke the surface, taking flight, with their wing-like fins sending them in all directions. Several landed on the schooner's deck, flapping their fins and tails frantically.

Trish filmed with her video camera just as a fish glanced off her neck, then fell to the deck. "Damn, that hurt." She looked over at Sally. "Keep your head down, Sally, these buggers hit hard."

Gilley came back on deck with a cat under each arm. "Din-din, kitties." Bear was the first to make his attack, by putting his paw on a fish to hold it down. He looked up at the group as if to say, "what do I do with it now?" A moment later, his instinct kicked in and his jaws opened for the kill. They both picked up a fish and crawled under the Whitehall, where they meticulously stripped the flesh off and devoured them. Trish zoomed into their dining area.

Gilley collected a bag full of fish to put it in the freezer for future dinners. Trish and Sally continued their vigil with the school of porpoise until a flying fish ricocheted off Sally's shoulder and landed, flapping, on the deck behind them. "Come on, let's get out of here before we get one in the chops."

They had to step carefully as they went aft, avoiding fish that were scattered over the deck. Gilley filled another bag with fish. "These are really tasty fried with onions and mushrooms. They're not bad raw either. I ate a lot of them in the life raft, a little bony but good sushi, even without wasabi."

Trish took the bag from him. "Say, aren't we in mahi-mahi waters now?"

"We sure are, and as soon as I take a noon latitude, I'll rig the fishing pole. Would you be a pal and put those in the freezer, and start the generator? We're getting low on volts."

He wrapped his arm around the shroud to steady himself, then swung the sextant in a slow arc, following the sun to its highest point, noted the time, then went below to plot the noon latitude.

Trish sat beside the chart table, watching him pencil a line on the plotting chart, then transcribing it to the north-Pacific chart. "That looks very good. At this speed, we're going to ramp up on the doldrums pretty soon. Let's go and rig the fishing pole. I'm tasting mahi-mahi."

38

For the next two days and nights, *Romayne* sailed toward the equator. Gilley remembered Alfi's warning: "A prudent mariner always reduces sail at night." So they dropped the gollywobbler before dark just to play it safe. Trish scanned the sails. "So we have maybe one more day and night with this great wind before we hit the doldrums. Why don't we leave the gollywobbler up tomorrow night? Maybe the old girl will crack off four-hundred miles. It's a hell of a strong sail, triple stitched. Remember what you said to the cute Coast Guard lieutenant that we all have to take a little risk once in a while. Right?"

"A little risk? And what if we get lambasted with the mother and father of a white squall in the middle of the night, blowing sixty knots, just so we can brag to the guys in the bar that we did four hundred noon to noon? But, we blew the gollywobbler to rat shit."

"Daddy always left the golly up at night. Granted, we blew one to smithereens and we had one left. But we've been in squalls before, so we run off downwind, the main'll blanket the golly, and those squalls never last more than ten minutes, fifteen tops. Think of the ride we'd have. It's just a thought. It's your call, sweetheart."

"Look, your dad was in a race that he'd kill to win. He also had a lot of spare sails and a crew of ten. I remember him telling me they blew a few sails. We've only got one golly. So let's see how she blows for a while. I'll think about it. So, you thought the lieutenant was cute?"

"Well, yeah. You know—dreamy eyes, not as dreamy as yours of course, but a close second. Besides, I much prefer older gentlemen;

they're more mature in the ways of the world and women. Well, I don't need to explain that to you, you're the best friend and sexiest lover a gal could have, and besides, I love you. So there."

Trish's Log: Days 5 & 6

My noon fix; 10°14' N Lat. 119°32' W Long. Wind NE 20-22K. Speed.Av.13-15. (384 NM noon-noon): Sea 8-10Ft. Friendly trade wind clouds. Cumulus.

Well, we did it. We really did it. Unbelievable! Gilley decided to take the little risk and leave the golly up last night, even though it was blowing 22K, and the schooner was doing 13-15K. It wasn't until we got our noon GPS fix the next day we actually did 384 NM over the bottom noon to noon. Gilley's fix was 380 NM and mine was 392NM. What a thrill! We got one squall, which gave us a big kick in the ass; we were in it for about 15 Min. Gilley was steering dead down wind and he saw the wind gauge kiss 45K and the hull speed through the water was 18.1knots for a good ten minutes. Awesome.

I sat beside him to watch the action. Man, what a ride. It would have been better if we had daylight to see the rooster tail coming off her stern. We shouted our heads off, but Sally slept through it. Funny girl, the next morning at breakfast she asked, 'I had a weird dream that we were on a very fast train; did we get in another silly squall'?

Anyway, that was something, and I'll never forget it. Gilley figured that the seams on the golly must have stretched a bit in that squall, but no rips. Now it's day seven, 1800 hrs. and the wind is down to 15K and the old girl is taking it easy at 8-10K. Good thing, too, we've been driving her very hard the last 4 days and nights. We're on the latitude of the Panama Canal, which, according to the pilot chart, is where the doldrums are.

Trish was driving. Sally, happily sitting beside her, closed the book on her lap. "This account of the Smeeton's scares the be-Jesus out of me. My God, they got pitch-poled and rolled. You read it, didn't you?"

"Yeah, a long time ago. As I remember, his wife was at the helm and went overboard when it flipped; terrifying."

"Right, but she was thrown back on board with another wave, and had a broken shoulder and a big gash on her forehead. Tough lady."

"It wasn't her day to die. Gilley knows all about that crash, he actually met the Smeeton's and they gave him some tips how to avoid that hairy situation."

"What was that? Don't go around the Horn?"

"No, basically it was using anything to slow the boat down when you're running before it, drogue, tires and warps. Also oil bags to smooth the spindrift down."

They were suddenly startled when the cowbell on the end of the fishing pole clanged. The rubber shock cord stretched aft. "Hey, we've got a fish. Take the wheel, I'm gonna pull this puppy in."

Trish pulled the fishing line, but it was yanked away from her hands. "Damn! It's a big one. Sally, put Arthur on and give me a hand."

Sally grabbed the line, and together they tugged on it, then watched the tarred line angle off from the stern. "Let's put the line on the winch. It's too much for us, and I'm not going to wake Gilley."

With great effort, Trish guided the line into the fair lead and wrapped a few turns around the winch. She gasped, "I don't know what we've got, but it sure as hell isn't a flying fish. Sally, will you grab that winch handle and start cranking? I'll get the gaff."

Sally knelt beside the winch, cranking it slowly until they could see the flashing silvery side of a large mahi-mahi that veered quickly the other way. Finally she winched it up to the surface, where it twisted and splashed.

"Okay, winch it up so I can get the gaff into it. That's it, two more feet, perfect. Now wrap the line around the cleat and lock it. Good girl." Trish gaffed it in the gills and held it. They dragged the wiggling fish over the stern rail and onto the deck, where it flipped and flopped. Trish grabbed it and held it down with her knee, then walloped it several times on the head with the winch handle until blood started to flow. "Well that's it. There's dinner; we landed our first mahi-mahi."

They stared at the dead fish as it gradually changed from silver blue to a greenish hue. "Trishy, it's changing color, or am I seeing things?"

"Yeah, that's what they do when they die; it's very strange. Who knows, maybe its soul is going up to fish heaven. I can't believe Gilley didn't wake up with all the noise we made. He's really out. Wait till he sees this."

Trish took the rigging knife out of the seat locker and felt the blade. "It's been years since I cleaned a fish, but here goes."

She inserted the tip of the knife into its belly, slitting the full length up to the gills. Then she cut the front section of the gills away from the head.

"Hold the head while I try to separate the cartilage."

"Oh, yeah, I remember. There's a little more to cut up in here."

She cut the cartilage away from the head, and then pulled the gills again. Gradually the front fins and the guts separated from the body. "Here we go, nice and easy does it, now one more cut at the stern end and *voila*, they're out." She dropped the entrails over the side, then removed the hook. "We should get a few meals off this guy, what do you think, chef?"

"Yeah, that's a big fish, and what a strangely shaped head, so blunt. Trishy, I'll fillet it in the galley. I think I'll bread it with some garlic butter, then maybe some green onions and white wine. What do you think?"

Trish smiled and held up her hand to high-five Sally's. "I'm salivating as we speak, but I better decapitate and de-tail him first. Let's take it down the forward hatch and surprise him for dinner."

Day 7

5° 22' N Lat.: 111° 34' W Long. Wind. N.E.12-14- K. Speed.8-10 K: Sea 6' Clouds Cumulous. Noon – noon, 204 N/M. Current approximately, 18- NM/day

We caught our first mahi-mahi. It's a good thing we washed the blood off the deck so Gilley didn't see it or the fish. But he did see the coiled-up fishing line; I told him we had a fish on and lost it. So when we all sat down to dinner at the cockpit table, I served the meal. Gilley took a bite and smacked his lips. He asked Sally what was the delicious fish. With a straight face she told him, just tilapia with special sauce. He said, 'I've never tasted tilapia this good, it tastes more like mahi-mahi'. We couldn't hold our laughter. It really blew his mind to find out we'd caught, cleaned, filleted, prepared and served a mahi-mahi without him knowing. He was over-the-top-mast pleased and figured it weighed about 30 lbs. Sally filleted the rest of it and committed it to the freezer with the flying fish. What a day.

The wind kept dropping during the night, then after Gilley's watch we dropped the main to give more air to the golly, which just filled. Then we had the golly and ballooner up, making good about 5-6K. Then, on my dawn watch 4-8, the wind went on strike. The sails were hanging like limp pricks (Gilley's phrase), and there wasn't enough wind to blow out a paper match. No wind, but the sea was like a pig's belly, choppy and from all quadrants. Romayne is rolling like crazy. Mast creaking and all kinds of new noises that we'd never heard before.

Then, Gilley says that we will deploy (love that word, totally military) the flopper stoppers. I helped him get them out of the engine room. I had never seen or heard of this amazing invention.

The design is so simple and completely effective. They're aquatic anti-roll breaks that create resistance when they're deployed overboard. 4 Nylon pendants, attached to four-foot-square angle irons welded together. Rubber mats with diagonal cuts are bolted on the edges of the boilerplate under it. I couldn't believe the immediate effect. If the yacht attempts to roll, the diagonally cut rubber mats open up, allowing the water to flow up through it. When it tries to roll the other way, the rubber mats close and act as breaks so the water can't flow down through it. Now Romayne has enormous anti-roll resistance, with two floppers on each side. Thank you Mr. Flopper Stopper.

The scorching sun pounded the deck like a hot sledge and bounced back at them with blistering heat, making it too hot for bare feet on the deck. Not a cat's-paw of a breeze offered relief. They lowered and furled the sails; then, with sweat pouring, they installed the awnings over the main and fore booms and fore deck, giving them lifesaving shade. Gilley went down to the galley for juice and cookies.

Exhausted, Trish and Sally flopped down on the cockpit seats. "Thank God that's over, I'm done for."

They were suddenly startled to hear, "Arr, arr, what be this schooner crossing the line this day?" A gravelly voice coming from the foredeck startled them. A long-haired man wearing a green crown, sunglasses and black diver's flippers approached them. He carried a three-pronged trident spear and was partially draped in what appeared to be a wet green material over his shoulders. The rest of him was uncovered and dripping with water. He advanced with flippers slapping and the spear thumping the deck

"Arr, what do we have 'ere? two lassies, I see."

Sally giggled. "Well, what do you know, an uncircumcised King Neptune, I declare."

Trish broke up. "I don't think they do that procedure at the equator."

She turned to the King. "Your majesty, it's the good schooner *Romayne*, outbound from San Francisco, bound for Cape Horn, sire."

"Arr, so has either of thee been across the line before?"

"Arr, I have, your Majesty. T'was on the schooner *Bojangles*. Near three decades ago with Captain Alan Cameron."

"Aye, the name comes to mind, if memory serves. So did thee have the crossin' ceremony?"

Trish smiled. "I did. I had a bucket of equator water poured all over me; mighty good it was, too."

"Arr, so the other lass, has thee crossed the line before?"

Sally stifled a giggle and held her hand to her mouth. "No, Majesty, I nay be crossin' the line, but I sure look forward to it. Be it just like this on the south side?"

Neptune advanced a few steps; his gray hair dripping on his shoulders. "Arr, very nice over there, too. Now, I have a small ceremony for all sailors who've nay crossed over."

"Arr, tell me what we have to do, sire."

"Very well, lass. Thee do the crossin' in thy birthday suits. So yer best be doing it now so I can get on with me work. I have other ships to visit."

Sally remained silent for a long moment before she answered in a firm voice. "I don't think so, and I think thee is a dirty old man. In fact, thee is not fit to wear the crown on thy head, and furthermore, I'm going to report thee to the President of the Pacific Ocean. So there!"

"Well, thee is a feisty wench, I see, so if thee don't obey me rule, thee is forbidden to cross me 'quator; thee will have to swim back to San Francisco, so there!"

Trish held up her hand. "May I speak, Majesty?"

"Arr, what say you?"

"I would be happy to remove my clothes instead; she be very shy about her body."

The king stroked his beard in deep thought. "A bucket of equator water is nay a proper ceremony for thy crossin' these days; thee may disrobe, lass. And the other lass too. Be quick now."

Trish had her T-shirt and shorts on the table in a flash. "Come on, sweetie, I don't want you to have to swim back to Sausalito, it's too damn far, and besides, there are sharks. And, and—who would cook for us? Pretty please?"

Sally's serious face gradually turned to a sheepish grin. "Alright, goddamn it." She yanked off her T-shirt and shorts. "There, are thee happy now, Majesty?"

"Arr, very good, lass, thee may now cross me line nekked. So does thee have a captain on schooner *Romayne?*"

"Aye, he's below, please tell him his crew wants to go for a swim, right now."

"Arr, very well lasses, what be his name?"

"Captain Cornwall. He's also President of the Pacific ocean."

"Aye, I know him well, he's been across the line many times. I'll visit with the old salt. I wish thee all fair winds and safe anchorages. And mind the UV rays, burny burny buns and boobs."

He turned and entered the doghouse and disappeared below. Sally giggled. "Arr, Neptune's got a cute tush." They could hear Neptune's loud voice. "Arr, thee salty old sea fart, where ye be?"

They could just hear Gilley's reply. "Arr, me old friend, Neptune, I'm in the galley."

Sally sat down and laughed. "I guess a king could get tired of looking at the same old mermaids all the time. Must be a treat to see real women once in a while."

Shortly after the king went below, Gilley appeared at the table carrying a tray of iced tea and cookies. He was clad in shorts and wearing a neat dripping ponytail. He stood holding the tray with a surprised look on his face. "Well, how about that, nude is good, I guess it is a little too hot for clothes today."

Sally chuckled. "That silly old king made us strip before he'd let us cross his precious E-quator. So did you have a good visit with his majesty?"

He grinned. "Oh, yeah, the silly old fart, he goes on and on about how the Pacific is overloaded with cruising yachts, tankers and trawlers. He can't keep up with the traffic. He's gone back over the side."

Trish laughed. "Yeah, but he gets to see a lot of nude chicks; not bad perks for an old fart. Does he make the guys strip, too?"

"I guess so. That's his new rule, for first-timers to strip. He says most of them are naked anyway. I really think he's losing it. So as soon as we finish our snack, we've gotta get some water on the deck to cool it down, then we can stand down for a swim, and take it easy."

"Thank God. Did he say how many days till we get into the southeast trades?"

"About two, three days; he figures there's some wind down there. We'll see. Anyway, he's gone now, so get dressed if you like."

"Hell, no, I'm getting used to the altogether. It's a lot cooler, right Trishy?"

"Damn straight. So, sweetheart, aren't your guys kinda hot with shorts on?"

"You're right." He dropped his shorts and tossed them into the doghouse. "Ah, that's better, now they can breathe."

After breakfast and checking for sharks, they all took a relaxing swim in the warm Pacific, then back on deck, Gilley issued them buckets with lanyards, and together they poured enough water on the deck to cool the air above. "Good, that dropped the temperature a fair bit," Trish said, as she and Sally cleared the table and went down to the galley.

"Trishy, it's so strange not to be sailing. I still feel the motion, don't you?"

"Sure, I keep reaching for something to hold onto, like she's going to roll."

"So what do we do now?"

"Gilley and I are going to check the running rigging for chafe, because when we get into the southeast trades, we'll be hard on the wind, so we've got to make sure everything's ready to go. Then we can kick back, eat, read, sleep and—whatever."

After cleaning up, Gilley and Trish inspected every inch of running rigging and found that the foresail peak halyard was chafed where it was led through one of a mast fairleads. Trish noticed the outer jib sheet eye splice was ready to fail and needed retying. Gilley discovered that the new jib stays had stretched, so he adjusted all the standing rigging turnbuckles. The running backstays needed adjusting due to all the downwind sailing. He wiped the sweat from his forehead. "Well, I guess that's about it. We got lucky, especially with that peak halyard. When it's cooler in the morning I'll reeve it through a snatch block instead of the fairlead and retie the jib sheet. Hey, good eye on that jib sheet, I sure missed that one. And, I'll install a new outer jib halyard, too."

They descended to the cockpit and found Sally curled up fast asleep on the settee. Trish whispered, "Looks like she's got the right idea, I'm gonna have a shower and hit the bunk; you?"

"Yeah, I'm whipped too."

39

During their long, restful sleep, the confused sea started to lie down as the doldrums gripped the schooner and held it prisoner. The prevailing current from the northeast slowly took *Romayne* towards the equator, where she would soon pass over the famous invisible line on the ocean, without any fuss or jubilation from the sleeping crew.

The blazing sun passed over its zenith above the schooner, as did several passenger aircraft heading for various destinations on distant continents. They would be unaware that an old classic yacht and her crew were resting nude on the vast blue ocean, 35,000 feet below.

A school of bottlenose dolphins leisurely swam by the schooner, and a few petrels and fulmars flew by in their continuous search for food. However, no albatross flew over the schooner this day, as there was no wind which these graceful birds required to sustain their continuous gliding flight.

Gilley was the first to open his eyes to see his lady asleep. He watched her at rest and smiled. He thought that if he ever decided to install a figurehead at the bow under the jib boom, it would be this beautiful lady's likeness to grace it.

Trish awoke and glanced at Gilley, who smiled at her. She yawned, stretched and sat up slowly. "I don't care what they say about the doldrums, I could get used to this, even though it could metastasize into terminal sloth. But we'd never have to decide what to wear every day, and I might do nothing for the rest of the day, except stay naked, eat, swim and lie here, maybe take a few turns around the deck; how about you?"

Gilley rubbed his eyes and slid his legs over the side of his bunk.

"After I install the new jib halyard, I'm finally gonna read that book that Ish and Fern gave us. I've had on my list forever." He reached over to the shelf and showed her the book.

Trish nodded. "Well, of course, *Wanderer* by Sterling Hayden. It's a damn good autobiography. He was a good actor and a fine schoonerman."

"So what are you going to do, sweetie?"

Sally knocked on the open door and plunked herself down at the foot the bunk. "Well, as little as possible. I have some reading to catch up on. But, mostly nothing, and if I don't like nothing, I'll try to think of something else."

Trish went up to the doghouse flag locker, and shouted below to Sally, "Do you remember what I did with that package Helen gave me just before we left the dock?"

"No idea. Try the cockpit table drawer."

Trish opened the drawer as Gilley and Sally appeared. She pulled the long drawer all the way out. "Bingo! Now I remember, when we left I was crying and was sort of out of it. I shoved it in here and forgot about it."

She gave them a sheepish grin as she untied the gold ribbon and tore off the paper wrapping. She removed a white paper that was wrapped around a thin box, and unfolded it.

Darlings: This little offering from Eros (and I assume you are in the doldrums) is my latest formula. Make up the tea with 1 bag per bod, then add the white powder, then sip on an empty stomach; 20 minutes later, enormous euphoria will take you into a beautiful vision quest of love and fun. Enjoy. Finally, Bruce and I are thinking of flying to Tahiti to meet with you and enjoy a well-earned tropical rest. We haven't been back since

we sailed there on our voyage to San Francisco in 1960. We hear Papé'ete has changed a lot, and is expensive. So, dear friends, give me a call the minute you arrive. I so much look forward to hearing your voices and being with you again to smell the fragrance the tiare flower and you.
I miss you and love you, Helen.

Trish handed the letter to Gilley. "I really hope they visit us in Tahiti. They could stay on board so it won't be expensive for them. By that time, the freezer will be overflowing with mahi-mahi." He passed the letter to Sally. Trish opened the plastic box and removed a plastic baggie containing dark tea bags and a small post-it with Gilley's name and a happy face on it. "How about that? We each get our own ration of Helen's Magic Medicine. She's so cute." Trish grinned as she studied her ration. "We're definitely in the doldrums?"

Gilley nodded as he looked at his care packet. "Oh, yeah, no doubt about it. So that great quote by Wild Oscar, the one about temptation. 'The best way to overcome temptation is to yield to it.' I have a strange feeling that temptation is gnawing away at me as we speak."

Trish glanced at the clock. "Well, we haven't had breakfast, and as you said, we're in the doldrums, so what are we waiting for?"

Sally smiled. "I'll put the kettle on."

Journal: Day 9, 2nd in the Doldrums.

Position. Equator. Wind 0. Sea flatter than piss on a plate. Current, from the north Approx. 20 NM /day. Clouds, cumulus, morale high, still naked and euphoric. I promise to take sun shots today and teach Sally to navigate. Right?

Yesterday was beautiful and mind-blowing. Of course, it started with Helen's gift package containing the Magic Medicine. Gilley said the temptation was eating away at him. Then big surprise; Sally says, "I'll put the kettle on." Twenty minutes after we finished our tea, we were up into the stratosphere, taking us to places we'd never been before, alone or together; perhaps because we are on the equator and in the doldrums. Then Sally says, "Captain, sir, would you have any objections if I made love to my best friend? And I invite you to watch if you like." He answered, "I have no objections at all, Sally. You may proceed." Then, much to our surprise, Gilley casually reached in the drawer and removed a hand crank and lowered the table down to seat level, making it into a very large bed. He had never mentioned that you can do other wonderful things on tables.

Finally, after Sally and I had recovered from our incredible passion session, Sally leaned over to Gilley and said with a leering grin, "Now, Captain, sir, I believe it is your duty on this beautiful day to make passionate love to your gorgeous girlfriend. She's warmed up and ready to go, and if you have no objection, I would love to watch."

I don't think the three of us will ever be like we were before. Gilley is still in a trance; his mind is totally blown. I know mine is, and Sally now wears a continuous grin. Thank you, Helen, for an amazing day; we love you.

We lay under the awning and verbalized our thoughts and how we felt about each other, and this poor old planet in general. The day was pure, absolute, uninhibited love and respect, with doses of genuine fun and laughter.

40

"That shouldn't give us any more chafe trouble," Gilley said as he installed the snatch block on the foremast. Trish led the peak halyard through the block and pulled it hand-over-hand down to the pin-rail. They descended to the deck, where he retied the jib sheet, coiled it and draped it over the winch. Trish coiled the halyard, then joined Sally at the lunch table, now elevated to the normal level for their other favorite activity.

Just as Trish reached for a slice of apple, her paper napkin wafted up from the table, hovered momentarily, then drifted over Gilley's head and overboard. It took a few moments for the event to make the impression on them that it was a breeze. After three completely windless days and nights, this was the first hint that wind was actually out there waiting for them.

"Well I'll be dammed, do you suppose—?" The anemometer needle moved off the pin for several seconds, then back to the pin.

"Two knots; not enough to move the old girl. I want to make sure we get into the southeast trades before we take the awnings down. Tomorrow morning we'll know for sure. So continue relaxing, ladies, I'm going to wash her down; my upper body needs some serious exercise. Or feel free to join in."

They both picked up buckets and helped him with the wet-down. Sweat poured from their bodies as Trish filled her last bucket and splashed it over Sally's head. "Arr, now you can cross me quator neked. Ha, ha." The happy crew continued their splash-down until Sally held up her bucket. "That's it for me." She stowed her bucket in the deck locker. "Let's go swimming; I'm melting."

After a careful look over the side and finding no nasties swimming around, they dove overboard to cool their hot, tired bodies.

Back on deck, Sally glanced past Trish and pointed, "Guys, look over there, are they whales?"

Gilley reached for the binoculars. "Looks like a pod of blues. They're asleep, so with any luck we'll drift right to them. Get your video camera; we could get some action here."

It took a half-hour until the schooner approached within a boat length from the resting pod. The enormous mammals were spouting intermittently from their large blowholes.

Trish had them all in frame. "Jesus, Gilley, we're going to hit them, shouldn't we—?"

Then, as if by a soundless alarm, the whales woke in unison, and immediately dove directly under the hull, their enormous tails splitting the blue water as they sounded.

Trish and Sally screamed with delight as they all moved over to the other side.

"Wow! Talk about whale-watching in your back yard! That was amazing."

"That's the closest sighting I've ever had," Gilley said. "The reason we wouldn't hit them is, they have a sort of sensor, so they sensed our presence and dove to avoid danger. Clever, aren't they? By the way, blues are the largest animals on the planet, ninety feet or more."

At daybreak, Gilley was awakened from a deep sleep by the halyards slapping the mast. The wind had freshened during the early hours, enough to get him on deck to deal with it. Trish joined him to help him furl the awnings. "It looks like we're finally out of the doldrums. Oh, well, places to go and things to do."

"Yeah, we've had a good rest, and our special party. I'll always have a soft spot in my heart for this place."

"Me too." Trish shouted down the hatch to Sally. "Wakie-wakie, chef rise and shine, breakfast for three. We're about to get some sail on the old girl, if we can remember how to do it. Sally!"

They packed and stowed the awnings in the sail locker aft. Gilley hung the flopper stoppers in the engine room. Finally, they hoisted the sails and set the new course.

"This wind is south east, not bad eight knots, just right. We should have an easy day of it and get our sea legs back."

Romayne's departure from the doldrums put them in the southeast trade winds. The worst part of being close hauled was, the schooner's motion was more severe as the bow crashed into the oncoming seas, making it difficult to keep one's footing any-where forward of midships. "Daddy had a great saying about severe hull motion. 'Roll, roll goddamn your soul, the more you roll, the less you pitch; and pitch, pitch you son of a bitch, the more you pitch, the less you roll.' She's all yours; the course is one-eight-zero." The sails were trimmed to the new southerly course heading for their rendezvous at the shipwreck site for the memorial ceremony. After a few hours, they gradually eased into their old sailing rhythm for the next leg of the voyage.

Trish joined Sally at the helm. "I've been thinking about Gilley's memorial service. According to my calculation, we'll be there in about twenty days. I really hope this wind picks up a bit. It's a way lighter than the northern trades, but what the hell, we're in no hurry, we'll get there when we get there."

"That we will, and you're off watch."

Sally stood up, yawned and stretched. "I am, and I bid you a pleasant watch. I'm a little weary, what with all the physical activity, so I'll hit the bunk for a few zs. If you need Gilley, he's making love to his engines; speaking of which, you two were ab-solutely amazing together, but of course, I got you warmed up."

Trish's Log: Day 11

Lat.5° 16' south. Long: 120° 32' west. Wind east 13-15 K. Speed 9 K. Course175.

Sails; main top'sl, fore top'sl, fore'stay'sl, inner jib topsail. Morale maximum high.

Romayne is now hard on the wind because we have to make a lot of southing until we find the westerlies, then we can ease sheets to lay the course for the memorial site and the Horn. It seems strange and great to be under way again after 3 days of restful R and R. It looks like we'll be making our southing right down the longitude 120. The motion is pretty wild, so the galley is not a fun place to be. I'm helping Sally so we can get the grub on the table faster, without hurling. Gilley calls it a technicolored yawn. Our main diet is fish, which is very healthy and always delicious with Sally's super sauces, and frozen green vegs. I think we're all maintaining our weight; lots of calories and carbs.

41

After 19 days of hard sailing, *Romayne* approached the memorial site at 54°32' S latitude; 83°20' W longitude; just above the southern tip of Chile. They had been on a broad reach for nine days, enjoying idyllic sailing. At last they reached the crash site. Trish confirmed their exact position on the GPS.

"Well, ladies, here we are." Gilley glanced at Sally with the bagpipe over her shoulder and Trish with her fiddle under her chin. Stationed at the leeward rail, they stood on either side of him. He was wearing his beaded headband with the two eagle feathers.

Gilley played the first few notes of Amazing Grace on his harmonica. Trish and Sally joined in. Then, as if on cue, a school of bottlenose dolphins came alongside and started their ritual crisscrossing in front of the bows. "Isn't that something; all we need is our albatrosses to join in. Oh, look aloft, there they are."

He gave his shipmates a loving squeeze, then raised his arms to the bright sky. The first note of Gilley's chant was almost a whisper and barely audible, but slowly increased in volume into a soulful native chant, ending in a wail melding into a yodel. The increase in volume of his chant seemed to release some deeply held emotion, now visibly flowing out of him. He bowed his head to mourn the death of his beloved Daphnia and their unborn child. The child that he would never see, never hold, never kiss, never take by the tiny hand, never love, never take to school, never teach how to sail, swim and play the piano. Never—Never—Never.

He picked up the first wreath of dried roses, then held it up to the sky for several moments and let it drop into the ocean. The next was held high and released like the first. He paused with the next wreath, then embraced and kissed it tenderly, and let it fall. He held the last, smaller wreath to his chest, and with a cry of anguish, let it slip from his hands, into the southern ocean.

He turned towards them. Their tears fell to the teak deck to be absorbed into it forever. They watched the wreaths on the wave tops until they disappeared. They looked at each other and somehow found a way to smile. Trish went to the foremast and rang eight bells, four times.

Day 19

Lat 55° 30', S: Long.84° 35' W: Course 135' Stb. tack: Days run 240 M. Wind 270' @ 15-18K: Speed 10-12 K. Barometer 29.8, steady. (Hope it stays.) Sea 8-10' long swells. Clouds cirrus, replacing cumulous. Morale-Terribly sad. The memorial went beautifully. Now Gilley has closure at last. This will remain with me forever.

We're in the westerlies, making a direct course for Cape Horn, sailing on a reach, with full main and fore, fisherman and ballooner. Romayne really loves sailing off the wind; it's what schooners do best. Again, we have porpoise and two Royal albatross escorts. Gilley thinks we should round the Horn in about two days; he wants to sail about 10 miles off, just to play it safe. Lee shores are to be given a wide berth, especially in these waters. Then we'll head for a safe anchorage at Wollaston Island that a Cape Horner friend told him about. As soon as we have the hook set, we'll rest until we're damn well good and ready for the return to double the Horn. Then we can call ourselves Cape Horners.

Gilley took a couple of turns on the jib sheet winch and looked at Trish. "How's that?" She held up her thumb.

He sat beside her and patted her knee. "So, the day we do the transit, will we have enough time to sail into that anchorage you mentioned?"

"I hope so. I want to start rounding the Horn well before daybreak, so we'll have time to sail up to Wollaston Island, drop the hook. And, if we have enough wind, we'll certainly sail into the anchorage."

Two days after the memorial ceremony, they encountered a ferocious rainstorm. Gilley looked concerned at the lightning strikes piercing the water like rockets around the schooner. The smell of ozone filled the air.

"What's that strange odor?" Sally asked.

"Ozone, we always get it when the lightning strikes salt water this close, and if I was a praying man, I'd start about now. Those bolts are sure as hell trying to hit this old girl."

Trish and Sally, in yellow foul weather gear stood beside him, watching in awe as the rain poured down on them. Trish gave him a quick glance, then looked back to the powerful electrical display around them. "So what happens if we take a hit?"

"Both masts have lightning rods that are connected to the standing rigging, and then onto the chain plates and the keel bolts. It's anybody's guess if we'd come out of it without some damage. Just don't hold onto the standing rigging, or poof, adios amiga. We'd better douse the ballooner, we're gonna get some wind here."

The three of them managed to capture, bag and stow the big jib and toss it down the fore hatch. They double reefed the main and fore'sl and tightened the gybe preventers.

Gilley told them if it really started to blow a gale to be ready to drop everything quickly, as they would run before it under bare poles. Finally, after a very worrisome hour, the squall and the lightning moved off to the east. The wind picked up, and the following seas increased in height. They were unable to get a sun sight due to the complete overcast. Trish got a GPS noon fix in seconds, which she recorded in the logbook. Gilley plotted it on the chart.

"Well, with these conditions, it's nice to have a GPS, but I'll plot a dead reckoning position just to see how close it is to your fix."

"When Alfi gave me this, he said we can get wave heights from it. I think he said by getting the elevation. Have you ever used a GPS for wave heights?"

He looked over her shoulder at the instrument. "Yeah we did, look just below the Lat-Long, you'll see elevation. What does it read?"

Trish watched the elevation slowly go from minus fifteen to plus fifteen. "Whoa, that couldn't be right, thirty-foot waves?"

He watched the readout for a few more cycles. That's it, thirty-footers and building, speed eleven to the hour. I'd say we need about a hundred miles more of southing till we can lay fifty seven south, then we'll alter to zero-nine-zero and line her up for the Horn."

Trish knew when Gilley was concerned about the weather; he kept looking at the clouds and the seas more than usual. She was sure that these waves were more than just the "roaring forties" on the march, especially when she saw Gilley open the tops of the drogue deck lockers. She watched him take out the eye splice and loosened shackle pin, then return it to the box and do the same with the other drogue. He disappeared down to the engine room and returned with a small truck tire with a chain wrapped around it and lashed it to the mooring cleat.

He joined her at the helm seat and massaged her shoulders. "How's it going, shoulders sore?"

"Yeah. It's keeping me pretty busy; those quarter waves make it very tough. I'm steering about five degrees high, I'd rather steer her straight downwind."

"You're doing fine. It's best to stay a little high; we need plenty of sea room for our debut into Horn country."

"Right. So, you were checking the drogues?"

He squinted at the overcast sky, then aft at the rollers behind. "Oh, yeah, I'm sure our friend Wild Oscar would say, 'better safe than sorry.'"

"This looks like it's really making up."

"Yeah it is, and all of the research I've done on the southern ocean, and what the Cape Horners say, it's either flat as piss on a plate, or it's blowing a fucking gale. The way the barograph is sliding down and these seas ramping up, we want to be ready. Before nightfall I want to slow her down a bit. We should be doing seven to eight knots so we can line up at dawn to round. We'll know if it's serious when the wind hits sixty and the wave tops start blowing off; then we'll get busy. Of course, this could just blow through and head for South Africa. Anyway, we're good for now, and I'm gonna put my head down for a few. Call if you need me."

"I will, sweet dreams."

Trish was tired by the time her three-hour watch was over. She could see Sally in the doghouse putting on an extra sweater. A few minutes later Sally sat beside her, and looked aft at the seas marching behind them. "Tired?"

"Yeah, I'm having trouble seeing the lubber line. She's all yours. Make damn sure you don't let her get below that course."

Sally slipped in behind the wheel and glanced at the compass, as Trish made room for her. "I'll sit with you for a bit to make sure you get the feel of her. Ready now, here comes a big one, so be ready to give her port rudder." Sally was now an expert at the helm. She slammed the wheel to port and the wave passed smoothly under the hull.

"Alright you nailed it, nice going. Just keep looking back at them; some are a way bigger, like that last one."

Sally glanced aft quickly as the next wave approached and corrected for it. "Yeah. I see what you mean, but don't we need some more southing?"

"Yeah it's fine, because when Gilley comes on watch before dusk, we'll drop everything except the staysail and stream the drogue. We'll see. The wind's picked up to forty-three knots."

After two hours on her strenuous watch, Sally's arm and shoulder muscles were burning with fatigue.

Gilley's hands on her shoulders startled her; his massage was a welcome relief. "You look like you could use a few days off."

"Oh God Gilley, you really know how to treat a gal. Oh yeah, right along the top of my wasted shoulder blades." He continued the massage until she straightened her back. "Thanks, you saved my life just as I was about to mutiny."

"Good girl, take a rest. You're a terrific sailor."

The wind had increased, so Gilley and Trish managed to drop the main and fore'sl without any difficulty.

Sally, much relieved and on Gilley's order, altered course to 90 degrees due east. He looked at the huge waves rolling astern.

"Now, isn't that a lot easier on the shoulders?"

She gave him a half-hearted smile. "Sure is, and less pressure."

"Terrific, so you take her while Trish and I stream the drogue. You can have an extra scoop of ice cream."

"Thanks. Go stream your silly rope!"

Gilley shackled the eye splices together at the end of the drogue, and then shackled the chain around the tire to the center of the drogue. They carefully flaked about a boat length of the drogue line on both sides of the deck. Because of the howling wind, they had to shout at each other. Gilley on one side and Trish on the other took a few turns with the lines on the large bronze mooring cleats, then took the inboard ends forward to the anchor windlass. Trish nodded that she was ready. Gilley saw the knot meter reading eleven knots, then lowered the tire over the stern. They slowly eased out several feet at a time until the tire opened up to create a powerful drag, allowing them to ease more drogue into the sea. The canvas cones opened up to create more drag as soon as they hit the water. Finally, all of the flaked line on deck was in the water. They both looked at the knot meter. "Just right."

"That's not bad for a hundred feet out; it slowed her down to seven knots. I'm happy with it, and we've still got another hundred feet or more if we need it. Let's see how Sally likes it."

Sally was laughing and holding her arms up in the air. "Way to go, guys. Now we have a friend for Arthur, amazing, we have a new auto-pilot." She squinted at the compass. "Would you believe she's steering, zero-nine-five?"

"Well done." They all looked aft at the drogue.

Sally squeezed out from behind the wheel. "Trishy, you can drive; I'm going to the galley. Dinner in thirty minutes."

42

Romayne was right on course. Gilley was satisfied that the schooner was under control with the drogue keeping the speed at seven knots. He'd calculated they would approach Cape Horn at daybreak, hoping they would have visibility for any shipping traffic, but if not, the radar would give him visibility of any enemy. During the night, the wind speed had increased to sixty-five knots, and the hull speed gradually climbed back to nine knots, requiring them to let out more drogue.

The VHF transmitter was set on channel 16. In the event traffic showed up, he would contact the vessel approaching to find out the ship's intention regarding any impending course change. He would also warn the vessel's bridge officer that his schooner was towing a drogue sea anchor and he had very limited maneuverability.

Gilley knew he'd be awake for at least 24 hours and probably more. He made sure that the web jack lines for the safety harnesses were in place and taut. He had installed seat belts at the helm in the event the schooner lost control, pitch-poled and rolled, the helmsman would not be ejected from the seat, but would be thoroughly soaked, possibly half-drowned, but alive.

Except for the complete overcast, it was still reasonably light up to midnight at this time of the year in the southern hemisphere. They were hot-bunking it now, so the one coming off watch would climb into the warm sleeping bag vacated by the previous occupant. The one coming off watch would bring cocoa and a snack to the relieving watch, and would make sure the other was up to speed, on course and familiar with the overall situation. The temperature continued to fall as night approached, so sweaters, life jackets, safety harnesses, gloves and hooded slickers were needed as the ferocious wind pummeled their backs constantly. They found it impossible to breathe facing the wind, so they always faced forward. Gilley relieved Trish at 0300 with a towel wrapped around his neck under his slicker. The wind was so strong, Trish had to pull his hood back and shout in his ear. "God. I'm glad to see you. Wind is steady seventy-five and gusting eighty-five. Scary, but the old girl takes 'em one after the other."

Gilley checked the compass heading and nodded. "Yeah, the drogue is keeping her right down to seven knots, and we still have some left."

Trish was shivering and ready to climb into his warm bag. "Right. I'll get you a thermos of cocoa. You want anything to eat?"

"Just cookies. One more thing Trish, pull like hell to get the door open, and watch your fingers."

Gilley had checked the radar and was satisfied there were no ships on the scope. Once on deck, he clipped his safety harness to the jack line, crawling on hands and knees to the helm seat, where he fastened his seat belt. He felt slight resistance on the wheel. Trish was having difficulty pushing the doors open to squeeze her body out. Finally, she tugged his pant leg and handed him the thermos and cookies. "Thanks, and tell Sally I'll take her watch."

"Will do, steer small see ya. Oh, by the way, there's something on the radar; it's due east, big and coming west really slow."

"Got it. I may have to call you, so keep your slicker on."

He wanted to test how much maneuverability there was with the rudder, mindful that he must not steer far off course for fear of broaching in the trough. He wasn't surprised there was a ship in these waters. He knew there would be some tankers and freighters too large to transit the Panama Canal.

In spite of the wind screaming in the rigging, he thought he heard the rush of a breaking sea rolling behind and quickly glanced aft. He saw nothing, until half a swimming pool alive with sparkling phosphorescence cascaded over the stern and swept the aft deck and cockpit, slamming hard against the doghouse bulkhead then, losing its force, dissipated through the deck scuppers. It was a nasty rogue wave exploding spray in all directions.

"Alright, time to get busy."

He crawled to the doghouse to see how the women managed the slamming wave. Just as he got to the doors, one was being opened. Trish shouted, "Jesus, that was a big one!"

He climbed in. "Yeah we got royally pooped. You okay?"

Sally was awake and popped her head out of the bag. "We're fine, but this old house shook a bit and a little water came in."

"Okay, Trish, I've got to put oil bags out. I need you to take the helm for a bit." He glanced at the radarscope.

Trish pointed at the blip. "She's steering a crazy zigzag course, looks like about twenty degrees either side of west. Is that normal?"

"Hell, no, he should be heading right into it; this wind couldn't be blowing the bow off course. They've got plenty of power to blast straight through it. After I set the oil bags, I'll give 'em a call. You ready?"

Trish nodded and crawled out to the deck behind him. She buckled herself in and watched him disappear down the engine room hatch.

He slid into the dark space and turned on the lights. He'd prepared six big hemp canvas bags with many small holes. The bags were filled with cotton waste, also four bottles of oil in each bag, ready for quick release inside the bag. He took four bags and slid back to the aft deck. Lying on his side, he clipped onto the jack-line. Poured the bottles into the bag, he pulled the drawstring tight, tossed it off the stern, then slowly played out the line. After making it fast to a cleat, he repeated the deployment with the remaining bags, then crawled back to the helm.

"Alright you cheeky, liquid bastards, there's a dose of ten-forty for you."

He could still feel the extreme motion of the rolling waves lifting the stern, then sliding under the hull as he climbed up beside Trish and shouted at the seas. "Alright—settle down back there!"

The oil bags had a gradual effect on the spindrift from the wave tops as the film of oil spread over the surface. "Yeah, that'll help, and I've got two more when we need 'em. Hey, it looks like dawn out there, damn well time, too."

A blurred thin gray line formed on the eastern-horizon. He reached for the VHF mike from the seat locker and flicked the transmit-button a few times.

"This is Canadian schooner *Romayne* calling the ship heading west in the Cape Horn area. Over."

He waited a minute or so with no reply, then repeated his message and waited. No reply. He tried another ship-to-ship channel with no reply. "Goddamn it, answer you pricks." He switched the selector back to channel 16, cradled the mike inside his hood to shut out the screaming wind and called again.

Finally, after a long pause, the VHF came to life. "Canadian schooner *Romayne*, this is the M.S. *Islandia*. Ve are heading vest, ten miles off Cape Horn. Good morning sir. Sorry for the delay, ve have breakdown in steering compartment, our hydraulic steering is kaput, and the autopilot is down. Ve are on auxiliary steering, but it is not vorking vell in these conditions. The sea is most enormous and not in our favor today. Over."

"*Islandia!* Good morning, sir, I'm sorry you have a problem. I hope you can make repairs. Do you have me on radar? We need to have plenty of separation when we pass. Over."

"*Romayne.* Oh, yes, ve have you on radar, strong blip. Ve are tracking your course at zero-nine-zero degrees, making good seven knots. Please to understand our course is not straight. Ve are only able to steer between two-six-zero and two-nine-zero degrees. Ve have thirty-meter head seas. Ve can only make five knots. I pray to have a new hydraulic steering pump installed; my engineers think maybe a half hour. Over."

"*Islandia,* roger that, good luck. We will pass to the south of you, so we have enough sea room between us. Thank you, Captain. *Romayne* standing by on channel sixteen."

"Thank you, Captain, you vill pass to our south, ve stand by on sixteen."

A dirty gray seascape of boiling white wave tops was blowing to leeward as if they were sprayed out of powerful fire hoses. Gilley and Trish looked aft to see a series of enormous liquid mountains on the move. The schooner was riding on them as they passed under the hull. It was like a miniscule cork in the midst of these giants. The ocean appeared like a thick layer of white smoke, with visibility about two boat lengths. The sea was alive with a destructive rage.

Gilley poked his face into Trish's hood. "Those poor buggers have a serious problem, and now it's ours too. I'm going to check their course on radar. Hold on here for a bit? It's getting real dicey!"

After crawling back into the doghouse, he perched on Sally's bunk and studied the scope for several minutes. The ship was approximately eight miles directly ahead. First, it would be on its course of 260 degrees, and then slowly alter to 290 degrees, then swing back to 260 degrees. He put their closing speed at 12 knots.

Sally watched the action on the scope. "Why is it all over the place?"

Gilley was silent for several moments. "Steering gear's fucked; their course would break a snake's back." He handed her a walkie talkie, "If we're close to a collision course, press this talk button and tell me. Just keep telling me what he's doing. Ya got that?"

"Sure do."

He pocketed the other walkie and pushed his way out the doors and back to the helm. "Sally, do you read me?"

"Got you, Gilley. It's swinging to the south, like it's aiming right for us. Now it's holding for a bit, now back to the first course."

"Thanks, I've got the sequence. I'm going to alter more to the south. Let me know if he goes crazy."

He relieved Trish and took the wheel. "Good job, Trish. We're three miles from closing, so keep your eyes peeled. I'm heading south as much as I can. We gotta get outta his way."

The rumbling of a wave slapped hard like a cannon shot along the port quarter. He ducked as the spindrift blasted over them and was blown to leeward.

Sally's strong voice came on the walkie. "Gilley, it's on two-nine-zero more than the two-five-zero course. Just a minute, now it's two-five-zero again, and staying there, now two-seven-zero. Oh, Jesus Christ! It's coming right for us!"

Trish shouted and pointed. "There it is!"

They saw the ten-story-high bow dead ahead as she screamed. Gilley cranked the wheel hard over to port, and held his breath. He could read *Islandia* clearly on its starboard bow, dead ahead. "Hold on, this is—"

The wheel would turn no further, as Gilley tried to twist the wheel and the shaft. *Romayne's* bow slowly swung to port; the mountainous wave that would normally have lifted her stern and push her down wind, now slammed into her port topside and lifted the hull up and over toward *Islandia's* enormous steel hull. The wave rolled until it crashed against the immovable steel barrier and bounced back with such force that it hit the schooner's hull and pushed it away from the ship. Only eight feet separated the ship's hull from the schooner. The ship's course had altered again to port, and its stern was swinging onto their course.

Gilley and Trish looked up in horror to see several thousand square yards of black steel, and above that, stack after stack of colored steel containers. Several dark-skinned faces peered down at them with their arms waving.

The next breaking wave rolled the schooner's hull to starboard. He kept the wheel hard to port. Then another wave pushed the schooner over to the ship's side. *Romayne's* starboard quarter hit with such force that it slammed Gilley's upper body onto Trish, pushing her onto the bench. Her head hit the armrest so hard she was knocked unconscious and lay slumped over. The schooner's stern sideswiped off the ship's quarter, which ripped a section of the bulwark and cap rail off like it was a dry twig Then it continued on clear of the ship's propeller wash. Gilley looked up at the massive stern, with *Islandia* in white lettering, and in smaller letters underneath, *Monrovia*. He brought the schooner back on course. The drogue kept the schooner heading straight downwind again. Miraculously, the drogue avoided being caught by the ship's propeller.

"Trish! Trish, can you hear me?" He gripped her shoulder and moved it. She didn't respond. He raised her to a sitting position. Her head flopped onto his shoulder. "Trish, for God's sake, wake up!"

He pulled the slicker hood away from her face and saw the blood running down the side of her forehead and cheek.

"Gilley! Are you guys okay?" Sally's voice was loud and panicked.

"For Christ's sake Gilley, Trish! Oh, please, please answer. Are you alright?"

It took him a few moments to find his walkie. "Sally! Trish is out cold and bleeding on her forehead. Come out here."

Sally forced her way through one of the doors and crawled to the seat. She took Trish's face in her hands and examined her forehead. She shouted, "Let's get her on the bunk."

Gilley slid over to the other side to take her limp body under his arm, dragging her on her back into the doghouse and lifting her onto the bunk.

Sally felt her carotid artery. "Boy, she took a bad hit. Trishy!" She patted her face. "Trishy, it's time to wake up." She glanced at him. "Her pulse is okay, but she's concussed for sure."

Gilley kissed her cheek. "Trish, we want you to wake up now." A weak moan was barely audible. She partially opened one eye and mumbled something incomprehensible. Sally leaned over her closed eye and carefully opened the lid.

"There's my Trishy."

Trish mumbled. "Toto, where the fuck are we?"

"We're at Cape Horn. Do you know who the President is?"

"Captain Gilley Cornwall—He's President of the Pacific ocean."

"That's right, Trishy."

She groaned, and whispered, "Oh, God, my head hurts sumpen awful." She squinted at Gilley. "Oh, hi, Mr. President, are you alright?"

"I'm fine."

"So who's driving—and what happened to the enemy?"

"Drogue's doing just fine, *Islandia's* outta sight. I'll be back in a few."

As soon as Gilley returned to the helm, he looked aft to see blurred gray spindrift spewing from the wind-torn seas. He had his last radio conversation with the ship's Captain, who was relieved to hear that no one had been seriously hurt. He was sincere with his apology that his ship was out of control. "In a berry soon moment, praise be to God, Captain, ve vill be steering vell." His final sign-off message was that he would very much like to meet the courageous Captain and his crew on the Canadian schooner *Romayne.* "I love your country and Canadians are berry good peoples, aye?"

Sally was fussing over Trish. She was lying secure on the bunk with an ice pack to reduce the swelling. Sally gave her a strong analgesic to minimize the pain. She cleaned and dressed the cut. "Maybe I won't need to stitch. It's under your hairline and won't show; the butterfly bandage will hold it together."

Gilley was enormously relieved that they had narrowly escaped a terrible death, but worried that the impacted bulwark could result in structural damage. Fortunately, they'd been belted to the seat, as ejection overboard would have meant certain death.

"Sally, will you give me a bearing and distance to that headland just to the east of the Horn, which is Isla Deceit? And how's Trish doing?"

"She's sleeping. Give me a minute; I'll figure out the bearing and distance."

He realized how close they'd come to being killed. He was shaking with delayed fear and extreme fatigue.

"Gilley, you with me? As near as I can plot it, we're nine miles south of the Horn and the bearing to Isla Deceit headland is zero-four-five degrees; the distance is about thirteen miles. And good news, I just tapped the barometer, the needle jumped up a bit. Do you suppose?"

"Great, bloody well time. As soon as I get her on a safe course, I'll come in and check the chart. Any more enemy around?"

"Just *Islandia*; oh my God, would you believe she's steering a straight course. Anything more?"

"Thanks Sally. I'll let you know when you can come back here and enjoy the scenery."

The wind speed was down to 73 knots. A quarter turn to port gave the schooner more control. He felt she was happier on this heading, but now he had to steer and couldn't rely on the drogue as autopilot.

"Hey, Mr. President, how about a sandwich and tea?" He woke with a start as he felt Sally beside him. His hands were on the wheel with the master spoke straight up.

He wiped his face. "Jesus, did I drop off?"

"Yes, and as ship's nurse, I order you to get some rest. We'll need you later. Trish is asleep, so you can keep her company."

43

When the schooner rounded the headland two hours later, it seemed that they had entered another world, with a completely new ecosystem. The wind had dropped to 26 knots, as they were protected in the lee of the headland. Also, the temperature increased dramatically. Most unusual of all was that for the first time in twenty-three days, the schooner had actually stopped, dead in the water. The drogue had sunk below the surface, and the drag of the cones prevented the schooner from any movement except drifting with the current. Trish had recovered somewhat and stood holding onto Gilley. They peeled off their slickers, safety harnesses, and life jackets and tossed them on the cockpit table.

After a group hug, the women locked arms with Gilley, who started to dance a sailor's jig. Physically and emotionally exhausted from their terrifying transit, they allowed their aching bodies to slip to the deck and lay on their backs, panting like spent marathon runners.

Sally rolled over and embraced her shipmates. "Oh, thank you, thank you, we did Cape Horn."

Trish raised her bandaged head from Gilley's heaving chest and moaned. "I'm so relieved to be out of that bloody gale, and *Romayne* is the most incredible schooner afloat. I hope you didn't get hurt too much, old girl."

Gilley kissed Trish's forehead. "I'm blown away by what we've done, with only a few scars to prove it. Speaking of scars, how's your noggin, sweetheart?"

Trish rolled over and touched her bandage. "It hurts, but I'll live. As Daddy used to say, 'You bruise easy, heal quick.'"

The black-and-blue bruise on her forehead had migrated onto her cheek. She glanced over at the open doghouse doors just as Robin appeared with her large, panicked yellow eyes. Bear followed, mewing, obviously spooked by the extremely violent motion from the sudden crash. They walked cautiously, looking all around as if they were expecting an imminent attack "Aw, come to mummy, Robin, everything's going to be alright now, I promise. No more nasty storm and bang. All gone."

After lots of coaxing the cats stepped over Sally and stopped when they approached Trish and Gilley, who picked up their furry friends for a cuddle. "Poor little buggers." Gilley held Bear and scratched his head. "I haven't been paying any attention to you for a while. We've been a little busy up here, but everything is cool now, big Bear. We'll get ya something to eat in a bit."

Gilley and Sally winched the drogue on board and flaked it on deck to dry. Trish was excused all duties until further notice, and sat at the helm with her face basking in sun that had slowly pierced through the diminishing stratus.

It was the first clear weather they'd had in four heavy weather days.

The morale onboard was improving quickly. Gilley and Sally shook out the reefs in the main and fore'sl, hoisted the jibs, and headed for Bahia Scourfield on Wollaston Island, 17 miles to the north. Gilley and Trish studied the chart and plotted their course to leave Isla Deceit and Isla Freycinet to port. "As soon as we round Punta Martin, we steer right into the bay. It's well protected and depth sixty feet. *Romayne* should fit in there."

Trish smiled and hugged him "Just right. Oh, man, I can't wait to get the hook down and shower, rest, eat and sleep."

Sally steered with a smile on her face. Trish watched Gilley trimming the jib sheets, then took his hand as he returned to the helm bench.

"God, I feel good, even though my head feels like it's in a vice. I just feel so relieved. And all the more so, because we did Mr. Horn when it was blowing ninety five with ninety-foot seas. Daddy, that was for you. How about that, you guys?"

Gilley faked a frown. "Oh, it was okay, I guess, but I don't think I'll be coming down here again unless it's on a cruise ship with no wind and all the luxury that goes with it. But seriously, if it wasn't for that hairy go-around with *Islandia* and that big blue monster that came aboard, it was an okay transit, and I think the oil bags settled some of the spindrift down; the first time I've ever used them."

Sally glanced at him for a moment. "Well, you know, when I saw the ship through the windows, sliding by like a black ghost, I thought we were in big trouble, but what do I know? I knew our Captain would get us through it, and I did pray—hard."

"We got lucky. *Islandia* was right out of control, and when we were bow-to-bow, it looked like we'd bought the farm. Anyway, we're alive, and that's all that matters."

The landscape of Tierra del Fuego was unlike anything they had ever seen. Austere, jagged rocky headlands, sparse vegetation. They saw mossy rocks, low bushes and ocean kelp sloshing around the small bays. Sea lions were hauled out and resting on rocks.

The exhausted crew took in the bleak landscape of this remote southern tip of land on the South American continent. They could only wonder about the utter loneliness of such an interesting and strange place.

Sally was in the doghouse looking at the chart and radar. "Hey, I'm pretty sure I've got Wollaston Island on radar. Have a look."

He looked over her shoulder. "Yeah, that's it. It's time to show the colors. Gilley hoisted the Maple leaf to the leach of the mainsail, then reached into the flag locker for the Chilean flag. "So here we are in Chile, time to hoist the courtesy flag, thanks to Jon Ewer."

Sally stretched her arms and did a few squats. "I think I'm getting my second wind."

She grinned and looked at him. "So, Gilley, how close were we to a head-on?"

Gilley held up both arms and spread them, and gave her a nod.

"Jesus."

For the final two hours, *Romayne* sailed north in a light fair wind, now well protected from the rapidly vanishing westerly gale. No waves were produced in the lee of the islands they passed. The deep depression that had captured and locked them in its ferocious grip for so long had finally passed on to the east, on a course to the south Atlantic Ocean and the African continent.

Gilley unlashed the anchor from the starboard bulwark, then hoisted it with the davit tackle and swung it over the cap-rail, ready for anchoring. They sailed into the anchorage and kept to the plan that this voyage would be entirely under sail. He instructed Trish to steer directly into the center of the bay. He showed Sally how to trip the snap shackle to release the anchor. The wind had dropped just enough to keep the schooner under way into the opening of the bay. Trish shouted. "Gilley, sixty feet!"

"Let go, Sally!"

She yanked on the trip line and watched the anchor pierce the surface and disappear into the bay. The rattling of the studded chain as it passed through the hawse pipe was a new and exciting sound; her first anchoring, now close to the bottom of the world.

Gilley watched the chain run out and saw the three white painted links indicating 300 feet. He locked the brake on the windlass as the bow swung around and stopped when it was headed to the entrance of the bay.

He went astern with the engine to ensure that the anchor was well dug into the bottom. With Sally, he lowered the sails and lashed the gaskets around the booms. Their anchoring was completed so quickly that they looked at each other in amazement. "That's it ladies, welcome to Bahia Scourfield."

Gilley slowly walked over to see what was left of the starboard bulwark where it was blasted apart by *Islandia's* stern. The women followed and leaned over to inspect the damage. Trish glanced at him. "It looks bad."

"Yeah, it does. One of the topside planks is stove in and the seams have opened up. Well, ladies, we'll be here for a few days to fix the old girl. But thanks to Sally praying so well, we're alive, and we'll get it together somehow. Now I remember why Ish told me to save a few teak planks from the refit. He said they might come in handy someday. Thanks, Ish."

For Gilley's last duty, he launched the Whitehall, took a line ashore and secured the stern to a large rock. Physically and emotionally well beyond exhaustion, they eased their strained bodies below to collapse on their bunks. Their numbed minds had been severely stressed beyond what any of them could think about. They slept.

44

Day 34

(Bahia Scourfield, Chile) Speed 0: Wind 8: heading, 185 degrees, at anchor, in sixty feet.

I have never been so grateful to be alive, and I can honestly say that my dearest shipmates and I were terribly close to meeting the grim reaper. It was touch-and-go, then WHAM! We side-swiped and bounced off the stern of the container ship Islandia from Monrovia. Gilley did everything in his power to get us around Cape Horn. Sally prayed, and all I did was hold my breath. I got a nasty concussion. I'm okay, but I wish the ugly bruise would go away. Powder helps. It took Gilley and Sally two full days to make the repair to the stern of our wounded schooner. (No physical repair work for me. I'm cooking, resting and slowly recovering.) Gilley had to replacee one broken hull plank, then sister two broken frames in the engine room. All of the outboard repair work was done while standing in the Whitehall lashed to the hull. He said he could never have done it without Sally's help. They caulked and filled the seams and painted the new plank. He decided not to repair the broken bulwark and cap-rail but have it done in Tahiti. We finally got the schooner shipshape, and we are more or less physically and mentally back together for the next leg of the voyage. We took it easy for another two days, and went ashore for a walk around the bay. It was remote but beautiful, and we all agreed that we would not want to live here. We had our Cape Horn celebration dinner with all the trimmings, candles and Helen and Bruce's Mumm Champagne. We toasted them, and all of our friends, but especially Romayne and us.

45

Trish leaned over to Gilley and touched her mug to his, then Sally's. "Cheers, mates. I've been wondering about the next leg. How many days do you estimate to Tahiti?"

"I was just looking at the pilot chart. We'll be on a close reach for about sixteen days, then reach up toward Tahiti, say our average two hundred miles a day. I figure about twenty-five days, and if we get lucky with a soldier's wind, twenty."

"What about the doldrums?" Sally asked.

"No doldrums this leg, Sally, they're a way up north by the equator, remember?"

Sally giggled. "Oh yeah, how could I ever forget that? So I guess we don't get naked and all that fun stuff for three days under the awning on this leg?"

Trish wrapped her arm around Sally's neck and squeezed. "Come on, you horny little bugger, you don't have to be in the doldrums to get naked and all that good stuff, you can do that right here."

"No way, it's too cold; besides, someone on shore might be looking at us."

"Honestly Sally, you're absolutely incorrigible. What are we going to do with her Captain?"

Gilley shook his head. "I really don't know, it's getting serious. Maybe we better lock her up in the foc's'le with the cats; put her on bread and water. Naked."

"Okay, okay, I get the message. Twenty days to Tahiti; so what the hell are we waiting for?"

Gilley nodded and glanced up at the masts, then down to the two smiling faces. "Why not, we're squared away, well rested and the wind is light, and the barometer is high. Let's get some sail on this old girl."

Gilley started the Gardener that powered the hydraulic windlass. He and Sally went ashore to release the stern line from the huge rock onshore and coiled it in the Whitehall. The three of them slowly hoisted the main and fore, then the two jibs. They weighed anchor and lashed it to the bulwark.

There was just enough of a breeze to drive the schooner out of the bay and on their way to double Cape Horn.

Trish sat behind the wheel and headed for Punta Martin on Isla Freycinet Island to the southeast. As soon as the schooner was clear of the mouth of the bay, the wind freshened from the west. Trish shouted happily, "Here we go, guys. Tahiti, here we come. Yeah!"

Romayne on starboard tack rounded the southern point of Isla Deceit and set course for Cape Horn, eight miles to the west. It was crystal-clear, with not a cloud in the sky, but the wind was light and from the direction they wished to go. Gilley closed-hauled the sails and set a course that would give them a good look at the foreboding Cabo De Hornos. Trish set up her video camera to capture the scene that had been denied them during the ferocious gale.

"I thought I better get this shot in case no one believes we doubled Cape Horn. Come on guys, let's all get in the shot." Trish jumped in with them while they waved to the camera. Gilley mimicked a fast Charlie Chaplain walk back and forth to add some comedy to the production.

Sally was sweeping the horizon with the binoculars for traffic. "Hey, look! We've got company yonder." She passed the glasses to Gilley.

"Well, what do you know—a big cruise ship; it seems to be steering a straight course what a relief."

Trish set up her camera on the port deck, ready to record the passing of the enormous ship. Gilley exchanged greetings on the radio with one of the ship's bridge officers and gave a brief accounting of their ports of embarkation and destination. They agreed to pass port-to-port. As the ship was moving at 18 knots and *Romayne* was pushing eight, they passed each other much sooner that they'd estimated. The ship's side decks were lined with waving passengers, cameras flashing. The ship's deep-throated horn blew several loud blasts as a nautical salute to them. They waved to the passengers as the ship's bow wave hit the schooner.

The clock in the doghouse chimed six bells. Trish squinted at the clock. "Was that five or six bells?"

Sally looked at the clock. "Six; you're off watch. Gilley, would you mind taking the next watch? I'm a bit tired, and I want to take a nap before I make dinner."

"Sure thing, what's for dinner?"

"That, sir, depends on what kind of a fish you catch. We're out of mahi-mahi, but we have flying fish."

Gilley set Arthur on course and streamed the taffrail log, locked it and looked up at the sails. "Well, she's trimmed, right on course, next stop Pape'ete. Forty-eight hundred miles northwest, here we go."

"Good." Trish smiled. "I could sail on this old girl forever, as long as you're onboard."

"That can be arranged, as long as we don't meet any out-of-control freighters."

DAY 20 from Cape Horn

1200 Hrs. 20°42' S. Lat. 130°10' W Long: Noon-noon 244 NM. Wind 270° @ 12- 15 K. Speed: 8-10 knots. Sea 6': Sky starry clear. Next landfall Pape'ete 1058 NM northwest: ETA Tahiti 5-6 days with luck.

Well, here we are on big blue again; we've been under way for 20 days and nights, heading for the Society Islands. Tahiti, Moorea, Bora Bora. We called it paradise in the old days. Daddy used to tell his friends after the Tahiti race that we were there at the best of times, before the girls were charging for it. I know some of the crew on Bojangles got laid (even some of the married guys, naughty boys). And a few got the clap and had to go to another race boat to get their butt shots of penicillin from the sympathetic wife/nurse of their skipper.

Sixteen days ago we sailed over the memorial site. We took our sun sights together, and we both knew we were sailing over that sacred patch of water, which will never be the same since Gilley's wonderful memorial service.

So here we go again, but this time we really are chasing sunsets. We so much look forward to revisiting Tahiti; of course, Gilley has some friends to see after eighteen years away on the high seas. It'll be interesting for Sally to experience this fascinating island society, and I'll have fun showing it to her. We are five or six days from our landfall, and we've been sailing very carefully, especially at night. It seems the nasty squalls hit us at night, so we just run off and they only last about 10 minutes. But I always hate them at night because you can't see them, but we're getting good at handling the old girl as they blow through.

46

"You awake, Trishy?" Sally whispered from her bunk.

Trish grunted. "No, why?"

Sally sat up and looked at the clock. "It's six bells, your watch."

"No way, I just went to bed."

Sally slid off her bunk and stuck her face next to Trish's pillow and kissed her cheek. "Wakie wakie, you've been down for six hours. I'll get some breakfast."

Trish stretched and eased herself out of the sleeping bag. "I'm going to complain to the stupid management; I'm not getting enough sack time." She looked out the doghouse door to the unmanned helm. "Where's Gilley?"

"Probably walking the deck. I'm off to the galley."

Trish put on her shorts and sweatshirt, and barefoot went out on deck. Gilley was leaning on the forward bulwarks, looking ahead. She snuck up behind him and wrapped her arms around his waist.

"A penny."

He looked around at her. "A penny?"

"Yeah, a penny for your thoughts."

He turned around. "Oh, I was just looking at the Albert Ross family over there, and I was thinking about some of my old pals in Tahiti that I haven't seen for too many years."

Trish watched the pair of Royal albatross as they swooped over the wave tops. "Old girlfriend pals?"

"No, my good friend, Daryl Pritchard, who crewed with me on the *Tiara Topero*. Later he became a five-star restaurateur. I figure he should be good for a meal or two. Also Gigi Gullete, he was Chief of Customs, he recommended me for the job on that trading schooner. Come to think about it, he did the same for the skipper's job on *Te Vahine*. The best Frenchman I ever knew; I owe him a lot."

"And beautiful vahines?" She gave him a leering grin. "So only five more days, lover boy, and we'll be in paradise and check everyone out."

"They're probably all fat and have lost their teeth by now, the way a lot of them go when they hit fifty."

"Aw, no, I'll bet they're still beautiful. I remember some of them, they were a lot of fun too." Trish watched two albatross skim over the wave tops, then abruptly pull up and land ahead of the schooner, right beside a bright orange, partially submerged container. It broke the surface momentarily, then submerged again. It took a moment for the unusual image to register the danger into her brain. She pointed. "Gilley! Container dead ahead." She spun around and ran aft to disengage the wind vane.

She heard Gilley's heavy footsteps behind her.

"Unlock Arthur, I'll get the wheel!"

Trish reached for Arthur when the schooner's bow impaled itself on the sharp corner of the large steel container. The sudden impact lifted the bow out of the water, which knocked her onto the deck. Gilley tripped and sprawled onto his stomach and face. At that moment, the shackle on the running back stay block exploded with a loud pinging sound. The main topmast was no longer supported from aft. The large fisherman sail was putting a severe bow on the mast. Trish was dazed from hitting her head on the deck. She rolled over and looked aloft to see the topmast bend forward. Gilley shook his head, wiped the blood from his nose. He got onto his knees. They could hear and feel the container bumping and scraping under the hull until it broke the surface like a whale. The strange sound of the top-mast cracking shot down to the deck. Trish held her breath in horror, as the mast broke at the upper mast band. She screamed, "Gilley! Look out, the mast!" He looked up quickly and rolled under the Whitehall. The jagged end of the mast came straight down, blasted a hole in the bottom of the Whitehall, and smashed Gilley's left leg. The large spar slowly fell forward onto the deck and lay motionless.

He let out a blood-curdling scream. "Aw, goddamn son of a bitch, the fucking mast got my leg!"

Trish ran forward and knelt beside him, then Sally appeared, stunned. "Oh, God, no!"

Trish held his head. Sally looked at his flattened and twisted lower leg and foot. The skin and muscles were ripped open in a long gash, and several splinters of bone were protruding from the wound. Blood was seeping out of the torn flesh and onto the deck.

"Gilley, don't move. I'm going to get you a shot of morphine right now. Trishy, don't let him move. We'll have to get him inside as soon as I shoot him up, then I've got to tourniquet his thigh to stop the bleeding." She looked into Trish's' terrified eyes and shook her head as if giving her a signal. She left them and disappeared below.

Gilley's eyes glazed over, then partially opened and blinked in pain. "Oh, man! I got a load of hurt here."

Trish leaned over his face, smoothed his disheveled hair and kissed his forehead. "Hold on, darling, she'll be back with the morphine right away." She glanced up at the mainsail and jibs still pulling hard and driving the schooner with Arthur steering the same course to Tahiti.

She was too shocked to consider what could happen next, except the pain-relieving drug and Sally. Yes, Sally would know what to do. She could put a cast on the broken leg. And—and. Let's see, where are the crutches? Sally would know; she's the nurse, the R.N. Twenty years in the operating room, thank God for Sally. And of course she would pray. I know she's praying right now.

Sally slipped on rubber gloves and knelt beside Gilley's prone body. She loaded the syringe with a quarter-grain of morphine and injected the pain-relieving drug into his thigh muscle. "Gilley, take deep breaths. You'll be out of pain by the time I've finished this sentence. I can see that you are almost there. You'll experience euphoria just like Helen's magic medicine. How's that now, okay?"

"Holy Jesus, the pain's going. So what now Doc, a cast?"

"Now I'm going to put this tourniquet on." She carefully wrapped it around his thigh and tightened it with a wood dowel until the blood flow stopped.

"Good, now I've got to splint your leg and foot so we can move you into the doghouse and onto the bunk. How do you feel, Gilley?"

"A little woozy and high, but there's no pain."

"That's good. Just hold on, I'll be right back."

Trish made a quick look around for enemy, then kneeled beside him and raised his head, cradling it on her knees. Her hands were shaking as she stroked his forehead and leaned over his face. "Sweetheart, you're doing fine and Sally'll be—oh, here she is."

Sally laid wood splints on both sides of his leg, then slipped some cloth ties under and tied them firmly on top. "There, that should do the trick. Now, Gilley, this won't be easy, but we have to get you inside. I want you to sit up and try to scoot backward on your butt. We'll help you."

He sat up slowly and put his hands on the deck beside his thighs. "That's good, just kind of do a butt walk and push with your other foot. We don't have far to go." Sally glanced at Trish and nodded. "Okay, here we go, slow and easy."

The two women pulled his shoulders as he inched his way along beside the doghouse and around the corner. Finally, with enormous team effort, Gilley was lying on the bunk, gasping. Trish propped him up with pillows and secured the weather cloth to prevent him rolling off the bunk. "Comfy?"

"Yeah, so far. Hey, is that water, you hear it?" He looked over the edge of the bunk to the steps below. Trish and Sally looked down and saw nothing. "That goddamn container must have punched a hole in her. Trish, go to the foc's'le quick!" Suddenly the auxiliary generator started. "Close the watertight door if—"

The noise from the generator muffled his last words as she jumped down the steps.

"It's water under the sole!" She shouted, and raced forward to the galley, through the crew's quarters to the closed watertight door to the foc's'le. She heard water on the other side and under the bunk. Panicked and confused, she opened the locking dogs. An enormous gush of water forced the door open and knocked her down. Water poured in through a large open gash in the hull. Several teak hull planks were stove inwards and two frames were splintered, protruding at strange angles. She looked around at the crew bunk and pulled two pillows off and tried to stuff them into the opening. The force of the water ripped them out of her hands and drenched her. She was blown back onto her knees. "Shit." She pulled the mattress from the upper bunk and tried to stuff the end it into the hole, but it was forced back as well. "Fuck!" She pushed on the door with every ounce of her strength, but the force of the water overpowered her.

She kneeled to look under the lower bunk. The watertight bulkhead had broken away from the hull, allowing water to pour through the opening under the bunk, then into the bilge and the mate's cabin. She quickly opened the sole hatch to let the water drain into the bilge to be devoured by the series of bilge pumps. She retreated to the galley and realized that she had to close the second watertight door.

The force of the water against the door made it impossible to unhook the locking latch. "Oh, come on, release, you bastard." She put her shoulder against the edge of the door and one foot against the bulkhead behind her and pushed as hard as she could, then reached around the edge of the door and lifted the latch.

She was just able to hold it until she inched her feet into the galley. Suddenly her wet feet slipped out from under her and the steel door slammed with a loud bang. Out of breath, she got to her feet and dogged the latches. "Bloody hell!"

Gasping, dripping wet, she went through the salon and up to the doghouse. "Oh, man!"

Sally was mopping Gilley's face and looked at Trish's disheveled wet hair.

He turned his head. "How big's the hole?"

Her shaking hands indicated about two feet. "I couldn't close the foc's'le door because of the force of water, and the bulkhead is bashed in and the water's pouring through. I finally got the galley door closed and that stopped it. I opened a hatch so it would drain into the bilge; I guess that's why the genie fired up."

"Yeah, yeah, the automatic sensors fired it off. Sure hope they can handle it."

Sally looked at Trish with a concerned expression. "Trishy, will you give me a hand? I need to bring some stuff up here. We'll be back in a minute, Gilley, hang in there."

Trish quickly went on deck to check for traffic again. Seeing nothing, she joined Sally.

They entered Sally's cabin. "Trishy, it's bad, really bad. His tibia is completely smashed, it's just splinters. The calf muscles are ripped to pulp. His leg is only holding on by some muscle and skin. It's virtually severed. A cast is out of the question. There's no choice, Trishy; I have to amputate right away. This is life-threatening. I just hope his heart is as strong as he is."

Trish's mouth opened but no words came for several moments. "Oh, no. This is terrible. Sally, do you—?" She stared into Sally's bright eyes, held her and whispered, "I'm scared, are you?"

Sally shook her head. "No, no I'm not. I should be in a panic, but the surgeon I worked with on many amputations always said to me before an operation, 'Sally, we are going to save his life.' So, Trishy, I'm counting on you to help me."

Trish helped her up the steps with the plastic box that contained the operating equipment.

Sally took his hand. "Gilley, I'm sorry to tell you that your leg is very badly smashed. A cast won't work. I have to amputate your leg below the knee, and I need you to give me permission to operate."

He stared at her. "Holy Jesus, are you—sure?"

She nodded and glanced at Trish, whose tears were rolling down her cheeks, then focused on Gilley again.

"I'm absolutely positive your lower tibia is smashed to splinters for about eight inches above your foot. The calf muscles are torn to shreds. I've never personally done an amputation, but I've assisted at hundreds of them. Gilley, I'm confident that I can do it. And I really have no choice. What do you say?"

He looked at her, then at Trish. "Umm. Well, I guess if you put it that way."

He glanced down at his twisted foot. A slight grin creased his face. "How about that? Well, you know Sally, as a kid, I always wanted be a pirate and have a peg-leg. Arr! You know, so I could wear an eye patch and have a parrot on my shoulder squawking, 'Pieces of eight.' So did you bring a peg-leg in your box of tricks?"

She forced a weak smile. "Damn it, I completely forgot that, but I brought crutches. I'm sure we can get you a peg-leg in Pape'ete." Her expression quickly turned serious. So I assume that's a yes?"

"Yup, okay. Let's go for it." He looked at Trish. "Sweetheart, you're skipper now."

Trish took his hand from Sally and held it tightly to her lips and kissed it as if trying to draw some strength from him. "Sally, will you give me a hand? We've really got to stop the old girl and heave her to."

"Fine, let's slow this motion."

"Yup, I'll get her set up. I need you to drop the jib."

Trish unlocked the wind vane, took the wheel and very slowly brought the bow up into the wind until all the sails luffed and the schooner lost all forward motion. "Drop 'em." The jib flapped and shook until it piled onto the deck. The main and foresail were luffing and completely depowered. She slowly brought the wheel all the way to starboard and locked it so that the rudder was acting like a hull break. *Romayne* was simply put to sleep. Together they furled and lashed down all the sails except the foresail, which they left up and sheeted in to act as a steadying sail. "Well, that went a hell of a better than I expected. Let's back the staysail over on the shrouds and we're done. So, old girl, you're going to have a good rest, and for Chrissake, don't hit another container, okay?"

"So, Trishy, all I need you to do is to pass me instruments and shine the flashlight if I need it. I'll show you what they are."

Trish put her hand on Sally's shoulder. "Sure. Are you alright?
"Yeah."

Gilley was obviously enjoying his morphine-induced euphoria, and smiled at the women wearing surgical masks and caps.

After scrubbing their hands, they put on rubber gloves, and Sally slipped her fingers under the tourniquet to check for tension.

She told Trish what the instruments were.

Sally removed the splints and prepared her instruments on the other bunk, then draped a sterile cloth over his thighs. Trish put a sterile rubber sheet under his legs.

. "Gilley, are you comfortable?"

"Oh yeah, just fine, never better. Say, that juice is terrific; how long does it last?"

"Until it starts to hurt, then I'll shoot you up again." She looked over at her assistant. "Are you ready?"

She nodded. "Yup."

Sally held Gilley's leg just below his knee and felt the pulverized bone from below the knee to below the break. She drew a line with a marker around the leg where she would make the incision. She loaded a syringe with Marcaine and injected all around the line. "This'll take a few minutes, so just relax and take deep breaths."

She held out her hand. "Scalpel." She pricked the tip on his foot and leg, and looked for a reaction. He didn't flinch.

Trish watched the scalpel slice into his leg and looked at his face. The blade penetrated and Sally stopped just in time for a blood vessel. "Whoa, don't cut that one. Hemostat." Sally clamped the vein, then tied if off and finished by piercing it and tying that off to insure it would hold; then she cut it away. "Sponge. One down."

Trish mopped Sally's sweaty brow and then her own. "Scalpel."

Trish heard the clock strike four bells and stole a peek at the clock. Ten o'clock in *Romayne's* doghouse operating room. The surgeon was still strong, with one knee braced against the bunk and the other foot back to steady her body from the slow roll of the hull. "Saw."

A very neat cut with the new saw blade made short work of the tibia. The smaller bone on the outer side of the leg, the fibula, was severed quickly.

"Scalpel, and now a slice through the gastrocnemius, the larger calf muscle and below it, the soleus. Now, someplace in here should be the peroneal muscle. Oh, there it is around the fibula. I knew that. Okay, now we've got the major arteries and veins called—called—what the hell are they called? Oh, yeah, the anterior and posterior tibial arteries and peroneal vessels. Gimme two hemostats. Tie off that last one, gotcha! Sponge. There's the one I'm looking for, the superficial peroneal nerve, tie that off, cut, goodbye. Gilley, I just want you to know your missing foot will either itch or hurt; it's called phantom discomfort. Now, all I have to do is gather the two flaps and close it up. Oh, wait a damn minute here. Trishy, will you release the tourniquet just a bit, so far okay, a little more. I have to make sure that I don't have any bleeders. Whoa! Hold it, there's a leaker. Hemostat! Now we'll tie that puppy off again. Got it. Okay—let the tourniquet off slowly. I'll wait a few minutes just to make sure. Okay, all the way off. So the best surgeon I ever worked with always made a final check that he didn't leave anything in the patient, no hemostats, no scalpels, sponges, yeah it's all gone, nothing left. Good, now I can close the flaps with a neat stitch, and another. Ten should do it and a few more, better safe than sorry. And let's leave a little opening for drainage. Now, some antibiotic powder all over the stump. And finally some absorbent dressing. Now, Trishy, would you wrap it with this Ace bandage? And I do believe we're done here. You didn't lose too much blood, Gilley, you'll make it back soon. Now I'll prop your leg up to keep the blood out of the stump. Finally a little mopping up, and we can all have a nice cup of tea."

Sally massaged and soothed his knee. "So now that you're about ten pounds lighter, how do you feel?"

"Oh, about ten pounds lighter, but no pain or strain. Did you save my tattoo?"

"Sorry, it was right below the incision. She reached for the leg, but a sudden roll of the hull shifted it from the edge of bunk and down the steps. They all looked down at it and laughed. "Oh well, I guess I don't need that anymore. I had that TE-VAHINE tattoo done in Pape'ete when I took command of her. So I guess I'll just have to have *"Romayne, Cape Horner"* done on my other leg, and you two should have tattoos as well."

Trish put her arm around his neck and kissed him. "Of course you will, and I still love you, even though you're ten pounds lighter." Sally wiped her tears with a bloodstained glove and leaned over to kiss her patient.

"You're a great patient, Gilley." Tears seeped through his smiling eyes.

"Thank you, Sally—for saving my life." They held him as he laughed. "I guess I'll be able to buy a parrot and an eye patch in Pape'ete."

Trish laughed. "Sure, why not? The cats will love it."

47

Physically drained after the operation, Sally gathered up the surgical instruments into the box and went out on deck for some air. As Gilley's morphine was wearing off, the pain started to seep back into his non-existent leg and foot. She gave him a booster, mindful that she would have to taper off his dosage, as addiction was just down the road a bit. Although he was cavalier about the amputation, she knew it was just machismo talking.

They were approximately five days from landfall in Tahiti. Gilley discussed with them how they could make watertight repair to the open gash in the bow. He told them that when the repair was completed, the schooner would be seaworthy enough to get under way again. He was absolutely adamant against activating the emergency position-indicating radio beacon to signal for assistance via the satellites and marine rescuers. He insisted that they could make the repair and proudly sail the wounded schooner into Pape'ete with all colors flying. Sally felt confident he was strong and would survive as long as infection was kept out of the equation. She also knew, and told him, that she had to operate quickly, and waiting for rescuers would have been out of the question.

"I know damn well you two can patch the hull; hell, you just did a major amputation. This should be a piece of cake for you. Trish, about how much below the water line is the hole?"

She paused. "I'd say about a foot below and two feet above it. The hole is out of the water most of the time, because she's heeled over now. I'd sure like to stuff the mattress in there; I know it would keep some of the water out. What do you think?"

"First, we have to stop the water coming in from the outside. Here's what I know will work, because I've seen a crashed bow that was patched this way. The wind is giving us a little chop on the holed side. I'm sorry; you'll have to work on the weather side, because we want the hole completely out of the water. The foresail and maybe the main will keep her heeled over. There's a storm staysail in the sail locker that we can use for a big bandage on the bow. Give me paper and a pencil and I'll draw a diagram and show you how to do it. And I really need to be there with you to give you directions. Sally, have you got a wheelchair stashed away someplace?"

"Afraid not, but I'm sure I remember wheels on the captain's chair before we left Sausalito. Right?"

Trish stared at him. "Yeah. Gilley, you took the wheels off the captain's chair; where'd you put 'em?"

His face lit up. "Brilliant, good girl, they're in the bottom left desk drawer, so all you guys have to do is get the chair up on deck. Yo ho ho, have wheels, will travel." The opiate had elevated his morale, and they rode the high with him as Sally handed him a pad and pencil.

He drew a simple sketch. "Here's what we do. We lay the foot of the staysail along the starboard cap rail, tie the clew down to a cleat and tie the tack forward to a shackle. Then we drape the head of the sail with a line on it over the hole, then lead the line under the bow and up to the port cap rail and secure it. Now we have a bandage. Are you with me so far?"

They both nodded. Trish pointed to his sketch. "Yeah, but I don't think that'll hold, because the force of the water on the bow would get in behind the sail and tear it away. Right?"

"Yes it would, but I have several pieces of thin plywood under my mattress that are perfect to place over the canvas to cover the hole and nail it to the hull. Also, I have a bundle of oak sail battens to nail all over the edges of the bandage so it won't allow water to get behind it."

Sally looked doubtful. "So how do we get over the side to do this, hang by our feet?"

"Good question. We rig a bosun's chair from the anchor davit, which has a block and tackle that we can lower and raise and also swing the davit fore and aft. We pass the plywood and battens to the installer, who does the job and Bob's your uncle. But, whoever does the job gets soaked. Okay?"

"And of course, you're going to volunteer as installer?"

He shook his head. "Nay, nay lass, I'm now handicapped, remember?"

Sally gave him an unconvincing stern look and held both hands up in front of his face. "Gilley, these hands just held a scalpel and now you expect them to hold a hammer?"

Trish held up her hand. "No problem, I'll do hammer and nails."

Gilley grinned. "Good, and I'll double the grog rations."

Sally faked a smile. "Oh, goodie, I can't wait."

They decided to rest and do the repair in the morning. The water that was coming in through the hull was immediately pumped overboard, and they felt secure now, with both watertight doors locked. They were more concerned for the cats that hadn't been seen since the collision. Trish searched the schooner from stem to stern. "Robin! Bear! Come out, wherever you are. I have some mahi-mahi." She heard a weak meow coming from Gilley's cabin and traced it to an open locker beside the bunk. "There you are, you poor kitties, no wonder you're hiding, with all the scary crash bang." She carried them to the galley and sliced some flying fish. "There you are. So when you've finished, come up on deck to see uncle Gilley; he's worried about you."

The next morning, rested and refreshed after breakfast, Trish and Sally lifted the Captain's chair on deck and installed the wheels. Gilley was happy in his new wheeled chair with his leg propped flat on a board. They guided him to the starboard bulwark and lashed the chair to it. Next, they dragged the heavy sail to the deck, and with difficulty, unfolded it. "God, Gilley, it's stiff as a board. We'll never be able to wrap it around the bow."

"Just attach the head of the sail to the davit block and dunk it in the water. It'll limber up fast."

Following Gilley's instructions, the sail was transformed to a tight-fitting hull bandage. Then Trish, secure in the bosun's chair, was surprised how easy it was with Sally holding the plywood, to nail the plywood through the canvas onto the hull, covering and sealing the hole. "Trish, space the nails about two inches apart. I want to make sure the plywood is really on there."

After two hours, Trish was soaked, but the plywood patch and sail battens were well secured by copper nails. They moved the davit to the port side so that she could nail the sail battens over the edges of the sail on the port bow. They had made a complete seal that would prevent any water from entering the hull.

"Now, Trish, you can do your mattress-and-pillow-stuffing plan. Just lay it between the busted hull planks and lash it tight as you can to the inner ceiling planks; that should do it."

They wheeled him back to the doghouse and helped him onto his bunk. Sally made him comfortable and propped up his leg. "I want you to get some sleep, and if you have pain, give me a shout and I'll give you a little boost. Sweet dreams."

Trish stuffed pillows around the broken frames, laid the mattress against them and lashed it tightly. She closed both steel doors and dogged the latches, then climbed the stairs to the doghouse, where Sally was changing Gilley's dressing while he slept. She whispered into her ear, "Seems to be a lot of blood, is it okay?"

Sally nodded, "Yeah, this is normal wound drainage. It's fine. The only thing to worry about is infection, so I'm putting a lot of antibiotic powder on it. Keep your fingers crossed."

"For sure, he's had a massive shock to his system and he needs lots of rest."

"We all do." Sally secured the ace bandage, pulled off her gloves and joined Trish at the cockpit table. "God, I'm totally knackered. How about you?"

"I'm on my reserve tank, which is right on empty." She rested her chin on her hands. And I'm gonna lobby for heaving-to for the night. What do you say?"

"Hell, yes. Trishy, you're the skipper, let's do it. I'm done for." She plunked down on the settee, and within minutes she was fast asleep.

Trish swept the horizon with the binoculars; no ships or containers.

23 Days from Cape Horn

Noon fix. 20° 25' S Lat. 146°52 W Long. Course 315°: 23 days from Cape Horn: Wind S.E @ 15 K. speed 9 KT. Sea, 6'-8'. Clouds: cumulus. Morale: I'm okay, but exhausted. Gilley is high, and surgeon Sally is so totally cool.

Bloody hell, we hit a big steel container with our name on it. It punched a two- by three-foot hole in the starboard bow. A hell of a shock to our beloved schooner; she really took it on the chin. Thank God for the two watertight bulkheads and 12 automatic bilge pumps that spat a lot of water out. Then, even more terrifying, the main running backstay shackle let go and the main topmast broke and came straight down. It punched a hole through the Whitehall and right onto Gilley's left leg below the knee. The bones were pulverized so badly that Sally had to amputate. I was terrified. I barely remember how I got through it. Pure adrenaline, I guess. Sally knew exactly what she had to do. Her self-confidence kept all of us together.

In my opinion, she is a surgeon extraordinaire. She should get a medal for saving Gilley's life. My intuition insisted that she really had to be on this voyage. Never in my wildest dreams did I expect that it would be for life-threatening surgery. He came through it like a trooper, and he should get a medal, too. After the operation, Gilley was high as a kite on morphine. We hove-to and let our wounded Romayne rest. Gilley made me skipper; I'd never been so close to collapse. We had zip energy left and had to leave the repair till the next day. Next morning, Sally and I, under Gilley's direction, managed to make a jury repair and patched the hull. Who said two broads can't sail a 108' gaff schooner and patch a stove-in bow?

The patch is still holding, with slight seeping around the edge of the canvas; no big deal. We check it every hour. Now I know what real pressure is like for skippers.

We finally got under way the next morning. We're still able to take our three-hour watches as Gilley can take his sitting at the helm with his leg propped up on a pillow on a plank. Arthur steers all the time now. Sally and I monitor the radar, very little shipping, just a few island cargo coasters.

Thank God, no containers. I happened to spot the goddamn thing, but I couldn't get to Arthur and the wheel in time to change course. Perhaps there is some mystical reason that this terrible event took place, which has yet to be revealed to us humble sailors. If that mast had just been a little more—No, I can't go there.

We are 328 miles from Tahiti, and if the S.E. wind holds, we'll be in Pape'ete the day after tomorrow. That'll be a great relief for us, because we really have been put to the test on this leg. (No pun intended.) Gilley still has pain in his non-existent leg.

Sally was thinking about cutting him off the morphine and putting him on Demerol, as he was getting to like it too much. He insists on keeping it going, and said if he gets addicted, "Fuck it, I can go to the Betty Ford clinic."

Romayne, now partially bald-headed and in spite of the broken topmast, was sailing well under the four lowers. Again, the crew's vital energy was spared with the faithful service of Arthur steering night and day.

Sally was sound asleep in the doghouse. Trish came on watch and sat beside Gilley at the helm. She checked the compass, now steady at 315 degrees. "Hi there, see any enemy?"

"Just a small French coaster heading for the Tuamotus. You know, sweetheart, I've been thinking, maybe we should honor Arthur with a knighthood for his outstanding service. Don't you think Sir Arthur McWindvane kinda rolls off the tongue a lot better than just plain old Arthur?"

"Sure does, but hey, doesn't the Queen have to do the honors, you know, be-knight the chap on the shoulder with her sword?"

"No, as owner of the good ship *Romayne*, I have the right to honor any member of my crew I want. And, as President of the Pacific Ocean, I have awesome power on the Pacific, much more than the Queen of England. It would be a very simple little ceremony. I would just knight Arthur with a sail batten right there on the aft deck."

Trish put her hand on top of his. "I guess that would work, but I suggest you say, 'Arthur, thee are one hell of a fine helmsman, and with the powers bestowed upon me, I knight thee Sir Arthur McWindvane. Good on thee mate, steer small, and don't even think about stealing my girlfriend in port'. Ya like it?"

He roared, "I love it, let's do it."

They watched a pair of albatross glide alongside them. Gilley paused for a moment, then faced her. "And then, how about if some nice person would ask, 'Do you, Mary Patricia Cameron, take Gilley Alexander Cornwall to be your wedded husband?' Of course, that would be a much bigger ceremony."

Trish gasped, her eyes wide. "Oh—Oh my God! Yes, yes, I do, I mean I will. Gilley Alexander Cornwall, I will take you to be my wedded husband!" She draped her arms around his neck and kissed him tenderly.

"And—and look, my love, we have the Albert Ross couple as our witness. Oh, God, how absolutely perfect. Pinch me; is this a dream?" She waved to the floating birds as they sailed by them. "They're looking at us." Trish stood up and shouted to them. "And you're both invited to the wedding!"

She sat down as Sally appeared at the doghouse door. "What's all the shouting about? Invited to what wedding?" She joined them at the helm and scrutinized their tearing eyes. "Okay, what's going on?"

48

The western horizon slowly devoured the fiery red orb at the closing of the unforgettable day. For the umpteenth time, Trish revisited Gilley's carefully crafted words in his proposal to her, and smiled. She didn't see it coming; there was no hint that he was considering a full-blown commitment to her. He'd also told her that he wanted to make out his will right away and name her as his sole beneficiary. He said it was because of the accident, and he simply had to get his affairs in order. And as she was the most important affair in his life, he had to legally include her.

She watched a small pod of porpoise frolicking in the fading glow from the sunset. She flicked on the running lights and tested the strobe light on the foremast, and shouted, "Lights are bright, sir; light your pipe, sir; like your wife, sir." She chuckled at her father's old saying. "Hey, Mom and Daddy, Gilley and I are going to tie our knot." She threw her fist into the air.

She was excited that they'd be making their landfall in Pape'ete at dawn, when she would be on watch again. She wondered what changes they would see in the old, magical paradise that she'd experienced twenty-eight years ago when she first met Gilley. Now she wondered who would be at the quay to greet and congratulate them for doubling Cape Horn and bringing a wounded Captain on a patched-up schooner into Pape'ete under sail.

"Yo, land ho, Tahiti dead ahead!" Gilley's deep voice boomed out to his crew in their bunks.

Trish and Sally woke immediately, and with hair flying, went on deck to see the sight they had been dreaming about. Gilley handed Trish the glasses. "You can just see the tip of Mount Orohena through the clouds."

Trish sat beside Gilley and gave the glasses to Sally. "Good morning, darling. What a great way to wake up."

"None better. Have a good sleep?"

"I never get enough, but today, it doesn't matter."

He squinted as he looked up at the sails. "Speed's down to six knots. I really want to her sail in. You know, someday we'll look back on this adventure and wonder just how the hell we did it?"

"Well, the first thing is the reason we did it, and that's because we believed in your vision. I'm damn sure we all needed a change from our fucked-up lives. That's why we did it, but how did we do it? For sure, *Romayne* is a major player, and she had three capable sailors to drive her. We also had Sir Arthur and a hell of a lot of luck. Does that make sense?"

"Yeah, but if it hadn't been for you getting me off the hash and my ass, we'd still be back in Sausalito, twiddling our—whatevers. So here we are, slightly bruised, but ready for the next chapter."

"Which is, we're engaged, I'm just getting used to saying it. And I'm going to lobby for Helen to marry us. I'm sure she's still a minister in the Universal Life Church, and I know she's married quite a few happy people. What do you think?"

"Perfect. She's the only person to tie our knot. And I want to have my old mate, Daryl Pritchard in Tahiti, for my best man, and Ish and Jon Ewer for groomsmen."

"Absolutely, and I've gotta have Alfi to give me away, Daddy would insist. I think we have the beginnings of a terrific wedding party, if we can get all of them to show up. I'll call Helen and Alfi as soon as we land. I'm so stoked about this; I am finally getting married at forty-five to the most wonderful man. Yeah!"

"Thanks, and to the most amazing lady in the world. Of course, we'll need a red-hot Tahitian band for those who want to dance, and with luck I'll have my peg-leg so I can dance with my beautiful wife. And what do ya say that everyone wears pareus — you know, make it a full-up Tahitian wedding in Cook's Bay?"

"Oh yes, yes, that'll be absolutely awesome!"

Sally stood before them, holding the breakfast tray, and gave it to Trish. "Absolutely, what?"

"We were talking about the wedding and dancing with my husband for the first time." Sally sat beside them and took her bowel of muesli. "How long before he'll be able to wear his peg-leg? Any idea?"

"Well, if there's no infection, maybe a month or so. The stump is naturally going to be tender for quite a while, and they have to custom-make the prosthesis. Let's see what a doctor says."

"We'll have a lot of loose ends this end; to send invitations and muster the regiment to make their arrangements for time off, book flight tickets, and then all the details. I better make a list."

49

Trish hoisted the small French tricolor courtesy flag under the starboard cross-tree, which was *Romayne's* formal signal that this visiting Canadian yacht with her large ensign flying was paying her respects to the old French colony. Then she hoisted the small yellow Q flag under the port cross tree, which indicated to the colony's custom and immigration officials that this vessel's crew is healthy and not importing any disease that could infect the general population. However, irrespective of the fact that her famous captain had his leg amputated at sea, and is certainly bruised, but definitely not diseased, no flag had yet been invented to signal that his vessel had collided with a steel container that punched a sizable hole in the bow; the main topmast carried away and smashed the Captain's leg to mush. All the bunting is signaling that he is requesting permission to enter this fine old harbor to take care of a few repairs, revisit old friends, and marry his sweetheart in Cook's Bay; and who knows what else?

The wind had died to a zephyr as the schooner approached the pass into Pape'ete harbor under mainsail and jib. Sally was standing by the mainsail halyards, ready to drop it. The Gardener diesel was quietly ticking over.

Gilley was intent on sailing *Romayne* through the pass and around the dog-leg to port, as he had done so many times years ago in the *Tiare Topero*.

Trish stood on the bowsprit to guide him in through the pass. She faced aft and shouted, "You can turn in now; all clear, nothing moving." Then she spotted a small French-flagged cabin launch setting out from the long quay, headed in their direction. "There's a boat coming our way. It looks official." She slid back to the deck and stood by the jib halyard.

Romayne glided into the center of the harbor as Gilley rounded her up into the dying breeze. "Drop 'em!" Trish released the halyard and watched the jib drop into the net. They quickly furled it and tied the gaskets. Together they lowered the mainsail and secured it to the boom.

Gilley watched the launch come alongside and immediately recognized Koko, his Tahitian engineer on the trading schooner. He jumped onto the deck and grasped Gilley's hand. "Ia ora na, Captain Gilley, you're a sight for sore eyes, you old salt, it's great to see you again."

He stood up, holding onto the wheel for balance. "Koko, my good friend, it's been too long, but wonderful to see you again. This calls for a hug, old friend. So you're a pilot now."

"Yeah, I took your advice and signed up. It's a great job, good pay, and a pension. Now, I come home to my family every night. So whose schooner you driving? Looks like you took a hit on the bow and the stern?"

"Schooner's mine, Koko, and we hit a goddamn container. The backstay let go; the topmast broke and busted my leg. Sally over there had to amputate it. But I'm okay." He sat down and patted his knee.

He looked down at Gilley's leg, shocked. "Holy Jesus, man, you need to see a doctor, eh?"

"Yeah, I guess so." He called Trish and Sally aft. "Koko, I want you to meet my fiancée, Trish Cameron. And this is Sally Brown, our good friend and my personal surgeon. Koko was my engineer; now he's a ship's pilot."

They shook hands. "Io ora na, ladies. Welcome to Tahiti. So,

Gilley, where's the rest of your crew?"

Gilley turned and pointed at Sir Arthur. "He's right there, Sir Arthur McWindvane."

Koko showed surprise as he studied the windvane briefly, then looked back at Trish and Sally. "Just three of you, amazing. Where did you sail from?"

"We sailed from San Francisco to Cape Horn, then here. Very happy to be here, too, because I gotta get her hauled for repairs. Is Boisson's yard still going strong?"

Koko looked over his shoulder and pointed to a large crane next to a long shed and fishing boats alongside. "Sure is. Old man Boisson retired, and his son, Jules, is manager now. He's doing a good job, too. Let's go over there; you can lay alongside. Customs and Immigration will check you in there." He signaled the launch driver to return to the pilot base. "So you finally got your big schooner. She's beautiful, Gilley, and Jules can fix you up. They have real good ship-wrights, a new dry dock and three rails." He pointed to the dock. "There's space on the holding dock." Trish and Sally dropped the fenders over the side as Gilley brought the schooner alongside. They tossed the lines to the dock crew. Koko stepped ashore. "Gilley, I'll go and get Jules to see when they can haul your schooner."

They watched him disappear inside the yard office. Trish sat beside him. "Sweetheart, do you suppose we can find a phone to call Helen, Alfi and all of our friends?"

"I'll ask Koko. They should have a satellite phone in the pi-lot's office."

Sally handed Gilley his crutches. "Can you ask Koko to call for a cab to the hospital? I want a doctor to check you out and get an X-ray. But right now, I want you to take a turn or two around the deck to get your circulation going, then I'll change your dressing. Up you get. I'll walk with you."

Surprised, he looked up at her. "Okay, if you say so."

He held the crutches and took a step. Sally held his arm. "That's it, start off slowly, one small step for whomever, one giant leap for you."

Together they walked to the bow, stopped for a minute, and then continued back to the cockpit. "Good, that's enough for your first outing, now sit and put your leg on the seat."

Sally slipped on rubber gloves and removed the bandage. Trish joined them as Sally examined Gilley's stump. "It looks good; minimal drainage and absolutely no sign of infection. Trishy, would you put the bandage on your fiancé, and I'll get some tea. Fiancée! I've gotta get used to it."

Trish had just completed the bandage as Koko came aboard with a young man beside him. "Gilley, you remember Jules, who was just a kid when you sailed away on *Te Vahine*."

They shook hands. "Of course I do. It's great to see you again, Jules. I remember you'd made a very nice radio-controlled sailboat, and you and I sailed it off the dock right here."

"It's good to see you again, Captain Gilley. I certainly remember you and the schooner when it was in the yard many years ago; I think I was about nine at the time."

He held Trish's hand. "Jules, I'd like you to meet my fiancée, Trish Cameron from Sausalito, a great little town across the bay from San Francisco."

Trish shook his hand and smiled at the tall young man. "It's nice to meet you, Jules."

"And you, Trish. I'm happy for you. He's a fine man, and some say he's a pretty good sailor." He glanced at Gilley and winked. "I'm very sorry to hear about your accident." He looked down at Gilley's bandage. "But I'm glad you are going to be okay."

"Thank you, Jules. I'm sorry we have to meet like this, but we've got some damage fore and aft."

"Yes, I noticed. We can haul you first thing in the morning and start the repairs. And I offer you anything you might need, phone, hot showers, two-twenty volts."

"Good, we have some calls to California if that's okay?"

"Yes, we just installed a new sat phone. So may I see the damage to the bow below so I'll know what we need to do?"

"Sure, Trish will show you. She and Sally did the repair."

Sally arrived and put the tea tray on the table. "Oh, here she is. Sally, this is Jules Boisson, the boat yard owner." They greeted and shook hands.

Trish led Jules to the foc's'le. He helped her undo the lashing and pulled the mattress away."

"Oh, mon Dieu, that was a serious collision! Did she take on much water?"

"Yes, but luckily, I was able to close the watertight doors. We'd installed twelve automatic bilge pumps before we left California, and they pumped a lot of water."

"Good work. So you and Sally made the patch?"

"Yeah, it was Gilley's idea that you can use a storm jib for other things beside sailing. He showed us how to do it. He really knows what to do when a boat gets in trouble."

"Yes he does; he's amazing. Now, let's see: there are three broken frames, and maybe four or five broken hull planks and four inner ceiling planks. Then we have the main topmast, which needs a scarf joint. And I noticed the starboard cap rail and bulwark are damaged. Um, this should keep us busy for a while."

"Oh, and the Whitehall shore boat has a hole in its bottom. So approximately how long do you think?"

"I'll put three of our best shipwrights and two apprentices on it. They work very carefully together. Perhaps four weeks should do it. Then we'll have to prep and paint the starboard hull, and there might be some damage to the underbody. I'll know better when we get her on the ways tomorrow morning. You've certainly had an amazing voyage with some serious difficulties. I'm very impressed." He took a small digital camera from his pocket and fired off a few shots to document the hull damage.

They returned to the cockpit. "Well, Gilley, it was a terrible hit, but luckily you have watertight bulkheads and your pumps. We can repair your hull and mast in about four weeks. I expect there may be some damage to the underbody, but we'll see tomorrow. So, Gilley, if you'll excuse me, I'll make up the job order and give you a quote for the time and materials. It's great to see you again after so many years, and let's have a longer visit soon."

He gave them a genuine smile and stepped ashore.

"Koko, I'd like to ask a favor of you if you have time?"

"Sure skipper, what do you need?"

"I'd like to call Daryl Pritchard; could you—?"

"Sure, I have his cell number in my phone memory." He scrolled for the name and hit the numbers.

"Here, it's ringing on speaker mode."

"Pritchard!"

"Daryl, me old mate, a voice out of the past, it's Gilley."

"No way, you salty old bastid. Where're you calling from?"

Gilley glanced at Trish and Sally and stuck his thumb up. "We're alongside at Boisson's. It's great to hear your voice. Any chance to see you?"

"God, man, we thought you'd sailed off the bloody edge. Yes, of course, I'm running the last errand in town. I need to pick up a case of plonk. How in the hell are you, mate?"

"Oh, a little the worse for wear and tear, Daryl, but I can still sit up and take nourishment. How about you?"

"Terrific, and all the better for hearing your voice. So you're alongside in what exactly?"

"Gaff schooner named *Romayne*; it's the only one here flying the maple leaf."

"Bloody good on yer, I'll be there in a flash."

Trish filled their mugs. "So, he's a Kiwi or Aussie?"

Gilley had a wide grin on his happy face as he handed the phone to Koko. "Yeah, a very wild Kiwi. How about that, he sounds just the same. Now, just to give you some background: When we met here umpteen years ago, he'd sailed in here as deckhand on a very boozed-up ketch from New Zealand. I sailed in from Panama, crewing on a yacht, about a week before, and the strongest liquid the owners had onboard was chamomile tea. So we met, became instant friends, and after we'd both blown what little money we had, we shipped out as deckhands on a copra schooner and went to work. He was a great shipmate, and could drink everyone under the table, even the Germans. It's amazing the two of us weren't thrown in the Bastille for life. I'll let him tell you about some of our more creative activities, always initiated by him, of course. He was outrageous."

Suddenly a Land Rover with the horn blasting pulled up beside the quay. A large man wearing shorts and a Tahitian shirt got out, waving a bottle, and approached.

"Arr, stand down me swabbies." He jumped onto the deck with a loud thump and held out his arms to Gilley, who stood awkwardly on his leg. They embraced each other for several moments.

"Goddamn, it's good to see you at last, my old friend. How are you, and who are these gorgeous ladies? G-dae, Koko, it's good to see you again, mate."

Trish and Sally looked on in amazement at this whirlwind of a man and how he dominated the meeting.

Gilley held Daryl at arm's length, grinning at his old friend. "Well, Daryl, to quote your old expression, 'I'm more like I am now than I was before,' but apart from having my leg amputated at sea, I'm just fine. It's bloody good to see you, white haired old bugger." He eased himself slowly onto the settee.

Daryl looked down. "Jesus Christ, Gilley, you really did. What the hell happened? Does this mean that we can't play football again? Just kidding." He stood holding Gilley's shoulder, stunned.

"Before I go into that, Daryl, I want you to meet my fiancée, Trish Cameron, and her lifelong friend, Sally Brown. We've just sailed from the Horn."

They exchanged long looks and handshakes. "I'm charmed to meet you, Trish and Sally; I can't wait to hear how you all met. My God, would you believe that I am, in fact, almost bloody speechless?"

Trish motioned to the settee with her hand. "It's good to finally meet you, Daryl. Gilley's told us a little bit about you; all good."

Daryl's big hand was still holding the bottle of Mount Gay rum on the table. He laughed loudly and held up the bottle. "I'm bloody sure that someplace on this planet the sun has gone over the yardarm, wouldn't you think? I wonder, would it be possible to have some glasses and ice so that we can toast each other with a long-overdue loving cup?"

Sally stood up, smiling at Daryl. "Absolutely, Daryl, but if you don't mind, I really want to have a surgeon check him out and get an X-ray, just to make sure there aren't any complications. Would that be possible?"

Daryl's expression immediately became serious as he studied her face. "Oh God yes, of course, Sally. I'm sorry, I wasn't thinking. It's something to do with age, I'm told."

Within minutes Daryl, Trish and Sally helped Gilley into the Land Rover and were headed for the hospital. Gilley gave Daryl all the details of the collision and amputation as they drove.

The orthopedic surgeon examined Gilley's stump. "The X-ray revealed a short split at the end of the bone, which will heal soon. Miss Sally, you are a fine surgeon and I am proud to shake your hand that did this operation under very difficult conditions."

He removed his gloves and offered his hand, which she took and smiled. "Thank you, doctor, but I had a wonderful patient and assistant; also, the scalpel and saw were very sharp."

"Excellent, Captain Gilley, I'd like to see you in about two weeks so that we can have you fitted for a prosthesis."

The top of the Mount Gay rum bottle was quickly removed, then sailed over the side. "So, Gilley, it takes your old friend to supply us with our long-overdue grog rations; shame on you, and good for you, Daryl. Oh yeah, the glasses and ice, I'll be back in a minute."

Gilley took the bottle and squinted at it. "Ah, the best sippin' rum, you remembered. Thanks for this."

"My pleasure. If memory serves, which it does occasionally, the last time we were together, we were drinking Mount Gay. So, Gilley, just the three of you on board, no mutinous crew ashore?"

"Yeah, just us, two cats and Sir Arthur McWindvane back there. He did most of the steering, while we just sailed, caught mahi-mahi, enjoyed delicious food and— whatever."

Trish listened to these two close friends catching up on the voyage, Gilley's memorial service and their forthcoming wedding. They were like long-lost brothers who had been regrettably estranged for many years, and finally found one another, both wondering why they'd failed to keep in touch over the years.

Sally put the tray on the table. "Belay the small talk, mates. Daryl, would you pour, sir, so that we can do some serious toasting?" Sally dropped ice cubes in the special glasses with *Romayne* engraved on them.

Koko returned from the pilot's office. "Looks like I'm just in time."

They all stood for Gilley's toast. "To old friends, and let's pledge that we never, and I mean never, get out of touch again, aye?"

Daryl held up his glass. "It's my great honor to toast Trish and Gilley on your forthcoming nuptials, and surgeon Sally. I reckon that's going to be a fair dinkum hoolie."

Koko stood and held up his glass. "To two of the best and wildest sailors I've ever known."

Trish stood and looked at Gilley. "Well, I want to toast Gilley, the incredible captain, and to my dearest friend, Sally. I love you both. Ohmigod, and to you Daryl, and Koko, for making us so welcome, thank you. We're delighted to meet you."

Over the next hour, they had brought each other up to date on their busy lives over the past decades. Daryl offered more rum, but Gilley held up his hand. "That's plenty for me, old friend. I'm meant to be on the wagon for the hard stuff; besides, my crew are slurring their eyes and crossing their words, and we have to go on watch." The doghouse clock struck eight bells. "It's your watch, Sally; course is three-one-five, steady as she goes there."

"Sally laughed. "Like hell, Sir Arthur is so well trained now, I'm going to turn it over to him."

Daryl looked at his watch. "Oh, I've got to get my rear in gear, we've finally sold the restaurant to our head chef and my wife Juliet, is putting on a home-cooked dinner for him and his family. Now, before I go, I assume you won't be living aboard and haven't made arrangements for lodging yet?" He glanced at Gilley.

"Not yet. Jules's secretary is going to find us a hotel."

Daryl held up both hands. "No, no, I won't hear of it. I have a ten-unit apartment building about four blocks along the waterfront, with a view of Moorea. It's a nice top-floor unit ready to take you in. It's yours, fully furnished, kitchen, full kit, two bedrooms, bathroom, linens, Jacuzzi tub, TV, the lot. So have your sea bags packed, call me when you're ready and I'll pick you up. It has an elevator and you can have it as long as you need it. Only five thousand a month—just pulling your leg, old man. Oh, Christ, that didn't come out right. Anyway it's on the house; no argument about that, I hope?" He drained his glass.

"Daryl, you know we've never argued about important things like a free apartment. Thanks, we accept, and I don't mind having my leg pulled, it doesn't hurt a bit."

Daryl gathered himself together, pecked Trish and Sally on both cheeks, then hugged Gilley and gave him a card. "My mobile number. Must dash, cheerio, mates; good to see you again, Koko."

He was about to step ashore when an attractive middle-aged Tahitian woman and a tall younger woman walked along the quay toward him. They stopped beside the schooner; the older woman noticed Daryl and called out to him.

"Ia ora na, Daryl, how are you?"

He paused and squinted at her. "Oh, my word, is it? Yes, it's Maeva. I haven't seen you for ages. I'm well, thank you." He looked over at the *Romayne* crew and pointed. "And look who just arrived, our old friend, Gilley, and his all-girl crew."

He shouted to Gilley. "Hey mate, you've got company. Please excuse me, dear, I'm running late, have to scoot, but I'll see you later." He stepped onto the quay and waved back at them.

Gilley looked over at the two women with a surprised expression. "Well, well Maeva, come aboard." He stood unsteadily as they approached. Maeva took Gilley's hand. "It's great to see you, Maeva. I'd like you to meet my fiancée, Trish, and her friend, Sally. Of course you remember Koko."

Koko smiled at them. "Hello, Maeva, it's good to see you again. Gilley, I'm sorry to say I have to get back to the office to log you in. I'll phone Customs and immigration. They'll be along soon."

Maeva appeared to be shocked when she noticed Gilley's amputation, then slowly looked up at his inebriated face. "Hello, Gilley." She then turned away from him and nodded to Trish and Sally. She studied their faces for a moment before she took their offered hands.

"This is my daughter, Micheline." Maeva said as she stared at Gilley.

Startled, Gilley took the young woman's hand and smiled at her. "It's a pleasure to meet you, Micheline. Please join us, won't you? Daryl almost succeeded in getting us drunk for his welcome party."

Maeva frowned. "I'm not surprised; I remember you two always drank much rum together, so it's just like the old days again." She glanced at her watch, then stared at his leg and pointed at it.

"What has happened, Gilley?"

He sat down and propped his leg on the settee.

Although a little drunk, emotionally exhausted and tired of having to repeat the story to everyone, Gilley tried to put a humorous spin on the event. "But the good part of it is that now I can have a peg-leg, wear an eye patch and have a parrot on my shoulder that squawks, 'Pieces of eight.'"

Micheline laughed and looked at her mother, who frowned.

"Mom, it's a joke. Gilley will play a pirate, like in the movies and his parrot will say 'Pieces of eight,' don't you get it?"

"Oh yes, I was—how do you say the word, I think, shock to see his injury. Excuse my English, I don't speak it much anymore. Yes, I remember, Gilley, you were always doing the silly jokes."

Micheline tried to put on a straight face. "You are a very funny man, Gilley. I can see a big red parrot on your shoulder, then it poops on your shoulder." She burst into laughter.

Maeva nodded. "So what brings you to Tahiti?"

He studied her handsome face for a moment before he answered. She had the exotic mix of a Tahitian mother and a Chinese father.

"Well, Maeva, I'll give the quick version. When I left here in *Te Vahine*, I knew that someday I'd come back, I just didn't know when. It's like I sailed into a completely new world. Anyway, the owners who I liked very much, wanted to cruise to every country in the world as a big geography lesson for their four youngsters. They had a crew of four, with teacher and a doctor on board."

He glanced at Trish and winked. She reached over and took his hand.

"Then, just by chance, I was anchored off the yacht club in Sausalito California, and I ran into Trish, who was teaching a Tai Chi class. Maybe you remember, Maeva, about twenty-eight years ago her Dad won the Tahiti Race, and she was the navigator?"

"No, I don't remember any of that; it was before I knew you. I was still living on Bora Bora."

"Well, anyway, after a lot of water passed under many keels, here we are, and we're going to be married on the schooner in Cook's Bay. After that, who knows?"

"Now, Maeva, what can I offer you to drink?" Trish asked. "We have some juices or tea?"

Maeva looked at her watch again, then over at the ferry that was berthed close by. She shook her head. "Nothing, thanks. We're going to Moorea on that ferry, and it leaves soon."

Trish smiled at her. "Well, maybe when you have more time to visit. I'm sure you have lots to catch up on. So please excuse us, we have to pack our bags because we're leaving the schooner early in the morning. It was nice to meet you, Maeva and Micheline."

Micheline smiled, then embraced Trish and kissed both cheeks. "Welcome to Tahiti." She turned to Gilley and asked with a grin, "Gilley, how did you decide which beautiful lady to marry?"

He grinned. "Ah—it wasn't easy. Well let's see. I had to toss a coin, you know, the best two out of three." He acted out the tossing of a coin, catching it and slapping it on the back of his hand."

Maeva looked on, obviously unimpressed. Micheline laughed and clapped her hands. "Wonderful. Trish, you're a lucky lady, and Sally, I know you'll find someone too, maybe a nice Tahitian man." She embraced Sally. You're very beautiful."

"Thank you Micheline, you're sweet to say so."

Trish waved to them as they entered the doghouse. "Gilley, I'll pack your bag."

Trish flopped down on the settee, Sally went to the galley and put the kettle on, then dropped into the captain's chair. "Jesus, how about that? I kinda gathered that Maeva wasn't pleased to see Gilley. Did you pick up on that?"

"Absolutely, and I assume they have some history together. Did he ever tell you anything about her?"

"No, he only mentioned Daryl and the old customs guy, Gigi. I asked him about old friends, you know old girlfriends, but he kind of blew it off. Actually, that was just when we hit the bloody container. But God almighty Sally, he was based here for six years; he could have had every girl on the island. Maeva had to be one of his squeezes, don't you think?"

The kettle started to whistle. "For sure, she's a knockout, just like her very beautiful, tall, blond-haired daughter. So what's that all about?"

"I don't know, but I'm beginning to wonder; a blond daddy?"

Sally handed Trish a cup of green tea. "This should sober us up. Man, that rum kicked ass; no more hard grog rations for this gal."

"Sure did, and it didn't last long the way Daryl was pouring it and we were inhaling it. He seems like a wild man. I'll bet he and Gilley cut a big swath around here in the old days. A pair of horny, handsome blond studs, all they had to do was wink at a vahine, and bingo."

"They didn't have to wink honey, they were probably fighting them off. Sailor's paradise, right?"

Sally topped up their cups. "Yeah, you know, Trishy, I've been thinking, maybe you could have some nice pillow talk and—Oh hell, I don't know, forget it."

After a short pause Trish leaned forward. "Yeah, and what?"

"Well you know—about Maeva."

They were shocked to hear Maeva shout something in Tahitian. They raced up to the deck to see Micheline crying. "No! I'm staying here. I'll get the next ferry." Maeva took off at a fast walk.

Micheline sat beside Gilley and reached over to hold his hand, which he opened to receive hers. He glanced at Trish and Sally, then back at Micheline. "Well, what do you know, I lost a leg and gained a daughter all in one week. That's got to be a first." He smiled up at Trish. "Sweetheart, would you and Sally hug my wonderful young daughter, and make her welcome on *Romayne*? She's part of the family now."

50

It was the first time Trish and Gilley had slept together in his cabin since they had anchored in Bahia Scourfield. She snuggled her head on his heaving chest and gasped into his ear, "Well, darling, that still works, not that I had any doubt about it." She kissed him again. "And now, besides our love for each other, we have your sweet, lovable daughter to love."

He stroked her hair, then, after a brief silence, said, "You're right, she is lovable and sweet. I just hope to hell I can get on an even keel with Maeva again." He paused. "I was completely blown to bits when she dropped the bomb on us."

"How did she say it?"

"These are her exact words. 'Micheline, now it's time to tell you the truth. Gilley is your real father, and he left me and sailed away before you were born.' I still can't believe it. I have a daughter. What an amazing day."

"Weren't you surprised when Micheline told us that her mother was married to a tall, blond Frenchman who she always thought was her father?"

"Yeah, he was her stepfather for a few years. Go figure."

"There's a lot of loose ends on this, like, we're they were married before she was born? But then she said they divorced and he went back to France when she was nine. It's all very mysterious."

"I have no idea. I guess Maeva kept her in the dark all those years. Maybe she thought it was best for her not to know until she was older, or maybe never. I'm sure she did what she thought was best for the child. It couldn't have been easy."

"If Maeva's looks could kill, you're the last person she ever expected or wanted to see. Now you have a daughter and a pissed-off mother who—well, doesn't like you very much."

"I was with her for about six months after I came back from the shipwreck. I was in bad shape. I'd lost a lot of weight. But I've gotta say, I owe her a lot; she pretty much nursed me back to health. And when I got back to normal again, *Te Vahine* was in commission and ready to go. I even asked her to come on as crew, but she didn't want to leave Tahiti and her family. So when the owner and his family arrived from England, we set sail for Panama and then to the Med. I had no clue she was pregnant. I doubt if she knew untill after I'd left."

"Were you in love with her?"

"Hell, what did I know about love then? It was just getting my health back, no strings attached. We never talked about marriage. I was committed for five years on the schooner, and she knew that. I honestly thought I'd go back to Tahiti someday, but by that time I was involved with someone else, and there were others, including my late wife. I was a very loose cannon then."

She rolled over and kissed him. "I don't think I'd want to be in your stable in those days. So how does the thought of monogamy grab you now? Do you think you can handle that?"

He held her tightly to him. "I really like mahogany, that's a very good dark wood for boat building. The salon and this cabin are paneled with it."

"Ha, ha, you know what it means; you'll have to be a good boy. Your days of sowing wild oats are over."

"Oh, that word, sure I can, and how about you? Will you still—you know, with Sally?"

"Hopefully not, if everything goes well and she gets involved with someone. And if that relationship doesn't happen and Sally needs me, I'll always be there for her. Would that be alright?"

"Of course, as long as I can be with you and watch."

"That'd be fine with me, but of course, it'd be up to her, you know. She may want privacy."

"That's a perfect arrangement, and for my final shot, there could never be anyone to compare with you, and if there was, I would kiss her on both cheeks and say, 'thanks, dear, but I'm a monogamous guy now, but my wife Trish, might be interested, she's ambidextrous.'"

"Ha, you still have a bit of the rogue in you. That's charming."

They were interrupted by Sally, standing at the open door, holding a tray with breakfast. "The top of the morning to you noisy lovers." She put the tray on Trish's lap.

"Good morning, sweetie. Thanks for breakfast in bed; that's a first."

Sally grinned as she sat on the side of the bed. "My pleasure. What time is Daryl coming by to take us to our new digs?"

Gilley glanced at the ship's clock as he munched on a muffin. "He said to call him when we're ready."

"Well, whenever, we're packed and ready to go. We just have to put the cats in their carriers. So Gilley, give me a shout when you're up. I want to change your dressing, and I'll call Daryl so he can take us to our apartment. Enjoy."

Gilley looked over at Trish and pointed aft. "You know, I was just thinking, we met about two hundred yards from here twenty-eight years ago on *Bojangles*. When your dad introduced you, I was bowled over that a seventeen-year-old girl had navigated the schooner that won the race. Do you remember that meeting?"

"I do, it was unforgettable. At first we were in shock that we were first over the line. We had no idea how far ahead because our transmitter packed up and we got no noon position roll calls from the other boats. Then, when the next boat came in about six hours later, that was unbelievable. Daddy gets the credit, because he figured the wind was stronger to the south. All I did was get noon fixes, no big deal. But the big deal for me was meeting you. You became my new pin-up boy. I even took a Polaroid of you, and I had to wait for a quarter of a century to see you again. This is like our first anniversary."

He leaned over to bury his nose in her hair and kiss her. "Happy anniversary, my love."

Daryl parked his Land Rover next to the quay just as the boat-yard crew were preparing the lines to pull the schooner along the dock and onto the marine railway. He jumped onto the deck.

"Good morning you salty travelers, I trust you're all rested and ready for your next adventure, which will be a bloody cake-walk compared to what you're been through."

"Morning Daryl." Gilley took his hand. "Yeah, we did, and you're just in time. They're gonna haul her right now, so we're in your good hands. All we have are three sea bags, two cats and their stuff. So let's watch her come out, to see how much damage the container did to her bottom."

"Of course, I'm completely at your service and we have all day, in fact, all week. My wife, Juliet, just left for New Zealand for a medical conference, and she'll be there for a week."

Daryl loaded the seabags, and Trish brought the cat carriers. Sally placed the litter box and cat food in the rear cargo space. Gilley led the way on his crutches over to the boatyard. They all sat on the viewing bench beside the rails, where the schooner was slowly pulled into position and onto the supporting blocks. When they were satisfied all was level and lined up, they waved to Jules.

He acknowledged their signals and rotated one arm in a circle, indicating that he was engaging the winch drum to the motor.

Gilley leaned over to Daryl. "Daryl, Maeva told me yesterday that I'm Micheline's father."

He swung around quickly, stunned. "No! I thought she was married to that French bloke, Jacques. My God, Gilley."

Gilley watched the activity on the ways as he spoke. "She told me in no uncertain terms. Micheline's eighteen now, and I left on *Te Vahine* eighteen years ago. Maeva and I were shacked up for about six months after I got back from the shipwreck. It all adds up, Daryl. Also, she's tall and blond, and Trish says we have the same eyes. Not much doubt about it, she's my daughter."

"Stone the crows. I remember meeting Maeva and Jacques and the girl about five or six years ago at our restaurant. She introduced him as her husband and their daughter. Come to think of it she was tall, blond and beautiful then. That must come as one hell of shock, just out of the blue?"

"Sure did. Micheline is delighted to meet her dad, and Maeva is totally pissed that I never made any contact with her."

"Well, so are the rest of us. You never sent a letter or Christmas card to anyone, bugger all. We really all thought you'd bought the farm, Gilley. A big bunch of demerit marks for you, mate."

"Yeah, I really failed on that one, but I was so involved with too many things and people. I was right out of the picture and in another world, another life. It won't happen again Daryl, for sure."

"Alright, you're forgiven." They all watched silently as the hull inched up the rails, gradually exposing the copper-sheathed underbody. Some of the copper sheets were torn and hanging where the steel container had raked them loose, but it had done no apparent damage to the hull and spared the rudder.

When the carriage came to a stop at the end of the rails, the crew quickly blocked the wheels and Jules walked the length of the hull to inspect the damage. He looked up at Gilley. "It's not too bad, Gilley, three or four hull planks are dented and scraped slightly. We can install some graving pieces and a few sheets of copper. I thought it would be much worse, so this is your lucky day. Yes?"

Gilley nodded. "Yeah, I figured we might have to replace a few planks. I'm very relieved."

Also, Gilley, I think it's possible that your collision could have split the container open so it would sink. Let's hope so."

"I'll have the funds for the repairs wire-transferred today, if my driver can take me to a phone."

He looked over at Daryl, who nodded. "I have a Sat phone in my car, which I'm giving to you, as I'm picking up a new one this afternoon that has more whistles and bells."

Jules nodded. "Very well, Gilley, we'll start the work right away."

With great forbearance, Daryl had learned to live with his constant peeve about the snail's-paced traffic flow on the roads in and around Pape'ete. With tires squealing, he parked the Land Rover in front of a large three-story apartment building.

"So here we are, monsieur-dames, your residence awaits you. Maybe you noticed there was a large food market a block away, also a clothing shop, a barber, and a few odds and sods for your convenience. Sadly, the bordello burnt down a few years ago, and I don't think they'll get a permit to rebuild. Oh, well, progress."

They dropped their bags and went out onto the balcony, with its glass-topped table and four cushioned easy chairs. "For your viewing enjoyment, we have Point Venus on your right, a nice place for a picnic, and yonder the one-and-only Moorea. Not bad for a port in a storm; this magnificent view will be yours for the foreseeable future."

"This is incredible, the view, the apartment, and oh, look." Trish saw the tin of Harrods' English Tea on the dining table beside a vase of Tahitian flowers. She leaned over to inhale the fragrance. "Ohmigod, tiare. Umm, Sally, fill your nostrils with this aroma."

Sally inhaled deeply as her eyes closed. "Incredible! This is better than air, I love it."

Daryl picked two of the fragrant flowers from the bouquet and placed one behind Sally's left ear. "There you are, dear lady, wear a new one every day, behind the left ear, which means you are available." He placed the other behind Trish's right ear. "Behind the right ear means you are not available."

Daryl set the sat phone on the table. "The kitchen is stocked with the bare essentials: cereal, milk, bread and whatnot, just to get you through for a few days. If there's anything else you need, the manager can get you anything; towels, sheets, skid or whatever. Her number's on the phone. She's a very sweet Tahitian, been with us for ages, her name's Jeanette."

"Daryl, you're a real prince, and you always were. Ladies, this is the kindest and most generous man I have ever known. Thank you, thank you, old friend. Now, Daryl, before I forget, Trish and I would be honored if you'd be my best man. I can't give you a date yet, but as soon as I can get my peg-leg and we can muster the regiment here for the big event, we'll set a day."

Daryl showed genuine surprise as he reached over and took Gilley's hand. "It'll be my great pleasure. I'm touched. Can you believe this will be my first time as a best man? Bloody wonderful, it was meant to be."

Daryl pulled the phone toward him. "I'll call the phone company and transfer ownership so you can get cracking on your calls right away."

Sally lifted Gilley's leg, put a cushion under the knee and rested it on the coffee table. "Gotta keep it up, Captain."

Daryl hung up the phone and put his hands on Gilley shoulders. "Now, dear friends, I have errands to run and I'll be back at about twelve thirty to pick you up for lunch at our restaurant. See you later."

Trish waved to him as he vanished out the door. "God, what an amazing man." She picked up the phone and placed it in front of Gilley. "Darling, why don't you give it a shot? Here's our list of names and numbers."

He looked at it suspiciously, then at her and nodded. "Well, I have the best man locked, and the most important person to call is Helen, so I defer to you." He handed her the phone.

She punched the numbers and crossed her fingers. Moments later they heard, "You have reached Dr. Helen Boyle, well, not quite. Please leave your name and number and I'll call you back with alacrity."

"Helen, it's Trish calling from Pape'ete. I'll call you back on the hour. Love."

She pushed the phone back to Gilley. "That didn't go well. But the phone really works. So here's Ishmael's cell number. Your turn."

During the next hour, they had contacted all of their friends except Helen. Everyone was overjoyed to hear about the wedding and would start to get time off, and wait for the actual date of the event to make their flight reservations. Gilley wanted to have them all on the same flight. "Have the regiment together, as they say, only one trip to the airport."

Trish stared at the phone, then dialed. "Helen, it's Trish, calling again. We have a sat phone so we can—"

"Oh, Trish dear, it's wonderful to hear your voice calling all the way from Tahiti. So how are things on the good ship *Romayne*?"

51

Daryl parked at the rear tradesman's door to his restaurant and preceded his guests into the kitchen, which was alive with activity. He introduced them to his chef, Pierre, who would soon become the new owner of Daryl's thriving business. The large dining room was packed with feasting and imbibing tourists. The Tahitian maitre'd seated them at a table that gave them a view of Moorea. On both sides of the view corridor, two marinas were filled with power and sailing yachts flying flags of many nationalities. "So now all I have to do is manage the bloody marinas and hope I can find a buyer for them. Now Gilley, old friend, how would you like to take them over in your retirement? They pay off better than preferred Exxon Mobile stock. And the fuel concession goes with it"

Trish glanced at Gilley, who laughed as he looked at the menu. "I don't think so, but you're kind to offer it. I think after we've cruised the leeward islands, we'll mosey on back to Sausalito and drop the hook for a spell, at least until we can figure out what we'll do for the rest of our lives. So you recommend the ahi, it sounds just right, a good change from mahi-mahi. Trish, Sally?"

Daryl caught the eye of their waitress. "Ia ora na, Marie, it looks like we'll all have the ahi with a Caesar salads and a bottle of Pinot Gris." Daryl's eyes swept over Marie's well-proportioned posterior and shapely legs as she left the table. Trish and Sally noticed his observation and smiled.

"Now, people, this morning it just hit me that you're having a full-up wedding in about two months, so we're going to have to put our skates on. Only one hotel in Cook's Bay is suitable for your shindig, where you can park *Romayne* alongside their dock, which is all part of the shaded outdoor restaurant and dance floor. I've called the owner, who I know well, and he has only one weekend available seven weekends from the one coming up. So I've booked it, you're on the calendar, solid. I suggest we tootle over there tomorrow on the ferry and size it up. I must say, they put on one hell of a wedding spread. I went to one last year and was very impressed. They have about thirty-five cabins, plenty for your guests, also a pool, spa, shuffleboard, sauna, massage, water skiing, kite boarding, the bloody lot. And there's an excellent local Tahitian band, which I've also booked. I suggest a case of Mount Gay, a few cases of good Australian plonk and a keg of Hinano, and you're off and running, mate. Whatever grog is not consumed, you can stow it in your liquor locker aboard for your cruise."

Gilley nodded. "Let's do it."

"Fine, now he's asked for a thousand dollar deposit to hold it, so if your funds haven't arrived by the time we leave tomorrow, I'll cover it. You know, a short-term bridging loan overnight, let's say about fifteen percent."

"And that'll cover your commission for the event, I assume?"

"Get stuffed, you old bastid. Anyway, you'll love it and so will your guests."

"Thanks, Daryl, I really appreciate that you've got the ball rolling. My brain is mush, like it's still at sea and looking for killer containers."

Marie opened the wine and poured a little into Daryl's glass. He tasted and nodded.

She filled the glasses and stood beside him. "Is there anything else for you, Daryl?"

"Anyone, anything? I guess not, thanks, Marie; I think we're all set."

Daryl toasted his friends. "To my old friend and to the beautiful new ones. Gilley, old mate, I've missed you terribly all these years, and I'll be damned if I'll let you get away again without a land address and a collar on your ankle for a GPS fix on you; and now, we can get together on the net."

Gilley touched his glass. "Thank you, old friend, I promise to phone you often."

"Now, Trish Cameron, a true Scots name—I'm extremely happy for you both. I wish your life with this great man is filled with love and happiness. You're a fresh breath of life; it's my great honor to know you."

He smiled at her, then turned to face Sally. "Sally Brown, you are an extraordinary lady to be involved with this amazing voyage, you've faced extreme danger and performed an operation under very difficult conditions. I'm honored to know you as well."

They touched glasses and drank. Trish looked at Daryl and grinned. "And you sir, are an amazing gentleman, generous to a fault. Thank you for everything you've done for us. You're everything Gilley said you were, but really you're a lot more. It's wonderful to know you."

Sally and Daryl clinked. "Thank you, Daryl, and I know the world's a better place with people like you helping others. Good health to you, kind sir."

"My God, ladies, you're far too kind, I'm—"Daryl's attention was momentarily distracted as his gaze settled on Maeva and a tall blond Caucasian man as they walked past their table. She stopped and looked back at him. Gilley, Trish and Sally looked over and noticed her as well.

Gilley waved, but she ignored him, turned and walked away. "Well, well, apparently Maeva has some reason to cast us off. I hate unpleasantness. But I still have close contact with Micheline, and she's coming to the wedding, so we'll have another bride's maid. Ah, what the hell, you win a few, you lose a few, and sometimes you can't tell the difference."

Trish laid her hand on top of his. "Who said, 'This too shall pass,' Kipling? Oscar Wilde?"

52

Pape'ete, Tahiti: Well, as luck would have it (and we've had lots of it, good and very bad) What a thrill it was, especially for Gilley, now eighteen years later, twenty-eight for me, to sail into Pape'ete. It was wonderful to see the old buildings, catch the intoxicating aroma of tiare flowers. And, of course, the early morning crowing of the roosters. Brings it all back in spades.

Hooray! Our wedding plans are moving along like clockwork. All guests are booked on the same plane from San Francisco. All it took was one very efficient travel agent. The Cook's Bay Inn will cater the dinner. Gilley had his first fitting for his prosthesis; one, a varnished Burma teak peg-leg; the other has a metal shaft attached to a foot. He'll wear that one at the wedding for dancing; and the peg for more informal occasions like pacing the deck with eye patch and parrot. We all have appointments to have a small picture of a schooner and 'Romayne Cape Horner X2' tattoos on our legs. Far out! Micheline is such a doll, and we all love her. She and Gilley have really bonded. She has an outrageous sense of humor, so we are all passing our naughty jokes to her. The only fly in the soup is that Maeva has tried her damndest to discourage her from having a natural, loving relationship with her father. Fortunately Micheline is very strong-willed and is going to do exactly what she wants. So be it.

The repairs to Romayne have been completed to the best marine standards. We'll move back onboard in a few days. We'll hate to leave Daryl's wonderful apartment, it's has been a life-saver in every way; incredible sunsets over Moorea, watching some fun TV movies. It also gave Gilley the opportunity to walk to the shipyard every day to check on the work. And have lunch with Jules. Sally and I got some much-needed exercise walking into town every day to see the amazing food and fish market and meet some of the charming Tahitians. They are sweet and extremely friendly. The town still has some of the old charm. What a thrill to experience and taste it all again.

We also found the most beautiful pareus, so we bought enough for everyone in the wedding party. Gilley and I will have a different pattern. We have topped off the fuel and water tanks and re-provisioned our larder, so the schooner is ready to go. We look forward to dropping the hook in Cook's Bay. It's been too long for me, and I need that beauty fix.

Am I nervous about the wedding? No. I'm very relaxed, and so look forward to being with Helen and Bruce, Alfi, Ishmael and Fern, Jon Ewer and Lynn.

Daryl invited Gilley to move *Romayne* to a mooring in front of his palatial hundred-year-old estate in Puna'auia. A lovely protected anchorage where the schooner can moor stern-to and hang out before sailing her over to Moorea.

The *Romayne* crew loved the new mooring and again enjoyed a view of Moorea. Trish continued her journal, but always made herself available to help Sally with the meals. Daryl became Gilley's personal driver and took him to his appointments with the doctor and the prosthesis fabricator. Daryl's lawyer prepared Gilley's last will and testament that would now include Trish and a generous allowance for Micheline's college. Daryl took Gilley to a goldsmith to commission a special wedding ring in the shape of two dolphins kissing. He explained to Daryl that

Trish had decided she wanted to come back to earth the next time as a dolphin.

The next morning, Daryl held Juliet's hand as they walked across the lawn toward the schooner, to introduce his wife to Gilley and his all-girl crew.

He shouted down below. "Alright mates, it's time to get up and face the day. Are you all decent?"

"You bet. Come on down, you're just in time for breakfast."

They were all seated at the rosewood table. "Gilley, Trish and Sally, this is my dear wife, Juliet, finally home from down under."

They all stood up. "Oh, please don't get up, but thank you. Gilley, it's wonderful to meet you at last, also Trish and Sally. Daryl has given me chapter and verse of your amazing adventure and your wedding. How lovely to finally meet you."

Trish made room for them at the table. Gilley gave her a warm smile as he took her hand and sat down across from them. "Thank you, Juliet, it's great to finally meet the amazing lady who has somehow been able to capture and partially tame this rogue. I congratulate you, and welcome aboard."

"Well, it wasn't easy, Gilley, but I dearly loved the rogue and the challenge was too good to ignore, but I'm sure you'll agree it is still a work in progress." She leaned over and kissed Daryl's cheek. "However, the work is very satisfying. Right, you darling rogue?"

Daryl nodded and patted her hand. "Yes, dear, but I thought the work was complete?"

"It will be on our anniversary, next year." She winked at Trish. "So, Gilley, I understand you're having your wedding in Moorea. How perfect."

"Yes, we plan to take our California wedding party right from here to the hotel in Cook's Bay, so you and his nibs can sail over with us if you like."

"Yes, we'd love to sail over. Now, you adventurous sailors, if you don't have plans for this evening, would you join us for dinner? I was given a large package of Kiwi venison chops by one of our members. Daryl can collect you for drinks and just come as you are, you all look absolutely marvelous."

Gilley nodded. "Thanks, Juliet, we'd love to come."

The next morning, following a wonderful, fun-filled dinner, Trish and Sally sat at the cockpit table and watched Daryl mowing the enormous lawn on his tractor mower. He waved to them every time he made a pass by the schooner. Trish waved back. "He doesn't seem any the worse for wear, considering how much rum and wine he put away last night. My God, that was a hell of a dinner party." Trish laughed at Daryl steering with his feet and waving with both hands "He really is a very sweet man, and don't you love Juliet?"

"I really do; she's a one-off. You know, she's very subtle, but I have a feeling she wears the pants, and is extremely clever not to show it. I'd say they have a great marriage."

"Yo ho, ho and a barrel of rum." Gilley's gravelly voice flowed up to them as he came on deck and slipped in beside Trish.

She put her arm around his neck and kissed him. "Well, well, it walks, it talks, it actually lives, considering that it drank a barrel of wine last night."

"Oh Jesus, tell me about it— Sally, have you got anything for terminal cranium dysfunction?"

Sally returned and handed Gilley two pills. "These should put you right in no time. If they don't help, you're done for. I assume you'd prefer your burial at sea?"

They watched the mower man as he made a pass standing on the seat on one leg and the other straight out behind like a figure skater. Next pass he jumped off the machine and ran behind, making it look like it was getting away on him; he faked exhaustion as he waved his arms, shouting at the mower to slow down. At the last moment, he caught up with it, climbed aboard, stopped the machine and limped aboard the schooner. They all clapped and roared with laughter. "Good morning, you outrageous party animals, I trust you slept well and the noisy mower didn't bother you too much."

"Morning, Daryl, we're fine." They all focused on Gilley and his bloodshot eyes.

Gilley made room for Daryl to join them at the table. "Them's pretty fancy circus stunts, mate. I'll bet you're still ripped ya bugger, how about a beer?"

"Just finished one thanks, put me right too. Nothing like being on the mower with all that fresh air. I like to keep our guests entertained. Juliet gets a kick out of it. She's even got me with the video camera."

During the remaining three days before the arrival of the wedding party from California, Gilley had been fitted with his prosthesis. His stump had healed with no complications and fitted well into the padded devices, with a modicum of discomfort. He was delighted with the beautiful gold dolphin wedding ring, as he put it into the velvet case. For his ring he'd selected a standard gold wedding band. It would be the first ring he had ever owned.

Daryl and Gilley made the final orders for the libations, flowers and the cake.

Trish and Sally made sure that their one-piece pareus fitted perfectly. For the third time, they counted the pareus for their wedding party guests, then folded them neatly and labeled them with greeting cards.

Daryl made arrangements for a fifteen-passenger van to transport their guests from Faa'a airport directly to the schooner to load their luggage onboard.

53

Trish, Sally, Gilley, Daryl and Juliet were standing where the arriving passengers would exit the customs and immigration doors.

As the Tahitian custom dictated for disembarking passengers, they all carried the flower leis to place over their friends' heads and to give the obligatory kisses on both cheeks. Trish kept looking at the arrival board.

"There they are!" Trish shouted, and ran to embrace Helen. "Oh, God, it's so good to so see you, welcome to Tahiti, love." She put leis over Helen and Bruce's heads.

"Alfi, my dear, how great to see you. You'll see a lot of changes here from the old days, but it still has the charm." She put the other lei over his head and kissed him. "Welcome to Tahiti, it's great to have you here."

Gilley introduced the Californians to Daryl and Juliet. They made the rounds to welcome Ishmael and Fern, now proudly showing her pregnancy. Trish embraced Chief Jon and Lynn. "Welcome everyone." She took Helen's carry-on bag in one hand and her hand in the other, then led the way to the baggage carousel.

"It's terribly sad about Gilley's leg, Trish, but I must say he looks very well; and my God, Sally-the-surgeon, super hero. Well, you all are. What an amazing voyage you've had; we're enormously proud of you."

After the luggage was accounted for and loaded onto the van, the group headed for Daryl and Juliet's estate and *Romayne*.

Sally and Trish served sandwiches and iced tea for lunch and joined in the conversation about the voyage.

After a restful lunch Gilley, stood up and faced their guests. "Now, good friends, as we have a two-hour sail to Cook's Bay, we should get under way as soon as the table is cleared. I'll need three volunteers on deck—Ish, Jon and Daryl. Just go and familiarize yourselves with the running rigging. And ladies, please make yourselves comfortable at the table. Trish or Fern will show you how to operate the heads."

Gilley assigned his crew to their positions for sail hoisting and sheeting, and asked Alfi if he'd like to take the helm. "You better believe it. It'll be great to take this wheel again."

They slipped the lines off the pilings and the mooring, hoisted and trimmed the four lowers and headed the schooner out into a fresh breeze. Within a few minutes, *Romayne* was cracking off eight knots, to Alfi's absolute delight. "Damn, I love this schooner." Trish and Gilley sat beside the old sailor and smiled at him.

It was a perfect day, with a fair wind for the short sail to Moorea and their entrance through the pass into Cook's Bay. They lowered the mainsail and foresail, then stood by at the foremast, ready to drop the jibs.

Gilley took his bearing on the dock at the Cook's Bay Inn, and then held his arm up to alert Ish at the anchor windlass. "Let go and give it all the chain, Ish." The schooner gradually lost way as the anchor dug in and slowly swung around, facing the pass. "Drop the jibs." Trish and Sally set the fenders and stood by the mooring lines while Gilley backed the stern to the dock as they threw the lines to the shore crew.

Gilley shouted to his crew, "Well done you guys, grog rations on the aft deck, just as soon as we get the awnings up. You're all on vacation, so, for you lovely ladies and gentlemen, your choice of rum, wine or beer." He put his arm around Fern's shoulder and shot a glance at her tummy. "And juice or tea for you, young lady."

She made a sad face, then broke into a wide smile. "I know skipper, no grog for mommy, only four months to go and then party time, yippee! I go below and make tea. I think I member how to boil water."

Trish and Sally brought rum, wine, beer, ice and glasses. "Help yourselves, folks, cheese and crackers coming up."

The owner of the Inn presented himself to Gilley. "Io ora na, captain, and welcome to Cook's Bay, your ship is very beautiful. I just wanted to tell you that our supply vessel comes to the dock at midnight tomorrow. They usually finish unloading in one hour, then you can return to the dock until Monday."

"No problem, Emile, we'll just slip the lines and Trish and I will spend the first night of our honeymoon in the middle of Cook's Bay."

"Excellent. Our dinner service starts at six."

Trish walked beside Helen, arm-in-arm, to her hotel room. "Here we are. Oh bravo, room eight, our lucky number."

Helen kicked her sandals off and flopped on the bed. "Now, I'm absolutely knackered from the flight and down for the count. I shouldn't have had that Hinano, but it tasted so good, just like old times. I think I'll pass on dinner, dear. Maybe I'll have poached eggs and tea in our room. Come by in a couple of hours, and do bring Gilley and Sally. Bruce has given me my sleeping assignment, so I'll see you later, I'm off to the land of nod."

54

The small congregation was seated on both sides of the aft deck. Helen, who would perform the ceremony, was the first to appear on deck, clad in a long pareu that fell just above her bare feet. She was wearing a tiare flower headband. Walking slowly, she took her place behind the schooner's helm. A smile lit up her face. "Ia ora na."

Gilley, Daryl and his three groomsmen, Ishmael, Jon and Koko, also wearing tiare headbands and pareus, followed next, taking their places to Helen's right. Then Sally, Fern and Micheline stood on Helen's left.

Trish's hand tucked into Alfi's arm, and holding a beautiful bouquet, entered from the doghouse. Her flowered pareu was the same pattern as Gilley's. A white veil borrowed from Juliet was tucked under her headband. All heads turned to watch her as she took her place beside the groom. They looked at each other and smiled.

Soft music sifted over the deck like a gentle zephyr. Helen slowly raised her arms in the air, then lowered them.

"Dearest friends, we are gathered here today on this famous schooner to give our blessing to the bond that growing love and respect have created between Trish and Gilley in marriage, and to wish them our love on their continuing journey of life. It is wonderful that they should be married here in this magnificent bay, where they knew each other twenty-eight years ago. There have been many famous sailors and sea-faring explorers who have anchored here. So it's appropriate that this couple should add their names to that group on the good schooner *Romayne* and tie their special loving knot in Cook's Bay."

She turned to the couple. "The growing strength of marriage will depend not only upon your love in giving to one another, but also upon your wisdom in helping each other to grow as persons."

Helen looked at the congregation before her. "If there is any person who has any reason that Gilley and Trish should not be joined in marriage, let them speak now; before you walk the plank, or, forever hold your peace."

Gilley slowly turned his head to the congregation and grinned as they roared with laughter. It was only a brief glimpse, but he saw Maeva observing the wedding from beside a planted tree in the background.

"Trish and Gilley, you were created to be together, and together shall be forevermore. But let there be spaces in your togetherness. And let the winds of the sky dance between you. Love one another, and let it be a moving sea between the shores of your souls. Fill each other's cup, but drink not from one cup. Give one another your bread, but eat not from the same piece. Sing and dance together and be joyous, but let each one of you be alone. Even as the strings of a lute are alone, they sing with the same music. Give your hearts, but not into each other's keeping, for only the hand of life can contain your hearts. Stand together, but with room to grow. For the trees of the forest stand apart. And the oak tree and the cypress grow but stand not in each other's shadow. Love one another, but make not a bond of love."

Helen joined their hands together. "Gilley Alexander Cornwall, will you have Mary Patricia Cameron as your wedded wife? Will you love her, comfort her, honor and keep her in sickness and in health, in sorrow and joy, as long as you both shall live?"

He looked into Trish's smiling eyes. "I will."

She repeated the same oath to Trish, who smiled as she looked from Helen and then to Gilley.

"I will."

"Who gives this woman to marry this man?"

Alfi announced loudly in his squeaky voice, "Because her beloved father cannot be here in body, but in his name, spirit and memory, I do."

Helen nodded to Gilley to take Trish's hand and repeat the same words.

"I, Gilley, take thee, Trish, to be my wife, to have and to hold from this day forward, for better or for worse, for richer or for poorer, in hardship and in ease, to love and to cherish, all the days of our lives."

Trish then repeated Helen's words to Gilley.

Daryl handed the gold dolphin ring to Gilley, who placed it on Trish's left hand. "With this ring, I thee wed and pledge my faithful love."

Trish had not seen the ring until this moment. She gasped. "Oh, kissing dolphins, it's so beautiful. I love it."

She took Gilley's ring from Daryl and placed it on his finger. "With this ring, I thee wed and pledge my faithful love."

Helen smiled and nodded to Daryl, who reached over to the helm seat and took a bottle of wine and two goblets.

"Trish and Gilley, would you now drink to one another? Fill each other's cup, but drink from your own. Let this act confirm your promise to one another to be yourselves and risk what you are, for the sake of what you yet can be."

They poured wine into one another's goblet.

Helen joined their hands. "Let the drinking of wine remind you that what matters most is the spirit, not the wine, not the cup." She smiled and nodded.

Their goblets rang together, and they drank.

"Now you will feel no rain, for each of you will shelter the other. Now you will feel no cold, for each will give warmth to the other. Now there will be no loneliness for you, though you are two persons, there is but one life before you."

"And as Trish and Gilley have pledged themselves each to the other in the presence of this company, by the authority vested in me, I pronounce that they are now husband and wife."

Helen smiled at them for a long moment. "Well?"

Gilley glanced at Helen and then at Trish. "Oh yeah, the kiss." He lifted her veil. With his arms around her waist and her arms around his neck, they kissed.

The congregation clapped and shouted. "Fair winds! Yeah!"

Helen came around the wheel to embrace them. "Good on yer, my darlings. I give you my love."

Trish held Helen closely. "That was such a beautiful ceremony. I especially loved the part, now you will feel no rain, no cold and loneliness. Where did that come from?"

Helen held their hands together. "It's an old Apache wedding prayer I've always loved. It was written just for you."

The happy bride and groom turned, overwhelmed by embraces and congratulations. Sally wiped her tear-filled eyes and kissed her old friend.

"Oh, Trishy, I'm so happy for you both, and I wish you the best forever and ever."

"Thank you, sweetie, and you're a terrific maid of honor. Come on, let's get a drink."

Daryl stood up on a chair and shouted, "Everyone! The bar is very much open and dinner will be served whenever you're ready, followed by music and dancing. Enjoy."

Trish brought a glass of Mount Gay for Alfi. "Here you are, dear, thanks for being the best stand-in for Daddy." She nudged his glass with hers. "Here's to you, and to you, Daddy." They held their glasses up to the setting sun as it took a slow dive behind Tiger Tooth mountain.

Alfi wiped a tear from his cheek and kissed her. "I'll tell you, Trish, Alan would be right at home with this crew, and he'd be damn happy to have Gilley for a son-in-law. You've got a great man. Be happy, dear lady."

Trish and Alfi joined Gilley, who hugged his daughter with one arm, while the other reached around Trish.

They were standing with the full congregation. Gilley turned and smiled at Micheline, then to the gathering. "I want to make sure that you've all met my lovely new-found daughter. She's the finest new addition to our family anyone could ask for. So, friends, please welcome Micheline."

"Merci, Papa. I want to meet all of you and learn how you all know my father. I understand he has some very interesting history, and I really look forward to hearing about that as well." She grinned at him. "It's not often that a daughter gets to be at her father's wedding. Congratulations, Papa and Trish, it's wonderful to be in your family." She smiled and reached for them.

After many toasts, the Tahitian band, wearing pareus and flowered headbands, fired up the wedding party with the percussive beat on the wooden toeres. This immediately set in motion an extremely exciting mood. The serious, non-dancing drinkers decided to carry on imbibing and enjoying the drumbeat and dancers doing their wild thing.

Chief Jon and Lynn toasted Gilley. "I've gotta tell you, Gilley and Trish, how honored we were to be invited to your wedding. The sail over here was incredible; *Romayne's* a dream to sail. Here's to you both, and as always—steer small, my friend."

Gilley and Trish touched their glasses. "Thanks, Jon, we're delighted to have you and Lynn, and I hope you can sail to Bora Bora with us. We'll be back in Pape'ete next Friday."

"Absolutely, we'll be flying home Sunday."

"Terrific, I'll give you as much time at the helm as you want. If I remember right, it's a soldier's wind both ways, and we'll set the gollywobbler for sure."

The happy newlyweds continued their rounds, chatting with guests, until Daryl blew on a conch shell to get everyone's attention. "Ladies and gentlemen, and you, too, Gilley, bring your glasses, find your places, meet your seatmates and let's carry on with the mirth and merriment!"

Gilley and Trish took their places as hosts at the ends of the long table. Trish had made sure that the hand-printed place cards would introduce couples to new dinner partners. Everyone would be seated next to a person they didn't know very well, or at all.

Daryl stood up and tapped his glass. "Ladies and gentlemen, I just wanted to say that it was a great honor to be my old friend's best man at his wedding to his adorable Trish. And, it's a great pleasure to be with all of you fine people who have come from so far away to support them in their new life voyage together. But first I must tell you what a great leader our Gilley was a way back then. Some of you know that he was skipper of the old gaff copra schooner *Tiare Topero*. I was mate, and Koko here was engineer. On one of our trips, we had just unloaded a hundred or so drums of diesel, general cargo, crates of beer and demijohns of rot gut and supplies at Taiohae Bay on Nuku Hiva."

He reached down for his glass of wine and drained it. "But before we loaded the schooner with copra and empty barrels for the return run back to Pape'ete, the captain and his four-man crew decided they should get loaded first. We were tired from all the hard work, but somehow we mustered enough strength to walk to the boozer to sample their Hinano beer, which we had just unloaded a few hours before. So, during the serious imbibing we were approached by a shipping agent, who told Gilley that we were to load a herd of oinkers as non-paying deck cargo in the morning. We were told that we must construct a corral to contain the pigs on deck with bags of copra and empty drums so that they couldn't fall overboard. He said it was very valuable cargo, worth much more than the silly copra. Gilley looked at the scrawny, malnourished agent and said, 'I do not haul livestock on this schooner, now go away, this is a private meeting.' Well, the agent became furious and tapped Gilley on the shoulder and shouted, 'You will follow orders from the owner of the company. Tomorrow you will load these swine on the ship and take them to Pape'ete,'"

Daryl waved to Gilley and gave him a wide grin.

"Then Gilley winked at me. We stood up and looked down at the miserable five-foot-nothing-of-an-excuse-for-a-shipping-agent. I believe I said, 'Apparently you didn't understand the captain. I repeat, we do not haul swine on the good ship *Tiare Topero*. You are dismissed, now go away.' Then Gilley very calmly picked up the man by the seat of his britches and shirt-collar, hoisted him out onto the dock and tossed him into the drink.

"Then he shouted at him, 'I said we do not haul pigs on our schooner.'"

The guests laughed and clapped. "Way to go, Gilley."

Daryl held his hand up. "Hold on, there's more. So after we'd closed the place after midnight, we headed back to the schooner, and as we approached the dock, we noticed the open doors of the warehouse at the end of the quay, and heard the sounds of pigs oinking. We investigated within and found a herd of pigs, literally hog-tied both fore and aft, lying on their sides. Gilley took one look at these poor animals and shouted, 'Gentlemen, this is an outrage, we must release them forthwith.'"

Daryl took another swig from his refilled glass and continued. "In those days, we always carried our deck knives, so we cut them all loose. Now, you wouldn't believe how fast pigs can move when they have the use of their legs. Approximately fifty very happy swine were out of the shed and on their way to freedom and to places unknown, through the town and out the other side. We were laughing so hard, we actually fell over when our great leader shouted, 'I repeat, we do not haul pigs on our schooner.'"

The guests shouted and clapped, some stood and held up their glasses. Daryl held up his glass. "To Gilley and Trish!" Gilley stood and adjusted his headband that had drooped over one eye. He held up his hands and smiled, and looked over at Daryl. "I thought there was a hundred of them. Whatever, at least they all had some more time to enjoy their freedom."

Gilley sipped his drink and laughed, then leaned over and kissed Trish. "Thank you Daryl and great friends, Trish and I want to thank you Californians for coming to celebrate with us. And I must tell you that it all happened on this end because my best man and shipmate, Daryl, rolled up his sleeves and got very busy. He arranged for this spectacular location and all the logistics that went into planning it. I also want to honor and thank Helen Boyle for making our wedding ceremony one that will be remembered with great joy for the rest of my life. I also want to thank Sally for saving my life, and Trish, who assisted Sally, and both of them for saving *Romayne* from going to the bottom. You are an incredible team, and it's been a privilege to be shipmates with you. Also, Alfi, I salute you, just three days before your eighty-fifth birthday. Here we are again, twenty-eight years after we met on Trish's dad's *Bojangles*. And to all of you wonderful friends, Daryl, Juliet, Jon and Lynn, Ishmael and Fern, Jules and Tina, Koko and Pepe, Tom and Marania, and my daughter Micheline." He raised his glass, with tears streaming down his cheeks. "Damn, this wine make my eyes water. So carry on."

After dinner, Trish and Gilley started their personal visitations.

He put his big hands on Ishmael and Fern's shoulders. "Yo, Ish, I hope you got enough to eat and drink." He put this mouth directly on Fern's ear. "Remember, sweet mother, you're eating for two now!"

"Ish eat for three, he always hungry, like goddamn moose."

"I'm two-blocked to the masthead, skipper. This wedding is something else, you rule, Mon."

Daryl's eyes followed Gilley and Trish. "Jules, I'll wager my last frank that their marriage will be, will be. Bloody hell, I can't find the right word. Help me out Juliet."

"Just like ours, darling, full of incredible surprises and—"

Jules topped their glasses and put his arm around his Tina.

The newlyweds, holding hands, approached the gathering: Gilley grinned. "Far too much mirth and merriment here, so I assume the best man is telling his off-color stories again."

"Not yet, I'm saving that for later."

Gilley reached for the bottle of wine beside Daryl's elbow. "Allow me, sir. As my best man, it's my responsibility to keep you as happy as a clam for as long as I can. Then you're on your own."

The Tahitian performers returned to the dance floor; guitars and toeres burst into life again. Jules and Tina were the first to swing into the otea, the fast pre-sexual love dance. They were soon followed by Daryl and Juliet. Tina and Juliet's hips moved at a speed that mesmerized the men. Tom and Daryl's knees and hands were rotating in the traditional manner, intent on backing their ladies into an imaginary, inescapable corner for the final act of seduction.

Trish took Gilley's hand. "Come on, darling let's do it; after all, we are the hosts."

She moved her hips much slower than the experienced ladies. Gilley opened and closed his knees and arms to the rhythm of the dance. He staggered slightly, as his prosthetic leg was not in a supportive position and would have sent him crashing to the floor but for Trish's swift rescue. She grabbed him under his shoulder. "I've gotcha, honey. If you go down, we go down together. Just go slowly, slowly, you're not twenty-five anymore."

Jules and Tina then changed partners with Daryl and Juliet as they did a quick circuit around the floor, to include Trish and Gilley into a foursome. Koko shouted to Gilley and waved his arms. "You're doing great, Captain, let her rip!"

Lynn looked at Jon and smiled. "Why the hell not! It looks like fun." She grabbed his hand and led him onto the floor, where they were immediately followed by Koko and Pepe.

Ishmael took Fern's hands and motioned towards the floor with his head. "What do you say, little mother, let's give it a go?"

Fern shook her head. "No, no Ish, not dance now, it hurt baby. No drink for me, no dance, no fun. Maybe I go to bed, give baby a rest."

Ishmael picked her up under her knees and shoulders and onto the floor, where he did a solo otea. The others formed a circle around them until the music ended and Trish came over to Fern. "Good job, you two."

After a brief pause to allow the panting dancers to catch their breath, the band played the anniversary waltz. Everyone joined Trish and Gilley, and Sally almost had to carry Alfi to the floor, but Helen and Bruce appeared just in time to help her support him.

The dancing continued at a furious pace. Gilley, feeling more pain than he was willing to admit, sat on the piano bench.

Trish joined him. "Uncle, uncle." She gasped. "I haven't danced for years; I can hardly stand. How's your leg, love?"

She could see he was in pain. "It's definitely uncle here, but what the hell, at least I did the otea with you."

The bandleader announced a break before the final set.

"Just in time, my dear husband." Trish stood and kissed him. "Do you know where the ladies' head is?"

He pointed. "Yonder, just to port of the dining area."

Gilley watched her walk to the restroom when one of the waiters approached him from behind and leaned over his shoulder. "Captain Gilley, someone wants to see you in the lobby." He pointed to the front of the hotel.

He glanced over his shoulder and then at the waiter. "Who is it? I don't see anyone."

"I don't know, Captain, the desk clerk told me to tell you."

He stood up and slowly limped over to the lobby. Seeing no one except the clerk behind the registration desk, he asked who was looking for him. The night clerk looked up and pointed behind him. "In the alcove sir, over there."

Maeva was sitting on a wicker couch. She appeared troubled as she looked up at him.

"Maeva, what is it?"

"Gilley, I have to talk to you."

His expression showed concern as he sat down.

She hesitated, then said. "Tomorrow I go to see Father Beneteau after Mass and confess my sin. My sin to you, Gilley."

"I don't understand, what sin?"

She hesitated again. "When you come back here after the shipwreck, I look after you, because I love you, very much. I want you for my tane, my man; and I want our baby for us so we can marry. Yes?"

The wine was playing tricks; he had difficulty understanding what she was saying. "Maeva, I never wanted a baby, or to get married, and you knew that. I signed on *Te Vahine* for five years. You remember all that, and I asked you to be on the crew, and you said no. What are you talking about, your sin?"

"I tell you now."

"All right, what?"

She looked down at her hands. "I tell doctor to take out my IUD coil thing so I can have our baby. Then, one month and two months, I miss my period, doctor tell me I'm pregnant. You sail away on schooner. Now I have our beautiful Micheline, but not Gilley for my husband."

She put her face in her hands and sobbed. Finally she looked up at him. "I watch your wedding—and I very sad."

Gilley sat beside her and took her hand. "I'm really sorry, Maeva. If I had known then you were pregnant, I would have—"

Maeva slowly pulled her hand away. "Goodbye, Gilley. You married now, so go to your wife." She turned and walked slowly out of the lobby.

"Maeva, wait!" He started to follow her, then stopped as he watched her disappear into the dark night.

Trish was sitting on the piano bench with Sally when Gilley approached, looking pained. "Oh, sweetheart, sit down and take the weight off it. Where'd you go?"

"Oh, just drawing off a pint of superfluous fluid." He faked a smile, then reached for his glass of wine and drained it. "Arr, that's better."

The Tahitian band that had been pouring down several Hinanos returned from their break and fired up their instruments with renewed energy, bringing the wilder dancers to the floor. Trish grabbed Sally. "Come on, honey, my lovely maid of honor." They danced and twirled then, cheek to cheek. "Remember the good old days, when we learned to dance together, among other fun things? Oh, God, what a great night this is, with all of our best and loving friends having a blast. I love you, Sally, just like when we were three."

They were all surprised to hear several rapid horn blasts

announcing the arrival of the small cargo vessel that was lit up like a cruise ship. Then a powerful searchlight swept the schooner fore and aft. They watched the vessel approaching the dock. Gilley shouted. "Holy Jesus, we gotta skedaddle."

Trish and Micheline got under Gilley's shoulders like human crutches and helped him aboard. Micheline handed Trish her bridal bouquet as she stepped onto the dock. "Trish, don't forget to throw this over your shoulder."

"Thanks, honey, I almost forgot. Gilley, watch this, it's important!"

"We gotta let go, you take the bowline, I'll get the—" Then he realized this was the final act for Trish to complete their wedding ceremony.

She turned around, kissed the tiare bouquet and threw it over her shoulder. It flew in a perfect arc to the three unmarried bridesmaids. They reached high, but Sally, the old volleyball player, jumped higher and one-handed it, clutching it to her chest. "Trishy, I got it!"

"Terrific. Wedding bells for you love." Trish pulled the bow line aboard, Gilley got the stern line, and the schooner slowly drifted out to the middle of Cook's Bay. She shouted to the waving friends, "Good night all, we love you."

He turned to his bride and picked her up. "Well, Mrs. Mary Patricia Cameron Cornwall, you are now half-owner of a one-hundred-eight-foot Fife schooner. Welcome aboard, which half do you prefer?"

"Oh, wow, let my boozed brain think a moment. Let's see. Oh yeah, that's easy, I want the half where you are." She threw her arms around his neck and kissed him passionately. "Thank you for half ownership of *Romayne*, I'm truly honored and extremely proud to—" She whispered into his ear. "To also have half ownership of her captain, which makes it absolutely wonderful. And now, darling, I have a very important question for you: do you have any idea how to do honeymoon? I've never done one before."

55

Trish's Journal — End of the Voyage

It gave me the greatest pleasure to write to Mom and Daddy to tell them their forty-five-year-old Trish is finally married to Captain Gilley Cornwall (President of the Pacific Ocean). You'll be happy to know that we're deeply in love, and I'm going to grow old with this fine gentleman/schoonerman. It's hard to believe that we met in Tahiti twenty-eight years ago.

The day after the ceremony, we took our wedding party on a cruise around the leeward islands, some of Gilley's old stomping grounds. I had never been to Huahine, Taha'a or Ra'iatea before, only Bora Bora, which now has many more hotels and tourists. It was a treat to sail these waters and meet more of Gilley's old friends. After the cruise, we said good-bye to our dear friends, who had to return home and resume their busy lives. We loved being with them.

We hung out at Daryl's and Juliet's estate for another week, fine-tuning the schooner, re-provisioning for the last leg of the cruise, the windward beat to the Bay Area. So it was just Gilley, Sally, me the cats and Sir Arthur McWindvane to sail her home. It was very sad to say good-bye to Daryl and Juliet, who had been so kind and generous. Even Daryl produced real tears when we left. He insisted that Gilley was to either send a monthly E-mail report or a call by his old sat phone. So, I'll have to teach my computer-illiterate husband E-mail and drag him into the electronic twenty-first century. Gilley invited Daryl to sail with us, but he had to turn down the invitation, as he had to complete the sale of the restaurant to his chef, Jacques, and train him to manage the business. Also, to find a buyer for the yacht marina.

The sail home was mostly uneventful, except that I taught Sally to navigate. She loves it, and navigated the last half of the leg. Romayne was hard on the wind for most of the leg. We had been told about the Pacific gyre. This mass of hundreds of square miles of plastic flotsam and jetsam is permanently lodged in the middle of the Pacific high. We were appalled at the enormity of it; zillions of plastic bottles, bits of wood, plastic toys, sheets of plastic, nets, styrofoam and rope. It will take centuries to break down. And we sailed through it. Mankind has not been maintaining our environment. Shame on us. Hundreds of birds including our beloved albatrosses have died horrible deaths from ingesting bits of plastic. Gilley was incensed at the sight of this environmental disgrace in his Pacific Ocean. And as he is the appointed President of this immense body of water, he feels it's his duty to write to the heads of governments of all the many countries in the Pacific Rim about the horrendous pollution. First, we'll have to map out every country and then find out to whom and where to send them; that could take some time. We decided that all the countries should contribute to the funding for the cleanup. Well, it's a beginning. Who knows, maybe we could get some help from King Neptune — he seems to have a lot of clout in that region; perhaps he and Gilley could team up and kick some high-powered asses.

Then, I got an idea that all the plastic that is collected could be recycled and made into intra-uterine contraceptive devices and installed in all young girls on the planet who have or are about to become sexually active. I'm convinced that this act of prevention would eliminate most of the unwanted teenage pregnancies and abortions, but it may increase their activity; better that than unwanted buns in the oven. It's just a thought. Helen thinks it's a terrific plan.

We made it back to Sausalito in pretty good time, 3600 miles in 18 days, 16 hours, averaging 200 miles a day. We even had enough wind from all directions to get us through the doldrums. We never used the engine; after all, this IS a sailing vessel. Gilley said, if Captain Cook and his crew could do it, then so must we.

Sally and I are extremely grateful to Captain, darling sir, for the opportunity to make this amazing voyage. I guess one could say that marrying the owner, and becoming half-owner of the schooner, is a great love bonus.

We dropped the hook exactly where we departed from six months ago and sailed the Whitehall up to my funky old home.

Gilley bought the old floating home adjacent to mine that had just come on the market. After a thorough survey, the inspection revealed it needed a lot of work and a new concrete hull, so he got it for a song. The reason he bought it was so we could lay Romayne alongside my float and his float. We are ecstatic, and so are the cats. They now prefer to live aboard the schooner, but they make occasional visits to sleep on our bed up on the third floor.

The best news is that Sally and my financial advisor, Tessa Cole, who lives at the end of the dock, have met and the sparks are flying. She has just invited Sally to move onboard. Sally said that one should be close to one's financial advisor. I agree. Who knows, maybe wedding bells; after all, she did catch my wedding bouquet.

The saddest news is we lost dear Alfi after a bad bout of the flu, which developed into bronchitis and then double phenomena. We are all devastated by his death, but I feel so fortunate that I had him for a friend for many years. He was first mate on

Daddy's boat when I was fifteen; he was a great sailor, a compassionate man and a wonderful human being. We sailed out the Gate with all of his friends on Romayne to spread his ashes to the westerly. He left me his classic gold pocket watch that had belonged to his father. I certainly will keep it running.

So here we are, Gilley and I living happily following our on-going whirlwind romance and a fantastic journey surrounded by the kindest people in the best small town on the West Coast. We will spend the winter here, doing a little of this and that, and we'll play with the Rag-Timers band at The Music Box.

Gilley informed me that he is wealthy, thanks to his friend and financial advisor on the Isle of Man, who, during the last twenty-five years, had diligently grown his personal wealth. We've had many discussions of what we're going to do or where will we go. Gilley wants to return to his family log house where he was born up the Sandman's Creek in British Colombia and visit his parents' graves.

We will sail Romayne up to the West Coast of BC and cruise along that beautiful inland waterway with its long deep fiords and the awesome Gulf islands with scores of exotic bays. I'm so excited to finally see Gilley's birthplace and meet some of his people there. I hope they'll have a pow wow in his honor. He will certainly donate to his tribe.

Gilley has kept his promise to make monthly calls to Daryl on our sat phone. They usually spend a good hour together, shooting the breeze, going over old times retelling their old stories, roaring with laughter on some new ones. Daryl's marina sale went through without a hitch, so he and Juliet are fully retired. Gilley asked him if he'd like to join us next spring on our cruise to BC. And Alaska; Daryl accepted immediately. We'll ask Helen and Bruce, Jon and Lynn (who are now engaged), Sally and Tessa to take the remaining cabins.

My dear husband finally told me during the sail home that at our wedding ceremony, when Helen asked if anyone had any reason why we should not be married, he turned his head to look at the congregation and got a quick glimpse of Maeva watching our ceremony from beside a tree. Also during the music intermission at the reception, when I asked him where he had been during a ten-minute absence, he answered that he was drawing off a pint of superfluous fluid, when in fact he had been told that someone wanted to speak with him in the hotel lobby; it was Maeva, who confessed to him that she had sinned and had her IUD coil removed so that she could be impregnated by him. Obviously he was reluctant to tell me about that meeting at the time, but decided to tell me later, when we were alone on watch one evening. So we are relieved that he finally has some closure with the mother of their daughter, Micheline.

Helen has finally anonymously released her recipe for the Magic Medicine on the Internet. So far, there are thousands of positive comments in print about it. She is sure that when the Drug Enforcement Agency gets a hold of it, they will ban it immediately and put it on Schedule 1, with all the other fascinating mind-altering substances.

Joy on the waterfront, a new life has come to our community. Fern and Ishmael are the proud parents of their 8-pound 7-ounce baby girl. They are calling her Romayne. Lucky baby with such loving parents.

Finally, Gilley has made arrangements and funding for his daughter, Micheline, to attend any university of her choice. She will visit with us while all of us investigate the colleges in B.C. and California. She has decided that she will become a doctor. She also wants to spend some time with her father; we so look forward her visit next year.

I am putting together my film documentary of our wonderful voyage, and having a great time with it.

Well, dear Helen, you did tell me to write my memoir, because by doing so you said, I'd be reborn. You were right, as usual; so thanks to you and some others along the path, I am reborn, and I'm extremely grateful to you.

Last evening Gilley and I sat in our chaises on the upper deck of our floating home so we could enjoy the magnificent fiery sunset to the west. To the south, we had a full view of the City for a while, until an enormous bank of fog rolled in through the Golden Gate. I had forgotten how much I missed hearing the foghorns. I mentioned to Gilley how I loved that deep-throated horn because it made me feel so safe. We sipped our wine and watched the orange sunset fading slowly to a deep crimson as it spread over the western hills. He agreed that it was indeed a very good sound, especially when sitting in a comfortable chair, drinking wine with his loving wife, watching the 'Red sky at night, Sailor's delight.' Now everything in our lives is in harmony, just like a perfect "Soldier's Wind."

P.S. did figure out how to do honeymoon. Wow!

Biography

Stuart Riddell is a 1929 Model, born on a farm on Vancouver Island. B. C. Canada. He has had many occupations and activities. In 1938 his mother moved them to London, in a failed attempt to re-unite with his father. Then they were evacuated to Canada when the bombs started to fall on Britain. After high school he attended the Royal Canadian Naval College and the RCAF. He has worked as a gold miner underground; logger; service station ; sheep rancher; partner in a sawmill. In 1958 he bought a 53-foot classic sailing ketch named Romayne, and with a crew of six; male and female (including his dear friend Emily) sailed to New Zealand via San Francisco, Mexico, and Tahiti. In 1960 Stuart and Emily were married in Auckland. They all sailed back to Vancouver having logged 25,000 miles on that voyage. They immigrated to Sausalito California. They raised a son and a daughter. He became a real estate salesman for six years. In 1970 the family went to England and bought a 43-foot sailing cutter and cruised Europe for two years. Then sailed to France, stored the mast on deck and motored up the river Seine to Paris; then crossed France and down the river Rhone to the Mediterranean and on to Greece. They chartered their cutter as owners for four years. They sold the vessel and settled in Florida where their youngsters graduated from high school and thence to college. Stuart took up yacht surveying and with Emily moved back to Sausalito, California. He sold his business after 20 years, when oral cancer struck. He took a year off to deal with it and recover from that illness and retire. He became immersed in creative writing which encouraged him to write his debut novel during the last decade. He has discovered that retirement and writing are excellent and awesome activities, and he says he will continue until his fingers can no longer perform on the keyboard. Stuart and Emily are living in their floating home in Sausalito after 55 years together. He agrees with Johann Wolfgang von Goethe. "Whatever you can do or dream you can: Begin it. Boldness has a genius, power and magic in it."

Additional copies of *A Soldier's Wind*
may be ordered through amazon.com or
www.createspace.com/5647696.